Judy,

Thank you for being
my Alison! She's a great
character and you fit her
beauty well.
Love

VAMPIRE SLAYER

Trio-Genesis

L.S.C. FERNANDES

Order this book online at www.trafford.com
or email orders@trafford.com

Most Trafford titles are also available at major online book retailers.

Cover Photo By: Jerome Stallings
Editor: Matthew Renfer and Samantha Kate Cassano

Print information available on the last page.

ISBN: 978-1-4907-5934-0 (sc)
ISBN: 978-1-4907-5936-4 (hc)
ISBN: 978-1-4907-5935-7 (e)

Library of Congress Control Number: 2015906632

Trafford rev. 10/17/2015

 www.trafford.com
North America & international
toll-free: 1 888 232 4444 (USA & Canada)
fax: 812 355 4082

CONTENTS

"Each of you should look not only to your own interests,
But also to the interests of others." - Philippians 2:4

To My Sister, Ligia,
who has heard the story from beginning to end

Nine o'clock rang the hallway grandfather clock that stood left of the stairs. It was raining outside the black mansion gates. Bolts of lighting and crashes of thunder raged on in battle as the rain came hard on the grounds. It should have been a quiet night, with a half crescent moon and a star-filled sky. But it wasn't as the man on the television had predicted—it was North Pole cold in Schroon Lake NY, though it was the middle of the summer.

Helpless in his own estate, the figure of a man sat close to his wife, watching her as he held her hand and hoping that his love for her would be enough. Her name was Savanna B. Montgomery—a wife and mother who brought along a child that would change both the good and the evil.

"Olivia, my sweet, it will be all right," she said. "Your Father is here with you. He can protect you. He will take you to Trio-Genesis whenever you want, and someone very special will help you with your powers. You'll see all your friends again. We are not going to be enemies forever, I promise you. One day we will be safe and love each other like brothers."

Savanna's dying words slipped from her mouth slowly. She was pale against the dark red sheet. Her hands were cold; her eyes, watery. Her light brown hair fell over her face in a graceful manner as she laid blank-faced on the bed. Savanna's sweet calming smile had gone, her bright eyes and perky cheekbones were no more. Somehow, her voice sounded hopeful.

Savanna looked into her husband's eyes and told him everything with one look. His hurt gaze changed to happiness and then misery again.

"Take care of our little countess, my Angel," her hoarse voice spoke again.

"I'll protect her with my life," he promised.

"Olivia, I love you," Savanna said with her last breath, and before a moment had passed, she was gone. Her body disappeared, and Olivia and her father were left with nothing to hold on to but each other.

Panic filled the child's eyes as she hopelessly looked around the room and lifted the bed sheets to look underneath. Olivia's big, brown eyes stopped to look at her father's sad, blue ones.

"They took her somewhere where she will be safe," he told the confused child as he held her in his arms.

"Is she coming back?" the child asked, her eyes never leaving her father's. The shaking of his head was enough for her. This was the second time in his lifetime he had cried. The first was when Olivia was born. Those tears were different from these.

"I'll protect you, daddy," she whispered, not fully understanding what had happened now. Olivia would understand later when she missed her mother and realized that she wasn't returning; when she realized she was left alone with her father for the rest of his life; when she would not see her little school friends and family anymore—only then would Olivia fully grasp what happened. Only then would Olivia know what death was.

Time passes so quickly for a child. The mind only truly begins to collect memory at five—lest the memory be traumatic. Her mother's death was just that for Olivia: A horrid memory locked forever in her brain.

CHAPTER 1

Birthdays and Deaths

If not for his powers and other inhuman things, one would not think that this was the man from the stories who kept the little children afraid. No—that man was gone. That man was now a husband and a father to the most precious little five year old.

His wife, Savanna, had been the person to turn him good, the one who kept him alive, the one who drove him to be a better man, and kept him going in his fight to be good. She would go down as the enemy's wife, the one who turned the most evil man human.

Savanna B. Montgomery, mother of Olivia Brook Montgomery, daughter of the most evil man alive, Count. Stories of him have been told, unbelievable ones at that, but this did not stop him from being evil. It's what drove him, kept him going, kept him alive. That was then, before Savanna, before Olivia, before he became good maybe even human.

His last name was not known—only by Savanna and Olivia was the name revealed. For it was their last name, the name that his father gave him before he died, the name he was known by before he became Count; for he was then known as Mr. Montgomery. He was never addressed by this awful name, but only known as Count Dracula. Dracula M. Montgomery. Never would his name be forgotten.

"Olivia? Olivia?"

"Yes?" She turned around and looked at her father. The cold night of her mother's passing was only a memory now. Today was her seventh birthday party. She stood by the fire watching the flames dance up and vanish and dance up and vanish again, as it gleamed in her eyes and reflected her emotions.

"Is everything okay?" he asked. Olivia nodded. "Let's go, then. Everyone is waiting to cut your cake."

These were not the average vampires from scary stories. They were not the blood-sucking creatures they once had been. Under Dracula's new rules no one was allowed to kill, but they all did anyways. They weren't as violent as before but they were still evil creatures, who dreamed of overthrowing the Count and returning to their natural actions: killing for pleasure.

To vampires, killing humans was a game and they were just a crowd of over grown children who took the game too far. After all, they didn't have to kill them: they could drink a little and let them live on with their normal lives, or they could turn them into Vampires. But as it was, the community of vampires—those who had turned—was overpopulated, and soon the mansion would have to be enlarged. Instead, they decided to suck them dry, down to the very last drop of blood. They left their bodies cold and empty on busses, park benches, driveways, street corners, cars, and anywhere else they found a person alone at night.

Killing in the morning was far too dangerous, and they had not yet grown accustomed to the light of day. Even though born vampires did not have the slightest problem with sunlight, it was a rule that no one could kill during the day. It was an old rule made decades ago, and it was something that no Count would change. From generation to generation, Counts came and went, just as rules did, but this was one that had been untouchable. They learned to approve of the rule, since it was the only rule everyone always agreed with.

Traditionally, new Counts were chosen to rule by old Counts, but this was changed the day Olivia was born. Becoming Count or Countess is a birthright made possible only by being in the family line. It was a smart rule any Count would have made, and since

2

Dracula Montgomery was first to have a child, he benefited from it. But other vampires were opposed to the new ruling. Vampires like David, who was a runner up for Count, secretly hated the rule.

Dracula and Olivia ran to where the others were. Around the table, waiting for the birthday girl and her father, stood hungry little children and the hungry parents.

Hungry for blood, that is. Vampires—sweet vampires—all there to celebrate the little countess' birthday. Olivia blew out her candles and made a wish—a wish she thought would never come true. The atmosphere was filled with delight. The little vampires all came together laughing and playing while the big vampires—the parents of the little ones—stood and made small talk.

They were filled with the laughter of running vampire children. Balloons filled the ceilings and ribbons covered the stairs. Joy was everywhere and in everyone. Everyone but David.

He stood from his seat at the corner of the room, where he had been watching the whole ordeal, and walked over to the grand stairs. He was tall and lean, with bold shoulders and long legs. His skin was pale; his eyes dark blue, the color of the sea when a storm was raging. Dark black hair covered his head. He had thin lips for a mouth and a five o'clock shadow to match. On his left hand was the empty spot where his wedding ring was once worn. Someone "accidentally" killed her and that same someone faced dire consequences. Besides his punishments, David was a good man—a man with a fake attitude, a fake smile, fake feelings, and a cold heart. Cold enough to kill his own kin if need be.

"It would please me to make a toast, if you would please raise your glasses. To Olivia: may you grow in happiness and love," spoke David. He was Dracula's most trusted friend.

"To Olivia: May you grow in happiness and love," the room repeated. Soon after his toast, David left sight along with Dracula, but the party was ending, so their presences weren't well missed.

David and Dracula walked down the corridors of the Mansion, laughing and joking about old memories they had together. The two were like brothers and acted as such. Dracula, the eldest; head of the family, and David the youngest, picking up the leftover glory.

"My good man. The past years have been hard on us both— you more than me, I'm sure," Dracula said. "How would I ever have survived without a friend like you?" His face was overflowing with joy. "You... have been my right-hand man for as long as I remember. You've been there for me all along. I don't believe I've thanked you," he said as his feet stopped moving. David too stopped walking and looked back at Dracula. "Thank you."

They looked at each other for a moment and roared with laughter.

"Oh, you are quite the joker, Dracula, old pal."

"Old?"

"Not in age, my friend, not in age."

They kept their walk down the halls and kept their light-aired conversations about battles and fights and women and old lovers—man-talk.

"I am a better swordsman than you," David said like a child as they argued about fighting skills. "I can fight with both hands. I read my opponents like a book. In fact, I know all your weak points. If you and I, right now, were to battle, I would have the upper hand, having more skills as I do. You'd have little chance in defeating me."

"Well then, bless my soul, for not having to fight you." Dracula laughed, and David joined. "By the way, what are my weak points?" he asked half-serious.

David thought for a second while they walked in silence. He looked over at Dracula who was almost breaking into a smile. "I'm sure I know them." He said, though his voice was unsure. Dracula laughed again.

Little Olivia ran down the halls to find her father, wherever he may be. She found herself coming to a halt at the sound of angry voices, which she recognized perfectly.

"Dracula, my friend, she is not allowed to be here," David said. "She is not our kind. She is our enemy—one of the ones who lives to destroy us: a slayer. She is not welcome h..."

4

"She is only half slayer, David, and she's my daughter. Of course, she is welcome here. Olivia has been living here her whole life. We are all she knows. We are all she understands. She is just a child." Dracula explained to him.

David was resistant still. "You are making the biggest mistake you have ever made as Count. It's treason, Dracula."

"Count Dracula," Dracula said putting his foot down. "And Olivia will be taking over when she is of age, and you will keep silent about this," Dracula spoke in an angry tone.

David was not pleased with the discovery he had made early on in the day. He trusted Dracula, but Dracula had not felt the same way. David had known hours before the party that Olivia's mother was Savanna Brooks, the slayers all vampires fought to kill. She was powerful and dangerous; beautiful and kind. His rage filled his veins, and his eyes grew dark and misty. The happy feeling was gone completely, and his hands were fisted into tight balls. He was doing his best to hold himself back as his nails dug into his flesh.

Dracula laid down the law that his daughter would rule. His face red and his voice firm, he moved in on David as their eyes fought. The evil in his heart was rising as was his promise to his late wife.

The door creaked and their attention was taken away from the argument. She had stood there innocently listening, but when the silence fell over them, her little feet could not help but move closer to the door to have a better listen. The Count stood down from his evil thoughts and made his way over to his daughter.

"No... no... I will not bow to this half breed," David said as a ball of fire went flying out of his hand straight to the small child standing at the door. As it moved toward her, her eyes grew to the size of a full moon. Dracula's biggest fear was being realized at this moment, and everything happened as if in slow motion for him to get a better view of her death. Olivia stood frozen by the door unable to move, her feet stuck to the ground below her, pulling her under the wooden floor as the hot ball of fire got closer to her face.

Dracula quickly screamed at his daughter to surf way, but Olivia's ears would not hear. When his hands met her stiff body, he pushed the child out the way. His eyes turned red with anger as his pearl white fangs came from their hiding place. David was not joking as he too revealed his fangs—yellow and sickening from all the blood he stole in his life.

"Are you mad? Think this through, David. Olivia will fight on our side. We will have power beyond power. Dreams will be reborn the day she rules us all. She can make this a better place for you, for me, for us, our people," Dracula spoke carefully.

"She is not part of our people. That is something you must understand. All I wish to do is help you get rid of the pain that this girl will cause us in the future. They are all the same. They all believe that we are evil beings out to destroy the world, when all we want is to save our people." His words were of good intentions, but only in his own mind.

"She is young, we can use her still!" His heart ached as he glanced over to his daughter and saw the desperation on her perfect face—tear-stained eyes meeting his truest form for perhaps the first time.

"Your thoughts deceive you." With this, David made a ball of fire that not even Dracula could survive. The heated light was glowing in the brown eyes of the small girl as she blinked down the water that washed her face. Dracula's promise roared in his soul, and when the child opened her eyes she was faced with a sea of red that stained the gray rug his body was on.

He grabbed a hold of her hand and sobbed his last words—words that she did not hear, for the only sound in her ears was like the ringing after a large bomb had gone off.

David's knees buckled beneath him. A river flowed from his eyes, and his bone collided with the wooden floor. The screeching sounds from his lips could break glass. David watched the light fade from Dracula's face and the blood-covered girl sobbing into his lifeless body.

The noise brought in the guards, whose hands immediately grabbed tight around Olivia. She kicked, pulled, and screamed all the way out of the crime scene. David looked up at different faces with pleading eyes. His eyes would also see a bright light of red followed by a world of deep and unawakening darkness.

The skies cried for three days, wetting the black stone on the leafy grounds where a new leader was shaking in the downpour. The black fabric enveloped in lace covered her body like a cloud of rain floating in the gray havens. Her face contained red eyes and a hot peppered colored nose against a pale white skin. The tears left behind streaks on her cheeks. She felt a pair of eyes watching her from afar. They were not the same pair that watched her when she stood at her mother's grave. They were not warm and comforting. These eyes were cold and evil, and they were the blue eyes of a small boy, two years older than she. With dark brown hair and an evil glare, this look could only belong to one little boy: Joshua Lensen.

CHAPTER 2

A Pointless Meeting

The sun shone brightly on the courtyards outside the mansion gates. Olivia lay peacefully in her large bed sound asleep. Pieces of her brown hair fell gracefully over her face; she slept on her left side with one hand under her head and the other over the blood red sheets. Her chest rose, fell, rose, and fell as she breathed. Her light olive skin was soft and creamy. Her face was stoical, yet calm. Her dreams seemed one in which she rarely ever had.

The bloodshot curtains must have been ajar, for the sunlight seeped through the window and touched the sleeping countess' hand. She felt the warmth of the sunlight and moved her hand over to her eyes. She turned on the bed twisting the sheets on her body, covering herself in a cocoon of red blankets. Olivia yawned and stretched her arms then legs, pointing her toes to the window. She opened her eyes and pushed the sheets away from her face and upper body, as her pupils shrank and her hair shined brighter.

It didn't bother her, the sun, but it made her tired. Olivia sat up on her bed looking out the window at the grassy field and a bit beyond the hills past the gates. It was as far as her eyes could see that early in the morning, but her mind wandered passed the window in her bedroom, passed the grass on the fields, passed the big black gates that kept her inside even being free, and passed the hills.

Olivia imagined, way beyond the hills, a red and white checkered blanket lying on the green grass with a large weaved basket lying on top of it. She saw a man and woman laughing aloud and then telling the running children not to wander off too far. only problem is that children never listen and they go where they aren't supposed to.

They ran wherever their little feet took them, far beyond the view of their parents, passed the green grass and into the dark woods, where clouds floated just above the ground, trees moaned with the darkness, and dead leaves covered the dirt.

It's a good thing that when children are having fun, they forget to look around at the bigger picture and miss the chance of realizing they have gone too far before becoming completely lost. They ran.

The boys kept playing and running until the older boy fell, cutting his knees on the wooden sticks and rocks sticking out through the dead leaves. The younger boy ceased his running. His body went cold and his muscles tightened up at the sight of his hurt brother, but he promised to get help.

He ran, the trees cut his arms and little legs. Tears flew down his face as his breath quickened. A dark hooded figured appeared in front of him and offered help. The younger boy led the way without ever looking back to notice that the hood had come off and a face was revealed. He had bloodshot eyes and a thirsty mouth with bright proud fangs. Turning back would have done nothing for the boy. It was useless. The man was no longer following the little boy but following the fresh smell of blood he was tracing with his nose. A cry of pain came from the older child awaiting his brothers' return. He saw the younger brother's red face from running and his own face filled with a bit of joy at the sight of his brother.

The boy kneeled next to his hurt brother and the fog parted for the hungry man coming from behind the boys. He also took a knee and ran his fingers over the cuts on the little boy's knees. His head was down and his emotions well hidden. He brought his blood-covered fingers up to the nose and took in the sweet smell he longed for. The man lifted his face, uncovering his sharp fangs in their full glory.

Her thinking came to a sudden halt. Olivia didn't want to know what happened next, although it was very clear. She buried her face into the sheets and tried taking a breath and clearing her thoughts. She brought up her head, and her eyes were immediately met by hills that reminded her of the picnic and the parents and the boys—their bright green eyes tearing with fear and their blonde hair wet from the sweat on their brow. The killer showed them no mercy. He was an old-fashioned vampire. He did not turn his victims. He did not play "can I borrow your blood." He killed for food. He killed for fun. His biggest joy came from feasting on the blood of the helpless. That's why he was always around. Someone always wondered into the forest on a sunny day.

That is where he rested; that is where he hid, waiting for them: Lovers, on a mindless walk, runaways, children playing and running away from their oblivious parents during a picnic.

Black birds shot up and flew away from the trees in the mist of the forest at the sound of screams of terror. Back at the picnic, the woman's body shot up as she felt the pain of her children being taken from her. The blue sky that took their attention wasn't a distraction anymore. They noticed their missing boys and screamed their names about the hills, but it was useless. Dead children cannot respond to the call of their parents. The woman stopped screaming, she stopped running, and she stopped completely. Her knees shook beneath her and she fell on them. She looked at the forest that rested in front of her, far away from the lovely family picnic she had packed. The sky above her seemed to go from blue to gray. She spoke softly, telling her husband that it was too late. They were gone, and if there was anything left to find it would be their lifeless bodies without a drop of blood inside. She regretted not warning them of the creatures of the dark who spent their lives seeking blood, jealous of the lives that lived and died because they could not.

Olivia's thoughts were a controversy of what she believed. She lay back down on her bed, and since the thoughts couldn't go any further and the story could not be changed, she closed her eyes and slept a bit more. She wasn't much of a morning person anymore.

When she was small she would wake early ready to play with her little friends.

Now she had duties to attend to when she woke up, and play was the furthest thing from her mind. It had been 12 years since Dracula's murder, and her days of waking up early and being happy about it were gone. She liked the night.

During the night she could ride the streets for as long as she pleased and as fast as she wanted. Olivia would go out and drive for hours without a destination or a map. She went where the road took her. If the road curved right, she curved right with it. If the road went straight, she straightly followed her path. The road did not judge Olivia; the road did not call her and her people killers. The road did not know any better.

Every time Olivia got on the road, she was accepted. The nighttime was the only time Olivia had to herself. During the day she was covered by work and things she had to do in the mansion. Olivia never thought she was ready for the job anyway. Secretly, she never really wanted the job, but it was the only thing she had left of her father and it was what he wanted for her: to be ruler and rule over them all. So during the hours that the sun was out, and a few hours after it had set, Olivia worked.

That's why she loved the night. In the darkness of 2 a.m. she could visit Patrick, who knew her ever since she was born. He was a handsome 24 year old, and he respected Olivia on his own time. He didn't address her formally when she came around. He didn't have to, and Olivia didn't want him to. He took care of her like an older brother—not overprotective, but always there for her when she needed him most. Wherever Olivia decided to go, Patrick had sworn to follow and respect her leadership. He was her right-hand man; the one person she really listened to.

Patrick didn't live at the mansion. He lived above his work place, Eclipse. He was the manager of the most popular vampire bar in all of Toronto. The only vampire bar in Toronto. Others were scattered around the world, but this was the closest one to the Mansion, not that it matter; everything was a short surf away.

Olivia loved going there and judging the new drinks that the "bar" had. There were no alcoholic drinks there. Vampires do not like alcohol, and they had no need for it.

Olivia didn't like alcohol either; she had seen its effects on humans. Still, she didn't base her opinion on what it did to the humans. For Olivia, the smell of alcohol alone was enough to dislike it.

Just like any other vampire, she treasured the taste of blood. She and her friend Patrick opened a bar for vampires that had everything but a name. The day the bar was ready, Olivia and Patrick stood outside on the roof looking around at the street and thinking of one.

"How about: car, asphalt, lights off, lights on?" asked Patrick.

She laughed. "Lights off, light on?" Olivia looked at Patrick.

"It was just a thought," Patrick said honestly.

"Or: the old man, homeless, the beggar," Olivia said, looking at the passing stranger.

"Harsh. That man has done nothing to deserve your bad mouthing," he said, regarding the old man on the street below. She nodded halfheartedly.

"Hey, sir! Down there. How's life treating you?"

There was no response. The man kept walking down the alley. His hands were in his gray coat pockets and his eyes looking down. His old buckling legs unsteadied his walk.

"He's wasted."

Patrick and Olivia sat there observing the night. Looking at the sky and the stars and as they thought of more names. "Hey, look at that. It's a lunar eclipse." Olivia looked up in awe. It was the very first eclipse she had ever seen. It was probably the only eclipse she would have seen considering she didn't have time for such events.

Patrick howled at the disappearing moon. "Bring the wolves out."

"A lunar eclipse," she whispered to herself. Something in the name bothered her. It was charming but not attractive. She tried to think of a play on words but nothing satisfied her running thoughts.

"Lunar... lunar eclipse," she kept repeating, while the handsome vampire beside her howled at the moon like a lunatic.

12

The sky blackened as the earth's shadow swallowed the moon completely.

The words escaped her lips naturally. "Eclipse."

Eclipse became a big hit for many vampires, including the ones who chose to roam on their own, though there weren't many; eight in total. They all knew about Olivia. She was Countess of all of them, but as long as they did not live under "her" roof, they were not under her demands. The eight that didn't live at the Mansion, not counting Patrick and the vampire from the woods, choose not to dwell among the others because they did not appreciate the idea of having a leader. They came around from time to time, met with Olivia, and were civilized while under the Countess' care. She reminded them that they did not have to be under her ruling but they were welcome to join whenever they wanted and even if that was not their desire Olivia had no reason not to trust them. They never wronged her or anyone, according to them, and they lived in peace, something Olivia could understand. The eight spent their visiting time at Eclipse, along with the rest of the vampire who respected Olivia as more than a ruler. These vampires respected her as a friend. They were the ones she could count on. She might not have known their birthdays or last names, but she knew every face in that bar and would recognize them anywhere she saw them. They looked out for the Countess more so than the others did, and Olivia had a soft spot for them in her heart.

Every time she walked in everyone would stop and look at the door, which bothered her a little because she didn't like being the center of attention. Olivia was high class, but she knew just how to be down to earth. Blood of the father and heart of the mother. Sweet and fun to be with, serious and angry, lovely and graceful, crazy and wild; and yet, she was just as any other normal person found walking in the streets of a big city.

Eclipse was a nice place to go and grab coffee and if you happened to be a vampire the other drinks would be delightful as well. The walls were painted dark brown, and from the ceiling hung dark yellow lights. There were round tables surrounded by four chairs. There was a bar, with tall stools that had cream brown seats just like the ones from the chairs. On the walls, where the dark windows were sat cozy booths for the more intimate vampires. It looked just like a coffee house with over a hundred things to drink, but only three drinks were named and favored by the countess.

Xixi was a yellow liquid served in a tall water glass that was open wide at the top and got smaller at the bottom. The rim of the glass was decorated with crystal brown sugar. Olivia had this drink on fun party nights when she had just raced Patrick in one of her many cars. Whoever lost would pay for the drinks, but since the bar belonged to both of them the money went nowhere. One of the other drinks was the thick, milky drink, White Ape, made with white blood cells and placenta. The mixture looked sweet but tasted just as thick as it looked. Olivia only drank this when she was upset at something or on her birthday that she didn't like to celebrate. It felt wrong celebrating something the same day of the year her father died, so in respect for the dead, her birthday was celebrated a week after. She drank the last drink—a Bloody Mary—most often.

Rich, thick, creamy virgin's blood, served in a large round glass with silver lining wrapped around it. It was delicious and left no trace that anything had been in the cup. This is how Olivia spent her nights. Driving and drinking. Her nights were completely devoted to Patrick, the road, and that welcoming bar. It was good, since her mornings weren't as lovely as she wished.

The sun touched her face, Olivia decided it was time to wake up and smell the roses. She wanted badly to stay in bed, but time didn't allow, so she hid under the covers and waited a bit. She heard footsteps outside her door. They were getting closer and closer until finally it stopped. The door opened. A woman with long, blond hair walked in the room as if it was her own— fixing things, grabbing dishes left there from the night before, picking up clothes, opening the curtains in the room so the sun light could shine in brighter. She walked over to the bed and started making it with Olivia still in it.

"Olivia there's a meeting at the Hall in a few minutes," the woman spoke in a loud whisper. "What are you still doing in bed? The time to wake up is now; there is much to be done." She spoke quickly and stopped in front of her bed with her back to the window before speaking again.

"The day is not our friend," the woman said. Olivia's brain wasn't working this early in the morning. She could barely hear what the blond woman was saying.

"Why are you whispering?" Olivia asked with a hoarse voice, but she was gone. The door was left open and Olivia was left annoyed.

"At least go out the same way you came in so you can close my door," Olivia screamed. She sat up in bed and gave the door a look.

"Why bother having doors? It's not like anyone knocks before they come in." Olivia looked around her room to see if she was alone. After realizing it was her room and she was alone, she looked back at the door and blew at it. It shut. She lay back down and…

"Olivia." The door swung open again. "These papers must be read over before the meeting today," James said, dropping a stack of papers on her bed.

"Yes, James. Come right in," she said sitting up again.

"Don't give me that look," he spoke, and he was gone in a hot, fiery blaze.

"Sure, use the door for coming in, but let's all just surf on out, so the door that we came in from is left open." She got up, walked over to the door and closed it. "Really, it isn't that hard to close a door. Why can't people just come in here to say hello, or bring me coffee, or cookies, or a plate of bacon and eggs or something?"

"Coffee?" There was a voice behind her. Olivia turned to face her future husband.

"Good morning, Joshua. Will you be using the door or are you leaving the same way you came in from?"

"No one walks anyone. We are beginning to gain weight," he said handing her the coffee cup. He sat on her bed. "Bad morning, Grumpy?" Olivia nodded. "I'm going to let you get dressed and read all these papers," he said, smiling at her and picking up some of the papers from the bed, as he looked them over. "It's nearly eight, Olivia. You should hurry." Joshua got up and leaned his face down at her, giving her a soft kiss on the lips. He lifted his face and spoke. "I think I'll walk to the Hall, or at least down a hall," he said and walked out through the door closing it behind him.

"At least he can close the door." She walked slowly in her room, the floor creaking under her feet. Olivia's hand caught on fire and her body quickly became a walking campfire as she surfed herself to the bathroom. She put down her cup on the counter and began to brush her teeth. The lights, still turning themselves on, illuminated the dark floors, and the gray walls revealed a very large bathroom that looked beautiful under the yellow glow of the light. Olivia got dressed quickly and made her way to the Hall.

She reached the tall, black glass doors. Pushing them open, Olivia saw everyone inside sitting calmly and all ready to start. The look on some of their faces was of disappointment. Some didn't even look her in the eyes, just down at the floors shaking their heads in disbelief. The faces of the elderly were aged from waiting—the faces of the young, red with anger. Vampires were not patient creatures.

"Yes, I am a huge disappointment, and if her father were still here we would all be better off. Yes, I know I'm not much of a leader, and I'm not the first choice for countess either. Some of you won't even look me in the eyes, hoping maybe I'll become invisible and completely cease to exist, and maybe someone else can run this place. Others think, 'no, she's not late because she was doing something important, she's late because she overslept because she's still just a teenager. This girl is going to run us all down the drain. We are doomed, doomed! Oh, Olivia, do something right. Can I be Count now, I'm sure I'll do a better job than this bimbo does. Unbelievable!'"

There was a long pause. Silence covered the room. "Did I miss a thought?" she asked, looking into every eye. "If not, since I am already late maybe we should start to concentrate on more important things. I don't suppose anyone even started looking at anything while I wasn't here?"

Another long pause. "Then I am to believe that not one person in this room has come prepared?"

Not a soul spoke. "Please don't all speak at once, I'm having trouble understanding all of your great ideas," Olivia blurted out.

"Shall we get started?" a voice from behind Olivia spoke. A man: tall, with dark eyes and dark skin, his clothes ripped and his face bleeding. "Now that we've all been harassed by the Countess, maybe we can get things moving."

Olivia turned to look into the eyes of the man she hated most: Glover. "It's nice to know I'm not the only one who gets to places late," she whispered. She sat down on her large leather chair and looked at the glass table that sketched across the room. Olivia could never concentrate during these meetings. All she saw was the shining light from above their heads. It made a particular irritating sound, as though the light needed to be changed. Every once in a while it flickered very quickly and it was almost impossible to notice. Olivia had been the only person to sit starring at it long enough to realize it and even count the seconds. She didn't look directly into the light. She used to, but after a long time her eyes would grow tired and everywhere else she looked there would be a large yellow spot. She looked at the reflection it made on the glass table.

Glover, now acting as if he were in charge of things, started the conversation. He was, once again, being completely overdramatic and acting like an overgrown teenager who's been bossed around by his parents for too long. His words were immature and melodramatic. He walked around the table over and over as if he were presenting something to a large corporation he knew didn't want him.

"For years now we have been destroyed, abused, used, and more importantly turned over by those whom we like to call slayers…"

It was the only thing Olivia heard before her thoughts trailed off. For a while, she concentrated on the light, but it reminded her of her thoughts of the children in the forest, and from there, her brain raced everywhere. She thought about her mother and father, her old childhood friends, the days that she didn't have to care about the rudeness of the world and the fate of her people… her people… what made them "her people"?

She did not by any means give birth to any of them or create any; in fact, Olivia had never even turned a human before. It was completely against what she believed to be morally correct. It was also something that every other vampire hated about her. How can a leader—a true leader—not believe in growing their army?

Olivia stopped her thoughts for a second and once again switched them. She was their leader, not because they appointed her, but because she was born to be so. She did not have a choice, which puzzled her greatly. If, in fact, many of the vampires did not approve of Olivia being the Countess, what kept them from stripping her of the title?

Her father? No, it couldn't be. Dracula was dead. Dracula dead… this thought froze her body over. She had a perfect image of her father in her mind. It was the image of his dead body by her small feet. It couldn't have been Dracula. Maybe it was her powers—the powers she had yet to discover and learn to control.

Thirty or so minutes went by and Olivia missed everything that had happened in the "oh-so-very-important" meeting. She only looked up when her name was finally mentioned by someone.

"Yes. What about the countess? No one would ever suspect anything coming from such power. After all, it's not every day that Dracula's little girl goes out into battle," spoke a man from the far left of the table, as the other vampires laughed. Although he only meant to mock her, he spoke the truth. Olivia never went out to battle. Once or twice of course, but never enough for the slayers to discover that she was in fact the Vampire Slayer. Nevertheless, she was great in battle, and she was an incredible swordswoman.

"No, I will not have it. This will never work. Olivia is strong but she is too stubborn. She would ruin everything that we have worked for," a woman said, pounding her fists on the glass.

"But if she were to…"

"No, it's too dangerous. I will not have her running around fighting for us," spoke an older man. "If Dracula was alive, and he heard this idea, he would drop dead before us all."

Joshua stood from his seat and stepped into the argument about the countess. "The Countess is to be kept safe from harm, and here you are trying to put her into the fire. I disagree completely and will never allow any of you to put her life in danger."

"Oh, you only speak so highly of her because you are in love with her," a man said smirking across the room for all to see.

"In love? Please, Joshua is incapable of such things," said a young blonde woman. A short silence fell over the room before another person spoke.

"You should restrain yourself from saying stupid things, boy. The Countess is smarter than you think. She may act childish at times, but it does not mean she is weak. If she were, we would not show her such respect," said an elderly woman across from him.

"The only reason we show her respect is because she is the daughter of Count…"

"Stop it! This is silly. The girl is powerful, yes. She is smart, yes, but she is still too young to take such a great responsibility…"

"Excuse me…" Olivia spoke suddenly. "Would it be possible if we didn't talk about me considering I am still in the room?" All across the room there were cold glares that still somehow showed respect. After a strange moment of silence she spoke again. "Just a thought."

The argument continued as if she had not even spoken. Olivia rolled her eyes in disbelief over how childish they all acted. She leaned back in her chair and rubbed her temples. Olivia then proceeded to speak again.

"Why... why…. Hey, shut up!" All eyes were on her. She motioned for those standing to sit and rose from her own chair. "Why don't we just forget the last plan and start fresh? I mean the last plan was a bit of a long shot, and now we can start from scratch with something we all agree on."

Glover's eyes narrowed on Olivia. He stared her down until her eyes confronted his. Glover had no choice but to oblige to her commends, even if he knew that there was no other way to lure in the slayers. His plan would work, but unfortunately, the risks came at too high a cost.

"All in favor of a new plan say 'aye.'" Joshua took command after no one else did.

Once again, Glover was first to speak. He set his dark hands on the glass table and looked across the room. He asked many questions to which no one had answers, and stated many facts that nobody in the room knew or cared to know. Glover took up his own 10 minutes of glory by only stating what had already been said and disagreed on. After he had done so, he sat down and remembered more again. He spoke for another eight minutes. In the ninth minute, Olivia told him his voice was beginning to bore her and that his ideas were as restless as his tired face and body posture. She then continued by advising him that if he had no bright ideas and would keep proposing the same useless junk, he would be better off excusing himself, taking a hot bath to get rid of the dirt under his fingernails, and taking a well-deserved nap. Ashamed from the laughter in the meeting hall, Glover sat down and hid his hands in his coat pockets.

After what seemed like hours, another argument broke out. "But if we are to take them by surprise?"

"It's not going to matter taking them by surprise..."

"Of course it's going to matter..." The voices grew louder as anger grew also. There were vampires standing on chairs while others stayed sitting down banging their fists into the table. The room was shaking with anger as the argument raged on. Olivia couldn't help but notice that the light above them also shook and shook and flicked more often than before.

"She will not go alone..."

"And we are to say that you will join her?" "... There is nothing we can do..."

"It doesn't matter what the cost is..."

"HER father would kill you if he knew such things."

"HER father isn't here!" "...and what of the damage done?" "Is it not possible that you people can stop thinking of yourself for once and..."

"Why not have someone else take charge of this? Why not have someone with more..."

"If you interrupt me one more time..."

"What will you do?" At this, a fireball was made and as a fight was about to begin...

"ENOUGH!" Everyone froze. Olivia stood from her chair and asked everyone to have a seat once again. She took a breath and spoke. "This is the same plan we had four hours ago. The same plan we started fighting about. Is this what we have been reduced to? This is the reason anyone on the other side would hate to be us because we are always fighting each other. This is ridiculous. Fighting will solve nothing. It's been over five hours and we have come up with an awful plan that will do nothing but get me killed. We are better than this. In this room, we have all the brains it takes to make a good war plan, and here we are wasting my time arguing about me and bringing my father into the conversation. He is dead, I'm trying to move on, and it would sure help if you people would stop speaking of him as a beast that is going to come back to protect me."

She took another breath as she calmed herself. "Now we are not leaving this room until we have this problem solved. The first vampire to try and start an argument will..." Olivia stopped and thought for a second. What could she take from them that was worth a great deal? "...will... suffer great loss of... one of their fangs. On that note, who would like to go first?"

She took her seat and waited for a brave soul to speak. The hours ran late and the sky grew dark. Dinner was brought to them, after having skipped lunch. The light flicked and sang its dying tune. Olivia ran her finger through her hair and scratched the back of her neck. Glover picked the dirt under his nails and flicked it on the floor.

Joshua sat back on his chair and paid close attention to everything said. His handsome face and mysterious eyes narrowed at Olivia's direction occasionally. She felt his eyes on her and looked at him. Now, Joshua and Olivia were not the type of people to back down if caught staring at another, so both of them sat there looking at each other.

There was no emotion in their eyes. They were blank, even though both minds were racing a thousand miles an hour. Olivia's brown eyes starred down Joshua's cold, blue ones until Glover spoke.

"May we join the staring contest or would you two like to join the conversation?" his icy voice filled the room.

Joshua stood and spoke, knowing if he had not, Olivia would have, and her words would not have been as kind. "You are beginning to overstay your welcome here, Glover. Do not give me reason to return you to where you were."

"And where was that exactly, Glover?" Patrick's smooth voice cooled Olivia's temper, taking over the conversation entirely. "The bottom of a bridge? I hate most the vampires in here, but you are the only one I'd feed to a slayer, dead or alive. You have not begun to overstay your welcome, you have overstayed your welcome. Which means you must leave or you must die. I myself am a fan of you dying, but since Countess Olivia would not approve of such ideas, although she might make an exception in your case, I believe it's time for you to leave." His eyes were boiling with anger, the palm of his hands sweating. As he finished speaking, Olivia met his gaze, and by the smile planted on her face she did not disapprove.

Olivia stood and began clapping her hands loudly. Olivia's idea wasn't to praise Patrick and put him above what others had said, it was only the simple fact that Patrick could quickly quiet a room with their own words and fears.

"Bravo! Bravo! Bravo, Patrick! This man has made this entire meeting worth my while. Brilliant! Bravo! I couldn't have it said it better if I had said it myself."

Olivia couldn't have said it at all, because she had already given up on the pitiful vampires she lived with. She knew that they would argue, fight, and in the very end, they would end up betraying and killing each other. She stood there a moment thinking back on all that she had previously said and what she had just done. In the mansion everything Olivia did was recorded, not on paper, but with eyes and looks and in blood.

The praise she had given Patrick would not be vanquished smoothly, and although she was the authority in the Mansion, it was rare to hear of Countess Olivia not being in some kind of trouble.

The light recaptured her attention, and Olivia realized that all eyes were on her and that she had not finished speaking. Every vampire in the room gazed at her and wondered where her mind trailed off. She took a breath and looked over at Glover and saw an angry dog with his tail between his legs; kicked out, cold and in the rain crying his pathetic sobs, hoping his barks weren't loud enough to dismiss his owners forever. A pitiful sympathy filled her brain and she spoke again, in a softer tone.

"However, Glover... without you, these happy moments would never even happen, and for that you are welcome to stay forever if you'd like." After relieving some of Glover's pain, Olivia felt a small deal of satisfaction and pride, and yet she felt shameful for putting up with his misbehaver and his constant fight for rule and power. It wouldn't have been wrong of her to kick him out and leave him to fend for himself. It was what he deserved, minus some. She knew that if Glover stayed more than two days away from a "safe" place to call home, one of two things would happen: he would either go on a hunger crave, killing anyone and anything he could find, day or night, crowded market or dark alley; or he would be killed by any slayer who recognized his bloodstained teeth. Although it would have been even more satisfactory if she had heard of his death, Olivia could not trust Glover with keeping every secret he knew. To stay alive, any vampire would give anything away to a despicable slayer who would end up killing them anyway, and Glover was the last person on earth Olivia would trust.

Patrick's smooth voice emitted from his mouth again. "To be honest with you, Countess, if I may?" Olivia nodded almost on command. "I am quite the fan of Glover's plan." Even if Glover could come up with such a great plan, he was smarter than anyone gave him credit for, or he was shadowing a bigger demon. "It's diabolical, and you would have a great deal of fun."

Olivia sat trying to regain her thoughts. Eventually, she came to the conclusion that Glover wasn't smarter than what she already knew, which meant he must have someone else giving him all the great ideas. Whoever it was, it was a great idea, and suddenly she could not agree with it more.

CHAPTER 3

Browns Wing Park

Patrick held open the door as the vampires stood to exit. He watched closely as Joshua spoke to Olivia. He watched Joshua place his hands on her. The moving of Patrick's lips were barely noticeable as he counted how many times Joshua's cold eyes blinked.

There wasn't a vampire who spoke as fast as Joshua did when the time called for it. His words—no matter how incredible a lip reader was—could not be made out. It was as if his mind was racing and he had to get all the words out before forgetting. Joshua spoke like this only when Patrick was around.

Olivia rested her back against the chair and exhaled. She rubbed the sweat of her hands on her jeans. His hot breath was present again as he inched closer to her face. Olivia took in a breath and her shoulders rose slightly out of place. She swallowed hard, blinking her eyes slowly. As Joshua spoke, she pinched the bones on her upper back together and let out short moans. For some unexplainable reason, her eyes stayed locked on his. Yet her breathing started to steady as she moved away from him.

Joshua leaned in, placed a soft kiss on her right check, stood, and walked out, giving Patrick a distasteful look of envy.

Time passed slowly in the darkness as vampires went for their kill. Outside the moon shined behind the clouds. The dew of the summer night left its tracks on the dark green grass. Her heels clicked and clacked on the stone floors outside the walls of the Mansion. Olivia pushed open the black doors and walked in, her shoes bringing in the dirt and mud. She walked to the base of the stairs and stomped her feet repeatedly, letting the dirt go from the bottom of her shoes onto the clean floors. Her brows frowned as she placed her hand on the railing and stomped harder. The noise her heels made as they met the tiles echoed throughout the entrance of the Mansion.

Two of the Mansion's janitors walked in and stopped dead in their tracks. Olivia turned her eyes their direction. The three vampires stood for a moment looking at the clean floor and then where she stood and then at each other again. An awkward silence filled the air. The two men watched her every breath while holding theirs. Once more, her attention went to her feet and the mess around them. Olivia sat on the first step of the wide stairs and very slowly pulled her shoes off, each foot revealing her black stockings. When her feet were completely visible under the stockings, she stood on the same first step and looked at the men, gave them an apologetic smile along with raised eyebrows and raced up the stairs like a child in trouble.

She kept running down the halls. The dim lights darkened silver lined walls. Olivia came to a sudden stop and looked back. She shook her head and touched her eyes. Her father's fear was instilled into every vampire. That's what gave her the undeserved power.

She kept her pace slow and wondered the giant museum she called home. Everything was always different, older things presented themselves as new. New things were exhausting to look at. Aged faces hanging from the walls served as dark eyes in the emptiness. She had wondered so far off that every place she walked dust would rise and dance in the air. Spider webs hung from places, and the ruby red carpets were a deep burgundy. She noticed the stubs of candles hanging from the chandeliers above and the insects wrapped in thin lines that were stronger than iron—numb and waiting to die. They knew their fate. As lifeless as their small disgusting bodies were, these small little insects knew the way life worked. The bigger ones ate the small creatures. Soon they would be nothing more than bloodless—drained dry by the spider in whose web they laid.

In a way, Olivia was grateful for spiders. They are delicate and strong—easy to kill by the ones who are above them—but some are deadly, evil, and cold. They were like vampires— setting a trap for their prey and going out for the kill. They suck dry the victims and those that got in their way. "Eat everything that is on your plate," mother says. There are children in Africa starving! Why is Africa always picked on for its poverty? Other countries have starving children too.

Olivia rarely ever walked down this cold place. The paintings were haunting. Her skin would form tiny bumps all over. The hairs on her arms would arise and the lump was visible from outside her throat. The most recent painting in the halls of death had been of her birthday. She stopped in front of this picture painted perfect. She touched the frame and the red painted on her small lips. Her hand traced over where Dracula's heart once was and she retreated the hand, as if it had caught on fire. A large web hung over his face. Even the spiders knew he was gone. After Dracula's murder Olivia wanted no more pictures painted. She threw fits and rages over being painted. If a camera came within her eyesight she shouted, yelled, and fought. This particular image was finished after Dracula was murdered.

She kept on while the floorboards creaked under her feet. To her left up ahead was her old room and right across was her father's bedroom. It only revived hurtful memories that taught her to be stoical and imperious to pain. There was a time when that hallway had life, had light, had love. Now it was damp, forgotten, lost. Then again, the Mansion itself wasn't a lovely, living safe haven. Half of the vampires were dead and the living, who were vampires from birth, acted as if they were dead. They all hated life the same and all secretly wanted death upon oxygen, but their pride was too great to admit defeat and to crumble under another's feet.

The Mansion wasn't all bad. It had to have life, for there were living vampires there. It had to have light or else everyone would bump into each other in the darkness, she laughed, and it had to have love because… because it had to. Joshua! Josh loved her. In his own way of course, but nevertheless, he loved her.

"This place isn't bad at all. It smells good, we eat good food, and we drink good blood. We have good torture chambers, it's nicely lighted, the black tiles are shiny, the wallpaper isn't peeling off anymore, we have a dining hall and a dance floor and parties and music and… and there is a brand new library that not many vampires use, but I mean it's good right?" She was nuts.

Olivia walked and thought aloud, not realizing where she was headed. Her feet stopped suddenly as she reached the end of the hall where she was greeted by large, dark doors that ran from the carpeted floor to the dark misty ceiling. Her smile died at that door. Although Olivia walked here almost every day, she never walked far or fast enough to reach the end of the corridor, much less be face to face with those doors. She reached for the cold handles, which should have been covered in dust, but was not, and as Olivia went to open the doors, a familiar voice stopped her.

"Olivia?" She turned quickly and was greeted by the glowing of candles coming her way. "It's late. What are you doing here?" Concern filled Joshua's voice as he spoke.

"My apologies," she said. "I must have forgotten to ask your permission." She bit forming a thin line with her lips. "I do what I want. This is, after all, my house. What's your reason?" He was up to something. He always was. Trusting Joshua was worse than trusting the enemy.

"Josh, what's going on?" Michael stopped dead in his tracks. "Countess." He bowed his head carefully. "Didn't expect you to be up so late." He too gave Olivia the fake and icy look of concern.

Now, Michael was Joshua's best friend. They had grown up together and they had become like brothers. They looked nothing alike; Joshua's pale skin and dark, blue eyes couldn't look more different from Michael's dark skin and chocolate eyes. They were all meant to be good friends and always fight together, but as the years passed, Olivia's powers grew stronger than both those of Joshua's and Michael's combined. The jealously was written in stone. The friendship between them and Olivia was broken. Michael hated Olivia, it was clear to everyone, but to him it was a secret. The envy he had of her powers and the envy even of his best friend and their so-called love. He only put up with her because of Joshua. He knew that Joshua loved her and respected her, and so out of respect for the future Count, he respected the Countess as much as he could.

"I would think that you were in bed by now. You've had a long day, Olivia. Maybe you should get some rest. Should I walk you to your room?" Joshua said placing his hand around her as he led her back from where she came.

"Quit treating me like a child." Her tone had changed completely. This is was a restricted area, a sacred place for her to mourn the death of family. He was out of line completely. Olivia's eyes grew red with anger. Her fangs came from their hiding place and her jaw tightened. "I think you should go, Joshua. And as for you, Michael, try not to be so fake. Your thoughts are overflowing with rage."

"Michael and I meant no harm...." Joshua said, calmly removing his hand from her shoulder before it became nothing but a stub. Her fangs disappeared and her eyes returned to their natural brown color. He came closer to her and ordered Michael to leave. His look wasn't of approval but he did as asked. Joshua slowly came closer to Olivia and wrapped his arms around her. She stood there being hugged but not hugging back.

"What did you and Michael want up here?" she asked coldly. Joshua let go of her and backed away a bit. His eyes were calm and dark. He explained he was looking for her. Worried about her, Olivia walked away leaving with the words, "Don't be, I'm fine." Joshua watched her leave.

When he was sure she was gone he looked at the dark doors and down at his hand.

Putting the bronze key into his pocket, he walked away with a smile on his face. Soon, he thought, very soon.

Olivia woke up with the sun. Except for the place where the sun had risen, the sky was still dark. It was early too early for Olivia. Her dreams were tormenting and mocking her. The shattered illusions of a day with light that shined brighter than white pearls were set in her mind. The sooner she got up the sooner the day would end. The sooner the day would end, the sooner the next day would start. Life would on go with this simple ritual and then she would die. Or so she hoped.

She dressed and walked over to her window, opening the red curtains to let the sunlight touch her face like a soft blanket. She inhaled the sun and exhaled with an open mouth. Every time she got close to light it seemed to call her closer. Patrick once told her that he felt the same way. "The light is calming. There is place were the sun never hides, it touches and reaches everything," he explained to her. As much as she loved the night, after being awake she enjoyed the day like a pelican on the beach. Olivia let a soft flame take over her body and surfed to the kitchen. She enjoyed the simple freedom of collecting her own breakfast. She wasn't much for being waited on hand and foot.

As Olivia had predicted, the day went by in a rush. Night fell upon the Mansion.

Olivia stood in the large gymnasium punching the red bag that stood five feet tall. Sweat dripped from her brow down to her red cheeks. She breathed heavily and moved quickly, kicking and punching repeatedly. Red flames appeared behind her and vanished, revealing no one other than Joshua.

"Come on you can't still be mad…. are you?" He asked playfully. She didn't respond or even turn around. "You're still mad at me? That's not Countess-like." With this, Olivia turned and punched him right in the jaw. His face turned a bit and his eyes burned with hate. The other vampires in the gym stopped their actions and looked closely at the heated Countess.

"You must have a death wish! What are you not telling me Joshua?" She spoke loudly and her voice filled the gym.

"You always get right to the point! Don't hold back or anything, Olivia. Punch away!" He said turning his head to face hers. His eyes widened as her fist came at his perfect squared off jawline again. "You think you're so good at being bad, Olivia? Stop pretending!" He shouted after turning to face her again.

"Who do you think you're talking to? Unlike Michael, I am not your pet…. I can kill you faster than you can think. For some reason you told yourself that, you would someday be Count of this awful place. News flash, Joshua: you are nobody without me. You have no power. The control you have over anything is given to you by me." Olivia calmed her voice speaking only so he could hear. "You want all this power? Have it. I don't want it…." Her face was pale now. The sweat dripping from her forehead dried up. Olivia was no longer panting; it almost seemed that she was calm. "I have to go…. I need to get away for a while Joshua. I need some time."

"Olivia, I…." white lights started going off and a loud siren joined in. The speakers overhead called the OPS, Olivia's Personal Squad, to report to Whitefield Hall. The urgency of the announcement ceased the argument between the two.

Five of the six members stood in the Whitefield Hall; Olivia, Josh, Michael, James, and Sarry. In front of them stood a tan man with glowing red eyes and fangs white as starlight. Maybe before being a vampire he was dentist. No one's teeth were that white. He really took brushing and flossing to a new level. His name was not important.

Some vampires even wondered if he had a name. The ones who were forced to address him called him Nameless. He was a nice vampire, always about his own business.

Olivia stared at his fake tangerine looking tan.

"Why are you orange?" Olivia shocked the room to glares. "Do you know that it makes you look less intimidating? It's like, you couldn't even get tanning right."

Nameless looked at her a bit disappointed. He didn't just look like a tangerine, he was sweet like one. Nameless waited for Olivia to smile and give him play punches on the arm, but the closure never came. Nevertheless, the short, red-eyed, orange man stood in front of some of the most powerful vampires in the Mansion. It seemed strange that they were young vampires and maybe not very wise. But the younger the stronger, the older a vampire got, the more control he/she got over their anger and hunger. An angry, hungry vampire was a powerful vampire.

"Caleb has been spotted at Browns Wing Park having some dinner," spoke Nameless. "Of course, our friendly slayers interrupted his meal. He is injured and he's fighting six slayers. Act quickly; in and out. Don't forget his meal behind... If he is still alive."

The five surfed to the park and before they could see Caleb, they found themselves in a small battle fighting very smart slayers who knew how to attack. Olivia ran to Caleb who was fighting off three of them. A dark haired man, a tall brunette, and a beach boy. They had silver stakes and little water glasses hanging from belts. They seemed almost unarmed and defiantly pathetic. Her eyes grew red and her fangs came out of their hiding place. Not ten feet away Michael fought a girl in a pink shirt with straight, black hair. The tips of her hair were brown like dirt, or maybe it was dirt. Whatever color hair she had didn't matter. She stomped her foot on the ground, the earth shook and Michael went flying up. His body collided with a small tree and he fell limp on the ground. The girl wasn't done yet as she kept going at him. Wrapping his ankles in the grass, she lifted him up and threw his body around like a stick.

A blonde girl behind Caleb and Olivia was where the real action was taking place; she was fighting James and Sarry. James made quick fireballs and threw them at her without aiming much. His muscles flexed under his black shirt as he again brought his arm forward and released the balls of fire. She used water from a birdbath close by to defend herself, making a shield of water in front of her blocking the fire as quickly as they came. With a swift move of her hands, she flung the water at James and Sarry. The wall made a direct hit and threw both James and Sarry to the ground. Sarry was quick to rise running at the girl, who pulled a silver stake and began to charge at her also.

Joshua's gaze was taken away by the running blonde. In one quick move, he struck his opponent and stole his weapon from him. Joshua surfed in front of Sarry, "Ali, watch out!" came the voice from the boy who had been fighting Joshua. Within the same second, the blade in Joshua's hand stabbed her side. Alison held her wound and fell backwards, screaming on the ground.

"Alison!" called one of the boys fighting Olivia. He was distracted long enough for her to knock him right off his feet, making the boy fly fifteen feet in the air before coming back down. Blood ran from his lips and nose once he hit the ground, and he rolled in the dirt a bit. The beach blond boy pushed Olivia away and made a run for the injured Alison. By this time, Michael had released himself from the weeds and made a run for Caleb who was at the mercy of the black haired girl. As the beach blond boy reached Alison, the one who had been fighting Joshua screamed instructions.

"Rick, get her out of here! Go!"

The girl with black hair held her grip on her silver stake, ready to kill Caleb. Sarry had gotten Alison's blood on her clothes. It began burning through the fabric and would soon burn through her skin. James grabbed Sarry and backed away from the slayer's blood that was spilled on the grass. Joshua and Michael ran at the black haired girl.

"Kelly!" screamed the bleeding boy on the ground drawing her attention back to the fight. She saw Joshua and Michael coming at her and surfed behind them. Michael kept running to aid Caleb. Joshua came to a halt.

"Joshua, behind you!" screamed Olivia as she lifted her body. Joshua looked at Olivia when he heard his name. Kelly kicked his back, bringing him a lot closer to the ground than he liked being, then backed away from him. His piercing, red eyes and deadly fangs looked furiously back at the girl. She ran to help aid her bleeding friend.

"Tom, help me with Alison!" called Rick next to the bleeding girl. Her shirt was covered in blood. The dirt and grass stuck on her bleeding skin. As Tom walked away from Olivia, he kicked the brunette boy in the face, causing more bruises to his porcelain skin, and raced at the one on the ground trying to get the feeling back into his legs.

Kelly raised her eyes at Olivia; her hand was burning with red flames. She was headed for Joshua's unfinished business. "Jason! Surf!" the panicked words came out of Kelly's mouth. Tom reached Rick and the dying Alison. Joshua barked orders at Michael to get Caleb to safety.

"Josh!" Sarry screamed at the blood burning through her clothes.

"Get out of here!" Joshua screamed back, giving her aid.

Olivia stopped dead in her tracks when she saw the slayer, Jason, had surfed away. Olivia froze and extinguished the fire from her hand. Tom and Rick held on to Alison's hands.

"Ali, look at me. Look at me, it's Rick. We are going to get you out of here. I need you to lock your eyes on mine." Her eyes danced, blurring the images in front of her. The warm hand on her cheek held her face still. She could feel her entire body moving in circles.

"Alison! Look at me…. Hey, look into my eyes." Once he had her gaze, his attention went over to Tom. "Take a deep breath, Tom. This is going hurt you a little." Rick concentrated for a second and a large wave washed over them as he surfed them out of danger.

James ran to Olivia, but before he could reach her, the brunette boy surfed in front of him and stabbed James a centimeter away from the heart with a silver stake.

"I got that little trick from your friend. You can thank him for me, if you live." He said spitting the blood from his face as he spoke.

Jason surfed behind Olivia and grabbed her by the neck. Joshua was too busy watching James fall to a deadly grave to notice Olivia losing air or the black haired girl getting closer behind him. His skin grew hotter and he was taken by fire as he surfed next to James and threw a hard punch to the brunette boy right in the chest. His body flew into the birdbath, cracking his back and dislocating his shoulder. The cold water crashed on his body and face. It kept him from passing out, but not from letting out a faint scream of pain.

"Mark!" Kelly ran to him. Surfing would have been faster, but her body was in panic mode and her legs ran.

Joshua held James close to his chest. James's heart was beating right through his jacket and hot blood was creeping down his clothes onto Joshua's leg. James was going to die. Joshua's eyes and hand ran over James's wound. Joshua's eyes began to fill with a clear, salty liquid. James's body was cold, his face pale, and he held Joshua's hand tight as a sea of red flames came over them. His possible last glance at Olivia was apologetic. He wouldn't come back for her... He couldn't come back for her. It was her life or James' life. He picked James. She picked James. It was Joshua's only choice.

"Mark, are you OK?" Kelly asked looking at the cuts on his arm. "Your shoulder is ruined." He looked up at her, gave her a sweet smile and nodded his head. "You have to get out of here. Jason and I can handle this."

"Push it in place." Kelly looked at him before claiming he was completely crazy. "Kelly, we can't leave Jason alone. Put my shoulder in place." She hesitated and told him she couldn't. Although the bone was clearly popped out of place, Kelly argued she couldn't see the wound clear enough. "Kelly! I am going to keep fighting and it's going to be a lot easier on me if my shoulder is where it belongs. Now please, I know you can do this..." Before he could finish his encouraging words, Kelly grabbed his arm and shoulder and popped it right back in the socket. Mark let out a painful cry that echoed thru out the park. He breathed heavy and spoke, ".... you could have warned me...." Kelly laughed before trying to convince Mark he still needed to get his shoulder checked and they should leave. "You're right," he said, still slowly touching his shoulder. "And we will, right after we help Jason."

Jason was defending himself with a shield made of air. The strong wind came from his hands. Olivia threw out her hands and lit the grass in front of Jason on fire, and in a circular motion, surrounded the ground around him in red flames. The fire grew hotter as the flames burned brighter. Jason's shield was taken down in the hot disaster. Olivia lifted her hands to raise the fire all around him, creating closed walls of heat. There was a complete look of bewilderment on his face. Her power was unseen. Her intelligence in battle was alarming. Jason was helpless. If he tried to blow out the fire it would feed it, and make it stronger. His own element at this point would practically kill him. He was trapped. Olivia lowered her hands and watched the fire burn. The sick smile of evil played on her face. Olivia raised her hands and gave herself a loud few claps. Mark and Kelly began racing towards her but before they could reach her, Olivia ran into the flames that kept Jason captive.

There she stood, watching him choke to death. Sweat was running from his brow, the whites of his eyes were red from the smoke. Jason knelt on the grass coughing and holding on for his life. The flames had ripped through his right arm and burned through his skin. Blood crept down his arm. Olivia walked up to him. Jason looked at her feet and raised his head to look at her. His face was dirty, and his light hair was covered in black smoke. He looked like a firefighter caught under a house fire after rescuing the damsel in distress.

She laughed. "I bet you're asking yourself if it was really worth it. Did you get what you wanted out of this? Was one measly, hungry vampire worth your life?" Olivia rested her right foot on his left shoulder and pushed his body back. "I can smell your fear. I can see it in your eyes. You hate this… this weakness." She walked away from him and turned her back. Jason took this time to lift his body and gain some strength. "My father always said, once you have them in your grip and they are completely helpless… You let them go. I never understood that. Think he learned it from my mom. I'm not going to kill you," she said as she turned. Jason had been standing right behind her. He balled his fist and punched her across the face knocking her to the ground. "I said I wasn't going to kill you!" she screamed with eyes wide and mouth open. It wasn't about death. She was just pissing him off and she deserved it. Olivia stood and punched Jason back. "I said, I wasn't going to kill you." Olivia put out the fire. The cool wind hit Jason quickly, knocking him off his balance. Olivia backed away from him.

Kelly and Mark had been waiting for the wall of flames to be put out. Kelly ran over to Jason, who was sitting on grass recovering. Mark grabbed Olivia by the neck and stabbed her back with a silver stake piercing her heart. She screamed and fell forward. The ground kissed her face hard and quickly. Olivia reached behind her back, pulled the stake from her body, and threw it on ground. Her blood stained the silver and dripped down her back.

Mark ran over to Kelly and Jason. "I had to kill her," he said. Jason and Kelly looked at the rising Olivia, wiping the blood from her hands. Kelly looked up at Mark, who was already giving Jason a hand to help stand.

"Mark, you didn't kill her," she said standing and also helping Jason up. A light blue light came from Olivia's wound, healing the stab. Their mouths dropped. Jason's eyes scanned the stake on the ground covered in blood and then scanned the fully functional vampire.

"I think I took in too much smoke," Jason said.

"No, I saw it too. She's not even bleeding," Kelly said. "You should be dead," she screamed at Olivia.

"If not dead, at least injured," Mark whispered. Olivia walked toward them her eyes red and her fangs ready. "I think we pissed her off."

"You did," Olivia spoke as she approached them. Kelly came at her but was pushed away violently into a park bench. The wooden seat broke against her body and came close to killing her with its sharp broken edges. Jason charged at her with an angry look in his eyes. Mark followed right behind him. Olivia put out her hand and a rush of air came from it fast and hard, knocking both of them to the ground. Mark and Jason exchanged knowing looks.

"Kelly, be careful, she isn't what she seems," Jason said.

"Thanks, but I think I figured that from the healing of the stake to the heart." She dusted off the bits of wood from her clothes.

"This vampire is on steroids," Mark commented to Jason as they stood. Jason's eyes searched for an answer and a smile broke his thoughts. He walked toward Olivia. She didn't move or look like she was going to attack; instead, she waited for him to make his move, just like Jason knew she would. One foot from her, Jason surfed. She turned around expecting him to be right behind her. Jason surfaced right back where he was, and when Olivia turned around, he caught her by the neck lifting her in the air.

Her body was light. His strength served him well now, and Olivia no longer had the upper hand. Olivia grabbed his arms with both hands. She dug her nails into his flesh, cutting the skin. His blood dripped on the ground. Mark watched from the distance, and he swallowed hard.

"I can smell your fear. I can see it in your eyes. You hate this… this weakness." He mocked her words. Jason took a deep breath out and a big breath in, and the air around Olivia was no more. The bits of oxygen she was breathing in had completely vanished.

Kelly ran over to Mark who was still watching silently. He couldn't take it anymore. His hands rubbed his chest and he breathed heavy.

"Stop it, Jason. You're going to kill her," he said. The words fell on deaf ears. "You're better than that. You're better than them. Don't become a murderer. This isn't going to bring him back. You are better than her!"

Jason let go of her. Olivia's body fell to the ground and crumbed in front of Jason's feet. He backed away from her and watched her body for any movement. She was ghostly. Her body laid there in the grass motionless. Jason was still, his eyes empty, his lips parted. Her chest didn't rise and fall like it should have been. Mark and Kelly stood in place, waiting for something to happen. Jason knelt down next to Olivia and half-expected her to grab his ankle—she didn't. He checked for her pulse.

"Jason, is she dead?" Kelly asked. Mark's breathing was short and his eyes were pleading. Kelly asked again if the unconscious vampire was dead. Jason picked up her body and shook his head. She was still alive. Mark took a deep, calming breath.

"What are you doing?" Kelly asked. "No… No… No! You're not seriously thinking of bringing that thing back with us?"

"We have to, Kelly. We can't leave her here. What would happen if someone were to walk by and see a girl on the ground with fangs sleeping? She's coming with us." Jason's veins filled with blood. The scratches on his arm faded slightly. The burnt off skin healed a bit. Jason stood taller and straighter than before. His voice sounded deeper and his muscles looked bigger. Kelly and Mark protested. Sleeping or awake, the vampire could be dangerous. Trio-Genesis was a safe place for slayers. Not one vampire knew its location. Kelly told Jason that he couldn't just invite the enemy for a sleepover, but Jason would have none of it. There was a certain confidence in his voice now.

"She isn't going to get away, Kelly. She's asleep, and she's not going to see where we are taking her. It's going to be fine. Don't you want to know why she's so strong? Don't you want to find out why, how, she has so much power? We can keep her and maybe make her an ally. Make her work for her life," he said, madly.

"Jason, listen to yourself. She isn't a pet. She's a vampire. Did you forget what that means? She is a cold-blooded killer and we don't know how to kill her. How do you expect us to convince her that she has to be on our side? This same person almost killed you. Do you have any idea how dangerous she could be? We can't leave her here passed out on the grass, but she can't come to Trio-Genesis." Mark looked at him for a while. Jason's stare was cold and blank. Mark looked at Kelly and spoke: "Do whatever you want, we aren't part of this." He and Kelly surfed away, leaving the sleeping vampire in the arms of the diluted slayer.

Jason laid her body down and knelt next to her. Olivia's chest rose and fell. She was breathing peacefully once again. He brushed the hair from her face and stared at her full lips. His heart raced. He couldn't bring her into Trio-Genesis without setting off the alarms. Vampires weren't allowed. Jason sat there for while hoping she didn't wake up.

Dark whispers entered his ears and swam in his mind. His heart was beating faster and he closed his eyes with slow flickers. The voice was louder and more smoothing as he listened to its horrible advice.

He grabbed his arm, opened her mouth and pierced his wrist with her fangs. His eyes shot open. His lips smiled wildly. The bruises on his face healed completely and his arms grew new flesh over the scratches and burned off skin. His veins showed under his skin. He could see the blood running quickly through every little vein. He exhaled a long breath and picked up the sleeping Countess in his strong arms. A hot wind rushed over Jason and Olivia, and they were gone.

CHAPTER 4

∗

Caged Animal

Olivia used her hands and arms to cover her face and shield from the brightness of the light. She rolled around some, reaching her hands around her she pulled on invisible blankets. Goosebumps rose all over her body and the half-asleep Countess shivered. She murmured under her breath and tossed and turned some more. Again she hit beneath her with an open palm and yawned, blinking and rubbing her eyes like a child. The brightness of the light was a plague. She rolled around but was stopped by cold bars that kept her from falling off the edge of the bed.

"This isn't my bed…" she groaned. Reluctantly, Olivia opened her eyes and looked up. The white walls and floors weren't anything like her warm, red bed. The ceiling was one bright light.

Jason watched her move like a delicate flower. Olivia's hand made a small amber and quickly died out. She brought her hands closer to her face, flipping them over twice. Her fingers ran over her palms, and then her hands met as she rubbed them together and shook them out. She took a deep breath and again tried to surf, starting with a small fire. Jason laughed to himself. Her back was still turned to him. She tried again to surf—nothing.

"It won't work," a smooth voice spoke, stopping her. Olivia turned quickly. She walked forward and touched the long, silver bars. The metal sparked blue and Olivia withdrew her hands swiftly. Jason laughed at her pain. She once again tried to touch the bars and again they shocked her. Jason looked at her with frowning eyebrows.

"If it shocked you once, what could have possibly changed?" She exhaled, gritting her teeth before grabbing hold of the bars once more. Her hands began shaking—the erring sound of electricity grew ringing loudly. He rose with knitted brows as his thoughts betrayed him. It would soon stop her heart and she would fall dead in her cage.

"I am not crazy," Olivia said, letting go of the bars. Her hands burned bright red, but soon the color faded and not the slightest scar remained. She was completely unharmed. Jason composed his stance and shook his head calmly.

"You read minds," he noted. A talent only Slayers possessed. He watched her carefully.

"Really? I didn't know that. What else can I do, oh-powerful-one?" Jason wasn't amused at her attempt at sarcasm. They watched each other for a moment before Olivia spoke again. "Do you expect me to stay in here? I'm not an animal."

"You act like one." Jason looked at her blankly. She revealed her fangs as her eyes turned red. His look held its empty stare, and so Olivia returned to her normal self. He sat back in his chair. Olivia sat down and waited for him to speak. She was powerless, and although she had many moves up her sleeve, Olivia was forced to wait. She had played her pieces and now it was his turn, but all he did was sit and watch. He watched her move the hair from her face. He watched her scratch her arm and neck. He watched her tap her nails on the ground of the cell. If he wasn't going to kill her, or attempt to kill her, he could at least amuse her by trying.

She began humming. Olivia hummed the most annoying song: "Row Row Row Your Boat." She kept humming. Jason took a deep breath. Olivia smiled, but just as he began to release his breath, Jason hummed along. They sat humming the song, one after the other. Taking turns on who began humming and who hummed second. They even harmonized to it. He wasn't breaking. Olivia stood, still humming, and grabbed ahold of the bars. Her body shook and sweat, Olivia kept humming along. He stood from his seat again and walked over to her cell. They looked into each other's eyes, humming "Row Row Row Your Boat." Neither stopped humming until Jason did the unthinkable—he touched her hands. Olivia's eyes widened. She let go of the bars and ceased her humming. Jason also stopped.

"No point in hurting yourself," he stated coolly. "If you keep touching the bars they will drain your energy and if they don't do that fast enough—because you're a freak—they'll stop your heart. If you have one that's beating. This was created to keep your kind in. Try to burn it down, and it will burn you. I'd rather not watch you torment yourself so if you'd please restrain yourself, maybe someone will come to your rescue, though I highly doubt it."

"You seem so sure of yourself," she barked at him suddenly.

"You're just another vampire. A measly life means nothing. Why bother? Another can be made just as quickly. You and your kind take people from families and out of homes, hunting down good slayers to turn them evil. I know! I have spent years never hearing from the missing—wondering only where he has gone. And now, I finally have one of you, and I will do to you as you've done to us." His face reddened as he spoke. His hands became fists and his eyes narrowed. Jason took a second and gathered himself. He walked out of the room closing and locking the door after him. A man with this much rage would do well in the vampire community. A large portion of him was dark and evil. His mind could be easily corrupted.

Minutes passed and Jason came back with a large, turkey sandwich cut in half and a glass filled with a clear liquid that could only be water. He sat back down on his chair and looked at Olivia. "You hungry?" he asked, taking a large bite of his turkey sandwich.

"Yes. I'd love a large medium rare steak with a side of mashed potatoes and a Bloody Mary," she answered. Her mouth watered as she swallowed hard and licked her lips discreetly.

"Yeah, that sucks," he said, taking another large bite of his delicious sandwich.

Olivia sighed, yawned, and her stomach grumbled.

Olivia could stay silent no more. "What do you want? Why are you keeping me here?"

After he swallowed what he had in his mouth, he explained to her that after she passed out he couldn't leave her in the middle of the park or it would cause trouble for both of their clans. He also said that he never caught a vampire before and the idea of having a pet sounded fun. He mocked her strength and people with his insensitive words. Olivia stared at him blankly. This was all a game to him. He went on to explain that because she hadn't died when she was stabbed, he was confused and wanted to study her to find out why. He also told her the only people who knew she was there beside himself were Mark and Kelly.

"Where exactly am I?" she asked calmly.

"What does it matter? No one is going to come save you, I've already told you that," he said coldly with a smirk planted on his lips.

"I'm not one for being lost. It stings the heart," she answered, perhaps a bit too honest.

"That might just be the feeling of the stake from earlier." Everything out of his mouth was just as cunning as hers. "But I've been silent long enough. I'll humor you. You are sitting in cage—a white room in Trio-Genesis."

"This room is white? I hadn't noticed." Her pitiful attempt at sarcasm rose again. "What's a Trio-Genesis?" She asked innocently.

"It's not a Trio-Genesis—just Trio-Genesis. It's a building." He laughed softly, trying to be just as sarcastic as she was. It didn't work as well because she didn't laugh or smile. "It's a safe place for slayers. I'm sure you've heard of it. I mean—we slayers don't know where vampires hide, but we know you have a safe haven like we do—a place you can call home. Except ours offers classes so that each slayer can use his or her powers to his or her fullest abilities. We believe in helping people and those who have lost family and friends to the likes of you."

"You live and study here." She stated. Jason nodded. Olivia didn't ask much more.

She had heard of Trio-Genesis before from her mother. When she was little, Savanna used to tell Olivia that she would take her to study at this big school for slayers when she was old enough—that her powers would grow and she would learn more than she could ever imagine from Trio-Genesis.

"Do you have a name, slayer?" She asked after the silence seemed to have settled in.

She couldn't do much with his name, so he answered, "Sharpie. Jason, Sharpie."

Olivia frowned. She didn't understand the reference. "Sorry, I've always wanted to do that. I'm Jason. Just Jason," he said.

"I'll call you slayer," she told him. "You've lived here all of your life?"

Jason nodded. There was more silence. Jason took out a notebook and began writing in it. He looked up at her every so often and took notes. "You live with vampires don't you?" She nodded and watched him write her answer in his notebook. He had torn papers falling from the sides, crumbled around other pages. There were staples and paper clips on every page. "I was thinking of killing you, but you might be of use to me after all," he spoke again. Olivia looked at him in disbelief. He kept talking. "What do you know of The Vampire Slayer?"

"Any news?"

"Not yet," Michael answered Joshua, who paced the grounds. His eyes never blinked and sweat ran down his face. Michael offered a towel to his best friend but Joshua rejected it. Joshua looked down at the floor. He had gone back to the park several times to check if she was there. He looked in all the places he thought she could be. Unfortunately, the vampire mansion was too big and they had not yet finished searching for her. Joshua even sent out search parties of children to look in small places where the average adult wouldn't seek. He told them that the Countess was playing hide and seek and that the first child to find her would win a big prize. The children needed to be tricked into looking for her, but the adults were commanded to seek until told otherwise. The mansion was upside down. Joshua told them that no one would rest and that the searching would not cease until Olivia was found. Everything was put on hold until they had news of her whereabouts.

The last time Olivia disappeared was because she decided to go to the Bahamas and tan without letting anyone know of her absence. But this time was different. They were all together fighting slayers at a park. She should have been back by now.

"I shouldn't have left her," Joshua said as rushing vampires ran behind him. He was the last one there with her. She seemed to have everything under control—of course, there were three slayers fighting her—but still, the daughter of Dracula could handle 50 slayers alone.

The two sat at the base of the main stairs. Joshua's face was stained from what seemed like tears. "I'm incomplete without her. As much as we fight and argue or disagree, we are reading the same book. We might not be on the same page, but we are on the same chapter." Joshua looked square at the main door. "What if something's going sour?" he whispered to Michael.

"She will come back," Michael reassured. "Olivia is big girl and can handle herself." Michael stood and placed his hand on Joshua's shoulder. "They've worried long enough. We should call off the search until morning."

Joshua didn't want to seem too dramatic. "Right. I'll make an announcement. Fetch Patrick, will you?"

"You have got to be joking," Olivia started. "The Vampire Slayer?" She laughed and crossed her arms over her chest. "Doesn't ring a bell." Jason laughed at her. Surely everyone knew of The Vampire Slayer. Maybe the rumors were true. Maybe the vampires never found out she was also half slayer.

"You... you're funny." he stated. "Unfortunately, I have to write about Olivia and that's about all I know: her name. I looked at her family line to see if I could find anyone that was related to her." Olivia's eyes gleamed and a smile formed. "But I couldn't find anyone. If she does have any family around, the secret is kept very well," The smile faded. "My parents used to be close friends of her mother's. I think I even met Olivia when I was a child because of

Savanna, but I don't remember much…It's been such a long time and…" Jason went off in his own thoughts.

"You knew Savanna Brooks?" Olivia asked quickly. "Do you remember her well?" The slayer shook his head and the vampire girl exhaled. "So tell me more about this project of yours." She tried to change the awkward subject.

"It's for my history/present class. It's just another bad idea, of course. But because it's ignorant not knowing our past, I have to do it. The assignment was that everyone had to pick a name out of a jar and write about him or her." Jason wasn't much for schooling, but he got very good grades. "My teacher put her name in the jar as a joke. But I'm way too stubborn and I decided that her name must have come to me for a reason. Maybe it's my calling to know more about her." Jason looked down at white tiles on the floor, staring at his glassy reflection. "When I saw her name written in prefect cursive, I got chills," Jason continued. "My spine tingled and my heart pump faster. I think there's something about her. Something I can't explain yet and might never be able to." Jason had once again in the presence of Olivia gone off into his own world—a feeling that was new to him. Never before had he been so distracted by his own mind. The very sound of her name paralyzed him, taking him into a deep spell that could not be easily broken. Olivia watched his every move: the way his breath changed as he spoke her name, the way he wiped the sweat from his hands on his jeans, the way his eyes lit up at all the possibilities.

"I've had these dreams where she…" Jason looked up, Olivia had an evil smile planted. His words amused her. "My teacher is giving me an extra week to do my project because no one knows much about Olivia Montgomery. The vampires don't even know that she is the Vampire Slayer." She was puzzled. Jason leaned in and looked her in the eyes, "They didn't know Savanna was a slayer, the most powerful who's lived. Your Countess is half slayer, and I just told you one of the best guarded secrets." Jason sat back in his chair rubbing his temple. He rested his face into his hands and brushed his hair with his fingers a couple of times.

Sure, for the first couple of years no one had a clue about Savanna, but it was out in the open now. She could tell him all of this or she could play along.

"That explains a lot. All the things she did—things no one understood." Olivia played along as best she could. "Her ridiculous rules about not turning. She's been lying to us all along." She paused again to check his expression. He was putty in her hands. "We've had the daughter of the most power vampire and the most powerful slayer in our hands and it's gone to waste." Another pause. "If no one knows her, how is your teacher going to grade you?" she asked honestly.

"That isn't my concern. I propose a deal," She nodded. "You tell me what you know, and I won't kill you," he said gleefully.

"Any other options?" There weren't. "Then I'll take death please."

"Fine," Jason conceded. "Is there something you want? Besides the obvious."

She wasn't going to waste any more time. "Back at the park when I was stabbed..." Olivia stopped. She needed another lie and she needed one quick. She obviously wasn't going to get away with a clean shot, so she needed something to make him believe she wasn't as bad as they came.

"I'm not a normal vampire." She had no response from him. "I'm a lab rat—a genetically grown vampire." He leaned in a bit closer.

"When I was a little girl, my parents and I were walking back from the premier of a movie I had been dying to see. It was late at night, and my mother and father held my hands. I remember to this day the clothes we wore, the way they smelled."

Olivia faked a pair of sad puppy eyes and continued her story. "We got in the car to go home. Ten minutes passed, we were on a long highway. It was late. My father said, 'Looks like we are the only ones out here,' then did this creepy laugh he used to do to scare me. When my mother screamed, he hit the brakes inches away from hitting a man. He was pale with dark, mysterious eyes. My father got out of car, and walked over to the man and spoke to him. I couldn't hear what he was saying. I remember telling my mother I was afraid. She told me everything would be all right. That's when my father's body flew into the windshield of the car. His body broke the glass, and the broken glass cut up my mother's face and arms."

Olivia stopped for a moment to take a breath and looked down in an attempt to choke up. "I was so afraid," she whispered. "There was so much blood everywhere. My mom's door came flying off and I heard her scream to me to hide as her body got dragged out of the car. I didn't know what to do. There aren't many places in a car you can hide." Olivia took a breath to muster a tear or two.

He was buying whatever it was she was selling. "The last thing I remember from that night was his face popping back in the car and lunging at me. When I woke up the next morning, I was in a hospital bed, but it wasn't a hospital. The air was foul and heavy. There were newspapers at the end of my bed with my parent's faces on it. I couldn't read the headline because I wasn't old enough to read the big words. I only remember it said: 'Freak Kills Mortons.' I was all alone in the world, my parents were orphans and I an only child. A blonde woman came for me and told me where I was. They ran tests on me. I don't remember being turned, but I was, I guess. They're engineering human children into vampires. I am one. There are others." That last part was true. Jason kept quiet and let the words sink in.

"They took my family and destroyed my life. I've been waiting for my revenge. No one will come for me, you're right. I'm a creation. Disposable. You asked me what I wanted in return if I helped you. I want to stay here, in your school, as a student."

She didn't let him speak, for she feared he would simply deny her. "I want to become a slayer," she pushed. "I don't think I'm asking much—after all, I'll be giving you vital, top secret information on the Countess. I will be committing high treason against the people who have raised me." He did not speak still. Olivia would have to go the extra mile if she was going to get what she wanted. "You should know better than anyone how revenge feels." Jason ceased all thought.

"Excuse me?"

"I know the pain of loss when I see you. You've lost one. And you wait for your day to take revenge." She resorted to personal information in her desperation.

He began questioning her about the Mansion—about Olivia mostly. He jotted notes down and asked bizarre questions not even Olivia knew how to answer. Jason was taught that Olivia was a horrible, evil, and cruel coward, hiding in the shadows of the mansion. The Countess was their protected gem. Hidden from battles, fights, and all slayers at all time. Had it not been for his incorrect schooling of Olivia, Jason could have had a better chance at unraveling the mysterious vampire girl before him. She answered honestly to all his questions. She just left out the fact that she was the Vampire Slayer. Jason finished his questioning, rose from his chair, and headed for the door.

"Where do you think you're going?" Olivia asked angrily. He thanked her for helping him find out everything he needed to know about the Vampire Slayer, but he wasn't really going to let her go. After all, she was a vampire and this was a slayer's household. Besides, Jason's real plan couldn't unfold if he let her go. She wasn't his first "project" but she was the most useful one. Olivia stood in her cage red in the face, eyes glooming with hate. Olivia argued that he promised that he would help her get her "revenge" but he told her that he changed his mind.

"I thought vampires were the ones who couldn't be trusted, not you."

Jason stopped dead in his tracks. "Slayers can be trusted."

But Olivia was just as quick with her words. "I didn't say slayers. I said you."

"If you're quiet, I'll bring you a blood bag later." He smirked and headed for the door, but as he reached for the handle, his hand caught up in flames. His whole body was soon engulfed in the hot fire as he was surfed inside the cage alongside Olivia. He was right about one thing when it came to Olivia. She did not approve of treason, unless it was her own. His betrayal would not go unpunished.

"I won't need a bag. There is fresh blood right here," she said smiling at him.

"How did you do that?" He asked, backing as far away from her as he could without touching the bars. "I am not letting a vampire roam around Trio-Genesis. You want revenge, go somewhere else. This isn't revenge school. This school is for born slayers. You were born human. Nothing here can help you. You don't have what it takes," he explained, his voice cracking as he spoke.

"I held up my end of the bargain, and now it's your turn. So you'd better start thinking of something."

Jason looked around. His heart pumped faster, and his arms flexed as his veins rose from beneath his skin. The distance between him and Olivia wasn't much. He could smell her brown hair and could feel her soft breath on his face. The slayer swallowed hard. "Unless there is someone in your family that was a slayer, I can't help you."

It was time for Olivia to come up with another lie. "My mother used to tell me that my great grandfather had special powers. No one ever really knew him too well, but she used to tell me these wild stories of a man that could control the winds. I think maybe he was slayer." Jason raised an eyebrow at her. She never ceased to come up with some ridiculous story to say.

"How convenient. Your orphan mother knew her grandfather." He answered her quickly. Olivia was getting rusty with her storytelling.

"Just because her parents died doesn't mean she was raised in an orphanage." Bam!

That should save it. "It makes perfect sense. At the park, I used a power that came from my hands I didn't know I had. Maybe my great grandfather's power is now also mine. It must have skipped over a few generations. Or maybe they were slayers and they didn't know." When he wasn't looking at her she shook her head and rolled her eyes, but once his eyes met hers again she composed herself back into the mess of lies. "Slayer, she's making an army."

This grabbed his attention. She was feeding him all the information he needed.

"I'd like to sympathize with you, but I can't. It's a tough process. Not everyone gets in. There are people who have been living here for years, trying to learn, trying get these powers that only slayers are born with."

"I could just kill you..." she pointed out, hoping it would scare him beyond thought. They were simple words that got to the point of her feelings and worked wonders at the mansion, but not here, and not with him. Jason had no fear when it came to Olivia. From the moment she could have killed him and didn't, all the fear he could have felt from her words were powerless. Olivia didn't wait for a response. She admitted to a truth that one day would puzzle even the most educated slayers. "...but I'm not that evil," she confessed.

He watched her defeated mind give up and sit in the corner farthest from him.

The sound of a clocked ticked and bounced throughout the room, filling in the empty spaces. The ticks seemed to jump off the walls and back into the clock. He resorted to the last option he had.

"HELP! Someone!" His attempt was pathetic, he did not give up. Jason kept crying out over and over, running his hands through his dirty hair. The strands fell across his forehead again. His blue eyes, tired and weary, kept glancing at Olivia.

He shouted louder every time, hoping that someone would hear: "Anyone... please....hello?" Nothing. "Help... help...help..." His voice grew horse and soft until his endless cries were only but a whisper in the night. "Help..."

"Will you shut up?" She asked finally. "No one is going to help you. If you haven't noticed, no one has come by in the last hour and no one is going to come by in the next hour either. I am hungry, tired, and pissed off! It's bad enough that I'm stuck in here with you because you won't keep up your end of the bargain, so will you please shut your trap?" Olivia was boiling. At last, not even she could take his consistent pitiful cry.

"You are the rudest vampire I have ever met. You think I'm not tired, or hungry, or sick of your blood-soaked breath filling the room? If you haven't noticed, I am stuck in a cage with a monster who, just a while ago, tried to eat me but realized she couldn't. You pretend to be so tough and think no one is going to stand up to you. You're not royalty, you're just another vampire trying to scam her way into our lives."

Olivia rolled her eyes at him. "You have to get over the killing you thing. It was an hour ago! The only reason you are in this cell is that you can't keep your word. What were you going to do with me, leave me here until I starve? I eat too, you know! Not just blood, real food!"

She looked away and then back at him to continue her argument. "You sit here, 'help, help, help, please, someone, anyone.' Whining like a baby! I can't even believe I'm arguing with you, so just shut up!" She screamed releasing some fury but the hate remained still.

They sat for another half hour without speaking. Time kept ticking away as they sat deeper and deeper into the night. Her eyes closed and opened repeatedly. Her hands wrapped around her legs as she rested her head between her knees. Olivia took deep calming breaths, and when Jason wasn't looking, she breathed into her hand, hoping she didn't really smell like blood. He was messing with her brain just like she was messing with his. Neither of them looked at the other. Neither of them said anything.

Jason's heart pounded in his chest. The heat from his skin surrounded them. The sweat running down his back wet his shirt even further. The shockwaves of electricity made the hairs on the back of his neck stand still.

"Fine," he said, getting her attention. Olivia raised her head and looked him in his piercing eyes. The hairs on his arms stood at her gaze. "This is childish. Let me go. I'll open the door, and you can get out. I'll help you." Now it was Olivia's turn not to believe a word out of his lying lips. "This isn't me giving in. This isn't me giving up. This is a part of me no one knows. Keep that to yourself, and we'll get your revenge." Jason reached out his hand to hers looking at the dirt on her face. Olivia raised her hand and wiped her face. "Please stay out of my mind," he smiled softly.

Her comeback to his words knocked the air out of his chest. "Keep me out of it." She smiled at him. Jason laughed a bit and was silent.

"Stay very still," she warned him. "This will burn a little."

Olivia stared him down. She pictured his body bursting into flames, burning his flesh off his bones. Surely enough, two seconds later, he surfed out of the cage. Jason didn't have any second thoughts as he rushed over to large green button that sat on a gray table among buttons of different colors. He pushed it, and a small door at the top of cage opened. Olivia stood where the door was and poked her head out.

"Creative," she said lifting herself out of the cell.

CHAPTER 5

A Simple Test

The halls were wide and the walls were eggshell-colored. The ceiling stretched miles high, as if the building had no end. Her eyes glistened at the beauty in that one hallway she walked through. Her lips were parted with a nearly invisible smile. Her brows close together. Olivia exhaled as she watched the astonishing walls. They were bare but fulgent like sand on the beach. Perhaps she couldn't help herself, or maybe she wasn't thinking; she reached out and touched it to find her hand went right into the wall and the white sand ran down her arms like little bugs, then fell on the floor.

Jason pulled her hand out of the wall. "Please don't touch anything," he said. He shook his head and continued. "This is why we can't have nice things."

After living there all his life, it was easy to miss the marvel of the building. It was as equally easy to forget others were affected by the magic of the elements. They kept walking. It was late, and curfew was enforced for anyone in the building, especially students. Noise should not be a reason another slayer who works, studies, or parents, cannot sleep.

Olivia's eyes looked everywhere. In this corridor the walls were light blue and rather cold. The standing hairs on her arms were proof enough of that. There were no lights in this hallway. In the other, there were hanging lights in golden accents. Here no lamps were found, no wall lights, no chandlers. This hall had the same blue glow of the walls. Jason warned her again of the danger of touch. She kept her hands to herself.

"It's water if you were wondering," Jason warned. "Very cold, it could kill you with one touch. I can't touch it either. But don't worry, from your little act in the park, I know just where to take you."

Finally, they reached an open space where the floors were no longer carpeted. There was nothing in the space but a little window that looked like a ticket booth. The room was very large and plain. The marble floors were light gray and the walls were made of thick glass. To the far left side was one chair—just one gray, folding chair sitting there all alone and facing whoever happened to come by. There was no evil or danger in the space before them. It was just an odd, open area. It was simple. It was safe.

Jason walked in front of her as they reached the booth. There was a light inside and the shadow of a person. He knocked on the window and waited.

"Don't judge an old woman by her looks," Jason cautioned. "She's a powerful old woman. Trust me, I know. Once a human was promised immortality by a vampire, the only trade was that he had to penetrate our hideout, Trio-Genesis, and feed the vampires as much as he could. She knew. No one can ever explain how, but she knew. And while he was sitting in that very chair," Jason said as he pointed to the silver chair, "she cut his throat." He swallowed loud. There was a possibility Olivia could lose her head tonight. She agreed to follow his lead on this one. An old woman walked over to the window. She had white hair and hot silver eyes that burned across the faces of whom she looked at. The bags under her eyes had bags, and she gave the impression that she had a desperate need for a glass of water. Her skin was pasty and her cheeks fell to each side of her face. She didn't look happy even when she was.

"Mrs. Seymour, it's been a long time! Too long I think. Isn't it time they take you out of this rat hole and let you teach something? Something exciting… that gives you life? You're looking good," he lied.

"Puffery won't work, Mr. Sharpie," she croaked. Clearing her throat she began speaking to him again, "So, what is it that you need this hour of the night? And Mr. Sharpie, please try to make this quick. I was watching the square box, and my favorite comedian is on," she informed him rather faint.

"I'll try not to keep you," he said with respect. Olivia stood behind him quietly. For the first time in a long time she was doing as she was told without complaining. "This here is... umm..." After all this time had gone by, Jason never bothered to get her name.

"Brook," Olivia answered filling in his blanks.

"Brook..." His voice, as he repeated her name, was filled with suspicion. "I found her in the park this evening, and she is claiming that she is a slayer." The next words he whispered so only the old hag could hear, "But you know people are, everyone wants to be a hero. I want to help her, but I don't trust her very much. Can you help me?" Jason backed away from the window. "We'll fill out the paperwork, and you can give me the test. I'll run it myself—don't want you to miss your show."

"Nice try, Mr. Sharpie, but they have changed everything. She needs to take a test and I will be deciding what she is or isn't. Young lady," she called out, looking at Olivia, "I'm going to need some blood. And I see there is some on your shirt and arms and... face. Where did you find her again, Mr. Sharpie?"

"The park..." He answered with shaking words and half-closed eyes. He turned to Olivia as Mrs. Seymour collected the things she needed. "I was hoping she would let us take your blood on our own. That way, we could have used my blood. The test is super hard, too—could take you hours. You'll never pass it," he told her, giving up. "Sorry. I tried."

They turned back to where the old woman stood—her eyes burning at Jason. He gave her a half honest smile. "Mrs. Seymour, it's very late and..."

"And I'm sure it wouldn't be a problem for you to take some blood, and for me to fill in some circles," Olivia spoke over Jason, whose eyes were wide.

"Very well, Miss..."

"Morton," she said.

"Miss Morton." She handed Olivia a piece of paper and explained to her that she had to fill in the circles that applied to her, and if she skipped any questions it would not count against her. Then she took a small needle from the top shelf and plastic tube. She asked Olivia for her left hand, pricked her ring finger with the needle, and let her blood fall into the tube. Once filled, the tube went inside a gray tin can that spun quickly. Olivia walked over to the chair, sat down, and began to read her test.

Jason walked in circles. He was done for. Every alarm was sure to go off now that her blood was out in the open. He paced slowly, waiting for the coming hours to go by. He wasn't allowed to talk to her. Jason listened to the spinning of the can slow down. The can became slower and slower until it finally stopped. The old woman could not believe her eyes and nether could Jason. They looked over at Olivia, who also looked up. Jason looked as if he had seen a ghost. The old woman simply smiled at her.

"What?" Olivia asked as she got up from her chair and walked over to the small window.

As Olivia got closer to them, he saw she was done and every circle was filled in completely. What took him three hours took her only three minutes. The blood was the fastest on record. She placed her test down in front of Mrs. Seymour's window.

"How come it took my blood work hours?" he asked, honestly.

"Tests are only as effortless as the person taking them, Mr. Sharpie. According to this, Miss. Morton's blood is easy to understand." Mrs. Seymour smiled at Olivia who kindly smiled back. "Wait here."

Now Mrs. Seymour did something she had never done before. She walked to the back of the messy booth she practically lived in, stepping on large books and old papers that laid on the dusty floor. There was a door just her size at the very back of the room. To get there, however, she had to walk over more books and paper. Soon, she came out the booth from around the corner.

"You wouldn't believe the mess I had to go through to get here." She was a lot shorter than she seemed behind the booth, but her aging face was the same.

Mrs. Seymour handed Olivia a paper that contained all of her classes, but no times or number. "There are no times. No locations," the unfamiliar student stated matter-of-factly.

"The elevators," Jason answered, smiling. Trio-Genesis was full of surprises, from its sand walls to its talking elevator.

"Just take the elevator." Mrs. Seymour had a friendly grin on her face. She walked closer to Olivia and took her by the hands. "Let me look at you." Olivia looked at Jason who shrugged his shoulders and waited for the woman to move. Mrs. Seymour spun Olivia around and caressed her hands. She took in a deep breath and looked straight into Olivia's eyes. Not a thought went through her head that either Olivia or Jason could hear. "I don't usually come out of my booth. But tonight..." Mrs. Seymour's eyes filled with tears. Jason opened his mouth, but words did not come out, so he closed it. "I wanted to be the first to welcome you," with what seemed like her final words to Olivia, Mrs. Seymour pulled her close and hugged her. Olivia wrapped her arms around the old woman and hugged her back. They pulled away from each other—the woman wiping her tears and getting back to her booth.

Jason and Olivia went on their way back to the cold and melting halls. All the while, Olivia looked at the paper before her. There weren't any numbers for the classes.

There were only words and information about her. Once they had gotten far enough from Mrs. Seymour, Jason took the paper from her hands and looked it over.

Brook Morton   October 29
Level 18   BT: O-
Element: Unknown

ID: 962910

Vampire   Browse
Elements   Kerrigan
Defense   Craips

Slayer History   Pinkelburg
Unknown   B

Olivia was the same skill level as Jason, perfect. He rolled his eyes and sucked his teeth. "Computer couldn't tell what you were…" he showed her pointing at the paper. Olivia read the words "unknown" and shrugged her shoulders as she walked on. "It could just mean that you don't have an element," he paused, still looking over the paper with no regard for the vampire girl. "We'll work on it." Jason looked to his side to speak to Olivia, but she wasn't there. "Brook?"

She stood a few feet back, looking at a picture. It was the first painting she had seen since she had arrived. It was the only picture in the hallway so far, and it stood alone, as if it had been forgotten. Olivia looked at the picture—her breath shaky as she read the name at the bottom of the painting. Jason walked over to her and stared with her at the picture. His lips pressed tightly together and he swallowed hard. Jason licked the corners of his mouth. "That should have been taken down," he said, walking away from the picture of the blonde teenage boy. "Come on." He grabbed Olivia's arm and pulled her away. They walked in silence. She didn't ask and he didn't speak.

"Are you in any of my classes?" she asked.

He cleared his throat and answered her, "All but one." A class titled unknown was rare. It could easily be the class to determine her "Unknown" element or it could be a boring lecture about being a slayer. In place of the unknown class in his schedule, Jason had Aerodynamics. Or at least that was the class name for slayers whose element was air. He didn't have a direct answer for her when she asked more about unknowns. There wasn't much to say, so he told her not to worry, and that it could just be that they wanted to get to know her because she was new.

"They play all kinds of tricks at this place. Be on your toes," he told her. He didn't tell her that the slayers she had fought were in their classes too. There was no point in upsetting her or making her worry. He could handle the coming fire on his own.

Jason was too transparent. His constant rubbing of his temple, frowned eyes, heavy breathing, and occasional loud exhale was enough evidence for Olivia to preach some warming words of reassurance. "I'm no trouble at all. I'm quiet, nice, sweet, kind, caring, and lovely; I'm a great person," she promised.

"Ton, the Countess is missing," an old Janitor spoke to the other with a smiling face.

The man mopping the floors stopped his work and looked with disbelief at his old friend. "Oh, please let it be so. That girl is two hands full. She's loud, she's rude, sour, mean, selfish, hateful—an awful person. Don't lie to me, Cal. Is she really gone?" he asked, hoping it wasn't April first.

Cal took the mop from Ton's hands and leaned it against the wall. "Out of our hair!" He laughed and kicked the yellow mop bucket on the ground. To two old men splashed their feet in the dirty water, shouting "Hooray!" at the top of their lungs until sleeping vampires screamed rudely for them to shut up. But in silent joy they looked at each other and whispered, "Hooray."

"I'm great!" she smiled out the words. Jason looked at her, eyebrows raised. Silence fell upon them again. They spent most of their time in awkward silence, trying not to think—hoping if they did, the other wasn't listening. Inside, Jason's heart ran circles, miles, and laps. His blood boiled and his teeth ached. His skin was hot but his hands were cold. The closer to her body his body got the more sweat his back would produce.

The walk to Olivia's room was long and boring. Jason wanted to crawl into his large bed and sleep. He was sure he was coming down with something. As for Olivia, she looked extremely awake—her eyes were wide open and her face had a huge smile as she recalled memories of Trio-Genesis. Savanna use to take her there all the time when she was little. She played outside in the yard with a brown haired little boy that looked like her. They ran up and down the grass laughing and tickling each other until one of them wanted to pee their pants. He was a year older than Olivia, but it didn't make him wiser. Olivia was skillful and always scheming, while the little boy covered in grass and dirt was honest and childlike. They were the best of friends and the closest enemies.

"You'll like it here. Every floor has its own unique aspect. There are a few things you need to know," Jason spoke, breaking the silence. "There are 40 floors, and only three can be seen from outside. Trio-Genesis is made from the elements, she is a strong building. Floors 15 through 20 are classes. On the first floor, there is a kitchen, two libraries, a ballroom, and meeting rooms. We are on the third floor right now. It has simulation rooms, cell locks, the registration hall and gym. There are two gyms, one for working out and a school gym, but that's on the 20th floor. Floors 21 through 36 are homes, rooms, and apartments. Floor two is the hospital. On the fifth floor, there is another library. Floors six, seven, and eight are forbidden, don't ask why, I don't know. Floors nine through 14 are student bedrooms. There is one game room or hang out spot—whatever you want to call it—on the 14th floor, and it's always filled with people so don't bother going there. Floors 37 through 39 no one goes on because it belongs to someone, and the 40th floor is the tower," Jason explained out of order.

"Don't you think I would have remembered that better if you had started on the first floor?" she asked him.

Jason took in a deep breath. He knew she was right. Why didn't he just start from floor one and work his way up? "Would you like me to explain them again?" he asked.

"Are you going to explain it like that?" Olivia mimicked his voice. Jason began walking. "Right..." Olivia said and walked alongside him. "What about your little friends," she asked. "Won't they remember me?"

"I'll talk to them before class begins. They need to be convinced that you won't do anything reckless. But they won't say a word outside of the group, we'll be dead if anyone knows you're here," he said honestly. Jason and Olivia finally reached golden doors that opened at their arrival. They could have surfed to their rooms, but Jason did not know where Olivia's room would be. They stepped into the large elevator and golden doors closed behind them. There were floor buttons: floors six, seven, and eight were missing. Floors 37 through 39 were circles with no numbers. At the bottom of the numbers were two holes, Jason instructed Olivia to put her index finger in the left hole. A small needle pricked her finger quickly. A shocked Olivia pulled her now bleeding finger out of the elevator and watched the blood run. "You'll be fine," Jason said, then grabbed her hand and sucked the blood from her finger. Her eyes were the size of watermelons. Someone was being very polite today. Jason opened his eyes, removed her finger from his mouth, and apologized. As he did the elevator spoke welcoming Miss Montgomery to the building, an indication of the building's knowledge neither of them noticed. The 14th floor circle lit up, and the elevator began to move.

"What the hell, slayer?" she asked her voice with disgust.

"I can't let you run around bleeding everywhere. The alarms could go off," he answered rudely and watched the numbers at the top of the doors. Olivia cleaned her finger on her dirty pants and inspected the circles with the glowing numbers. The small cut on her finger had healed so that her finger looked like new. The numbers beeped at every floor. They waited peacefully as the elevator took them to their destination. At the 14th floor, the doors opened and the elevator kindly said goodbye.

Olivia looked back at the golden elevator. Her mouth dropped open and she snorted a laugh from deep in her lungs. Trio-Genesis was wired to act as a human being. It knew everything and everyone by their blood. It had feelings.

"Look for your name on a door," Jason told her.

"How can we be sure it's here?"

"The elevator knows what floor your room is on. Just look for your name or initials," he said, walking away as he looked at doors.

"How do I know which one is mine?" she asked standing by the elevator still.

Jason stopped walking and looked back at the persistent vampire. "Do you know your initials?" Olivia nodded as her eyebrows raised and lips pushed together. "Do you know your name?" Again she gave him the same look that said: 'I'm not stupid.'

"Good," he mocked her. "Now look for the door with one of those two clues on it." He kept walking and shaking his head.

"So you're saying I'm the only person in this building with my initials," she stated.

Jason's feet came to a halt. He turned slowly, daggers shooting from his blue eye, "Just look for it," he said very slowly. Olivia mouthed a "fine" and looked on the other doors. It was a narrow hallway, long and dark. The lights were dimmed for the hour of the night. Some doors were brown and chipped. Others were clearly decorated by the element of the slayer living within. Each door had a silver oval platelet with a name.

Some were blank, some were scratched out, and some had added letters done by hand. Jason looked at one side of the hall and Olivia the other.

"Are they in any order?"

"No, Brook. Just keep looking," he sighed as he read the names of students he has never even met. No one before had ever taken the time to read the names on every door. No one had time for that. The building was one of the two people who knew all residents. It knew every creature, every slayer, every human, and every threat.

Olivia whispered each name under her breath. "T. S.C., M. Brooks, K. A. G., L. D. F., W. Schneider, V. C. B., R. Surfer, Matthew R., V.S.C.K., O. Brook M." Olivia looked at Jason who was ahead of her a little then looked back at the initials. "Olivia Brook Montgomery," she muttered and touched the silver letters on the door. She looked back up at Jason who was still reading names off doors. Olivia raised her fingers to the O, and a small, red flame came from her fingers, melting the metal around the letter. "I found it," she called out.

Jason walked back to her and stared at the door. "Brook M. You sure this is yours?" he teased her.

"I'm sure," she beamed. They looked at the large, brown door. It was old and dirty.

The glass door handle was cloudy and covered with dust. If the condition of the door meant anything, then the room was an awful mess.

"Don't you want to see what it looks like?" he asked her genuinely. Olivia nodded. Jason grabbed the handle in his hand, turned it, pushed the door in, and let go. A light flickered a few times and went on.

Olivia stepped into her room. It was identical to the one she had at the Mansion.

It had a large king bed to the left of the door and a love seat at the base of the bed. Large windows took up the walls opposite her bed with velvet curtains covering them. Olivia knew where everything was as soon as she stepped into the room.

"It's so big!" Jason said, "It's so...gray," he said with disgust.

The truth in his words sat on her shoulders—the bed sheets, the love seat, the curtains, the tiles on the floor, the color on the walls. She expected webs of spider, not lack of color. "Is gray bad?"

"I'm not sure. Trio-Genesis is a system—a computer. These rooms have been here for years. It's kind of like a present your parents or family members leave for you when you discover your element. If you have no family here, the building just assigns you one. My room is, for example, for a lack of a better word, dangerous. Everything is made of glass, from the bed head to the nightstand to the armrests on my chairs. If it isn't glass, it's shiny plastic with white fabric everywhere. It's pretty boring," he admitted. "But kind of pretty," he half smiled, "like being in puffy white cloud." What a sap.

This couldn't have been what Savanna left behind for her daughter—a cold copycat of the prison she's lived in her whole life.

"It helps you get in touch with your element. Mark's room is covered in grass, and his bedposts are made of bamboo with leaves growing out of it. Real leaves. It's like the guy is sleeping in a tree. He has a hammock made entirely of vines and branches. The weirdest part," he kept going, "is it blooms in spring, gives life to bright green leaves during the summer, and in autumn, the leaves change color before falling in winter." His description of Mark's hammock was enough to keep her attention.

"Mastering an element isn't easy. Our rooms are our canvas or notebooks or textbooks. You can spend years getting to know it all, but you can spend decades trying to master the element. How do you breathe when there's nothing there? How do you survive under water if it's suffocating? How do you…"

"I get it," she interrupted him. "Sorry, I can be a bit rude." Olivia didn't have to apologize to him. "How?" She walked around the room, trying not to touch anything until he was gone.

"You have to become one with the element. And without it, you're completely lost. Hopeless," he said, answering her question. Olivia was still walking around looking with wondering eyes up the curtains and down at tiles.

"I'm going to see if I can find you something to wear tonight and tomorrow." She wasn't listening. Olivia was away lost in her own mind—she looked at everything in the room but felt nothing and remembered her red velvet curtains, but also felt nothing. The gray was just what the doctor had ordered.

"Brook?"

She answered him when he had said her name for the third time. "Yeah?" She turned to him quickly as if he had only called out to her once.

Jason caught her eye, and a cold wind brushed over him. "I'll be right back. Don't, break anything…" Jason said expecting the worst. He gave her one last look and surfed away. A slow wind told Olivia the coast was clear, and that she could go crazy.

She touched everything that was solid, opened every draw, looked under the bed, and even spun in circlers with her arms out. Olivia walked over to the velvet curtain and opened them to be greeted by the starry night sky, hugged by a large crescent moon. She rested her hands on the glass. "Goodnight moon," she whispered smiling softly. It was the one book Olivia remembered from her childhood, and so every night as a "thank you" to her parents, she walked over to her window, looked up at the sky and said goodnight. It was something no one knew about, not even Patrick. After jumping on the bed and racing around the room like a wild horse, she had calmed down.

She looked at the sky and counted the hundred stars above. She was on count 79 when an untraceable wind filled her room with warmth. Jason stood at the door watching her in awe. He laughed to himself a little, and his joy faded. His jaw tightened and he composed himself in an upright position to assert his manliness.

"Brook."

Olivia didn't answer. Jason set down a pair of blue pajama pants, white t-shirt, light blue jeans, and a pink cashmere on the already messed up bed. Without another word, he walked out of the room and closed the door. Every possible thought went quickly through his mind. He couldn't understand what had come over him—the power he felt standing next to her, the rush of energy that hit his soul. It wasn't normal for him to let his guard down. It wasn't like him to let himself be so easily persuaded.

He stood outside her door as regret covered his face. "I should have killed her when I had the chance," he said under his breath. His eyes wondered down the dark hallway. Jason took a deep breath. He couldn't image what would happen if things went wrong. When the feeling got back into his legs, he walked away from her room. His body was restless. Jason stopped in the middle of the hall and leaned back as if falling into a bed of feathers. Before his body could hit the ground, a cold wind filled the empty hall and took him.

His bruised body hit his bed, and the white comforters engulfed his body whole.

The blood from his forehead was dry and covered in dirt. His blue jeans looked brown and his dirty sneakers covered the white blankets in mud. Jason wasn't a slob, but he was no neat freak. After a long night like the one he had, he didn't care how dirty his white sheets got. He opened his blue eyes and looked up at his ceiling as his stomach grumbled vigorously. Jason sat up on his bed and removed his shoes. He reached for the back of his shirt and pulled the light blue t-shirt over his head and off his black and blue body. The other scars had magically healed from Olivia's bite, not that Jason remembered. Adjusting his shoulders and neck, he stood from his bed and ran his hand over his eyes. His mind thought "shower," but his body screamed "sleep."

"What I wouldn't give to master water right now, and take a shower right where I stand," he laughed.

Olivia walked over to the bed to inspect the clothes she had gotten. The first thing Olivia noticed was an ugly, distasteful, pink cashmere sweater. Olivia looked for the tag, made in Scotland. "How many small creatures were killed to make this awful piece of fabric?" Olivia looked then at the light pair of jeans, four sizes too big. "Gee, you'd think a guy would know your jean size after being locked up together." She set aside the pants on top of the horrid pink goat. "In what world would someone find me wearing a pink shirt?" Olivia looked around her room to make sure no one was watching her. A red flame burned the ends of the hair and soon took over her body completely as she surfed off to get clothes that fit her.

Olivia opened the large closet doors, looking around as the white light turned on.

She saw so many clothes—half of them she had never even worn. She walked in and smiled at herself, proud of her perfect wardrobe. She ran her hand over a few pieces and set them aflame. The burning shirts and dresses disappeared, hanger and all.

Olivia looked down at her shoes. She had a large collection of sneakers and flats in every color. Her boots and fancy shoes all had tall heels on them. Like most of her clothes, these shoes never worn. Some still carried the price tags on them: $300, $500, $2000. Those were the perquisites of being a Countess. But the downside of being a vampire was that she never had anywhere to wear them to. She knelt on the carpeted closet floor and picked up black pumps with red painted soles on them.

Olivia held the shoes close to her chest and sighed. She knew she wouldn't be wearing those anytime soon, and despite what most people believed and although she wasn't very girly, the Countess still loved her shoes and clothes. To her it was un- human to dislike clothing and even more un-human to dislike shoes. Not that there was any human in her.

Olivia walked out the closet into the familiar setting. The room smelled like home. It was home. The sweet smell of hot blood, the warm smell of anger and violence—it was intoxicating. After a deep breath of all the things she loved and hated, Olivia walked over to her dark brown dresser. She looked at the piece of furniture for a while and shook her head slightly. The dark wood would never match the new setting she was in, but for now it would have to do—at least until she could buy herself a new one. Maybe a white wood one, or one covered in broken mirrors; yes, she always did fancy those. Olivia placed both hands on the dark wood, and like a forest, the dresser caught on fire and was instantly surfed to Trio-Genesis.

She took one last look at her rosy red room, walked over to the window, and pulled her curtains shut. Without turning around to say goodbye, she let her body be consumed by fire and surfed away.

Her new room was empty, colorless, cold, and uninviting. Not even Jason had liked it. It looked like her room back home, but it didn't feel like it. The gray décor was dragging all the life she had away. Olivia's body burned into the middle of her room.

She was facing the bed, and the dresser she had surfed just a few minutes before was directly behind her. There she stood, without much of a plan, and hoping the one she had would work. She stood there as if the boring blankets on the bed would turn to a vibrant red. When Olivia turned around, the dresser wasn't where she wanted it to be. She thought of surfing it to a different location, but she wasn't sure if the alarms would go off. After all the surfing she had already done, she didn't want to take any chances. There were fire alarms everywhere! If someone ate hot sauce the building would declare it. So she pushed the dresser across the floor until she found a nice place for it.

Olivia pushed it to the left of the bed.

It made a loud noise and it ruined the floors. Olivia was never one for caring that others were asleep, and as she pushed the dressed all over the bedroom, her new neighbors could hear very clearly the loud noises coming from her room. It wasn't too long before someone shouted, "Could you keep it down in there. Some people like to sleep at five a.m.!"

That was enough to remind Olivia she was not at the mansion where what she did went and what she said was the law. She had to be quieter. But that meant not being able to move her dresser around. So she left it there, by the window where she had last pushed it to.

The motions of reorganizing tired her out a lot sooner than normally. Olivia decided that a shower would be a good idea and headed over to her bathroom. To no surprise at all, it looked just like her own bathroom back at the vampire mansion. She looked in the mirror and saw the mess she was in. Her face and arms were covered in blood and dried up dirt. "On the bright side, I won't have to pay for a spa." She laughed at her own bad joke. Olivia tied back her hair and turned on the hot water.

The sink filled with the boiling liquid, and Olivia splashed the water on her face, rubbing her hands around her neck then over her face again with more water. To anyone else, the water would have burned their face and hands, but to Olivia, or any other vampire, the heat was comforting. She washed her face until the water in the sink spilled over. She looked up at the mirror and turned off the water. The blood on her face was cleaned, and there weren't any scars left behind. It looked as if nothing had happened at all.

To her left was a welcoming toothbrush that she took without hesitation and covered the bristles with toothpaste. Olivia walked over to the shower and turned the hot water on full blast. After shining her fangs and teeth, she stepped into the hot water and took a long, deserving shower.

When the bathroom door finally opened the hot vapor came rushing out into the bedroom. Olivia walked out fully clothed in cozy pajamas with little white sheep covering her pants and black shirt that said "the black sheep" with an arrow pointing up. She saw this on sale once at a store and couldn't resist buying them. And since Patrick had loved them just as much, she left the store with a new pair of PJ's.

Her mind flashed back to that day.

"I just want to buy one thing and then we can leave," she smiled sincerely.

"I will never understand you. Yesterday you wanted to try goat's blood, today if you don't buy pajamas the world is ending?" Patrick replied, rubbing his legs to get rid of the feeling of the long walk they had taken around and around the shopping mall earlier that day. "Why can't Joshua shop with you?" Olivia raised both her eye brows at Patrick's question. He laughed.

It was just a memory now. Olivia dragged herself into bed, the gray sheets cradling her body and hugging every piece of skin. She couldn't smell sweet blood in the air around her or any smell that reminded her of home. All that she breathed in was dirt and dust. But she fell right to sleep, the exhaustion hit her body quickly and knocked the clean showered Countess right out. The light eventually shut itself off and the bedroom door locked quietly. The night was calm and Olivia hadn't slept that well since she was a little girl. Something about that dirty, old, forgotten, bedroom calmed her and gave her an instant peace.

Morning came quickly. The sun was beating brightly on the yards on Trio-Genesis.

People filled the halls with noises and laugher. An alarm went off loudly in Olivia's room. She hadn't set it herself, so the noise took her completely by surprise. Olivia jumped from her bed and searched for the annoying noise. The ring of the alarm only got louder, Olivia couldn't find a clock or secret button anywhere. She lifted sheets, moved the mattress, opened the side table drawers without finding anything. Not a sign of a clock or an alarm anywhere.

In her anger, she found no other solution but to scream at her bedroom. "Alright! I'm up!" she screamed at the ceiling of her gray room as the noise stopped instantly. As mad as she wanted to be at the building for waking her up, Olivia found the self-room alarm neat.

For a second, she looked around, taking in everything that had happened the night before. The thoughts came racing back to her as she realized she wasn't in her normal surroundings. Olivia cleaned the corner of her eyes and dragged herself to the bathroom. She yawned, scratched her back, brushed the hair off her face, and then proceeded to brush her teeth. For five minutes she brushed, making sure every tooth shined. She went about her regular morning routine: a hot shower, a long disappointing look in the mirror, opening the curtains, looking at the yard—the usual.

But things weren't the same. The air was lighter, the room was brighter, and everything had changed. From one day to another, Olivia had taken on a new identity. She wasn't a different person, but she couldn't be herself. Still, things seemed better that way. She finally worked up the courage to leave her bedroom and head to class after the ceiling spoke to her and told her she would be late. Olivia jumped out of her skin but thanked the bedroom and left.

There were so many people in the hallway. Some were polite, others weren't.

Olivia looked at every face, noticed every eye color and every hair type. She bumped into different strangers and kept walking to the elevator. She heard so many "hey, watch it!" that she could see them coming. She tried staying out of people's way and soon found that she wasn't bumping into anyone any longer. People were moving out of her way.

She noticed the odd looks from the people around her. No one knew who she was and they seemed bothered by a stranger walking among them. She could feel all their blood boiling. Olivia was the natural enemy, and she didn't get off unnoticed. She tried getting into their heads but no one gave her leeway. It was strange having the path cleared for being a stranger. She was used to moving crowds, but it was always because of her power and title. Now she was a walking caution sign and no one wanted to come close to her. Trio-Genesis was safe. No one could break its foundation, but everyone always wondered. She reached the elevator, the doors opened quickly and the Countess couldn't be more relieved that the elevator was empty. Not many people took the elevator since the students surfed wherever they needed to go in the building. Once the doors closed, Olivia looked around and down at the little finger-pricking death hole. Her bottom lip pouted out and her eyes were like a little puppy asking for food. After standing still for a while the elevator spoke.

"Good Morning, Countess," it greeted her. Olivia's eyes widened, she shook her head in disbelief and cleared her throat.

"Good Morning… elevator," she responded very slowly as she looked around for a camera or a microphone. Neither were present. The elevator spoke again giving Olivia permission to call her Goldie. Olivia smiled a little and asked the one question on her mind. "Goldie, what do your records say my name is?"

"You are listed as Brook Morton, Countess," Goldie answered her accordingly.

"I'm sorry, am I under as Countess Brook Morton or Brook Morton and you were simply addressing me as Countess at the end of that sentence?" Olivia held her breath a while. Goldie did not speak. They stood in silence and then final she spoke.

"You are listed as Brook Morton."

"Right. That's who I am. Just plain old Brook Morton. Regular, loving, simple, slayer...Brook Morton." Olivia said, trying to convince herself.

"I love to stand here and chat, Miss, but you are going to be late for class. Would you like me to take you to your floor?" Goldie broke the awkward tension Olivia had created.

She stood there for a second and confessed to Goldie she wasn't sure what class she was supposed to go to. Goldie informed her she had class with Dr. Craips now. "Then by all means, please take me there."

"Certainly." Olivia didn't have time to notice she had moved until the door opened and she was in a completely different hallway.

"That was fast. Thanks, Goldie," Olivia said walking out.

This hall, too, was teeming. They all wore bright lively colors and Olivia wore black jeans with a gray shirt and a black zip up. Her hair was tied back and she had on black army boots. Olivia still received mean looks from people. She was already stigmatized, and she hadn't even been there a whole 24 hours.

A girl with short, red hair stood by the elevator doors, she looked like a crazy person. Her eyes were wide and green, and they couldn't be more opened if she tired. She looked about 10 years old. The girl did not blink and her chest did not rise and fall as it would if she were breathing. She was smiling and looked all around herself as if she had a twitch. Olivia didn't know where she was going. She thought about asking the girl where the class was, but the crazy redhead frightened her a bit.

"Are you lost?" the redhead asked bluntly.

Olivia hesitated, but she turned around and looked at the girl. The girl smiled at Olivia and asked again.

"I'm not sure. I haven't tried to find my way yet." She paused to look at the girl's green eyes. "Is there a reason you're..."

"Staring at you?" the girl interrupted her. Olivia nodded and raised her eyebrows. "Yes, there is. I think I know you're lost. Canada is a beauty in the winter isn't it?"

"What does that have to do with me being lost?"

"See, I knew you were lost." The girl smiled wider.

"Do you usually creep everyone out or are you just a creeper to strangers?" Olivia asked the red head coldly. "And by the way, it's summer. And this is New York."

"It's beautiful in the summer also. I love the grass, it's so wet and green." She blinked and her smiled left her. "You have to go straight ahead and turn left then go down the stairs. There will be big doors to your right down the hall. That's where you have to go. And if anyone asks you, you aren't in New York. You're in Canada. Quebec to be exact."

"Thanks for the directions." Her tone was sharp. Olivia turned to leave.

"Have a good day, Countess," the redhead answered her.

She stopped dead in her tracks and turned around bewildered at what she had just heard. Olivia's blood froze in the very spot they ran in, her heart beat slowly. She had been discovered. "What did you call me?" she asked. But the girl was gone. Olivia looked around a moment. She assured herself that it was only her mind getting the best of her, and so she turned and walked back in the direction she had to go in.

Jason was waiting for her at the double doors to the class, but Olivia wasn't used to seeing Jason, so she walked right by him. Jason grabbed her arm, and Olivia suddenly went on the defense. She pushed him against the wall. Her jaw tightened and her eyes glowed red. All the bodies who were busy moving came to a screeching halt. Every eye looked at Olivia and Jason, and the entire hall went on high alert. The once cheerful faces were serious. Jason looked Olivia in the eyes and whispered to her, "Are you out of your mind? It's me. Jason. Relax." Olivia let go of him and came back to her senses.

"Just a drill, everyone," Jason announced, and the armed bodies went back to their own actions. "I should have seen that coming. It's good that it happened to me and no one else. You have to be more careful."

"You can't grab a vampire by the arm and just have a nice chat, Slayer," Olivia informed him. Her hands were in a fist and her face was still a light shade of red. "First that creepy little girl, now you. What's her deal anyway?"

"What girl?" He shook his head, "I went to your room to find you, guess you got a head start. We have to go to class, and I still have a few things to tell you, so for one hour just please get it together," Jason told her.

Olivia took a breath and calmed herself a little. When she was all right she asked Jason what she needed to know.

"Doctor Craips… is fairly mental. He'll be inquisitive as an attempt to display your level of comfort. Keep your cool. There are days he won't speak, his anger over powers him and he shuts down. On those days he expects his students to known what to do. We continue with his previous lesson until the time expires. It gets ridiculous in there, you'll need to practice your patience. Testing is done in the open for all to see, he wants to rid us of our inhibitions. Just try what he shows you and move on if you can't do it. You work by levels in this class. There are eight levels and you start at level one, but he thinks that one should be eight because he thinks the people on top should be number one not number eight. So technically you start at level eight. There's no time limit to level up—you just level as fast as you can. Groups: they are made up of the three elements with two slayers per element. Each group is under the instruction of their leader. Usually new students are up for grabs by any group with an available opening. Your lack of one certain element gives me the advantage of looking after you. You'll be placed in my group until someone else fights for you. Hopefully, no one else wants you, we wouldn't want another 'drill'. My team might not be as welcoming as I have been but you have to deal with it. Be nice. For the most part everyone is a level one or just about there. We have a final for his class in two months, but like I said, it's not by level, it's by survival. Any questions?" He was completely out of breath from his ramblings.

"Yes. Will you be giving me pointless information I'm sure to forget every day or is this a right now thing? I wonder if you wake up with a scripted monologue ready to use when needed."

Jason shook his head. They were so completely different. The only thing they had in common was their lack of sensing when people were tired of their presence.

"I almost forgot," he blurted "The people in my group might or might not look familiar to you, in a bad way. Keep an open mind, your first impression of them was under difficult circumstances." Jason pushed open the doors and walked inside. "Might" was a strong adjustment to the reality of it.

Olivia watched him go in for a moment and whispered under her breath. "They can't be any worse than you." She made her way in behind him. It was a large gym with bleachers covering the left wall. The students sat waiting for the professor to arrive. He was never on time. All eyes watched Olivia and Jason enter as they sensed a threat. Their bodies tensed up, and every mind prepared for an attack. Their blood was boiling at the sight of her. She swallowed hard and kept walking—this time a bit closer to Jason. If they attacked, she knew he would be her shield.

At the very end of the bleachers, familiar faces watched Jason, and the now welcomed vampire, walk in their direction. Mark could hardly believe his eyes. "Did I take a hard hit to the head or has Jason lost all his senses?" he questioned to his friends who were just as bewildered. The five sat in puzzled thought as Jason and Olivia got closer and closer.

"I think he is still losing it," Tom spoke up, answering Mark.

Kelly and Alison sat in silence, reading only each other's minds. The girls' dying looks at one another spoke the most hated violence. Alison took a deep breath and tightened her jaw, she kept breathing slowly and softly; trying dearly to calm herself before she lost control.

"She's really pretty." Rick smiled at his angry friends. "Maybe I can teach her to surf. You know—the one you do with water, not the one you do to water..." He stopped as even he got confused.

Jason stopped in front of the five and presented Olivia. He had rehearsed this all morning and the night before.

"Guy! Gals! This is Brook." He smiled at his bathroom mirror. "Great, now I'm a cowboy. He dropped his head. "Howdy, Partner, this here be Brook. She'll be staying with us a while, so y'all best make her welcome..." Jason shook his head and kept trying different things he could say. "Alright, I know this seems sudden, but this is Brook and she's going to staying with us... No." He ran his fingers through his hair. "Brook, this is Mark, Kelly, Ali, Tom, and Rick."

The sun rose suddenly and Jason was taken from his sleep. He rolled around in his bed a while, and looked up at the ceiling of his bedroom. "This is Brook. I know she's a killer vampire but she's a student here now..." he sighed. "Nah."

He opened his mouth to speak. "...hi..." Jason said breathlessly.

"Hi!" Rick answered joyfully. Olivia smiled at him. Blood filled her face and her heart began beating again. "I'm Richard Connor Surfer," he spoke "I'm 22 and single," leaping from his seat to kiss Olivia's hand. She felt right at home. "It's a pleasure. May I be the first to introduce you to Trio-Genesis?"

"I'm flattered, but I've already been introduced." She told him kindly. "I'm Brook."

"You're not welcome, Brook. Despite what Jason has told you, you're a killer," Alison spoke up, also moving from her seat. Alison's mother was one of Trio-Genesis greatest scientist and her father was a math professor at the school.

Alison could have been an ugly nerd who sat in front of every class and pushed her glasses up closer to her face because the prescription was never just right for her sight. The kind of student with only two friends and both of them nerds. Neat freaks with allergies to cats, pollen, and dust. Her hair should have been extremely messy all the time; even if it was perfectly straight, it would be frizzy, uncombed, dead and split. The genius in her needed braces.

Surely then, she would be seen as smart as she really was. If she had looked like this, she would wear the same jeans to school every day until she decided they were dirty and she would mix-match socks that would come all the way up her ankles. She wouldn't wear girly framed glasses either; it would be grandmother's old reading magnifying glasses that enlarged her eyes. She would be in desperate need of a make-over.

But she was not the girl that stood in the back of the picture; no, not her. She was the one who you could spot in every shot, even the ones that weren't of her. She looked like a Barbie doll with her long blonde hair and blue eyes and delicate lips; everything about her was breathtaking.

Kelly stood quickly and held on to her friend's shoulder. "I'm fine, Kelly."

"You should sit and nurse your wound," Kelly smiled sweetly and walked over to Jason, took him by the arm a little further from the others, Mark stood and followed, instructing Rick to keep an eye on the vampire. Rick smiled uncontrollably and began to entertain the Countess.

Jason faced away from Olivia as the three spoke in whispers. "Are you mentally sick?!" Kelly questioned him. Her tone burned her words into his soul, almost as if to mark every ounce of mistakes he was currently making. "Mark, please tell him this is crazy. Talk some sense into him. Jason, please, please, tell me that you're joking. I'm all for making new friends, you know I am. I keep the peace between us, that's what I do. But a vampire?" she barked whispers and hushed words at Jason.

"She's right, Jay. I know that you make the final call, but this is a suicide mission. You want to train this vampire to do what, exactly? Become a slayer?" Mark took a small breath and gathered his thoughts. Never in his life had he ever seen such stupidity from his best friend. Jason had always kept his head on straight. His decision was always the best one. But this time, not even Jason himself understood the method behind his madness.

Mark could feel his confusion rising as he and Kelly interrogated him on his choices.

"I know you mean well for this girl. But we can't keep her. She isn't a pet. I'll be the first to admit I didn't want you to kill her, but I didn't mean bring her home and show her around. This is a difficult situation." He took another breath, before realizing his worst thoughts had already happened. "You helped her last night… you took her to the registration hall and enrolled as a lost student… didn't you?"

Kelly could not believe the mess they were in. Her mouth slowly motioned the word "what" but no sound came out. She stood in complete shock taking in the complications they were about to face.

"I have a feeling about this girl…." As Jason began to speak, Mark cut in.

"This isn't just a girl, she is a blood-sucking vampire!" he said, a little louder than he should. The gym fell quite again. The words rang in the open space. All eyes were once again on Olivia.

"Yeah, I hear that movie was really bad!" Kelly jumped in, saving the conversation. The sounds rose again as students went back to their own task and small talk.

Jason recollected his thoughts and spoke. "The deed is done. There is nothing I can do about it. Maybe if you two hadn't left me with her last night, we could have spoken about other choices. It's too late now. Brook is a student in Trio-Genesis and member of our team. I expect us to watch over her carefully and make sure she doesn't cause any trouble," he said strongly.

"You may have signed us to our death with this girl," Kelly spoke and walked back to sit next to Alison whose eyes burned into Olivia's person.

Jason and Mark stood for a moment more looking at each other. "Jason, I've known you for a long time, and whatever you told that girl to convince her that you fell for her stupid sob story is benefiting you a lot more than any of us." Mark exhaled his disappointment. "I don't think this was a call you could have made on your own. You're putting the whole team at risk," Mark reminded him. "What if she decides to go rogue?"

"You have no idea what you're talking about. Mark, don't you get it? We can get her on our side." Jason came closer to Mark whispering only so he could hear. "Remember… remember when I discovered that they were taking our students, the youngest ones for a purpose much darker than we could imagine?" Mark shook his head in disbelief. Jason couldn't let the past go. "No, listen to me. I think that whatever they are doing, wherever our slayers went, maybe she knows. I have a feeling about this girl, Mark. Just trust me, you'll feel it too, come time. You've always trusted my judgment." He pleaded with his friend.

Mark's tone changed to anger. His voice was shaken, and his face grew red. "I trusted your judgment when it wasn't made upon vengeance. That's what this is about." Mark put an arm on Jason's shoulder. "You have to let it go, Jason. You have to let him go." His voice was calm again, sad even. Disappointment filled Marks eyes as he too walked back to his seat. Jason stood for a moment. He could not take what he had done back. He could not change the events that would happen. He gathered himself and walked back to Olivia… Brook.

"…and that's how I got my foot out of the can." Rick laughed to Olivia who stood smiling wildly. Jason motioned for Rick to sit down. He and Olivia… Brook sat down next to Mark.

Mark turned to Jason who sat on the other side of Olivia and spoke quietly, "have you told her she isn't allowed to drink while she is here?"

Olivia's eyes widened. She couldn't go without drinking. She ate regular human food, but blood is what gave her strength. Going too long without it for any vampire would be torture not only to their minds, but to their bodies. Olivia would have to use more strength to fight and work and even go from day to day. Blood was their water, their wine, their poison. "What do you mean?" she asked terrified.

"Before you got you here, Jason injected you with limeandisorin. It took away all the blood that wasn't your own from the last two days. It's the only reason the alarms haven't gone off yet. And since you've gotten here, I trust you haven't had a drink. The building can tell when things are out of the ordinary," Mark explained in a whisper.

"Can't I simply drink and then take one of these shots?" Olivia was determined to compromise.

Alison joined in the conversation. "Do you eat and throw up after?" Olivia stared her down coldly. There wasn't a need to answer Alison's hateful question. "I thought not. So unless you want to suck your own venom, keep your disgusting fangs away from blood. Those are the rules, those are our terms," she barked, stunning even Kelly who had explained to her the events of the previous night and had just told Alison, Brook was staying.

Olivia's blood boiled. She rubbed her arms on her black jeans and swallowed her pride. After all, Olivia was not used to any person talking down to her as Alison had just done. She was the Countess, she was the superior, and she made the law. Her word was final, not the word of others, and definitely not the words of a stuck up blonde bimbo slayer girl.

No one stood up for her. Joshua wasn't around to punch Alison in the face. Patrick was nowhere to be found to tell Alison to back off and give her a break. And Jason didn't like Olivia any more than Mark did, or so he thought. Olivia sulked in her defeat as Jason smiled at Alison's superiority.

Rick turned to Olivia as a last string of hope and assured her that Alison was just a jealous snob and she should not be offended. Olivia did not smile, she did not look at him, and she did not care. Her focus was targeted, like a lion to the prey. Rick touched her knee gently, Olivia looked at the slayer, her eyes glowing red. He smiled kindly at her red beating eyes. Mark rolled his shoulders to release the sudden discomfort rising in him as Rick smiled at Olivia. Her power took their innocence over, as Rick completely surrendered to her mind. Her eyes returned to their normal brown color and Rick removed his hand from her knee and turned back around. The seven sat in silence.—their minds' convicting each of them of their mistakes for not putting an end to Jason's madness before it was too late.

Olivia quieted her mind, trying desperately to hear their thoughts.

"I want everyone sitting down, now." Mr. Craips was finally there, and he didn't notice that everyone was seated. "I said now!" No one moved.

He was a weird man in about his late 40's, and he had a large wedding band on his ring finger. His hair was kind of grayish, but only because he was overworked. His wife had been long dead but he didn't know that. That was one reason he was crazy. When he was about 18 years old, he and his girlfriend, now his dead wife, were in an accident with some vampires. He watched some of his friends die and his girlfriend used as live bait for sharks and snakes. They both came out of it alive, but ever since then, his brain didn't work right. He got married soon after because he believed he was getting old.

"I'm 91, Barbara. We must get married before I'm too old," he would say, and because she loved him, she married him at 19. Six years later, she died in a car crash traveling from Mexico to Canada.

His crazy green eyes danced around the room looking at every student. He looked down at his clipboard and screamed as if no one could hear him. "I smell new blood. Brook Morton, show yourself," he said bitterly. Olivia sat playing with her fingernails until Rick turned around at her.

"Oh, that's me," she realized suddenly. She stood. Craips motioned for her to join him down and center.

He looked at her and walked in circles around her. Then he told her to walk in circles around him and she did. He was pleased, so he didn't ask her anything until she began to walk away. "Where were you born Miss Morton?"

"Rhode Island, my parents came back to Canada soon after my birth. Three hours, maybe less. Where were you born?" She sassed him joyfully.

He smiled at her. She was everything he had ever heard of. Smart, sassy, funny... to him. "You are smart. It isn't going to get you anywhere." His smile didn't fade. "California. My parents came back to Canada soon after I was born too." He looked Olivia up and down and began his class.

"I see here that Miss, Morton does not know what her element is. Therefore, she has no way to defend herself. As you young people may know, this is defense class. Oh, and Miss Morton, Welcome to my class." He looked much older than his 40-year-old body really was. His trials had aged him greatly. "We will continue our lesson from last time. So please get into your groups when I say so. Our new student will need some help, so if I could please have one volunteer from each element."

Rick shot up from his seat and ran down to the front. "I'll help her with water, Sir," he said smiling ear to ear. Olivia rolled her eyes and laughed to herself a little. Rick winked at her and blew her a kiss. Mr. Craips slapped Rick's hand and looked down at his clipboard.

"One is not the same as three people," Craips said disappointed that his students did not want to help the world's most powerful slayer discover her strength. Mark looked at Jason, reminding him she was his problem and he needs to watch after her.

Jason stood. "I'll help her with air." He made his way down to the front also.

"Ah, Mr. Sharpie. I knew you would warm up." Craips smiled wildly at Jason.

Craips turned to his class and pointed to a little boy. "Louie, why don't you come here? Help us out with the final element?"

Louie was an 11-year-old boy whose powers had been growing faster than he was.

He adjusted his falling glasses and stood next to Olivia. She looked over at him and smiled awkwardly. Louie sniffed and fixed his glasses.

"Don't be fooled by his age or allergies." Rick told her.

"Class, you may go on and continue your assignment from last class. Oh, and please watch the windows. The janitor complained that we keep breaking them." The class split into their groups and began fighting in their areas. Winds blew, the ground shook, water splashed everywhere. It wasn't too much later when someone went flying under the large glass windows. "Watch out for the windows!" Craips screamed.

"Now, Miss Morton, these are the three elements. Everyone is born with one if they are truly a Slayer. Some don't know what their element is until they are 80. It is not uncommon to be without your element for a time."

"If this class is defense, why are you teaching me about the elements?" Olivia asked the funny, old man.

"Your element is what you use to defend yourself. If a Vampire attacks you, you don't have time to dress in sword and shield. Your shield is what you know, and your only weakness is what you don't." His voice was raspy and dry. He looked deep into Olivia's eyes as he spoke. His emerald greens hypnotized her mind, easing her soul and calming her senses. He taught only with his words and never with his actions.

"Now pay very close attention to whatever these students show you. We'll start off easy, and depending on how well you do, we'll pick up the pace," Craips informed her. "Gentlemen, I'm sure you'll have no problem with her." Craips took a few steps back and nodded at Louie.

Louie took a deep breath and came closer to Olivia. "Hi, I'm Louie." He said putting his dirty little hand out in front of him. Olivia took his small hand into hers and shook it. Louie smiled widely and took his hand back, "Wow, you're really strong," he said, amazed by her power.

"Yeah, well… I hit the gym a lot." She laughed.

Craips voice rose over the roaring of the other students work, "Louie, show her dirt. You shouldn't have any problem with that."

She knew what dirt looked like, and if she didn't, all she had to do was look at Louie. He was covered from head to toe in dirt, mud, and little pieces of dried up grass. His light brown hair was gray with sand, and the strands that touched his forehead glued to his skin with mud. Louie needed a shower fast.

"The kid's a genius," Jason whispered.

The only amazing thing so far was that all the dirt he carried never left his body, never fell on the floor, and never got anything else dirty. He was the magnet and earth was the metal. Louie rubbed his hands together slowly. After rubbing them together for a few seconds, Olivia thought he must be ready to begin his trick. To her surprise, this was the trick... rubbing his hand against the other. Louie stopped suddenly.

"This really is a neat trick," Rick said quietly to her. Olivia watched Louie. If this was the trick, she was miles ahead of him.

Louie opened his hands slowly and carefully. As he did, the dirt from his palms began to levitate and glow a rich, brown color. Olivia had never seen such a simple little trick before. Louie watched the glowing dirt, controlling it carefully only inches above his hand. Craips walked over to the boy and spoke to Olivia. "This is dirt. With this glowing speck of dust, this small boy can probably poison your entire body. Of course, he is much too sweet to do such a thing and way too young to fight. But Louie came up with this all on his own. The possibilities are endless with this child. Earth has become him."

Olivia walked closer to him, her hands itching to touch his power. Louie took his eyes away from the glowing lights to look at the Countess. He informed her that it was safe to touch and he wouldn't harm her. Olivia took a deep breath and reached slowly for the dancing particles of dirt hovering above the boy's hands. It was cold and dry like the desert at nighttime. They stood in silence until Craips took their attention and told Rick to show the already amazed girl water. Olivia took her hand back to herself and Louie ended his trick. The glowing dirt flew up into the ceiling and the building ate it. Olivia watched as the walls took the power and then let her attention return to Rick.

Rick wasn't as advanced in his element as he could be, but he also knew some neat tricks. Water was a delicate element to master because earth played such a huge part in it. Fresh water was easier to control than salt water was. But nevertheless, every slayer whose element was water had to learn both. Rick was determined to learn all he could from salt water. He spent most of his time in the ocean trying to be one with the sea, opening his mind to the roar of the waves and letting the water become him as earth had become Louie. Of course, he wouldn't walk around dripping everywhere he went, Louie's dirt was simple to explain. He was a young, mastered earth slayer, and 11-year-old boys still liked the idea of playing in the mud.

Rick looked around for a second and spotted a puddle of water from the other student's tasks. Craips immediately shook his head in disapproval. Rick was on the limb, and as if water wasn't hard enough to control, Craips wanted him to take water out of thin air! A task much easier for someone with Jason's power. He looked around some more and found his answer. Olivia. There, on the palm of her hands, were little microscopic drops of sweat. Rick put out his hand for Olivia to take. She hesitated for second but couldn't help herself. As their hands met, a light blue glow came from the palm of their hands. Craips smiled at Rick. "Nicely done."

Olivia pulled her hand back at the sight of the blue glow and Rick held on to the inside of his hand with his life. He took in a breath and opened his hand slowly, Olivia looked at his hand breathlessly with her eyes wide open and mouth parted. There, before her very eyes was a tiny ball of water. Rick quickly released his power and the ball splashed on the wood floor. Rick lifted his hands suddenly as the water rose, making a large wall separating him from the others. Olivia had seen this before. A water wall was impenetrable, deadly, cold, and strong. Still, Rick's body came right through the water, and he came out from the other side completely dry without a drop on him. The wall still stood strong before them.

"If you're done showing off, Rick..." Jason said.

"Oh, yeah. Of course." Rick responded. He took the water back into the palm of his hand and once again made it into a small ball. "Brook, your hand please?" Olivia put her hand out before him and Rick shook her hand as before. This time there was no light blue light. But as he let go of her hand, the water was gone.

"Where..." she began to speak.

"Back where he took it from. One thing that is very important to know from Mr. Surfer is that he always puts back from which he took," Craips explained to the baffled vampire. "Mr. Sharpie, if you will please, and may I suggest.... a short flight." Jason broke out a smile. He was never allowed to take off in the middle of class. In fact, because no other slayer had learned this kind of power, he was hardly allowed to do it at all. "Ms. Morton. You will find that holding on will prove you very useful." Craips said, motioning the two other boys to step back with him.

Jason walked over to Olivia. He wasn't fond of her just yet but he, like every other slayer and vampire, could feed off of her energy. With every step he took closer to her, Olivia's skin wanted to take a step back. They were two negative sides of a magnet, and it hadn't been 24 hours ago that they were in epic battle. Jason put an arm around Olivia's waist and pulled her close to his body. "If you even breath on my neck, I'll stake you right here in front of everyone," he whispered to her.

"If I didn't know better, I'd say you wanted a little bite of the wild side," she hushed back. Jason showed his pearly whites.

"You think I'd look good as a vampire?" he asked still smiling.

Olivia laughed a bit. "Yeah, but you'd have to look good on your own first." She had wrapped her arm around him tighter.

"You're not afraid of heights, are you?" he asked playfully. Olivia shook her head. "Good. You can look down, then." They were about 20 feet above the class. Every eye looked up at them. Alison's face was red, her arms crossed over her chest, and her foot tapped the floor. Olivia gasped as she had never seen this before—a flying slayer. She wrapped her arms around him tightly; this time, completely conscious of her actions. Jason laughed at her. "I thought you weren't afraid, Vampy."

"Don't nickname me, Slayer," she said releasing her grip. Olivia suddenly understood Craips words before Jason took her flying around the gym... You will find that holding on will prove you very useful. Those were the last words that came to her mind before her body met the brown wood beneath them. Jason immediately came down and knelt by her unconscious body. Rick knelt down in front of Olivia. The class rushed to the scene of the fall. Mark came bursting through the crowd. He knelt down by Jason, who checked Olivia's pulse.

"Is she dead?" Alison asked grinning.

"No. She's just knocked out," Jason answered. Craips stood there in silence, his eyes never leaving Olivia's body. Blood dripped slowly from her mouth and her sleeping body recognized it as feeding time.

Her sharp fangs came from their hiding place, and the Countess wasn't waking up to put them away. Rick panicked a little and looked up at Jason quickly looking for an answer.

"Jason," Rick whispered, "did you know you could set fangs to auto pilot?" Jason looked at Olivia's mouth confused, and all his questions went away. His eyes widened and Jason did all he could, averting everyone's eyes.

"Look! What's that?!" he screamed, pointing up the ceiling. As every eye looked up, Rick also came up with his own idea.

"I know CPR!" he shouted then flipped her over and planted one big kiss on the bleeding Countess. Jason watched him closely. Kelly couldn't believe her eyes. Craips was still standing there dumbstruck. Rick enjoyed his sleeping beauty a little too long, and as the fairy tale goes, the princess wakes up. Olivia looked into the blue eyes of the cool surfer dude in front of her. His lips motioned the words "put those away," and Olivia hid her precious fangs.

No one had seen what just happened, but now that Olivia was awake, Craips instructed everyone to go back to their tasks. The class walked away in disappointment and tried to continue their lesson. Mark, Tom, Alison, and Kelly stood right where they were and watched Olivia.

"I .... I thought you were dead," Craips said as Rick and Mark helped the Countess to her feet.

"Yeah, like that would kill her," Kelly murmured under her breath. Jason looked back giving her his stinging look of anger. Kelly silenced herself at once. At least one thing was normal about Jason, he was still in charge even in his silence.

"Do you want me to take her down to get checked?" Mark asked, surprising even himself with his concern for Olivia. Craips nodded his head slowly, still shocked with amazement.

Olivia looked up at Mark he did not make eye contact with her. She wiped the blood from the side of her lip.

"I'm fine," she said. "I'd like to continue the lesson, if I have a say in this."

"You dropped 20 feet from the air. Are you sure?" Rick's voice was calming and caring. He looked at Olivia as concern filled his eyes. Olivia nodded and brushed herself off a bit.

"Very good," Craips said. "I have to check on the other students. The three of you show Ms. Morton something simple. Mr. Sharpie, no more flying for the day. You four, get back to work," he instructed to Tom, Kelly, Mark, and Alison.

"She hasn't been in class an hour and we already have to cover up for her," Mark said to Jason quietly. "I know how much you want this, but you're putting us all at risk. I get it, I do. She's really powerful. I feel it too. And, okay, maybe she knows something, but that doesn't change your past and it doesn't undo what's been done. It's inevitable. Let it go." Mark turned to walk away, but Jason grabbed a hold of his arm and stopped him. He took in a breath to speak, but no words came out, so he released Mark's arm and watched his best friend walk away.

A high pitch bell rang across the room and students began cleaning up to leave. Olivia, Jason, and Rick were joined by the rest of Jason's team.

"I'm talking Alison to get her gauze changed. We'll meet you guys at Kerrigan's class," Tom informed the others.

"There's more?" Olivia whined.

"Yes, there are two more. Kerrigan and whatever element is specific to you," Jason told her.

"Which is your again?" Alison asked.

"Fire," Olivia smiled, "Wanna see?" She opened her palm and Jason grabbed on to it.

Alison snickered and shook her head. Tom wrapped a protective arm around the blonde girl and led her away. They left through the double doors and walked down to the golden elevator. The hall was too crowded to mention the vampire girl who had joined their group but it seemed that Brook was the hottest topic in the school. The slayers leaving the class mentioned no other name, and with every passing student Brook's name was in every conversation.

The questions ranged from her coming, to her suspicious attire, to her odd survival of such a high drop.

In the elevator Alison and Tom were able to find refuge from the others. Students normally walked or surfed to class. Alison also was used to surfing to her next location but she was instructed to keep from surfing until her stitches were removed, good thing for her Jason's blade was thin and coated in holy water, the wound wasn't as damaging as it first seemed, and she would be back to normal in a couple of weeks.

"How does it feel?" Tom asked about her side.

"The medicine helps. My parents nearly had a heart attack after you and Rick left the room last night," she laughed.

"They worry about you," Tom gave the obvious reply.

"I worry about Jason. He's strange suddenly." Her brows were frowned and her eyes pensive. "I've been a part of this team since the beginning and I've never known Jason to make such a reckless decision. Something's off."

Tom was not as concerned, in fact to him maybe nothing was wrong and this was Jason showing his true colors, proving that he was unfit to be a leader and to provide protection for his team. Sure it had been unlike Jason to bring a stranger into their happy family but it seemed just as possible that everything before this had been a façade. Jason could very well be a double agent, working on both sides, waiting for the day he would help take down the slayers and kill them all!

Alison laughed holding on to her side, "Don't make me laugh," she begged the joking slayer next to her.

"Sorry, I thought you could use it," he smiled down at her. The door dinged open and the two stepped off on the second floor.

"I spy with my little eye I a new student!" Kerrigan was very enthusiastic when it came to pointing out new people. Besides teaching everyone's favorite class Kerrigan was in charge of showing around new slayers or students their homes. But from 9 a.m. to 3 p.m. Monday through Friday he was the most sought after Elements teacher. Each year hungry students signed up for his class with hopes that an opening would suddenly fall on their laps.

Besides Kerrigan there were two other teachers who taught Elements and though their classes were just as full of bright young individuals, Kerrigan's class was by far everyone's favorite.

"Stand up, darling and tell us your name," he said looking square at Olivia.

She rolled her eyes at Jason as he encouraged her to stand. Olivia stood, cleared her throat, and spoke, "Hi... my name is Oli...."

Chapter 6

Classes

"Oli… lee lee lee lee…" she stuttered. Olivia cleared her throat again and spoke very clearly, "My name is Brook," she said the name slowly. "Brook. That is my name. Um, Morton." Damn her throat was dry, "Yup, Brook Morton." Olivia smiled and began to sit.

"And?" Kerrigan said.

"and… and…" she stood and looked around, "I like daisies. They'll live for a long time if you keep changing the water in the vase, after they've been picked."

"Ah, an earth worm!" Kerrigan laughed.

"No, I don't like worms," Olivia stated and the class laughed loudly. Had everyone not been laughing they would have heard Jason slap his forehead.

Jason stood, "Brook doesn't know what her element is yet. My team found her yesterday,"

"Jason found her yesterday," Alison said from the door.

Kerrigan turned quickly to the late students who handed him a slip from the hospital and went to take their seats in the back near Jason and the others.

"Great! Welcome, Brook. Alison can you please tell us which element is most likely to change sides?" Kerrigan asked the slayer as she reached her seat.

They laughed under the one-lit light above them. There were dirty cups everywhere. Olivia sipped her green icy drink and placed her thumb on the roof of her mouth to stop the returning brain freeze. The table was sticky and Olivia kept wiping her hands on her jeans. He asked her if she wanted him to clean the table or if she rather sit at the bar. But she was leaning back with her legs extended out and Patrick's arms laid restlessly by his sides. So there they sat, drinking key lime and kiwi smoothies, since Olivia hadn't gotten her hands on limeandisorin.

"Oh! I missed the best part of the story." She took another gulp of her frozen grass. "So I fall about 20 feet from the air and land on my face." Another sip. "I wake up to the surfer guy I was telling you about, three inches from my face." They laughed again. "I'm pretty sure he was kissing me," Olivia said, rubbing her shoulder.

"Does it hurt?" She nodded once. Olivia had never felt pain this long after an accident. She was going to have to be more careful. As long as her name was a secret, Olivia was in danger. He changed the subject. "There was a whole search party out looking for you. I'm sure they weren't looking very hard." Patrick smiled and exhaled. "You haven't been the leader they've wanted, Olivia."

"Court is a joke. I know the leader they search for, but they won't find her in me. They would have me kill every vampire who looked at me wrong if I were the Countess of their desires." She sipped again. They sat there looking into their glasses. Olivia was the opposite of what they wanted in a ruler, but she knew the law.

Section III: Rule 17

Section A

If the Royal family does not provide the community with an heir, (any male or female coming from the direct line of Count Dracula,) then the power of Count or Countess is granted to the Vampire possessing the most power. On the account that there be more than one vampire believed to be most powerful, the vampires elected to rule will debate their power in battle against one another. If the battle comes to a tie, the court will vote on the vampire they believe to be most fit as their leader. If the court cannot agree, the vampires elected must fight to the death, lest one forfeit.

Section B

If any vampire petitions the court to battle the Royal family heir for the throne, the heir is allowed to accept or decline the challenge without consulting the court. The vampire who wins the battle, wins the throne. If the challenger wins, then the title of Royal family is stripped from the original or current family and placed upon the winning family.

Section C

If the heir wishes to give up the throne during his/her time of reign, he/she must consult the court. The title is passed down to the heir, If there is none, the Royal title is then stripped from his/her family line and the Count or Countess gives up all power to the Vampire he/she deems worthy.

Section D

The Count/Countess remains in office until death or until they choose to give their title of Count/Countess away to the heir. The court may not overthrow the Royal family or any Count/Countess in office. In the event that the Count/Countess dies while in office, the title of Count/Countess is immediately passed down to the heir. If the heir is too young, the court is in charge until the heir is mature of mind. If there is none, the title is temporarily given to the first member of the court…

Giving up her title wasn't an option for her, "Don't ponder it, Olivia. For what it's worth, I think you're a great leader. And if it's worth nothing than on the bright side of things, your mother would be proud of you… and Dracula would be proud, too." She raised her eyes to meet his and he smiled at her. "It's late. I have to clean the bar and you have to get back to your gray bedroom. You have class in the morning." Olivia stood up and gave him a long hug. She picked up her car keys from the sticky table and walked to the door.

"I'm going straight back to the fort. Put my car away will you?" she said, tossing him the keys. "I'll keep in touch when I can." The ends of her brown hair lit up in red flames. "Oh, and Patrick... clean that table. It's gross," she laughed, before the fire consumed her. The light burned out and Olivia was gone. Patrick grabbed the rag from his back pocket and threw it on the table where they sat. He pick up their glasses and carried them over to the bar. It was quiet, the only sound came from the bottom of his feet meeting the floor board and the bottom of the glasses touching the dark wooden bar.

The light above the table flickered on and off. "Flame's going out," he said, as he walked back over to the table and stood on the seat in the booth. He reached over to look into the light while the small red flame flickered some more. Patrick reached into the bowl where the light was held. He pulled out the dying fire and held it in his hand as he stepped down on to the floor, and while he walked over back to the bar, he closed his hand on the flame and the fire was gone.

"Brook! Brook! It's Rick. Can I come in?" he shouted, knocking loudly on her door. Several voices came from down and across the hall. Students screamed at the top of their lungs, informing him of the time and telling him to shut up. Rick knocked softer on the door and silenced his loud mouth. The voices of the restless students settled down.

Olivia opened quickly, knocking the blonde slayer flat on his face. "May I help you?" she asked, with anger written in her tone.

Rick helped himself up and grinned at Olivia. He leaned against the doorframe and crossed his arms to show off his muscles, although they were already very visible through his white, cotton, t-shirt. Rick took in a breath. "I... noticed you didn't have dinner with us tonight. And I came to see if you were hungry," he blurted out.

Olivia looked at the invisible watch on her wrist. "It's 12 a.m."

"How did you do that without a watch?" Rick asked, baffled.

He was really asking for it. "Oh, come on, you can't be that stupid." She didn't hurt his feelings, Rick was more than used to being insulted. It made him more confident—made him strive for things more than others.

"Okay, so I lied. I'm not here to take you to lunch. Jason wants you to join us downstairs. We need to talk," Rick said quietly. She had a few things she needed to say as well. It was excessively easy to get her to come, but he didn't process the thought long enough to say anything about it.

He led her to the elevator and pushed the down button. They stood there a minute in complete awkward silence. Olivia looked up at Rick. He was much taller than she was, but she was much stronger than he. He kept running his nails on the walls, biting his lip, and exhaling loudly. She intoxicated him. The elevator reached their floor and the large, yellow doors opened. He motioned Olivia to go in first and he followed after. The doors closed, and the elevator went nowhere.

"I'm almost positive you have to press a button for us to move." Rick reached over quickly and lit up the third floor button.

"So what's the deal with you?" he suddenly spoke. Olivia took in a breath. Rick sucked his teeth and asked again. It glowed all around him, like a bright fire burning into his soul. Her power was like a gas pump anyone could connect to just by visiting the station.

Olivia didn't answer his question. It was useless for him to keep talking.

But that didn't stop Rick. Nothing did. He kept going—never stopping, never breathing, and never giving her a chance to answer any of his question.

"Alright, Richard!" she finally shouted. He was quiet. His smile sunk into a frown. Rick didn't mean any harm, he loved talking and hated awkward moments like the one they were having. Olivia noted his gloom, "I'm not going to apologize to you."

"Why not?" Rick murmured.

Her shoulders moved back out of place, her eyes blinked open, and her mouth parted. She looked up at him with sad eyes.

"I don't know." She let the confusion escape her lips. Olivia quickly drew her attention back to the elevator doors. For the rest of the ride down they were completely silent, still, and distant.

The doors opened, and Rick and Olivia came out of elevator and walked down the corridor.

"Have you thought about the possibility that she isn't who she says she is?" Alison asked from the chair. Her legs were crossed and her eyes tired. Couldn't Jason have picked a better hour to talk about this?

"Yes, but right now we have to take her at her word," Jason said.

"Why?" Alison asked quite angry.

"Because Jason thinks she knows something about Ryan." Mark didn't mean to deceive his friend by telling everyone the truth. He wanted to get back to bed and it didn't help his thoughts that he hadn't gotten much sleep the night before.

"That has to be a sick a joke," Alison was not in the mood for poor explanations. "What are we suppose to do when she turns on us?"

"We kill her," Tom said.

"It's not that easy," Mark informed.

"Off with her head, what's so hard about that?" Tom argued. "Every vampire dies somehow. This girl is no different,"

"That isn't your call to make," Jason said calmly.

"But it was your call to doom us to our death! You're call to have a killer run around..." Tom almost shouted.

"We're all killers," Jason gave him the reply he did not want to hear.

"You know what I mean..." Tom looked away at Alison hoping she would have the words to talk sense into their leader.

They turned into different halls and walked through several doorways. Then Rick stopped in front of large mirror doors and pushed them open. It was a tremendous white room. To the left was a large table covered with buttons and levers. Right above it was a window that looked into another white room with white tiles on floors and walls. To the right of the table was a large glass door with a blue button on the side. Olivia and Rick were greeted by a suddenly silenced group of friends. "Speak of the devil," Alison let out, loud enough for everyone to hear.

"Rick is a nice guy, Alison," Olivia smirked, as Alison's eye burned through Olivia's face.

"I was referring to the bloodsucking demon my diluted friend, Jason, brought into our lives. You have way too smart a mouth, Vampire," she hissed at the Countess.

Olivia laughed at her pitiful mockery. "Your choice of words are certainly going to put a damper on our relationship." Alison moved closed to her—the stance ready to kill Olivia with her bare hands. Olivia inhaled the anger on her skin. She saw the hate boiling in Alison's blood.

"Down girl. You wouldn't want to get hurt again," the Countess mocked. Alison moved on Olivia to attack her. Jason saw the horrid scene happening before it did and stood from his chair. He moved quickly on Alison and Olivia to stand in the middle of them.

"Now that you two have expressed all of your hate for each other, let's move on," Jason said, saving the day. He looked deep into Alison's eyes. She took a few steps back and stood by Mark and Kelly. Her good friend put an arm around her shoulder and begged her to calm down before things got messy. Jason ran a hand over his flowing hair and motioned for Rick to stand by the others. There he stood, before his greatest friends, next to the enemy.

"I know we didn't have much time to introduce ourselves this morning and get to know a little about each other. It would be in our best interest from now on if we all tried to get along," he said, looking specifically at Alison. "Brook is here because she wants our help."

"And Jason wants me here to help him with his class project on a myth," Olivia added in quickly.

The puzzled looks were instant. "Jason doesn't have a class project due," Tom said.

"Of course he does. He wants me to tell him everything about the so-called Vampire Slayer... The chick is a myth. I tried to tell him she's just a vampire, but he'll have none of it. He's convinced. He needs to know all he can about her to get an A in class," Olivia explained sarcastically.

Mark shook his head. "You are unbelievable. Do you think that capturing a Vampire and telling her you have a mystery project on Count Dracula's daughter is going to help you find him?" Mark blurted. "Jason," Mark continued, walking over to his friend, "you have to let this go. He is gone. I know it seems like you can find him. But just because you want to find him, doesn't mean he is still there."

"I know what I discovered. I know what she's up to. Mark, I know he is out there. And she has him. I've killed enough vampires to find that out. She's the last link, and if I find her, I find him," he whispered desperately, sweat forming on his brow, as his breath quickened.

"What if none of it was true? They could have lied to you. And if you do find her, what do you plan on doing? Killing her? You can't go up against the Countess. You'd be declaring war on all of us. It's against the law," Alison chimed in. Alison breathed deeply and blinked slowly, nipping at her lower lip.

"I don't want to kill her," Jason explained in his anger.

"Let's everyone just stay calm," Kelly begged. "No one is killing anyone."

"I know what it's like to lose someone you love," Olivia sympathized.

Alison always had a gift for being the loudest in the room. "What the hell do you know about losing anyone?" she shouted, making sure all the attention was once again on her.

"Alison, enough!" Jason demanded.

"You're right, Mark," Jason said, letting the subject go. His revenge would have to wait until he could gain the vampire's trust and he could dry her out of information.

His plan wasn't perfect yet. Revenge is never completely planned out.

Mark nodded and stood once again by Kelly. Jason took a breath and spoke. He explained to his friends that Brook wasn't a normal vampire—or so she thought. He even told them the story of how her parents died—or so she says. Then he went on to explain that she wanted to become a slayer and train herself to kill any vampire trying to ruin families.

"Lovely. You two are like the perfect revenge couple," Mark stated. "So your parents were murdered by one of your own kind?" She nodded after all it had been true. "And you want revenge."

Olivia rolled her eyes. "I don't want revenge," she explained sincerely. "I've lived with them all my life, but it wasn't by choice. They took my parents from me. I was the first child ever to be tested on," she lied. "There is a project, I should say, that was created to make mortal children immortal. We are injected with immortal blood and bitten twice daily for two years. After bitten, you are instructed to bite back. The idea is to mix your blood with the vampire poison to turn you into one of them. You are taught the element fire to burn your enemies with. Nothing can conquer fire. Not the Nile, not the ocean, not all of the air in the sky. They train us as killers. So if I can be trained to learn the element of fire, can't I be trained to learn any other element?" Olivia had them eating out of the palm of her hand, kissing the nails on her feet and showering her with unquestioned trust. They looked intrigued. All except Alison.

"You can learn fire because it is your blood by force, but nevertheless it's there. It's what they do to all humans-turned-vampires. They feed them their own poison daily. We aren't going to feed you our blood," Jason told her. "We'll help you become a slayer, only because it wouldn't hurt to know a thing or two about the enemy. And if you want our trust, you'll have to earn it," he added with the support of his friends behind his words.

"I'll answer everything you ask if you teach me everything you know," she said looking at Mark and then at Jason. Mark walked over to Olivia and put out his hand for her to shake. She took it firmly and shook.

"Brook Morton, welcome to Trio-Genesis," Mark said grinning.

"Try this. All you have to do is stomp your foot on the floor lightly. The ground should only shake a little. Don't be too upset if you have to try it more than once.

Here, I'll go first," Mark said back in Craips class as he showed Olivia a few simple earth tricks. He stomped his heal ever so lightly on the floor, shaking the entire foundation of the gym.

Craips nodded his head, pleased at Mark's talent. "If I laugh when nothing happens, please don't be mad when I say I told you so," Alison whispered to Kelly and Rick. Tom, Mark and Jason also stood close by. They had convinced Craips that Brook was under their supervision and that they would take good care of her and teach her everything she needed to know. And since Craips couldn't find other students to teach the girl, he took the volunteers he had and added the oddly numbered group to the system, everything had to be recorded.

She stomped. The floor cracked and shook, making a path in the direction her foot was pointing. A boy across the room went flying up into the air. Olivia stood in shock. Mr. Craips turned, with his eyes wide open. All the joy he had felt was suddenly gone. He was in the same situation three days ago when Olivia came crashing down on the floor: completely in shock. He never knew what to do when a student got hurt.

The pandemonium ceased and all eyes were on her. The blonde girl too was silent, her mouth was wide open and Rick was smiling from ear to ear praising the skies that Alison got slapped in the face with her own words.

Mr. Craips ran to the boy on the ground crying in pain. After flying 15 feet up in the air and coming down, he only had two broken ribs, a cut up face from the little pieces of wood, and some internal bleeding. He would survive the impact, but he would need therapy for the shock.

"Unbelievable. Dirt lightning bolt," Craips said once he had seen the distance of the crack on the wooden floors 10 centimeters from where the boy lay. "Maria, get a doctor quickly," he said pointing to a student. "No, no, no. Get nurse Bas. Tell her he has been hit by a dirt lightning bolt. And tell no one else. Go now, Maria. Hurry up."

Every student was surprised. Craips spoke after a student got hurt. Little Louise was dumbstruck as he saw the boy lying on the floor bleeding from his mouth. Maria stood there still as a rock. "Maria, Go!" Craips shouted at the girl. She surfed out, leaving back a hot wind to fill the room. Not a second later nurse Bas was in the room. She came with a rush of green grass and summer lilies, Maria returned in her warm wind.

The nurse knelt down by the boy and asked the class to give them some space.

"His element. What is it?" she barked in a thick Irish accent.

"He is water, as I am," the boy's girlfriend spoke up, her voice trembling, her eyes watering, and her hands shaking.

"Good. I need another water student," the nurse said loudly. From the distance where they stood, Jason motioned Alison to go and to keep an eye on the boy and make sure he'd be all right. Alison spoke up quickly before anyone else could and ran over to the scene. "Hold on to his body, transfer him to O.R, room eight. I'll get the doctors right away," she said standing quickly. "Girls, be gentle, whatever method you use to leave here," she added in before they could surf away.

The two girls thought of softest way to transfer an injured man. Their hands became clear as water and the power traveled quickly through their entire bodies, consuming the boy. They were gone and not a drop was left behind. All eyes again returned to Olivia, including those of her new "friends."

Craips shouted for the class to be dismissed and every student surfed out of the room using his/her element. They left behind the echo of their voices as they spoke about the incident before surfing away. Jason, Mark, Tom, Kelly, and Rick were left behind with a soon-to-be-in- serious-trouble Olivia.

Craips walked over to the students and shouted once more. "I said class is dismissed. If you five did not hear, maybe you can also take the blame," he said angrily as he grabbed Olivia by the arm and surfed away with her.

"Sit," he said when they got into his office.

It was a square room with light green walls. Rich brown wood peaked around the large oval rug that covered most of the floor. His mirrored desk was held up by twisted copper legs. In front of his desk were two gray plush chairs with the same copper legs as the desk.

Olivia sat in one of the chairs and examined her surroundings. There was a book case to her left with only one book.

He walked close to her and spoke quietly. "Who taught you?" Olivia shook her head. "Liar!" Mr. Craips shouted. "You show up in the night, have my students convinced you are to be in their care. The power you used is forbidden on school floors. And you didn't learn it on your own. Who taught you?" he asked again. "That boy is going into emergency surgery because of you." Craips didn't take a breath and Olivia was silent. She had never been scolded for being strong. "So I should assume it was an accident?" he paused and looked at his empty book shelve. "I will let you off with a warning, however I am forced to inform those above me what happened. Be more careful," he said and surfed out of the room in a muddy puddle.

There was so much to be confused about, she couldn't let it bother her. Olivia lit her left hand on fire and soon her whole body erupted into flames and she was gone, leaving behind the smoke of her body. Seconds later she was back in the gym where Alison had already returned to. The six stood arguing about the situation when Olivia arrived in a burning red flame.

"Brook! You can't go surfing around the building with fire!" Tom screamed at her. She couldn't drink, she couldn't go out in the middle of night, she couldn't punch Alison in the face, and now she couldn't surf.

"This only proves my point," began Alison. "Having her here is bad idea. And if that isn't enough for you, Jason, just look at the huge crack on the floor. But maybe you won't be convinced then either, in which case you can make your way down to the second floor and watch a really nice family worry about their son!" She was right. Olivia was way too dangerous to have around. But there wasn't much they could do. They just had to keep a better eye on her.

"Relax girl, it wasn't all that bad," Rick smiled, putting his arm around Olivia who nodded at Rick's undying support. Their heads turned to the half-quarter mile crack on the wooden gym floors. "I said all…" Rick restated moving his arm.

"It was an accident," Olivia tried. She had just put a man in emergency surgery and there wasn't the least bit of concern in her voice.

"No. Accidents are things done unintentionally. You on the other hand, don't even care about this guy," Alison said fuming.

"Mark," Jason called as another potential fight was about to break between the girls, "Can you and Kelly can patch this up?" Jason asked.

"We'll handle it," Mark answered, smiling at a gleeful Kelly.

Jason grabbed Olivia by the arm and dragged her over to the large windows. Rick, Alison, and Tom followed. "Look," Olivia wasn't looking at him. She had her hand over her eyes where the sun was hitting her face. It didn't burn her, but she was dehydrated and sun wasn't helping her fragile skin. Jason waved his hands and wind blew the curtains closed.

Words of gratitude slipped from her lips before she could stop herself.

"I'm amazed at how quickly all of you are helping her," began Alison. "She can't even stay in the light! This is ridiculous. How long are we expected to keep this up, Jason. She isn't one of us. I thought that went without saying. What are we supposed to do if she wakes up one morning and takes everything she's learned here back to the swarm of vampires? Trio-Genesis has never been found and when it is, because of her," Alison pointed at Olivia, "the entire building will fall apart." Alison pleaded with him over and over. Her mind was set. Brook wasn't who she said she was.

"I'm not sure if you're blind or just plain awful, but I happen to be standing right here. I can hear you, Blondie," Olivia said with anger rising in her voice at every word that came out.

"Give us a second," Jason grabbed onto Alison's hand and led her a few feet away. "You think I want to trust her?" he asked looking down at Alison. "She has to believe I do. She has to believe you do, too. I know what she might do. But she isn't going to do anything or it will be the end of her also. We've outnumbered her, and we've outdone ourselves. Nothing is going to happen. And if anything does happen I'll be the first to turn to you and tell you how right you were. I have a few tricks up my sleeve too. Have a little faith in me." He walked a bit further away never letting go of her hand.

"I'm looking out for all of us. I'm looking out for you…" he lied.

"I know the dangers, but I'm hoping she trusts us enough to give them away, so that way, we are the ones with the upper hand."

"I want so badly to believe you. But you're not the leader I remember. I don't know who you are anymore," she almost sobbed. "It tore us apart to lose him, but you were over it. We all were. And then suddenly it was all back. The hate, anger, bad choices. The first two of those things is fine, but your choices affects five other people. And the last choice you made, to house a criminal, a killer, a vampire," she whispered the last word, "if it goes south, it's more than five people you're hurting. It's a good thing he can't see you like this. He would be really disappointed." The words broke Alison as it left her lips but they had to be said, "Get her under control, or I will."

"So if I wanted you to, could you bite me?" Rick asked Olivia. Tom immediately struck him on back of the head.

"Are you trying to get us killed? If even a drop of your blood touches the floor we'll be dead meat. All kinds of booby traps are set to go off if a vampire bites someone. Besides, it's suicide to bite a slayer. Every vampire knows that… and every slayer, with the exception of you," Tom cursed at him. Rick began chuckling under his breath. "What so funny?"

"You said boobies," Rick laughed loudly. His laughed roared in the gym. Mark and Kelly finished cleaning up after Olivia and joined the three.

"What's so funny?" Kelly asked smiling at the hysterical Rick.

Tom shook his head in great disappointment and looked at Olivia for help. "Tom said boobies." Olivia smiled at Kelly. Mark giggled at Rick's undying laugher.

"Yeah, that'll do it," Mark said, still smiling at Rick.

Alison and Jason returned from their small conversation. They no longer held hands, but Alison could still feel the sweat of his hand on her warm palm. It lingered there in her hand, the sweet fragrance of his touch.

"We can't repeat this little mishap," Alison said calmly. "Whoever you are, whatever you are, we have to get your powers under control. We need to make sure that whatever you do, unless you're showering, you have one of us around. I'd rather not babysit a grown woman, but if it means keeping us alive, then I'll have to deal."

"Speaking of Elements, what is your element?" Mark asked.

"Mark, I'm pretty sure after the show we just fixed, her element is earth," Kelly said.

He smiled at Olivia. "Welcome to the family."

"You shouldn't drink, you know? Besides it's the middle of the day," Patrick said sternly. Patrick didn't want to kill her fun or rain on her parade. But he had to remind her of the risks she was taking.

"Just get my Bloody Mary, please?" whined the hungry Countess sitting at the bar.

He turned and began to mix things. Olivia played with her nails and tapped them on the top of the bar. She yawned and rubbed her eyes. All this sneaking away left the Countess with no rest. Good thing for her, Patrick kept the bar open longer than usual now that she was away. He would sit there and wait for her hours after everyone had left if he had to. Eventually he would close up and go to bed, but he always kept waiting for her to show up. Patrick turned around and placed a red drink out in front of her.

Olivia smiled at him as she took the glass into her hand and sipped the drink.

"This is tomato juice isn't it, Patrick?" she asked defeated. He smiled back at her.

Patrick always held his side down, and he made sure Olivia would hold herself too. If she couldn't drink because of the building, than he wasn't going to let her. The front door of the bar swung open, and all eyes were on the tall man who walked in shouting. The sunlight streamed into the darkened Eclipse from the wide open door.

"I hate her. She's going to regret leaving me, she will, she will. What kind of woman treats a man ... why if I had a gun..." He noticed the eyes on him. "What are you looking at?!" The room was still. The man went over to the counter and sat down next to Olivia.

"Hey, buddy? We don't serve your kind here," Patrick said, kindly drying glasses behind the counter.

"Don't be rude Pat! Of course we serve his kind here," laughed a vampire in the corner of the room. The others joined in his laugher. The man shot a couple of cold glares around and looked back at Patrick.

"So what does one of my kind have to do to be served here?" he said, now smiling at Olivia, examining her body up and down. The laughter stopped, and every vampire in the room tensed their bodies as their smiling faces faded. The man kept looking at Olivia until he caught her eyes. She smiled at him. "So, what do I have to do, beautiful?" Olivia held her smile. The bodies in the room had all risen from their seats.

Their fangs were ready to drink, their hands ready to burn, their eyes, like hunters, seeking the prey.

"Why don't you take a look around mister?" she said, her eyes never leaving his.

The man looked up and around, grin fading. From behind the counter, Patrick asked the man, "Would you still like to be served?" The man looked back at Olivia, her smile now also had a pair of sharp fangs. "We have no problem serving you. How about it?" Patrick continued.

He stumbled out of his stool and ran for the door. The room roared with laughter.

Olivia turned back to Patrick and took a sip of her drink. "I forgot this was tomato juice," she spat. "It wasn't nice of us to treat a guest that way," she laughed a bit. "It's taking too long to see this through," she wailed.

"The preparations seemed much longer than this," Patrick reminded her.

"I've been with those idiots over a month now, starving myself from proper nutrition. They are despicable and at the same time, charming. I can't win," moaned the restless Countess.

"Alison watches me like a hawk. I'm convinced Tom would make a better vampire than he does a slayer. Mark can't decide if he's friends with me or not. Kelly keeps us from killing each other, which we really want to do. Meanwhile, Rick is the sweetest person I've ever met yet they each live to put him down." Olivia was beside herself as she spoke. "Oh! And Sharpie? His brain is a pile of mush, I could probably kill someone right before his eyes and he wouldn't know if he should congratulate me or scorn me!"

"Isn't his indecisiveness crucial to you?" Patrick asked.

"Yes but what fun is it puppeteering when you know you'll win?" She breathed. "This is why free will is such a marvelous gift! And once you take that away, everything becomes too easy..." She was oddly pensive. "I need a challenge to wake me out of this low," she exhaled her complaints. "Everyone is fighting to protect what he or she believes in, be it good or bad. Everyone has a side," she stood. The room stood with her. Olivia headed for the door.

"Olivia?" She turned back to him and he threw her, her car keys. "Which side are you on… Countess?" Patrick asked with all respect. She smiled softly as the fire consumed her when she surfed. Everyone took their seats again and went about their own business. Patrick sighed and went about his business.

Vampire class, taught by Professor Browse, was an extremely large lecture hall. It seemed like every student in Trio-Genesis took the class at the same hour. There were students of every age in the class. Olivia sat in the back of the class on the last row, three chairs from the window.

The sun lightly lit the class as it came dancing in through the large glass windows. It was a different light from the one that lit the vampire mansion.

There was a new law in one of the meetings at the mansion a while ago to train immortal vampires to build immunity to it. Born vampires could enjoy as much sunlight as they wanted. They were, after all, still alive. It was a good idea at first but then they realized that a lot of them were dying in the long run, so they changed all the windows in the mansion. The sun would come in, but it would do them no harm. Every window was protected by a large shield that took in the UV rays and blocked them as if the whole building had taken a sunblock bath. The sun shined, but the skin doesn't tan or turn to ash. That idea was better. Olivia came up with it all by herself. She was always looking out for her people. That's something her father taught her: the people who raise you are the ones who know you best; keep no secrets from them, tell them no lies.

"It's so bright," the words fell from her lips and echoed in the large class. Browse went silent. No one ever spoke in her class. The room was too sensitive to noise. A sigh would bounce off the walls and echo for days. For the past hour, Olivia had been gazing out of the window. The professor's voice had faded into the background to the point where she couldn't tell the difference when Browse spoke and when she didn't.

"Ms. Morton. Is there something you'd like to share with us?" Browse asked smiling sarcastically. She sat still looking at the light. "Ms. Morton… Ms Morton." The woman repeated until the student sitting next to Olivia gave her a little nudge.

Olivia looked up at woman standing in front of the class with her arms crossed over her small chest.

Olivia hadn't the slightest clue of the events that had happened, but by Browse's body language, she wasn't very pleased. Her natural leader, bossy-like attitude came out. "Can I help you?" she answered back.

In the silence, a pen fell on the floor and could be heard rolling down the side steps in the middle aisle. A desperate phrase came out of Alison's mouth. "Oh, God." Mark shot an angry look at Jason, whose head burned with hate. Kelly sat still as a rock with her mouth open as Tom shook his head rolling his eyes. Rick seemed to be the only one amused by Olivia's words. His smile revealed all his teeth and reached from one side of his face to the other.

Browse was so taken by Olivia's rude answer that not even she spoke. She stood still, stuck to floor of the lecture room, searching for an answer. It was a new experience for her. Olivia raised her eyebrows at the woman in charge.

"Well…" came out of her mouth again. The words only froze Browse to the ground harder. Olivia continued her out-of-mind behavior. "If you aren't going to scold me to amuse yourself with the power granted to you as professor, then will you kindly do your job and resume your lecture?" A laugh came out of Rick's mouth.

Browse took the opportunity of the laughing slayer to her advantage. "Mister Surfer, if you would please cease your laugher! And Miss Mont… Mont… Morton, if you would be so kind as to hold your tongue! My next topic might entertain you some," she finally barked out. Olivia wasn't the least bit taken by her answer. Her words had still counted as the last ones given. Browse walked over to her desk and returned to her teaching.

It was nearly 12 o'clock. Olivia wasn't fond of sitting in this class. At least the others offered some form of adventure. But this teacher, she was so dreary to listen to.

"Where was I? Yes. The myth that not all vampires are immortal is indeed a myth," Browse said, as a student raised his hand. She pointed to him, giving him permission to speak.

"So what about vampires who are born vampires? I always thought them to be mortal. They have strength and fangs and can control fire, but I always thought they aged and died," the student said.

Browse loved to answer questions. She had studied vampires for a long time. She even became good friends with some of the most evil vampires in the world. She knew enough to answer any question given to her. She wasn't, however, allowed to teach everything she knew. Her information came from inside sources, but since it was treason to befriend the blood drinkers, she could never give a source when she had a new discovery. Most of the information she gave her students was, what she called, "undercover work." She had been the woman who inspired Jason to do his own snooping around to find out what he wanted to know. "Well, many vampires look old because they are old. Those old vampires are usually turned at the age they are at. And turning a mortal into the immortal doesn't give him or her a new face from their past. It merely makes them immortal. These older vampires then spend a lifetime proving themselves to be placed in higher power. If they don't advance in their powers on their own, they are common vampires or janitors."

Olivia couldn't argue with any statement that came out of Browse's mouth yet. And she spent the rest of the class looking for moments when she could "raise her hand" and correct the woman.

"It's true, however, that born vampires grow and age to a certain point. Their minds mature forever, but their bodies mature only until they are about 40. After that, they remain in those bodies until someone kills them," she went on. "Yes, Clément." She pointed to another student raising his hand.

The small boy asked, "How is it that vampires have children? They are dead."

"Born Vampires are as alive as you and I. Anyone want to take a wild guess at how vampires conceive?"

Olivia didn't raise her hand, but she defiantly raised her voice and spoke. "There are a couple of ways. There is a whole group of vampires called the nannies. Their only job is to find pregnant mortal women and turn them. If the mother is Immortal, the baby will be also. Only a few of these nannies turn the father of these children and only because the mother, after being turned and giving birth to her baby, realizes her husband is missing from her fairytale family and cuts her own head off. It's a loss to our... their community to have vampires committing suicide. Another group of vampires are the healers. Their task is to find dying children and babies. They go to families of these sick children and offer them life—all of them: mother, father, and sibling. Not all families agree once they hear they were selling their souls to the devil. However, many are desperate for life. The same is done with the elderly. Veterans are the easiest to pursue. They are offered the chance to live longer, a once-in-a-lifetime opportunity to relive their glory days. And, of course, the field of medicine is never out of the reach for them." Olivia chooses her words carefully. "Many vampire women long to have children, and it's not impossible.

Many vampire men long to have an heir, which is also possible. The drinking and trading of blood makes the organs function. It's why vampires drink. Their thirst is for life."

She laughed. Olivia was already giving too much information. But her lips wouldn't stop. The class took in every word she gave. Browse drank from her knowledge like a thirsty camel.

"If a vampire couple longs for a child, they must drink pure blood that matches their original blood. The man feeds only on the man he has chosen to clean his blood. He must drink from him without killing or turning him during the period of one month. It is the only blood he is allowed to drink because it purifies his blood back to his own. His organs after a month become fully functional, and he is able to produce a living seed. The same goes for the woman. One host, one month, no killing, no mixing. Now, of course, the men have learned to freeze their live seed, and they don't have to endure the torture of being careful when drinking from the host. Women don't have the same luxury," she explained. "Vampires have seeds and eggs, they are just not alive. They are still and ageless in their bodies. Without clean blood, the sexual organs don't function. Luckily for them, the other organs work just fine simply by drinking any blood."

The loud sound of the bell ended Olivia's lesson. The class didn't hesitate when it came to leaving. As interesting as her information was, no one believed her. They all thought she was crazy. All except the six slayers who knew she knew the truth and the one professor in the front of the class who knew the truth for herself. Slayers, regardless of how much information they were given, only choose to accept some. The words could be written in black and white. They never took information without a source or proof. Olivia's words did her people no harm. The knowledge of the actions in which she had shared with them would not encourage any slayer to stop them.

The seven students left behind got up and began to leave. Olivia was stopped by Browse and asked for a word. But her desire to share information had vanished. She didn't agree to Browse's request, leaving the professor crazy for more.

As soon as Olivia stepped foot out of the classroom she changed her mind about staying to chat. The first words she heard from her newfound friends were filled with judgment. They began to scold her for her behavior in class.

"Are you completely insane?" Alison started. "I'm not sure you understand this process, so let me explain to you again." Her eyes were popping out of the head. Olivia watched Alison repeat the words she had heard from the six of them once again. She ignored the voice of reason. "Are you even listening to me?"

She wasn't. Rick decided it was time to stand up for Olivia. Everyone was always picking on her, and he had enough of it. He didn't think she was this terrible human being. Her ideas and morals weren't all that bad, and he couldn't understand why everything she did was such a big deal. "Leave her alone," he shouted. Olivia looked up at the tall, blonde slayer defending her. "Stop pretending that all of you don't care about her safety. Like it or not, Brook is one of us now. She has given us more information in one class than we have given her in the few days she's been here."

"Rick, she's been here for a month. We've spent most the time arguing about what to do with her," Kelly reminded him.

"Yeah, that's what I mean. In minutes she can tell us everything we want to know. We are doing a crappy job of giving our part. Brook is nice, and maybe if any of you took the time to hang out with her, you'd see that she is actually a good person." Rick turned to Olivia and smiled at her. He placed an arm around her and said "Brook, I don't care what any of these losers say. You're alright." Olivia smiled back at him and thanked him.

Her whole life, she had only one friend: Patrick. It was refreshing knowing that Rick cared about her and would stand by her side no matter what. And he spoke so randomly that when he did, no one really fought with him.

"We have an hour for lunch before our next class. If we eat quick we can do some training, like we used to, before we were obsessed with watching Brook. It'll be fun," Rick suggested. The seven of them turned and headed for the elevator and down to the cafeteria for a quick lunch.

Olivia walked into the chaotic room that afternoon with Jason and his team. Between the students loud voices and the residents annoyed faces she found her way to the silver door that led into the kitchen.

The cooks were distracted with their work and Olivia snuck up behind a tall man who was facing the stove and humming to himself as he cooked. He reached for the wooden spoon on his right and began mixing whatever delicious master piece he was making today.

"Anything special?" she asked and the surprised man dropped the sauce covered spoon on the ground.

"Brook!" he said spinning and embracing her with his dirty apron pressed between them. "I swear you have invisibility, how do you do that every time?"

"You're wrapped up in your cooking, it easy. Anything good today? The line is huge."

"You are not a patient girl," he said and walked over to the fridge to pull out some cold cuts. "How about a grilled cheese?"

"You better make it seven, we're trying to get out of here." She smiled.

Not a minute later Olivia was looking for the rest of the group in line. She found them still waiting but not too far from the buffet. In her hand was a tray of freshly made grilled cheeses, each sided with fries and a pickle.

"Everyone okay with a hot grilled cheese?" Olivia smiled.

"Where did you get those?" Kelly asked.

"The kitchen. I know a guy…" she said and they headed for a table to sit and eat. She informed them that the one with tomatoes belonged to Rick. The slayer felt very loved to know Olivia had made one special for him. But then she added that the one with bacon was Mark's. He thanked her suspiciously. They gobbled their lunches and headed out.

"Rick is really brave. He's strong too," Jason said, so only she could hear. Olivia and Jason walked a little ahead of the others. "He's right about you, Brook. You're not as bad as you seem at first hand."

"They say first impressions are the most important," she said, smirking at him. Jason laughed and nodded.

"It might be. But they are also filled with assumptions. And mine of you were wrong," Jason always had motives of his own, but this time he was putting his whole trust on the line. She could read his intentions like a book.

Kelly laughed at Alison's concerned expressions as she watched Jason walk oddly close to Olivia. "She's going to fall for him, you know?" Kelly told her friend.

Alison's face went pale, and she slowed her pace. "He doesn't really care about her, Ali. He wants information. She's going to fall for it. He has her wrapped all around his finger. Jason is a smart guy. He isn't going to trust someone he just met. Give it some time, you'll see. He is just using her." The words of comfort didn't seem to help.

Alison knew better. She knew the type of person Olivia was. "I'm afraid he'll be the one doing the falling. It's already starting, and he doesn't even know it." The doors beeped open, and a group of students walked out. The gold doors remained open and Jason ran for the doors to hold them.

They all stepped inside. "Hello, Mark," she spoke. Would you like me to take you to the hospital again?" Olivia turned around and looked at Mark.

"No, thank you," Mark answered quickly. Jason placed a friendly hand on his shoulder and instructed the elevator to take them to the third floor. The lights lit up, and she began to move up.

"She any better today?" Jason asked cautiously. Mark nodded.

The doors opened on the 3rd floor.

Jason walked in first and turned on the bright lights. He made his way into the fighting half of the room and looked at the others through the glass window. Mark turned on the control board and watched it, making sure everything worked clearly. The buttons lit up in the bright colors. Alison walked into the room with Jason and picked up a sword off the right wall. She walked over to Jason and lifted his chin with the tip of the sword. He smiled at her. "Just like old times, huh?" she said. He cleared his throat.

"Good idea. Brook, come in here. Maybe you girls can settle some of your issues." Alison dropped her hand and head. Olivia walked into the room and closed the white door behind her. Jason motioned for her to pick up a sword from the right wall. As the Countess chose a shiny sword, Jason walked out of the room and locked the door.

"You really think that's a good idea?" Mark asked smiling. Jason nodded and talked into the mic on the control board.

"Alright ladies. We all love a good girl fight. Play fair. Alison is great at swords, Brook, so I'd watch out." It was the first time Alison really smiled. She was looking forward to this moment. Olivia turned to face Alison and smiled.

Alison twirled her sword in her hand and pointed the tip at the Countess. Olivia ran the end of her sword on the floor and walked. Their eyes were locked on one another, their smiles never fading. Alison and Olivia walked in a circle for a moment staring each other down. "Can they hear us?" Olivia asked Alison.

She shook her head. "There is a microphone in here, but Jason never remembers to turn it on."

"Good," Olivia shouted, and ran at her. Their swords met. Alison pushed on Olivia.

The blades rang against each other. The girls moved quickly at each other. If Olivia swung right, Alison blocked her. When Alison swung down, Olivia protected herself.

"Why is it you think he doesn't like you?" Olivia asked when she was face to face with Alison.

The blonde's blood boiled under her skin. She swung her sword harder, the force knocking Olivia's sword down. Her eyes followed her falling sword. Olivia quickly raised her eyes at Alison, who was already swinging her sword at Olivia again. The Countess raised her sword and pushed away Alison's with all her might.

The fight kept going until Alison decided that swords weren't enough. She kicked Olivia right in the gut, knocking the vampire to the left wall. Olivia dropped her sword and grabbed her stomach. Alison walked at her, pointing the sharp sword at the resting vampire. Olivia got up, sword in hand, just as Alison moved her sword at Olivia's neck.

"That's how I kill you right? I cut your disgusting neck off? Or maybe I can stab you through the heart, though I hear that doesn't work too well," Alison said. "Drop your weapon." Olivia had no other choice. Alison wasn't afraid of killing her right then and there.

Marks voice came from the speakers. "Nice work Ali." Jason unlocked the door and walked in.

"We'll work on this a little more, Brook. You could use a few lessons," Alison boasted, returning her sword to the wall.

Jason agreed and volunteered his services. Olivia smiled and accepted, looking ever so slightly at the blonde, whose plans kept failing.

CHAPTER 7

Island Trouble

"Girls, if I have to break up another argument, I'll lock both of you up for so long you'll have no choice but to be friends," Kerrigan told them as the students sat down. "Every class…" he whispered under his breath walking away from Olivia and Alison. "After hours of discussion Dr. Craips and I have finally decided on a suitable challenge for this year. It's only right you each get a chance to prove yourselves here." Kerrigan was referring to how things happened in Trio-Genesis.

The annual challenge served to enlist different slayers into Trio-Genesis' Trio Army. Six slayers, two from each element, would come together to survive, hunt down, and discover something that could prove they were good enough to fight in Trio Army. When chaos arrived, the six slayers would venture out to bring peace and justice. It was the highest honor to be a member of Trio Army.

The age restriction for enlisting was seven years old with the consent of a parent or guardian. If the child was an orphan and had no responsible guardian, the age restriction was 14. Students who wished to remain in Trio Army would have to prove their worth in the annual challenge, until schooling was done. The challenge also served as an application process for any team who had not passed the previous years. There were loopholes into remaining in Trio Army as a student without partaking in the ridiculous task of the year, but they were hard to come by and filled with certain risk of permanent removal. Most teams of students took many years to pass one challenge and without the guarantee of success for the remaining years, Trio Army was known as the hardest and longest job interview. Then there were the occasional few, who proved themselves worthy without the help of a team. Upon graduation each student was given the chance to enlist one last time. If the graduate proved useful to a Trio Army team with an open position, they were recruited and forever adored by the slayers they protected. If they shamed themselves with failure they took on any other job available in Trio-Genesis. And though being a doctor or chef was just as important as being a solider, members of Trio Army were given the largest homes, best food, private events, and even priority with medical situations.

"I know most of you can recite the following words but I've gotten in trouble with previous classes for not saying them, so bear with me. Besides, we have a new addition in this class, since last year's challenge," he said and smiled at Olivia. "You along with your groups of six: six Slayers in each group, two elements of each, at least two upper level slayers. Blah, blah, blah." The students laughed with Kerrigan. "It's very important that you know the people in your group and are able to connect with your respective element. If you and your group choose to withdraw from the testing, you may do so at the registration hall on the third floor: leave our class, swing a right, take a left at Brookens Hall, walk 23 paces to the golden elevators, and go down to three—so on and so forth, or just do the normal thing and surf."

The class enjoyed his humor. "If you do choose to participate and every member of your group is emotionally capable to follow the rigorous tests you will be put through... that was added for you, Jason," Kerrigan said, smiling at the handsome slayer, who smiled and sighed at the back of the class. Olivia looked at Jason, narrowing her eyes she searched his mind for an answer...nothing.

"...then please listen to the following instructions and prepare to leave immediately. Your Trio leader will be a given a map, and the six of you will leave immediately for said destination. You must remain at your destination for three days and return to Trio-Genesis at midnight on the end of the third day, no later, no sooner. Any group who chooses to return sooner or fails to meet the time of 12 a.m. on the fourth day will be disqualified from the Trio Army and will be forced to wait another year for application. If you are a graduating student and wish to enlist… as I know all of you do… you will be forced to be retested physically and mentally. If the members in your group are not graduating students, you may apply for an opening in your element with an existing group. You are not allowed to bring any food, water, or extra clothing with you. No cell phones, beepers, pagers, video game devices, or water proof watches. If you have chosen to participate in the following task please fill out the medical form below, sign and date at the bottom." Kerrigan took a breath and looked up at his students.

"Take a form and pass it down," Kerrigan said, giving the student on the far left the health forms. "If you don't want to participate, you are free to go and enjoy your three days off. Don't forget to study for next week's quiz on 'Fire. An element of its own or a combination?' That should interest our dear new comer." He looked quickly at Olivia.

Every year the six proved themselves worthy and soon they would have to enter the challenge for the last time. It had already been discussed that they would remain a team and graduate into a permanent Trio Army. But this year things were different: they had Olivia.

They couldn't take her, nor could they leave her behind to bring turmoil to Trio-Genesis. Their one solution would be to withdraw, or so five of them thought.

The paper reached Jason and he took it, gladly filling out the familiar circles and questions he had done since age seven. "What are you doing?" asked Mark, squinting his eyes.

"We have to sign our lives away to participate." He paused as he signed his name, Jason Peter Sharpie, at the bottom. "I'm doing just that." The slayer looked at the faces of his depressed and puzzled friends. "Don't tell me you've all given up on our dream."

"Obviously we aren't overjoyed about staying, Jason. But what about, Brook?" Kelly asked.

Jason smiled down at Kerrigan, "I had a chat..." he breathed looking down at his teacher and smiling stealthy, "with a certain Element's teacher..."

Alison chimed in and cut him off. "Don't say it," she begged demanding.

"He thought it would be good for us. It hasn't been done before..." he tried to continue.

"Jason," Tom took his turn and opened his month. "I don't have a problem with this, but the contract clearly states six. We make six on our own without her," he went on. "If there was a way..."

"I found a loophole," he said, raising his voice a bit. "If a group takes on another member whose element is undefined, the member is allowed the choice to participate in the annual challenge or to withdraw from it," he smiled. "We've practically taken her in,"

Alison shook her head as she laughed sarcastically. Kelly spoke, "I thought we agreed that Brook's element was earth."

"She hasn't taken another placement test. Her papers still say undefined. To the school, she doesn't know yet. Taking her with us puts us in an even better position."

Olivia was silent still. Maybe she was trying to figure out what was it about her that made people talk to her face pretending she wasn't there. She couldn't be that well behaved or invisible. Maybe it was because she didn't take herself seriously and so no one else did either. No matter what it was, she was clearly tapping her nails much louder against her desk than usual, and the throat clearing was ear splitting every time her name was mentioned.

"Another bonus," Jason went on, "is if we take a slayer whose element is unknown and said slayer shows significant progression once returned, we don't have to apply next year or ever again. We're in." The news sounded better to him than it did to the others by the looks of disgust on their faces. "I know that our biggest dream is to fight in the big leagues. We all know school rats in the Trio Army are taken as a joke. Trio Army doesn't have to be a dream forever. If we can get into Trio Army permanently and make a name for ourselves while still in school, they'll be begging us to join."

"We aren't going to get another chance like this." Mark agreed. If Mark agreed, Kelly would too. And if Kelly was on board she would take Alison kicking and screaming. Rick never opposed anything that meant bringing Olivia along, and Tom didn't have much of a voice. "So it's done. Brook comes along."

Maybe it was the excitement or maybe it was the fear, but Jason forgot to mention that if they failed with a seven they would be disgraced and banded from enlisting in Trio Army. They would have to settle for teachers, doctors, chefs, or just commoners with a lot of power.

Kerrigan went into his desk and pulled out the maps. The leaders went down to retrieve their maps from the desk. "Kerrigan, I was reading further into the rules and I happen to know that Brook is undefined. My group and I were wondering if she wanted to join us. We could use the boost to the top." Jeff presented his question with a listening Jason standing close by.

"Jason has already picked dibs on our new hothead." Kerrigan's information wasn't easy to hear. Jason's team was already on top, and they didn't need the extra help. Jason stood and faced Jeff.

The boys walked over to each other. "I didn't know you liked her so much, Sharpie. Keep an eye on her or she might switch on you," Jeff threatened him.

"Jeffery, I was sure you would have joined the other side by now," Jason said holding his ground. Kerrigan stepped in the middle of the boys and pushed them apart carefully. He didn't have to say anything—the two knew what it meant.

After two months of seeing Jason fight with his own team, Olivia was finally about to see him fight with someone else. Suddenly, Kerrigan goes and breaks it up before it gets good. "Like children on a playground," Kerrigan said. "Hand in your forms and the challenge begins!"

"Now?" Olivia asked. They really weren't kidding when they said the clothes on their back. Her black tank top and beige zip-up with dark blue jeans and black boots weren't exactly adventure clothing.

"Well, yes." Kerrigan answered. Groups surfed off as Kerrigan spoke. No one was ever prepared for the challenge, but that was the best part and most crucial part. War doesn't usually send a letter advising the other side it was coming. It simply came like a thief in the night.

Olivia tried to quickly finish her health form. "We're going to an island?" Kelly asked insulted. "We've been to hell and back and best they can do is an island? What's it called?"

"Blood Island," Mark said reading off the map. Olivia's head shot up. She looked at them for a second and then went back to filling her papers.

Jason looked around, "We should wait for everyone to leave so we can surf; well, so Brook can surf. I don't want to start this off by killing each other," he said sitting down next to Olivia. They all sat to get a better look at the map Jason held. "Surf to the east side of the island on shore. We don't know what the weather is like so it's best to wait for everyone to arrive. Don't go off and do your own thing," he said looking Rick dead in the eyes.

"I won't!" he answered childlike.

Olivia finished her records and Kelly took all their papers down to the front with Alison.

"This isn't a good idea," Alison spoke as they walked. "I don't trust her."

"She isn't that bad," Kelly said as she turned her back on her best friend and walked back up the stairs. "That's the last of them. It's just us and Kerrigan," Kelly told Jason as she reached the top.

Jason looked back and nodded at Kerrigan who looked ready to leave, he took the forms and surfed away with a soft wind. "Now it's just us," Jason smiled. "Let's bounce," he said and a gush of hot air came over him, sweeping the dust in the room away. The wind gust blew his body away, and Jason was gone.

"Yes, let's," Rick said, water dripping from his head. A large whirlpool surrounded him and he too was gone. A wave came over Alison, and she surfed off as a wind blew in from the window and swirled around Tom's body until he too had vanished. Green leaves swallowed up Kelly's figure whole until only Mark and Olivia were left. A warm wind surrounded them. Mark smiled at Olivia and she smiled back. Mark kicked his foot down and a wall of dust came up from the classroom floor; when the wall went down the slayer had gone.

Olivia looked around to make sure the class was empty. Her hand was consumed by fire and in the blink of an eye her entire body was in flames as she surfed out of the class. From the door Kerrigan peaked into the classroom just in time to watch her go up in flames and leave behind a white smoke which quickly evaporated.

Kerrigan smiled and shook his head. "She's going to be a handful."

It poured from the dark sky. The clouds were heavy and gray. The moonlight was coming through the trees, but it was nowhere to be seen. There was no wind, just the spewing water and the heat. Lots of heat. The rain was not a cooling factor.

Every time she came up for air, it would once again crush her back into the salty grave called Ocean.

"This is ridiculous!" Alison screamed from shore.

Olivia came up for air again. Her head turned to the direction of the blonde's screechy voice. Her screwed up, red eyes found the shore as the most recent wave fizzed out around her. Olivia began swimming over to where the earth and the water met. Another unforgiving wave came for the drowning vampire.

After two months of regular food and no feedings, Olivia was weak. Her swimming wasn't up to par either. The juicy steaks she had every night for dinner weren't much help. The taste was incredible, but there was no satisfaction for her thirst. Still, Darren, could cook her a hell of a dinner. And since Patrick wasn't giving in to her pleas, the bloody cow would have to do, however disgruntled it may be.

Her eyes burned under torment from the salty sea, but a few moments of comfort were being sacrificed in order to keep herself from crashing into anything harmful.

Nothing, however, felt harder than the water at the moment.

Five of them stood on the shore while the rain pounded down on their bodies. "Mark?!" Kelly shouted about the island. "Jason, he isn't on the island," her panicked words cried from her lips.

"We'll find him," spoke Jason softly looking around the island.

"Ali and I are fine, we'll go look for him," said Rick looking down at the pretty blonde.

They had paired off with their elements. A buddy-buddy system: Alison and Rick, Mark and Kelly, Jason and Tom, Olivia... Brook, and, well, Olivia and Brook.

"I'll go too, Jason. He could be at sea." Tom's thoughts panicked the group. Kelly began shouting again.

"No. Mark is fine; he would have no trouble locating sand. Kelly, please stop screaming. We don't know what's on this island." Jason placed both hands on her shoulders and shook her about as he hushed the words. He looked around once more, eyes enlarging with each passing millisecond. "Where's Brook?"

"She's gone too." Alison informed them.

The water gave her no mercy. Her eyes were closed now. Once again, she surfaced for air, the clock ticking as another wave crashed her back into the water. Her body went for the large coral pieces decorating the beautiful rocks of the ocean as more waves came to make the impact harder. Her side went for the coral and cut her flesh open. Olivia screamed as water entered her lungs little by little.

Jason reached for his side and crumbed to the ground screaming. Alison ran for his side asking him what was wrong.

"I think she's hurt," Jason said as if he were out of breath.

"Who? Brook? You think she's hurt... you can feel her pain?" Alison's voice was dripping with confussion. Jason nodded not being able to speak. He started taking a few calming breath and he suddenly stood.

"She's under water," the surfer boy said looking deep into the ocean before him.

"There's a lot of coral where she is. It's hard to miss," Kelly added.

"Jason, she can't breathe!" Tom joined in, looking over for instructions. The ruckus spread and was visible on each face standing in the sand.

Alison, completely appalled, shouted at the astonishing slayers. "You sense her already?"

A hand grabbed Olivia's arm and pulled her away from more coral. He, too, was bleeding, from his leg. Olivia opened her eyes. Mark pointed up. She nodded, understanding they were waiting for the next wave to come to go back up.

Turn your body in the direction the waves come from when you surface. That way, you will see them coming, he thought to Olivia. Her hand was clutching onto her side; the other was holding Marks hand.

They waited as Olivia's lungs were dying inside her.

"Rick, tell me when the next wave hits. Mark is with her. I can hear him," Jason said looking at a tearful Kelly. Rick walked over into the water until it reached his knees and closed his eyes.

They surfaced, coughing as they did. The waves were coming right behind them. "They have to go back under. Tell me when the next wave is coming so they can move." Jason kept his cool in order to save them, but the rescue involved risking another life.

"Ali! Ali!" Jason ran over to her. "I need you." He was spitting the water from the rain as he spoke. "I need to get them." His eyes weren't watering from the rain.

"Jason! Wave! Five seconds!" Rick screamed.

"I need you to get them, Ali. I can't do it. I'm not strong enough to face the rage of the sea but you are, and I need you to get them." Jason begged her, grabbing her arms gently and pulling her closer to him.

"WAVE!" Rick shouted.

They went under—Mark, never letting go of Olivia's hand, his muscles tightening as he held her. They surfaced for air. Tom was on shore breathing as heavy as he could.

He could feel the water filling up their lungs. He breathed deeper and deeper. Kelly was mind in mind with Mark to warn him of anything under they could hit. "Can't you slow the wave down?" Kelly screamed from shore to Rick.

He looked back at her with dropped eyes, shut lips, and shook his head. "I don't yield that kind of power," he said and looked back. The sea was too strong for him. He was still learning to master his element. Savanna had been the only one ever to master her element and all the others as well. "Wave, in 3 seconds." Rick did what he could to help. He did as he was told by his leader.

Another wave hit them.

Alison knew the danger of surfing two injured people with different elements. She knew the storm was strong and that no matter how much she calculated the timing of the waves, the wind was not on their side. Mark's thoughts entered her open mind.

Stay calm, Jason knowns what to do.

Alison and Jason shared a look and her body became one with the rain as she surfed away.

A cold hand grabbed Mark's arm. He looked over and Alison smiled at him.

I need you to concentrate. Hold on to her and tell her to concentrate, she thought to Mark.

She can hear you, he thought back to her.

Alison's smile faded. *Just concentrate on the water. Try not to be afraid of it, let it become you. Hold on to me, and I'll get us out of here.*

Jason took a deep breath; both Mark and Olivia were hurt. Having Alison surf them back would wound them even more. But he couldn't let them die.

She surfed. Land and sand. The rain suddenly began to settle. Mark and Olivia collapsed on the sand of the beach beside Jason and Tom. Kelly and Rick ran as soon as they had surfaced back on land and kneeled beside Mark who was coughing and hugging the land saying, "land sweet land. Oh, I love you sweet sand." Rick and Tom also knelt beside him.

Olivia coughed and tried inhaling. She looked over to her side down at Mark who was still busy loving the land. The blood from his leg mixed with the sand. He felt her eyes on him, looked over at her and smiled. Olivia crawled away from the six and sat over by herself.

"Mark! Are you okay?" Kelly asked hugging him; he took her in his arms and held her back.

"I am now," he said into her ear. Kelly let go and started looking at the cut on his leg.

"You were seafood out there." Rick laughed at Mark and joked. "Getting kinda sloppy there." It was a little too soon for making marks that he missed sand.

"I didn't miss it. I don't know what happened." He began to explain himself. "I was thinking about Brook and my body took me to the water. I couldn't help but to surf where she was."

It was strange for no one to care for her and give her attention like they were giving Mark. If something like this had happened and she had been around Patrick, Josh, Michael or anyone from the Mansion, they would have carried her away, hugged her, and showered her with care; but here she was just the reason a good friend almost died.

Jason and Alison stood right where they were without moving. He thanked her. "He couldn't help but surf to her? Do any of you hear yourself? There is something off about that girl." Alison was firm on her beliefs.

"We are a team, we need to help each other, and we are all on the same side," Jason said. "The next days aren't going to be easy; regardless, I need you to understand that we look out for each other."

"The only person I'm responsible for is Rick," she said coldly.

"Fine. Then he will be the only one responsible for you. You at least deserve that right?" he said and turned away. He dropped down by Mark who was still coughing a bit, trying hard to breathe. Rick was laughing as he helped get the water out of his lungs.

Jason joined in on their laugher. As he laughed, Jason looked around to notice Olivia coughing silently in her solitude. He patted Mark on his shoulder as he got up. He looked at his leg and told Kelly to find something to wrap around it. As soon as he did, Mark looked down at his leg and twitched from the salt water, sand, and hot air hitting the wound he had forgotten was there.

Jason walked over to Olivia. She was sitting on the sand trying to breathe, and as she did, she coughed up water. "You okay?" he asked gently. Olivia coughed up more water. Her arms wrapped around the stomach.

He crouched in front of her and took her hand. She lifted her face and looked at him. "Breathe…" he told her and blew on her face. She took in the air and kept breathing. Every so often, she would cough up more water. Jason kept blowing on her face while holding her hand. They were in silence; their eyes never parting.

From the distance, Alison watched her enemy and her crush connect. Jason called Rick over to help Olivia take the water out of her lungs as Alison kept helping Mark.

Rick ran over and sat beside Olivia.

"Okay, open your mouth and cock your head back a little. Jason is going to keep breathing with you. It's going to hurt a bit when you inhale because I'm going to pull the water out so when you exhale, the water will come up. Try not to cough—more water comes out that way," Rick told her.

"Inhale through your nose and exhale through your mouth," Jason added. Olivia nodded. She let her head fall back a little and opened her mouth. Olivia breathed in through her nose and when she breathed out through her mouth, Rick lifted his hand and pulled a thin stream of water right out of her lungs through her mouth. The moonlight shined on the water. They repeated the process a few times until Olivia was better. She held on to Jason's hand and Jason noticed her other hand over her left side. "You're bleeding," he said letting go of her hand. Rick looked over at her wound.

She removed her hand from the wound, and as the air touched it, a light blue light came from inside her and it healed itself. Rick's eyes fell out of his head. "How did you do that?" the beach blond slayer asked very slowly.

As soon as her wound healed, Olivia stood up. She wasn't coughing anymore and she was breathing fine. Jason and Rick stood after her puzzled looks on their faces.

Olivia thanked them and walked over to Mark and the others.

Jason and Rick ran after her. "How'd you do that?" Rick asked again in front of everyone.

"How did she do what, Rick?" Kelly asked.

"Nothing we haven't seen before," Jason said before Rick could say something. He looked over at Rick and without having to read his mind, Rick understood he should just drop it. Kelly went back to bandaging up Mark's leg.

"Night one has been a complete disaster so far, but we have two more days to make this happy family work. We should find shelter and something to eat?" Jason said smiling.

Mark stood, putting his arm around Kelly and Rick for support. The seven went off looking for shelter in the dead of the night.

"I wonder how everyone else is doing with their destination," Kelly said. "You think there's anyone else on this island?"

"No, it's just us. This is a dead island," Olivia answered almost too quickly.

A large cave was ahead of them. It seemed like a good place to rest for the night, so they made their way. Once inside, everyone looked to Olivia to start a fire. It surprised her a bit, but she didn't mind. Mark had to rest his leg and it was too dark to go off looking for food. They spent the first night lying around the hot fire hungry and still a bit wet from the rain.

A huge waterfall fell into a great pond of water. The trees whispered in the wind and the moon shined down on the water lighting up the night. There were mossy rocks along the side of the waterfall and a body of water below. They danced, laughed, drank, and talked into the late hours of the night. Fires burned that illuminated the darkness around them, but the light wouldn't travel far. There were too many trees around for these creatures to be seen, and they were so deep into the forest that they would not have been heard either. The forest looked like a regular club in the middle of nowhere, away from society, on an island.

The night was getting hotter and hotter; the party kept raging on. A man stood up on a great boulder and whistled the party silent. All eyes were on him. The music had stopped and the dancing had ceased. The silence was perfect and the only noise heard was coming from the creatures in the forest and fires cracking. The cracking of the fire and the wood burning in it was calmed, and now even the noises of the creatures began to fade as the man opened his mouth and began to speak.

"Tonight, on this amazing summer night we celebrate a new beginning, established years ago: 2,000 years ago." The crowd clapped and cheered. "Years of leadership, trust, and power!" Once again, the people went wild. "Our house has been standing these 2,000 years. And tonight I would like everyone to grab a buddy, the person to your left or person to your right. For some, that person will be a lover; for others, a useful mate. For we will toast for our 2,000 years and many more. Power! Trust! Leadership!"

The crowd repeated his words "Power! Trust! Leadership!" They then took the hand of their "buddy" and bit the back of it with their sharp teeth. The toast was made and once again, every eye turned to the vampire standing on the large rock. Joshua stood watching over the vampires. He could make a great leader. His vision was perfect and his mind maniacal enough.

"As tradition goes, we must toast to our fearless leader," Joshua spoke again, "and although Countess Olivia is not with us tonight due to her mission, we drink on her behalf." His voice filled the empty spaces. The vampires poured out whatever was in their glasses to fill from the water on the pond. "This water does not have the blood of the Countess, but we will still be drinking from a leader's blood. Mine," he said proudly.

The crowd was silent.

"You don't have the authority to do that, Joshua." The voice came from behind the crowd. Every face turned to look her in the eyes. They all bowed their heads in respect for her presence. "In fact, you don't even have the right to run this ceremony. It is Patrick's duty in case of my absence. Where is he?" she barked at him with her unforgiving tone. With two sentences Olivia took all the power Joshua had built in the last two months, with no regards to the many vampires who thought they could look up to him.

They all lifted their heads and turned to the man on the rock, his eyes looking down at the water in front of him. Joshua raised his head feeling enough of a coward.

"Where is Patrick?" she asked once more. By the tone, Joshua understood she would not ask again. Olivia stood completely still. All eyes on her, Joshua's lips ran dry.

"It felt wrong to come to the celebration without you, Countess." Patrick's voice came from behind her. He was always ready to save Joshua's skin. She turned to face him and he took a knee and kissed her hand. "Although, I must say, I always knew you'd show up." He then lifted himself and took Olivia's hand to lead her to edge of the water. They spoke quietly as they walked.

"Your nobility is why I have appointed you second in the Mansion. You should have been here Pat. I'm counting on you to do this for me," she said so that only he would hear.

"What good is leadership if it's behind hidden doors? You very well know I don't care for the Mansion and its monsters. With all due respect, Olivia, it is not my place to take your chair in case of absence. I'm not sure this is a good time for you to come back. Your prick of a fiancé is making the Mansion all topsy-turvy. Shouldn't you be in class?" he joked. "You see me every week, but to them, you haven't been around in over two months. There are questions even the great Olivia Montgomery won't be able to answer to these blood suckers." Patrick always tried doing his best to look out for Olivia, but after she left, Joshua's dogs outnumbered him.

Olivia gave him a kind smile as they reached the water. "They are too afraid to ask them," she knew, but maybe that had changed.

"Is this return permanent?" Olivia would not answer his question; instead, she lifted her wrist up to his lips. He understood. Patrick took her hand into his own and sank his fangs into her wrist, letting go he held her hand over the water. "Countess Olivia! Power, Trust, and Leadership!" Her blood dripped into the pool of water below them as Patrick licked the sweet liquid from his lips. His breathing calmed and his eyes softened.

Every vampire went up to the water and filled their cups to drink. The party went back to its wild form. Joshua went after Olivia sitting by a tree making small talk with Patrick. He took her by the upper arm and pulled her away from him. Patrick had half the mind to stop Joshua, but he could do nothing; Joshua was within his power as Olivia's betrothed. It was a weird bunch of laws. Olivia had power over Joshua, who had power over Patrick, who had power over Joshua in case Olivia was absent.

"You should not have done that. They have been asking enough questions as it is as to where you have been. Now the mansion will be under complete chaos. How long will this trip take you?" he asked, leading her away from the crowd.

"You know the risks I'm taking by being here," Olivia quietly scolded him. "They would have gone into chaos had I not shown. How would it look to the council if tonight they had been drinking your blood, knowing Patrick was appointed by me in my place?"

"Patrick lost his rights!" Joshua flared his nostrils.

"I can revoke any and all punishments granted by Counts before me," she reminded.

"Not the ones settled under the death penalty," he bit.

Olivia sighed her body shaking with anger. She inhaled the summer air as her shoulders dropped. "Don't you have enough power?" she asked just above a whisper her voice sad and broken. Collecting her emotions she began again, "This plan is just going to take more time. And until then, I have to trust you." She hated knowing Joshua was in charge of things. His thoughts were only for himself and of himself. Anything that helped him was good. Anything that didn't, wasn't.

He looked into her eyes; her heart beating loudly against her chest. Joshua would get his way only because he was smart. All the power Olivia possessed was wasted by her free spirit and poor choices. He pushed her hair behind her ear exhaling his desire into the air she breathed. "Why do you torture me, love?"

She frowned. Joshua looked over in the direction Patrick stood and she smiled. "It was only my wrist," she flirted.

He raised her hand up to his chest. "It beats still, for you only. Why do you betray me?" he said, holding the side of her neck and running his thumb on her jawline.

Joshua pushed the hair resting on her shoulder off behind her back. His lips met the skin on Olivia's neck as he drank from her blood and poisoned her. He spun her around to shoot smirking looks at Patrick who watched the pair enraged. When he was finished, Olivia took her bite, standing up on her toes to reach his neck, which he had gladly turned to her. The blood filled her mouth, and as she recalled not having a certain vaccine, her eyes shot open. Her presence was like the wind on a hot summer day; there, and then gone quickly and suddenly. Joshua opened his eyes to the empty space before him and the cocked eyebrows of a certain vampire not too far away returning the smirk.

Morning came quickly. The cave they had slept in the night before was filled with the sun's bright light. She ran her hands over her eyes and yawned. The waves crashing on the shore had woken her from her peaceful slumber. They must have let her sleep in because she was the only one left in the cave. She sat up and looked out at the beach.

Tom and Kelly were standing with water up to their knees trying to fish. It was a very amusing sight. After many attempts to catch a fish, Rick walked over to put his hand in the water and caught one for them. "Air head," he said looking at Tom.

"That's not fair. You are in your comfort zone," Kelly joked smiling.

"That has nothing to do with it. My element is water, not animals. I'm just a better fisherman than you two," Rick ran away laughing.

Olivia laughed to herself. It must have been noon already, for the sun was high in the sky when she came from the cave. She looked around for Jason and Mark.

"Because it's in my nature not to trust them." Alison was getting very repetitive. Jason looked into her eyes softly. He couldn't lie to her. He had done so before.

Jason put his hand on her shoulder. "I understand that she is not one of us, but she is trying really hard to be, and some part of her must be. You saw with your own eyes how she was doing with the elements. She's been training every day with Kerrigan and Craips, even after classes. Kerrigan has practically adopted her. They say there is something very special about her, don't you remember her earth outburst?"

"I do, which is all the more reason we shouldn't trust her. How many vampires do you know have that great of a control with the elements?" she said standing and dusting the sand off her jeans.

"You're right. She is hiding something, but whatever it is, it can't be so bad. Trust me, I've been with her alone." Alison rolled her eyes at his attempt to make things better. "Not like that, Ali. When you're alone with her, all you feel is her power. Lots of it." Alison looked away from him. He looked down.

Jason prided himself in being a fair leader. He wasn't afraid to make mistakes-that was a good quality in a leader. But around Olivia, he was second best. He was simply trying to get a bit of her light. "I need her on my side. You know why." If nothing else, Alison understood Jason's pain. Having Brook on their side would be the fastest way to end it all. And if she could find it in herself to be civil to Brook, it would help Jason ten times over. "I'll talk to the others to keep a better eye on her. Just be less you around her," he demanded, walking away.

Her face fell, "What's that supposed to mean?" she asked heartbroken, then looked over at Rick and saw Olivia standing beside him trying to master water. Jason also looked over at Olivia.

"Okay, so concentrate. You are going to lift your hand and move it around in a curly motion. Let the water come to you." He moved his hand around and made a string of water in the air. Olivia watched the water dance and tried to do the same.

Alison walked over to her. Jason followed close behind. "What do you think you are doing?" she said, pushing Rick.

"Oh, I'm just teaching Brook a few tricks." Rick smiled kindly, rubbing where Alison had pushed him.

"You can't master water, Brook. You aren't a slayer. I'm not sure I know what you are. If anything, your element is earth. So leave the water alone." She lifted her hands, made a huge wave, and walked away.

Rick looked back at Alison, "Don't worry, Brook. She always tries to show off," he said, nudging the Countess.

Two can play this game, Olivia thought. She turned back to the water, lifted her hand, and made an even bigger wave. Alison heard it crash back on the water and turned to see. "Wow… that was amazing!" Rick said, slapping Olivia on the back. "How did you do that?" She looked over at Alison and smiled wickedly. After a few weeks of not having a drink, anything would tip Olivia off. And the torment of tasting Joshua's blood and then having to spit it out was excruciating. She was going to let it all hang lose. Alison wanted to play dirty. She would play dirty.

She raised her left hand, facing the sea, and a thick rope of water went flying at Olivia. Rick moved out of the way. Tom and Kelly moved out of the water. It wasn't their fight. Olivia made a wall of fire in front of herself. The water hit the fire and made a sizzling noise like burning hair, sending steam up into the air. She used the same wall to attack Alison with it, pushing her hands forward. The fire went for Alison, who moved out of the way and ran over to the water until her feet were covered by the wet element. A great wind came over them. The ocean roared and Olivia's hands were covered with fire. She put her hands out in front of her and fire came from them in little quick balls, her brown eyes reflecting the fire. One of Alison's hands was down and out by her side as the other she held out in front of her, holding up a shield of water. The fire and water were hitting each other with great force. Alison was being pushed back into the water as Olivia was being pushed back in the sand. Olivia's anger grew but Alison would not back down. Her hair started to freeze up and began turning blue. She was using more power than she had ever used before. Still, the fire began consuming the water. Olivia smiled and everyone got a full view of her sharp fangs as her eyes slowly grew the crimson vampire red. No one wanted to interfere, but they knew soon Alison would be vampire food and that they would have a dead vampire too.

He ran over to Olivia and tried pushing her hands down. She used one hand to push him off, and Jason went flying at the sand. Mark used the sand Jason was lying on to push him back up on his feet. Alison was kneeling in the water her waist covered by it. Olivia was fighting her one handed, but Alison's hate did not wear out. Jason took in a deep breath and Mark pulled the sand under Olivia's feet to suck her in the earth. She was caught off guard, and the water shield Alison held up suddenly shot out at Olivia. Alison's body jerked forward and her other hand flew up behind the left one. Jason blew a wall of air in front of Olivia so the water wouldn't hit her. Then he held his hand very still so the wall of air would not be broken. Alison's power grew stronger. Her hair went bright blinding blue and then back to blonde as she released her grip and fell forward on her hands. Rick and Kelly ran over to her and helped her out of the water.

Olivia was still fully vampire—her fangs still showing and her eyes were now red, but she was stuck in the sand.

"Mark, let her go," Jason ordered as he rested his arm. Mark let the sand soften and Olivia came out of it. She got up and took deep, quick breaths. They stood ready to fight her. She looked into their eyes. Her eyes bled back to brown and she fell on her hands and knees. Her fangs went back to their hiding place. Olivia looked down at the sand, her lip quivering and her body shaking. She stood, looked at the slayers, and ran.

They looked at each other confused. Jason ran after her. "Brook, wait!"

"I can't believe after all of that, he's chasing her," Alison said under her breath. Kelly held on to her friend in shock. They all were shocked. Olivia picked a fight, but Alison accepted the challenge, and in the end, it made her better. Kelly walked Alison back into the cave. The men followed.

Jason screamed for her again. In his run, he surfed off and in front of her. Olivia stopped on her tracks. "Listen to me for a second," he pleaded not knowing what had come over him.

"What is it you want?" She tried to get away from him. If he let her get away now, he would never get his revenge. "I could have killed her. It would have been easy. I wasn't giving half of what I've got. I could've taken her down. I was going to. If you and Mark hadn't intervened, I would have." Olivia had never killed before, but Alison made her want to.

She let the weight of her head bring her to her knees on the sand. He knelt down in front of her. "You aren't evil, Brook," he stated very sure of himself. The wind had stopped blowing, and the sea was calm once more, only for the little waves crashing by the shore.

"Where did you go last night?" He had noticed, after all.

She didn't look at him. She waited long into the night to leave, but Jason was keeping a close eye on her. "I was thirsty, and I wanted to find some fresh water. But I didn't find anything,"

"You know, Alison and Mark or Kelly can separate the water and salt? They did it this morning. Takes a little while, and it's tough work, but it can be done. It pays to have brains." Jason paused and looked out at the water. They sat side by side with a good three feet in between them. "Alison is a good person. She's just…"

"Jealous?" Olivia chimed in smiling.

"I'm not sure," he said then changed the subject. She could always sense a threat before, but this time, Jason knew Olivia would help him. It was his only choice. "I don't believe you went looking for water… I believe you were thirsty." Olivia looked up at him. Her eyes moved down to his neck. She looked at his eyes as they glossed over again and then looked away. "Must be tough, having to live at Trio-Genesis."

"What do you know?" her mood came back to her.

"I know you're dying to sink your teeth into someone or something." He stopped talking again.

Olivia played with the sand by her shoes. "It's just blood. No big deal," she lied. Jason looked back at her and kept staring until it was uncomfortable for her.

"How much control do you have?" he asked so softly it sent shivers down her back. Olivia laughed them off. He must be kidding. "You look thinner, weaker, whiter. So tell me, how much?"

"Enough to stop."

His eyes never left her face. Olivia finally looked over at him. "Can I trust you?" Olivia smiled, showing her fangs. Jason breathed heavy. "I hear it's deadly for vampires to drink from a slayer," he said changing his mind a bit.

"It is." Her words were soft and soothing. And every passing second he was more overcome with the tranquility her presence provided him. Olivia had already won what she wanted.

"But you aren't just vampire, are you Brook? If that's even your name?" he said giving her his wrist. She took his hand into her own and moved her mouth over his wrist. Olivia kissed the spot on his wrist where she would be sinking her teeth.

"Of course it is," she said looking up at him, batting her eyelashes. "Nothing will happen if I bit you here," she said as she moved his hand closer and closer to her lips. Olivia opened her mouth, went for a bite, and stopped.

"Don't stop," he breathed, completely brainwashed.

"Don't... surrender to it," she whispered and sank her teeth into the soft flesh of the handsome slayer. Everything was going smoothly.

CHAPTER 8

Countess Olivia

Mark limped into the cozy cave dragging bananas behind him. He grinned brightly at the others and placed them by the light of the fire. He sat down against the wall and nursed the throbbing pain coming from his leg. Every couple of minutes when no one was looking he would take a peek at the gushing, swollen cut. Kelly had already promised to grow more leaves to sooth the pain and quicken the healing process. Not everyone was a magic healer like Olivia.

Over Olivia's never-ending fire sat a thin, flat rock that Kelly had mushed to look like a pan. Inside their nature made skillet fried the little fish Rick caught. "We're doing pretty well for two days in the wild. And you thought this would be hard." Mark tried making light of the situation. He smiled at Kelly.

"Sure we are. You have an infected wound. For food today, we will be feasting on fish with green bananas, and Jason is off God-knows-where with a person who almost murdered me." Alison's words where filled with truth.

Rick, always amused by Alison's hate for Olivia could not help himself but to laugh, "Am I the only one here who thinks she isn't a bad person?"

"Aw, Richard. It's because you have no malice, sweetie." Kelly smiled sweetly.

He and Tom kept rubbing together rocks and sticks. Their grunting and moaning wasn't a reassuring sign. "Gentlemen, we have a fire," the blonde girl spoke.

"If Brook wasn't here, we wouldn't," Tom reminded her.

"And in case you kill her in her sleep, I want to be warm tomorrow." Rick was smiling as usual. As much as he loved the vampire girl, Alison hated her.

"That lunatic is going to get one of us killed," she defended. After a few more grunts and sighs, Alison spoke again. "Alright, move over and watch how a real fire is made," she boasted, standing and going over to the boys. "Why don't we try the elements? Fire isn't an element of its own, it's a combination of all three elements."

"She's right," Mark said standing. He put his weight on the good leg and limped over to them. Kelly stood and helped him walk over. "It beats sitting here."

"I'll go find Jason, and we'll try it out. Maybe all of our power combined will give us something," Kelly said, walking out of the cave to see the setting sun. Jason and Olivia were standing right before her. "I was coming to get you. We want to try and make fire... Jason, are you okay?" he nodded quickly. "Your eyes are smoky," she informed him.

"I'm perfect. Let's make fire," he said walking away from her and into the cave.

Olivia stayed close to him.

Upon sighting his best friend, Mark's eyes grew dark. He stood properly and bit his teeth together. "You've been bitten." The signs weren't hard to see: pale complexion, smoky eyes, composed posture, and fast heartbeat. The blonde girl saw Jason's hand and held it closer to her eyes.

"Don't surrender to it," she whispered and sank her teeth into the soft flesh of the handsome Slayer. Jason's body went numb as all the veins on his body rose from his skin. Pain sat at the bottom of his stomach and the pleasure at end of his lips. His eyes closed. Olivia didn't let go.

Jason breathed heavy. She opened her eyes and glanced up at him. His mouth was open and his brow frowned. The blood had been completely drained from his face. The feeding wasn't nearly enough to sustain her, but he was fading, so she let go. His blood tasted just the same as she remembered.

His hand fell on the sand and the blood ran down his wrist, staining the white pecks of dirt.

He could not remove his eyes from hers, "Your eyes are shining... are they supposed to do that?" She shrugged her shoulders. "Maybe you are dying," he said sounding perfectly normal. "If you are..." he continued, "...then it's the most beautiful thing I've ever seen." That was out of the norm. Her teeth went back to their hiding place. He leaned closer and closer to her.

She moved away and stood. "You aren't yourself at the moment... the feeling goes away."

"I feel fine." He stood towering over her petite frame. Olivia walked away from him and he followed.

"You bit him?" Mark screamed at the hiding vampire.

Alison's hand trembled as she held on to Jason's wrist. The marks were very visible.

"You aren't going to ostracize me, Brook. I see beneath your mask." She was careful of the tone she choose to address the fed vampire.

Jason came from his trance quickly. "It was my choice. I knew she needed blood, and I offered some. We're both fine, so there's no need to worry," he told them.

"How are we to get back into Trio-Genesis?" Mark pointed out, breathing every word very carefully.

Jason squinted his eyes shook his head, letting out a laughing sigh. "I'm not stupid, Mark. I carry limeodisorin in case our little friend does get too far from our view."

"She doesn't have to go very far when there are suicidal idiots keeping watch of her," Mark barked back, the anger was dripping from his voice. He touched the open cut on his leg and winced in pain.

Daggers from Jason's eyes stabbed Mark directly in the chest. "Let's drop it and eat," the leader said.

"My appetite is gone," Rick whined. Jason's glare was not a forgiving one. Eating was an order, not a suggestion.

Kelly patted Rick on the back and rolled her eyes before Jason could see. Then she tried to calm the worried slayer. "You aren't going to eat your own catch? That's not a like you. I think you should have the first piece," she said dragging the beach blonde boy over to the fire. She picked up the flat rocks she had made to be used as plates and handed one to Rick. They whispered quietly in the background.

"You could have died," Mark said walking away towards the flames.

They ate in silence.

Who knows what kind of damage she has done to his blood? The last time anyone heard of a vampire drinking the blood of a slayer, the end came soon after. Slow and painful. The blood was toxic to the vampires; the poison deadly to the slayers.

The night fell quietly on the seven who sat around the crackling fire keeping their thoughts to themselves. The rain rushed into the cave in steady waves that washed up higher and higher on shore. Mark and Kelly built a dirt wall leaving the top open for air, as instructed by their fearless but delusional leader, Jason. The water was rising with the rain and breaking through the wall. They should have built one of solid rock. Now it was too late. Once the wall came down, water would rush in.

They looked at the map for options. It was a large island and this side wasn't doing them any good as of yet.

Jason opened his eyes after following the winds around the island. "The winds are calm on other side. We will be safe if we go on foot. I don't want another mishap if we decide to surf again. We'll cut through the forest. There's a waterfall smack in the middle of island. We can set up camp there if we are too tired," Jason said looking at the map.

Olivia's blood froze over. "No!" she shouted quickly. "I disagree," she said calmly. "We are perfectly safe here. We have an ocean full of fish and other little crickets. We have nice, rich, freshly picked… green bananas. And a wonderful cave with a roaring fire," she swallowed hard and breathed.

"The other side has food, clean water, and no rain," Kelly informed the panicked vampire. The other side also had celebrating vampires.

Olivia fought back. "We don't know what's out there. Here, there's a good chance we stay alive. If we leave, that chance isn't so great," she told them honestly, yet indirectly. The 2,000 years celebration would go on for another two days. Avoiding the crowd would be too difficult and protecting six slayers against hundreds of vampires, while keeping her identity, could prove even too much for the Countess alone.

"Brook, this isn't a democracy. But since you'd like to make it one, we'll put it to a vote," Tom suggested. "All in favor of leaving the flooding cave?" as the words left his lips, water leaked in through the bottom of the wall and fizzled out by the fire. Their heads followed the burning stream and then looked up in unison at Brook. Five hands went up, not counting Tom's. "All in favor of staying here?" he asked. Olivia's arm shot straight into the air.

"Okay, then. Let's bounce," Rick said.

More water came through the wall. "Yes, let's," Kelly agreed.

"I'll lead the way," Jason stated, "Mark. Kelly. Keep an open eye to the forest and surroundings. Rick. Ali. Make sure we move away from the rain. Tom and I will follow clean air. Brook…"

"Stay out of the way," Alison said. Olivia had no problem doing that at this point.

"Mark, break down the wall. Alison, when he does, whatever water has collected at the foot of it, push it away so we aren't flooded in. Tom, you steady the air when the wall opens. On three. One… Two…"

Mark took down the wall and Allison pushed back the water. The entrance to the cave was on a downhill slope and the water collected had been at least four feet high. Jason led the way into the woods. Olivia followed behind them, biting her fingernails and looking around at every little noise.

The sky darkened as they made their way to the bloodthirsty vampires right ahead. The seven crept quietly through the island, each listening closely for trouble. Olivia disappeared and moved quickly ahead to see the population of the vampires gathered for the second night. She needed a plan; a way out. There were too many of them for the six to stop on their own. And Joshua would never let them go. When she had returned to where the tired slayers were walking she found them a few feet away from the celebration, she stayed back, hiding in the trees. Jason was following the map down to the tee.

"What's that noise?" Rick asked faintly.

"Rick, don't be ridiculous. There is no noise," Tom said. They kept on walking.

"Stop," Rick warned again. "Don't you hear the noise? That music?" he said again.

Leave it to Rick to find the party.

"No, I don't." Kelly stomped her feet and crossed her arms; she was wet, hot, and tired of bumping into Rick, who kept stopping directly in front of her. At least it wasn't raining here.

Jason stopped dead in his tracks. Causing Alison to run into him, "Ouch, Jay, watch where you're going. You could have..." He covered her mouth suddenly. Alison stopped her breathing. Her eyes widened. Jason looked down into the blue sea of mystery that were Alison's perfectly colored eyes. They glistened in the night. She blinked slowly.

"Listen," Jason said looking back at them.

"See, I told you there was a noise," Rick whispered to Kelly. "What is that?"

"Tom, do you smell that? The air. It's foul," Jason said looking at Tom, his heart beating uncontrollably. He moved his hand from Alison's mouth. "Blood," the airheads said together.

"Vampires," Alison said as her heart dropped to her feet. They looked back and Olivia wasn't behind them anymore. "Of course," Alison said, dropping her arms by her sides.

They looked around whispering Olivia's middle name trying to find her, thinking for a second she'd stayed behind a bit and was catching up with them. "Someone should have kept an eye on her." Jason hushed.

"No one was told to do that," Alison pointed out the obvious. "She's gone. We should stop calling out for her before we're caught."

"Would it be wise to find them so we can avoid walking into them?" Mark suggested. Jason nodded. They walked quickly and quietly in the forests of the island where the music got louder and louder. Rick spotted fire burning as the music got closer. They followed the music and the light of the fire burning in the night. Olivia was still nowhere to be seen. They reached their desired destination—the waterfall—and hid in the forest watching the unusual celebration.

"That's a lot of vamps," Rick whispered. "What do you think they're all doing here?" he asked his fearful leader.

He kept looking into the party, his eyes searching for Olivia. "I'm not sure, Rick."

"I strongly disagree with finding out," Tom said.

"We'll go around them. There's an open space here we can cut through and continue on," Jason said pointing back to his map. "Brook, where are you?"

"We are in more danger than she is right now," Alison said. The words stopped her in her tracks. "She knew about this. She was trying to warn us," Alison told them.

"Too late now," Kelly whispered. "Not that I don't like watching vamps for fun… but I think we should get going," she continued.

Rick dusted himself off, "Alright." They left their hiding places and moved for the open forest where they could run for it. Surfing would definitely be too dangerous now. Any change in the atmosphere would give away the group.

They reached the open space. There was only grass and pools of mud for about a half a mile. They ran for it. A man emerged from the forest behind them. The man spoke. "Hey! You six! Get back to the party!" His New York accent was very strong.

They stopped running. Their breathing ceased. They would have to fight; there was no other way around it now. If Jason acted quickly enough he would be able to silence him before he called for the others.

"I'm talking to you! GO BACK TO THE PARTY!" the vampire screamed throwing a fireball at them as a joke. Jason flew up in the air, did a backflip to face him, and opened his hand which sucked the fireball into a black hole of air. The vampire smiled wildly, his fangs showing, and his eyes glowing red. "DINNER!" he shouted.

The words had barely left his mouth and vampires surfed all around them. They looked at each other for a second.

"Dig in," James Coop told the bunch.

Their training prepared them for everything, even a hundred vampires. "You think Brook could have talked us out of this?" Rick asked laughing. No amount of training meant they could survive this without backup.

Tom laughed. "I wish," he said.

Fire lit up the hands of each vampire. They let the balls of heat fly in the direction of the slayers. They wouldn't have to do much. There was enough of them to take down the little air field Jason made around the six. Fire came from every direction. Jason's field would keep the balls of death out while still letting his team fire away, but it made the force field weaker faster.

Alison grabbed the throat of two vampires with thick strings of water that she controlled from the inside of the field. The water cut off their air supply. She held on tight as other vampires threw fire at the water ropes. The fire sizzled out, but it made the rope thinner. Kelly stomped her foot on the ground over and over. Each dirt lightning bolt struck four plus vampires as it traveled down the ground and made its way up.

Vampires went flying everywhere.

Rick swirled his hands around and shot quick darts of water. He aimed at their hearts for an instant kill. His method was the most productive so far. But every dart that flew by the field would hit Jason hard. It echoed around the field until it reached where the dark blonde slayer protected his five friends. The energy of their powers washed through his field and hit him.

Tom's job was harder than it looked. Because Jason was taking as much air around them to build and re-build the field, Tom had to keep bringing in new air from the outside of the field, so two things could happen: one; breathing, and two; so Jason could keep the field up. He held his hands low by his side, and air came from underneath the field into the area around them.

Mark's powers were more advanced than Kelly's. He knocked down the vampires in the very back, grabbing them by their legs with tree branches and sucking them into the hard dirt by pulling his hand down and closing it quickly into a fist.

Jason was done playing around. He was always armed. Tom took over Jason's job, but he wouldn't be able to do it for long. There wasn't any air being fed through. He would have just enough time for Jason to do something drastic enough to stop everyone. Jason reached behind his back and under his shirt. He pulled out a silver stake and went for the kill. He ran through the field, right ahead at the vampires throwing fire. With his forearm, Jason blocked his attacker's elements with quick invisible shields of air. He reached the vampire right in front and struck him in the heart.

Joshua surfed into the open and every vampire stopped attacking. Jason looking into the eyes of the vampire whose life he had just taken. James Coop, a close friend of Joshua's, fell to the ground with blood running down his shirt.

Joshua looked Jason dead in the eyes and spoke to his people. "Kill them all," he said coldly. Jason surfed back into the field and took over for Tom. They were tired and knew they wouldn't hold long. It was all over. The vampires began to throw fire at them; hundreds came flying at the weak wall all at once.

"Great job, guys! They aren't breaking through!" Kelly said trying to motivate the airheads holding up a very weak force field.

"I can't hold it much longer, Jason! It's too much." Tom screamed. Jason looked around them with questioning eyes. He had already released the wall. "Jason! I can't hold the wall anymore!" Tom said and dropped his hands.

But the protection around them only grew stronger.

Joshua followed a blade of fire and watched it hit an invisible wall, a light blue nearly unnoticeable light shown for a split microsecond, "This isn't the work of the slayers," he said under his breath to Michael who stood beside him.

"Olivia..." Michael murmured.

"HOLD YOUR FIRE!" Joshua screamed. The vampires stopped attacking. The slayers stopped also. The moon shined down on the strong force field held up by Olivia. Joshua walked up to the wall, looked Jason in the eyes, and punched the field. Shock waves from the punch were sent around the field. The blue light hit Joshua's hand and raced up his arm, raising the hairs in its path. He shook his hand and moved his fingers about. "OLIVIA!" he shouted.

"Olivia. As in, Countess Olivia?" Jason sent his voice around to the five.

Mark took in a deep breath. His heart skipped a beat. "It can't be." His eyes lit up.

"OLIVIA!" Joshua screamed once more. "Show yourself, or I kill them all with my bare hands," he threaten her. She stood her ground. "I can break through your little field, darling," he mocked her. Joshua looked Rick in the face and spoke his most threatening words yet. "And he's the first one I'll kill."

Joshua felt a bright fire. He turned to find her surfing in. "Leave them alone, Joshua," she said keeping the field up with only her mind.

Their eyes were 10 times wider than ever. Their mouths dropped to the ground and their head cocked forward. "Brook?" Tom and Rick said in unison. She turned to face them as every vampire around them got down on one knee. Olivia did not bother standing them.

"So it's true. It was you protecting them. And here I thought you'd be on my side, sweetheart. Where have you been, Olivia?" Joshua rather demanded an answer. "Two months. God, I thought you dead," he choked back fake tears.

She moved on Joshua never looking away. "It must please you to know I'm not," she grinned.

"Your fiancé, worried day and night for you, Countess," Michael hissed the s's out, smiling evilly at her.

"And you, Michael?" She knew the answer very well. Olivia turned to her subjects, "How easily you mistreat me, for leaving on a short vacation." She addressed Joshua. "Let them go. They are merely passing by."

Joshua looked down at his dead friend and up again at Olivia. He walked over to James' body. "James is dead, Olivia," he said kneeling down and closing the eyes of the dead body that laid before them.

Olivia looked at the body, then away at Joshua. Her teeth hugged her lips and she blinked back tears. James was her friend. Despite who he was and how evil he had been in the past, he was one of the ones who was close with Olivia; they had fought side by side. He was Patrick's friend also. They shared good memories together. James was only doing as he had always known. She looked back at Joshua. "And I wish no more blood be shed," she directed her voice at the vampires. She let the field down, figuring no one would attack.

"You are committing treason!" Joshua screamed at her. He moved on her and grabbed her arms. Mark moved from his spot a few feet to attack Joshua. Kelly stopped him.

Olivia came out of his grip and moved back. "Treason would involve betraying your own for another."

Sudden disappointment rested in Jason's figure.

"I am the Vampire Slayer. Never forget the meaning of those words, Joshua Lenson," and with that he was silenced.

"I want all of you to pack up your party and leave. Go to Eclipse. Patrick will be there awaiting you," she instructed, she owed Patrick big time for agreeing to take the wild party in.

The vampires began to surf away. The body of James Coop glittered black and was sent to the closest male relative. The only people left were the six slayers, Michael, Joshua, and herself, the Vampire Slayer. Joshua moved closer to her. He rubbed the area where he had grabbed her.

"Forgive me?" His voice was smooth, his touch was soft, and his hands were warm.

"Joshua, don't make me hurt you," she said softening her tone. Joshua was playing his part perfectly, but her task now would be extremely difficult. "You have to go," she told him as he put his arms around her and looked dead at Jason. He leaned down to kiss her but was rejected by her cheek.

"Fine. I'll go," he said. His hands covered with fire, and he surfed away. Michael had stayed back. He walked up to Olivia and looked down at her before surfing away.

Olivia was left alone with the slayers once more. She looked back at them and they still looked completely surprised.

Mark held tight onto his leg. The blood of his wound wetting the leaves wrapped around it. Olivia walked over to him and moved his hand away. She placed her hand on top of his wound. Mark moaned in pain as a light blue light filled his wound, and when Olivia moved her hand, the wound was healed. Olivia broke the silence. "So I guess we can stay at the waterfall after all," she smiled speaking as if nothing had happened.

"Let the record show, I was right." Alison got the words off her chest. She moved closer to Jason. Olivia had no words. They would have many questions, so for once she decided to stay quiet. "How long were you planning on passing yourself off as an innocent orphan?"

Mark's heart pounded loudly in his chest. "She is an orphan," he protested to Alison, whose voice raged with the fury she had been holding back for months. She turned to look at him, and then at Olivia who stood nearby. Mark rubbed the sweat from his hands on his jeans and looked up at Alison. His eyes threatened her very life.

The liar, who had them almost killed a second ago was still being protected by the closest friends Alison had.

Jason spoke softly. "They know," he said, looking deep into her brown eyes.

Olivia didn't back down. She fixed her gaze on his drowning blue eyes and stood her ground. The circumstances had changed now that the six slayers knew who she really was. She would have to play the part. Olivia did not want to lead; for once, it was refreshing knowing she did not make the decisions. However, she wasn't much of a follower either. Her role was picked for her; whether she liked it or not, leading was in her blood and engraved in her brain.

"They know you're the Vampire Slayer," Jason said moving away from Alison a bit.

He was closer and closer to meeting his own needs now that he had Olivia. He still needed her on his side no matter what lies she kept. "Tell us one thing, Olivia." The way in which he spoke her name gave them all chills. It rang in their ears. It was she: the real Vampire Slayer, in flesh and blood, right in front of them. Some were still in disbelief. "What is it you want from us?"

Mark could not help her now. His eyes were the only ones that whispered compassion. His aura was the only one that welcomed her. Olivia looked at Mark, his eyes speaking comfort, their clothes sticking to their bodies from the rain that had washed them moments ago.

"I had no choice," she said. A question mark hovered over each one of their heads. "I want to wage peace between our sides, but I cannot do so if my powers are not complete. You wouldn't have helped me if I hadn't lied to you." She paused for a second then went on, "You understand revenge, Jason Sharpie. You know war. But peace is foreign to you; kindness is for the blind who seek the light of day in their darkness." The truth stung him and struck him to silence. "Your intentions are not all good, and they are hardly selfless. Mark knows." Mark swallowed hard. Jason looked at his best friend, doubting whether Olivia had found out this information for herself or if a close insider gave away his thoughts.

"I can't help you, unless you help me." She looked around at the six of them and spoke as only a true leader would, "The six of you are different. Your power has combined you through your friendship. No other team has the potential to be more powerful. Alison's powers have grown. She's leveled up." Olivia smiled looking at the blonde slayer who knew just what she was referring to.

Olivia moved her gaze onto Rick and he smiled kindly at her. "There is a reason and each of you might have your own. But don't deny that there is a reason you've allowed me to be here this long. The intentions may not be selfless, and the reasons might not always be pure. But it works. I want to end this. Once and for all." She looked at Jason again. His eyes had not softened their gaze. His jaw was still tightening.

Alison shook her head and exhaled the laugh she was holding in. "I've been a good judge of character my entire life, and even now that we know who you really are, I still don't trust you," she persisted.

Olivia had nothing else to say. It was their choice to believe or disbelieve her.

Mark moved. "Why not tell us from the start?" his voice filled with disappointment. He, too, should have been smarter when it came to realizing who she was. But he let his training and few years of knowledge overpower his nature.

Maybe the beach blonde surfer was the only one who understood her situation. "How would this have sounded? Hello, I'm Olivia; the Vampire Slayer. Please help me start a war to end it peacefully?" Rick said mockingly. He wasn't the brightest of the bunch, and a group of kindergarteners could outsmart him; but every once in a while, Rick could be really smart. "We would believe her as much as the Jews believed Jesus is God…" He went on. "Except He didn't start out saying He wasn't. My point is, Brook… Olivia had no other choice." Rick walked over to the vampire and stood by her. He looked down at the bloodsucker and smiled his sweetest smile, then looked back at the others. "I'm not the smartest crayon in the box…"

"The brightest," Kelly corrected him.

He kept on. "Thank you… The brightest, but I trusted Olivia from the start. And she did just save our lives."

"She can't be trusted, Rick!" Alison screamed. The sky shouted thunder.

"I knew I recognized you from somewhere," Mark said, My grandfather used to tell me we were friends when we were children.

He said that one day you would come to Trio-Genesis and that we would once again meet. Once news got out that you were missing around the vampires, I thought you were dead. I remember you, Olivia Brook Montgomery. Brook…" Mark stopped and laughed a little to himself. "Nice touch."

Jason was no longer inhaling, he wasn't blinking, and he wasn't present. He was their leader, and Olivia being Olivia, could lessen that leadership. But deep down Jason was born to lead. Sometimes life got the better of him; many times, even. But he showed others that he could still get back up and lead his team. What made him such a good, strong, effective, leader was that we was willing to fail and try again. Failure wasn't wanted, but he knew it was unrealistic to walk into battle expecting to win every time. Life taught him that. It made him stronger, but also cold and distant from the world around him.

"Back away from her, Mark," Jason said. "You too, Richard." He only used their full names when we was serious. Rick did not hesitate. Mark did.

"I'm quite comfortable here," Mark answered Jason.

Jason's eyes were swollen with darkness, his hands were balled into fists, his mouth shut tightly together. Olivia watched his nostrils flare and his chest rise and fall with greater speed than before.

"Mark, back away from her." Jason warned again.

Kelly's voice trembled when she spoke, "Mark, listen to Jason." Mark shook his head, never removing his eyes from Jason's. Mark moved in front of Olivia a couple of steps. His body blocked her view.

"This doesn't have to end this way," Rick whispered, begging the angry slayer.

"Shut your mouth!" Jason's body slightly rose from the ground as he spat his words at Rick. Alison moved closer to Jason and reached out touching his shoulder. He forcefully pushed Alison's hand away. The girl stepped back to stand by Kelly.

"Jason, I think you need to get some air," Tom tried.

"I feel fine." The fuming slayer lied. He approached Mark. Mark reached back with both arms and felt for Olivia's body. She was still there. "Last warning," Jason said. Mark stood his ground. Jason's hands grabbed Mark shoulder and pushed the slayer out of the way swiftly. Mark stumbled to the side clearing Jason's away.

Mark moved quickly to cover Olivia again. Without looking Jason raised his hand and strong wind came from his palm, Mark was knocked off his feet and collided with the muddy terrain.

Jason reached out with his free hand and held Olivia's neck in his large hand. He dug his nails into her flesh. Olivia lifted her hand from underneath Jason's gripping hand and used her strength to move his hand away. She backed up grasping for air. Jason stepped aggressively at her lifting his right hand vertically out in front of him.

Olivia's body floated from the ground, catching her off guard. The vampire panicked looking down around herself. Jason pushed his lifted hand back down towards the ground and her body met the hard ground with great force.

It all happened so quickly, Kelly barely had time to reach Mark. She helped him to his feet. Alison watched in horror as Jason spoke her name.

"Ali, come help me kill her." The words bled from Jason's mouth. The blonde girl was paralyzed. Jason stood over Olivia and raised his foot off the ground to crash her skull into smithereens. As his foot came down his body was crushed by Mark's body.

The boys wrestled on the ground. Jason punched at Mark's face as the slayer struggled to pin Jason under him.

Rick ran over and helped Olivia up.

Mark found a way to grab Jason's arms behind Jason's back. Mark pushed Jason's head into the wet dirt with his elbow.

"You kill her and you start a war," he screamed at Jason. "Ryan is dead, Jason! Let him go." Mark pleaded shouting over Jason's struggles.

"I can hear his voice in my head. I can hear him!" Jason sobbed into the ground.

"I know..." Mark whispered to his friend. "I'm sorry."

In the distance Olivia asked who Mark had referred to. Kelly told her it was just a memory now. Jason settled after being held down a few more seconds. Mark released him and backed away.

"I can't let you hurt her," Mark said as he reached Olivia and the others. Jason helped himself up and composed his mind.

They could see themselves thinking back to things she said— things she did that only she could do. It was amazing they didn't call her out on it before. Alison, however, knew her lies from the start.

"Now what?" Tom blankly asked. It wasn't only he who wondered where they would go from here. The situation was odd enough as it was. "Countess," he addressed Olivia as if he had been under her instruction all his life, "what do you suggest we do now?" In his quietness, Tom always managed to stand in the background of things. He watched everything happen around him and to him.

"Olivia." Jason found the leader in him. "It would be completely unrealistic to return to Trio-Genesis without you." There wouldn't be enough words to explain to the school why a group of six well-trained, highly trusted, gifted, slayers, lost one girl on a mission that would decide such important things for them. It was reckless to even try and convince the school that Olivia had given up and had gone back to her old life, abandoning all slayers.

"Seems like there is no choice but to keep up this masquerade," Jason said as he turned to his friend. "However true that might be, we will tell," Jason informed the group.

Alison was the first to object to this. Confessing to knowing Olivia wouldn't solve their problems. Tom and Kelly weren't too fond of the idea of giving up the cover story either. Olivia had done such a good job with her lie, far be it from them to go around telling the truth. If the entire school knew who she was, it would only cause chaos. Everyone would want to meet her, kill her, teach her, or learn from her. Beside the fact that Olivia's life would never be the same, she had years of information that could help the slayers and give them an upper hand.

"How long?" Jason asked them. "How long before one of us calls her Olivia? How long before it blows up in our faces. It's a lot easier to keep a secret for two months if it's only your burden to bare. But seven people… it's impossible."

"A secret is between two people. If three know, one must die," Tom said quietly.

It rained on them once more. The thunder silenced them. "We should look for shelter," Jason said and began to walk away from them. The others followed. Olivia stood still. Mark turned and watched her.

"Olivia," he said, walking back to her. "Jason's been through a lot. You aren't his favorite person. But we made you promises. I'm sorry that had to happen. I'll keep an eye on him." She didn't look at him. Mark grabbed her hand and made her focus her eyes on him. "You can't stay out here in the jungle alone in the rain. Come on."

They walked for what seemed miles. They wanted to get away from the rain.

There, on the other side of the island, was what looked like a small hut.

Once inside, Jason asked Tom and Mark to make a small fire. After minutes of hitting rocks and rubbing sticks together, Olivia stepped in and made a fire for them. It wasn't a happy moment like before. They were grateful to have a vampire with them in the cave, but they were not so joyous to be sharing a little hut with the Countess. There was so much awkward silence. Jason never stopped eyeballing Olivia.

"I am face to face with the VAMPIRE SLAYER!" Rick finally shouted. "Is anyone else as excited as I am right now?!" Rick smiled after holding his joy in. She was his long time role model. Sure, he had never met her, and everything she stood for, as far as he knew, was against everything he was taught. But he had so many questions for her. "I have to ask: Can I have a picture with you? You are beautiful. Not that you weren't before, but now you're Olivia, Vampire Slayer! Countess of good and evil," he said in his most animated voice. "Kelly, I'm friends with the vampire slayer. I have class with the vampire slayer. I know the vampire slayer." Rick was truly amazed. He had-had his fill of the silence.

"He is truly this enthused about meeting you," Tom told her. "He often spoke about one day meeting you, fighting you, just being around you," Tom confessed his friend's dirty little secrets to Olivia. She, too, was enjoying his excitement. It wasn't every day that a slayer was happy to meet her. Rick practically wanted her autograph.

Rick sat by Olivia, a little too close even and looked her dead in the eyes. "It's a pleasure to finally meet you. I'm Richard," He smiled forgetting he had known her rather long to be introducing himself over again. He took her hand into his and kissed it.

"Rick, you loser, she knows who you are. She's been in class with you for the past eight weeks," Kelly reminded the slayer. Rick brushed off her comment.

As happy as the story was on one side of the fire, it was odd on the other. Jason poked the fire with a stick and Alison sat with Mark watching Olivia.

"So why come to Trio-Genesis?" Kelly asked her, giving her a good breather from Rick's ridiculous questions.

"I didn't really have a choice after Jason kidnapped me, now did I?" she tried desperately to joke.

Alison watched with Mark from the other side and murmured to him. "What does she want from us? So she's the Vampire Slayer. Big whoop! That still is no cause for us to trust her. She's been living with those things all of her life. Who's to say they haven't already brainwashed her and turned her into their evil puppet? I stand on my prior belief of things. She wants to be unstoppable." Alison was not giving in to the madness of being star struck by a killer. Olivia could have been a saint for all she cared. She would sooner switch sides to kill her than fight beside her under her command. Many others would too.

It would be ages before Mark could get Alison to shut up about Olivia. He couldn't even get his opinions in before she spoke again. "Alison," he cut her off suddenly, "drop it. Just for tonight. Let it set in," he said getting up and walking out of the hut. Jason also lifted from his seat to get some air.

Their heads followed the two out of the door. Olivia looked down at the fire and its light burned slower. The flames died down and the chill of the wet clothes on their backs began setting in again.

"Give it the night, at least. Mark..." Kelly paused, "and Jason both have reasons for their actions towards you."

The moon lit up the night as the clouds began to part. "We need to find out why she's here and what she wants," Jason said as he walked closer to his friend. Mark didn't look at him. He looked up at the clearing sky and then at the white sand below his feet. Far be it from him to betray Jason. "I..." Jason began.

"No. Don't. We both have our reasons," Mark said.

CHAPTER 9

Body of Lies

They waited patiently for her to answer.

She took in a breath. "It was treason for my father to have me, so my full potential was kept a secret." She said referring the past choices her parents had made. "Dracula would have been killed."

"Not a bad outcome for us," Tom said coldly.

"And Savanna would have been burned," she added, glaring into his flesh, plucking out his eyes balls.

"So your parents keep you secret, Savanna dies," Alison said nonchalantly, "and then your coward of a father is killed,"

Mark's eyes shot draggers at Alison. Sure, they didn't have a reason to trust Olivia, but this was too much. She was answering every question asked. The least they could do was show some respect.

Olivia smiled at Alison with distaste. "You really are the scum of the earth. How low can you get, Alison?" Olivia asked honestly. The blonde slayer knew how to hurt.

Olivia took in a short breath, collected her thoughts, and then kept going with her story. "Dracula was betrayed by his best friend, David. But David didn't escape. It was seconds after the body of my father lay lifeless on the floor that guards came in and took David away," she looked down at the fire. Olivia could see the day almost too vividly.

Mark and Rick sympathized with her.

"I'm sorry," Mark said quietly. Olivia looked up at him and smiled kindly, thanking him with her eyes. She felt a connection between them. It wasn't electric or burning, but it was real and warm; caring and forgiving. Mark was on her side. It was a sudden change but it was pleasant, and she wouldn't argue against it.

"It's hard for a little girl to control her powers if no one is teaching her better. They found out shortly after my father's death who my mother really was," she explained further. "My little mishaps weren't hard to miss. Flooded rooms, sand dunes, random trees growing out of my bedroom walls."

"The only reason they think the slayers don't know about me is because Savanna seemed to be with Dracula so willingly. No one ever came to look for her, or take her back," Olivia added for their amusement. "All the times I visited Trio-Genesis as a child with my mother, the vampires thought that we had gone on family trips."

"As I grew older, they knew I'd be a force to reckon with. A fear grew in their minds. Their fear turned into hate and into the longing to destroy." She looked around at the hut and down at the fire again.

"I was too young to be in charge. So the counsel was put in charge. Forced to attend all their endless meetings, I learned they wanted nothing more than power. They were willing to kill each other for it; willing to end life just to have all the power in their own hands. When I turned 13, I was excessively mature for my own age and decided to take back the throne that was rightfully mine. The council didn't approve, and although I was given back control, I hardly had any say."

Jason cut her off again, "So Alison is right. You want to master everything and run back and show them who's boss."

"I came here because they are planning a war," she said bluntly.

Their eyes were stuck open; their mouths agape. Their blood froze over. War? It was the worst word ever spoken. It was to war that most of them lost families and friends. Jason couldn't imagine going to war anymore. The group was the only family he had left.

He couldn't imagine losing another person in his life to death or at the hands of a vampire.

"They wait on me, I promised to try and speak peace to the slayers. Show my people… the vampires, that my other people aren't as bad as they assume. But I might not be able to change their minds. I fear they will attack whether I want them to or not. I hope that they won't move while I'm here. I'm here to warn you, to prepare you." She needed a minute to collect her thoughts, but she had to get in a few last words. "And to fight with you."

"So we stop them," Tom chimed in. "We know their plans now. We attack before they can. The element of surprise is on our side. Betrayed by their leader, it's diabolical." Tom smiled at them. It was too diabolical for them; evil, even. Slayers had been trained to attack only when being attacked. Their minds were programmed to create peace, not start ambushes.

"No," Jason said. Tom's ideas were never valid, never good enough. The darkness in him was too strong to make rational decisions. And Jason couldn't attack until his own agenda was met. "We have to take this information back to Trio-Genesis." Jason stood, trying to regain his place as leader in their eyes. "There are certain people who need to know your identity,"

Trio Army didn't matter anymore. Life mattered more. No one knew how much time they had, and it was better to act quickly before it was too late.

Mr. Kerrigan wasn't surprised to see them return early from their mission. He also wasn't surprised to hear that Brook Morton was really Olivia Montgomery, she wasn't very good at keeping it a secret around the instructors and professors. Joy filled his face. He hugged Olivia and shook her body wildly in his arms. His laugher could not be contained.

"It's amazing how a few years will turn a little girl into a lady!" He shouted too close to her face. His eyes sparkled and watched every detail of Olivia's face. "Oh, your mother and I were good friends. She brought you here all the time. You were a wee thing," he said using his hand to measure how far from the ground Olivia's body stood. "You're 19 now?" he asked smiling ear to ear.

Olivia was at home. This man knew her, knew her mother, knew her family. He knew who she was. He had waited for her arrival, as did many others.

"Twenty soon." She smiled knowing he already knew her birthday was near. "You must forgive me. I don't remember you," she said.

He laughed loudly in the middle of the night. "My dear! Remember me? You're alive and well and here. It matters little if you know my face. It hurts only my ego," he joked with her. The six slayers watched his excitement. Maybe Olivia's return wasn't all bad.

"I must confess: I knew who you were the second you set foot in my class," he told them all.

Jason stood from leaning on the desk. "How?" he asked.

Kerrigan moved around his desk finally letting go of Olivia's arms. He moved left to right on his messy table, picking up and dropping papers, opening and closing drawers, looking for the answer to Jason's question. All the time he moved he said, "Where is that thing? I have it here somewhere." He kept looking for the paper no one could help him find. "Ah," he shouted, opening a folder in the last drawer of the beautiful oak table. "Here it is,"

The parchment he searched for was Olivia's class schedule and records. He handed the Vampire Slayer the paper and watched her confusion. "Mrs. Seymour. She brought me a copy," he smiled, leaning on his desk while letting the students figure it out for themselves. After a short silence, which was much too long for the excited Kerrigan, he spoke again. "She knew it was you! She told me, brought me the proof! Oh Olivia, you can lie to our faces, but you cannot lie to the school," he chuckled.

"How many know that she's here?" Kelly asked.

Kerrigan looked at the students. "All of us!" he shouted. Olivia's smile faded.

Alison could not smile at his excitement. "So the six of us were kept out of this secret for our humiliation?" she barked.

"Lighten up, blondie," Kerrigan said. "The teachers know. The leaders know. The building... Trio-Genesis knows the blood that runs in her veins!" Kerrigan said looking again at Olivia and smiling at her.

She liked him. Rick's welcoming was heartfelt, but the joy in this man was extraordinary. He jumped off his table and his eyes widened. "I have to give you a tour!" he said putting on his shoes, which were under his table, and taking off his reading glasses. "Jason, go straight to Mr. Craips and explain to him what happened. Bring him here. It will cause his failing heart great excitement to know Olivia has come out."

Jason dropped his shoulders and sighed. He wanted in on the tour—the journey. He didn't like being left out of the conversation. After all, it was only right he went. He was the only one who took Olivia under his wing! He captured her. He brought her to them. It was his idea. She was his prize, not a trophy for the rest of the school to awe in while he became the delivery boy. His head was a jumbled mess and he couldn't make up his mind if he wanted to carry her on his shoulders, or if he wanted to breathe the air out of her lungs to slowly suffocate her. What was happening to him?

"The rest of you can go to bed. I'll inform the others later," Kerrigan said.

"I thought you said they already knew," Rick protested.

"Yes, but we all respected her choice to keep her secret," Kerrigan said. "They'll be happy to know Olivia has come clean," he smiled down at the short Vampire Slayer.

Alison turned with the others to leave. "If I had known there would be this much excitement, I would have disagreed with bringing her out of the shadows with greater persistence," she said as they walked away from the two.

Olivia and Kerrigan were left alone to talk. "I have something to show to you," he smiled brighter.

It was late and the sun would rise soon. Olivia walked in silence while Kerrigan went on and on about how excited he was to know she confided her secret to him. She didn't want to rain on his parade by telling him she was forced to do so, but she did believe that she would have more freedom now that her teachers knew her to be the Vampire Slayer.

He looked into her blank, tired eyes and smiled softly as he pushed the button to call for the golden elevator. "Enough of me talking. Is there anything you want to know?" he asked.

It came to her easier than expected but the question was stirring inside. "If you knew I was coming, why wasn't anyone waiting for me?" She paused. "I don't mean waiting to see if I would show up. I mean waiting to welcome me. I've been here two months. Had I not said something would my being here stay in the shadows as long as I did?" The elevator doors opened. Kerrigan place a hand on Olivia's back and led her inside.

"Good to see you using regular transportation, Mr. Kerrigan," the golden elevator joked. "Welcome back, Ms. Montgomery. You've returned early. I take it your trip wasn't well," she said.

"You're arrival was delayed, Olivia," he spoke honestly, realizing he had not pressed any buttons and Olivia did not know where they were headed. "The 37th floor please," he said looking at the buttons. The circle lit up and she began moving.

"Your father and mother promised to bring you here after your 16th birthday, to live. I assure you, preparations were made to the fullest." Olivia didn't look at him. "It was in their hands to bring you, to show you where it was. When you didn't come… we thought you'd never make it." He smiled at her again as he took her into his arms in a warm hug. "But we were wrong," he said letting go.

She was willing to let it all go for the love and comfort of a real home and real people who wanted her for more than her power. The doors opened and they stepped off. Olivia and Kerrigan walked down the hall a little longer. They stopped in front of large brown doors, torn and beaten up with time and neglect.

Kerrigan pulled a silver key out of his pocket. It was no regular key; at the bottom, there were two knots and the body of the key twisted all the way to the top where a final loop was made. "You're parents left it for you." He gave Olivia the key. "A Countess should have a mansion, your father used to say." He watched her smile. "Only you can open it without setting the alarms off," he laughed.

"Olivia, we are glad you've joined us. I'll leave you to explore the three grand floors. Get some rest. We will speak tomorrow." He walked away leaving Olivia in front of the room.

She placed the key in the lock and turned it. The door made a loud noise and air came out of the top and bottom of the door. The hall wall lit up in a sand color and for the first time since standing there, Olivia noticed a large crystal chandelier over her head. Her heart was at the top of her neck. She turned the doorknob and pushed open the door.

It was a large, open room with a grand bed that still needed to be put together.

The silver metal was rusty and covered in cobwebs. There were no tools in sight. Every corner of the room was covered in dust. There was a glass spiraling staircase to the right of the room and a wall with a large opening arch that led into another room.

The small bathroom to the left wasn't very pleasing either. The tile was broken and falling off the walls. The sink was rusty and the plumbing broken. There was mold growing off the ceiling and the window in the kitchen was stuck shut.

Olivia couldn't bring herself to go upstairs or anywhere else in the house. It was just more rooms filled with dirt and trash. Boxes of things, locked up by tape. Olivia looked at the bed. It didn't look like a bedroom. Maybe the bed was simply misplaced.

The only good thing was the sliding glass door that led to a balcony. Sure, the glass was cracked and needed replacing, but that room overlooked the largest part of the lake surrounding Trio-Genesis.

The disappointment finally sank in and Olivia headed for the door to escape the certain tragedies of the room.

Jason lay on his bed, arms crossed behind his head. He look up at his illuminated ceiling counting the many times Olivia did something or said something that would have given away that she was the Vampire Slayer.

Two months she was there, two months she lied to them, two months he believed every word that came from her mouth. He had gotten so desperate in his search that the biggest piece of information was in front of him the whole time, and he missed it. Then he messed up again by attacking her. If he had kept his cool, if he had held his own, if he had planned better, he wouldn't have to back track now.

Jason looked over to his bedside table at the family picture in a glass frame. A man sat on a park bench with a woman on his lap. On the ground was a baby boy sitting on a blanket holding his feet while a toddler eating a strawberry sat right beside the baby. It was a bright, sunny day. And it was the only picture Jason had left after the fire.

Olivia walked right in, with no regard to the meaning of knocking first. "This place just keeps getting better and better," she said walking over to the bar he had in the corner. Olivia poured herself a glass of water.

"Your sarcasm is more difficult to sense each time," he said sitting up on his bed.

Olivia drank the glass to the very last drop. "How can you drink this thing? It's completely tasteless," she said putting the glass down.

"You shouldn't be here," he said as he stood and made his way to her. They stood there for a moment just looking at each other.

Olivia saw his body shift slightly. Everything she did worked out so well. "Is this your way of kicking me out of your room?" she asked and moved her feet to leave. Jason grabbed her suddenly by the arm and held her still.

"It's incredible how stupid you've made us all look," he laughed, never letting go of her arm. It was a strong grip. "The best hiding place is where no one would ever look, right in front of them. Or something like that, right?" he said releasing her.

Olivia turned to him. "Something like that." Neither of them dare mention the previous events.

She walked around his room— the white rug, curtains, sofa, and bed sheets were like an overpowering sense of heaven. She liked reds—the color of blood—but then again, so did every other vampire. Olivia sat on the edge of his bed and talked for a while, complaining about the dirt and lack of items in the room she left.

"What did you do to me?" he asked her, the sweat visible on his forehead.

"What do you mean?" She smirked at him, sweetly batting her eye lashes and biting her lip.

He held onto his bedpost and wiped away the drops of sweat on his brow. "When you bit me, you did something." His vision was blurry and his legs shaky. He wouldn't last very long. He would either die of thirst or kill to quench it.

"I turned you," she said casually.

His eyes tried to focus on her as he lashed out screaming at the top of his lungs. "You did what?" His voice roared in the bedroom, bouncing off the walls and echoing in their ears.

"Only for a short time," she said trying to calm him down. "You're thirsty," she said walking over to his little bar and grabbing a glass.

The color of his eyes darkened, and he tried to follow her around the room with his vision, but it was failing him. Jason sat on the ground and leaned against his bed. The next thing he saw was Olivia's figure walking at him with a glass and thick liquid inside. She moved the glass under his nose so he could smell the sweet scent he longed for. He took the glass from her hands and placed it on his lips, drinking down to the last drop. He exhaled loudly and dropped his head to his chest.

Like nothing he had ever had before, his vision began to clear up and his eyes returned to their natural blue state. Jason looked down at his hand and into the glass.

Blood. He released it, letting the glass shatter on the wood floor. "You turned me," he stated.

"You should be grateful. I don't give my blood out to just anyone," she said and Jason noticed the large cut on her wrist bleeding down her hand and forming a puddle on the floor. There was silence again. "I'm sorry," she said.

"For what?" he chocked.

"Lying to you. I should really get going. The sun is going to come up soon," she laughed. "We both need sleep." Before he could say another word, Olivia surfed out of room in roaring flames.

Jason got up and attempted to go to bathroom, but he slipped on the blood and his body went flying for the floor. His eyes shot open as he hit the ground.

He was lying in his bed holding his family picture off the side of the bed. He sat up and looked around. There was no sign of her, no blood on the floor no glass. It was a dream. A nightmare. If he was going to dream about Olivia turning him, he would never close his eyes to sleep again.

It was times like these Olivia wanted Patrick around. He was like an encyclopedia to her life. Olivia raised her hand to knock on Jason's door, as guilt flooded her mind. Wasn't it enough that she had lied to him, bitten him, manipulated him, ruined his chances of everything he's fought so hard to get, and almost got him killed by his best friend? She backed away from it. It was nearly morning; the sun was rising over the hills. She walked away, down the hall to the elevator. The ding from the doors notified Olivia she could go inside.

"37 please,"

"Ms. Montgomery, maybe you should head down for breakfast instead. Or go to the library and read a good book," the golden voice suggested.

"You'll learn I hardly ever read. I'll get breakfast later. I just want to go back to my room, please," she said blandly without much effort.

The elevator hesitated and after a moment began her normal speed. It was only a few seconds and Olivia was getting off, not knowing how desperately the golden heart was trying to help her.

She unlocked the door and closed it behind her after walking in. The sun shined through the dust of the windows and lit the room some. Olivia stood by the window. She needed a mop and broom. There had to be some kind of closet filled with cleaning supplies in this place. If no one was going to clean for her, then she would have to do it herself. She walked over to the front door and tried to open it. It was stuck.

Rusty old room. The door wasn't even working. Good thing she could surf. Olivia put her hand out next to herself. Nothing happened. Surfing wasn't working too well. She attempted to open the door again but it wasn't jammed, it was locked. Olivia pulled the key out of her pocket and tried unlocking the door from the inside. It didn't work.

Surely, her strength could break down an old beaten door. Olivia pushed and pulled at the door with all her vampire might. Nothing. She was locked in. Olivia took one look at the window and ran at it, throwing her full body against the glass. She bounced back and hit the floor with a loud thud.

"I got out before," she said aloud to no one. Olivia ran up the stairs to see if maybe there was something there that could help her. Her legs stopped at the top of the stairs.

There were boxes upon boxes. All taped up shut. Different things were written on each box. Olivia walked into the open room. The sun beat in through the round window in the middle of the room. There were two arches on opposite walls facing each other. They lead into other rooms.

She ran her hand over the top box closest to her and read the words on it. "Baby Pictures."

Olivia picked the box up and placed it on the floor. She knelt down in front of it and reached for the tape as a light hit her eyes. Olivia moved her face and looked in the direction of the light. A crow bar! That's what she needed right now. She ran over to it, picked it up and ran back down, forgetting all about the special gifts her parents had left her.

Olivia learned from Patrick that these were great tools to break into or, in her case, out of something. She put one end in between the doors, and pushed and pulled with the other. It wasn't working. Restless, she threw the useless metal bar at the window.

Olivia rested her head against the door. There was a knock. She raised her head quickly and spoke. "Yes!"

"Hey. It's Mark. I heard Kerrigan showed you your private quarters. I figured I'd find out if you liked it," he said, kind of asking.

Olivia looked up and around her. "Prison doesn't agree with me." Olivia leaned her ear on the door.

On the other side, Mark was sitting down with his back to the door.

The elongated pause between them was jarring. He listened to her breath as she scratched the floor with her index finger. "It's very plain in here. The walls are dead and the dust is eating this place alive." She told him to make small talk.

Mark didn't respond. "It could use some lace curtains and a large sofa with room for four. Maybe a nice white wood coffee table," Olivia talked on. "I would love to have a round rug and a mirror just over the fire place," she smiled. "Some paint. Water and soap would help too." She laughed a bit to herself.

He still hadn't said anything. "Mark?"

"Still here. Don't worry." He paused. "You could have told us who you were. You'd find that a lot of people would have welcomed you with open arms." Mark looked down at the floor and up again at the wall. He took a deep breath. "I'm sorry, I can't come in," he said closing his eyes. "They thought it'd be best for everyone's safety. Just until they figure out how to break it to the others or if they should." Mark stopped for a moment. Some information was best kept a secret, but this couldn't do much harm. "Not everyone is breathless to meet you, as you might have realized. And I do mean all slayers when I say everyone."

They sat in silence. Olivia locked in the room and Mark locked out. "Why did you protect me?" she finally asked.

"The Jason I know isn't a killer. I won't let him become one."

"Do you have family, Mark?" the subject needed changing.

"Dead sister."

"Vampires?" Olivia asked softly, with the apology already in her voice.

"Accident." He sobbed the numbing tears. "I wish every day it had been vampires. There would be someone to blame. It was her time," he paused. "She was young," he stated without empathy but continued breathlessly, "I was young." Silence.

He spoke some more. "Dad's alive, just not around much. He can't stand to be around mom, " he breathed, hopeless, and shook his head. "Haven't gone to visit her in quite some time. I should go," he said standing. "I'll come back."

He left her there, locked with the dirt-covered walls around herself, sitting by the door waiting for an answer.

CHAPTER 10

Weird Little Old Man

Kerrigan exited the golden elevator and walked down the 37th floor hallway. He shook his head as he reached the door and ran a hand over his jaw line. Cracking his neck left, then right, he pulled an identical key to the one he gave Olivia out of his right pant pocket. He placed the key into the chamber and turned it.

The man reached for the knob on the door and turned it to the right, pushing the door open. He looked about the room for the prisoner. She was nowhere in sight.

The light from the sun came in through the doors and shined on his clean-shaven face. He walked towards the doors and stood by them a moment. Kerrigan crossed his arms over his chest.

Olivia came from the bathroom door.

Her face was pale and her eyes dark. Her lips were dry and cracked. Her hair had dried from the island rain and the brown waves were messy around her face.

She swallowed the last bit of saliva in her mouth and looked at Kerrigan impassively.

"God, in heaven," Kerrigan breathed out.

"So you have decided to let me go," she said not changing the expression on her white face.

Kerrigan uncrossed his arms and moved from the sun. "Cautionary measure, I'm afraid. You have any idea how many vampires and misguided slayers we find, trying to impersonate you?" he asked, explaining to the hungry girl. "We were talking to your friends and teachers about your presence the past two months."

"Amazing how difficult of a process it is. You must be confident in your discovery considering it took you only four days." Olivia watched his expression change to compassion.

She walked over to the doors. "Did you know," she started, sarcasm filling her voice, "that the plumbing here is crippled?" The sun touched her face and Olivia inhaled deeply and exhaled loudly.

"Your manners could use some work," he told her bluntly.

"Forgive me. Neglected orphans aren't the best adults." She returned his anger with sass. Her stomach made noises as she spoke. The dust from the room danced in the light that crept in.

Kerrigan reached into his back pocket and removed a bottle of water. He untwisted the cap and held it out for Olivia to take. She did.

Before drinking, she looked into the water, held it up to her nose, and poked it with her finger. "It's just water," Kerrigan reassured her.

"You'd be surprised how many slayer and misguided vampires try to kill me," she said before downing the bottle in seconds.

He smiled and looked away. "The power-blocking mechanism has been taken down in your suite. Your name has been corrected in your files, your blood has been added properly to the system, and Trio-Genesis is, as we speak, making you prescription pills of limeandisorin. We haven't found a way to make it so that you can surf using your fiery element without setting off the sprinklers yet, and it might be too risky to do so. But the ones in here have been disarmed," he said as she drank.

"Please do not bite our residents. You will find the side effects are eerie for them." He remembered the horrified screaming slayer Olivia borrowed blood from. "The hospital is willing to provide you with three bags of blood for the week until better arrangements can be made." He paused.

Kerrigan continued on. "For fear of your life, few know of your identity. Please, please, please, try and behave. It's amazing how like your mother you are when it comes to trouble,"

Olivia's face finally lit up. She smiled stupidly. "Mom was a trouble maker?"

He laughed a roaring sound. "She married Dracula!" he shouted, still grinning. "Well, you better be off to class." Kerrigan finished and surfed out without giving Olivia a chance to reply.

She looked at the door and ran for it. Once in the hallway Olivia closed the door and opened it repeatedly. She walked inside and slowly closed the door holding her breath. Olivia closed her eyes and turned the knob pulling the door. It opened. She let go of her breath. Her head turned to look at the balcony doors. She bolted towards the door and held the silver-braided handle, sliding the door open. It, too, was now unlocked. She took one last look at the space and left, leaving both doors open.

Olivia looked at the direction of the elevator and then in the other direction. At the end of the hallway not far away was a red light above a door. To the right of the door was a sign:

STAIRS

She pulled open the door and walked in. Olivia looked over the edge. They went on forever. She better start now if she was to get food and be in class on time.

Ten floors later and Olivia was exhausted. Maybe she should have trusted the elevator. Never mind that now; her name was being called.

"Olivia?" Mark's voice echoed behind her. She turned and he spoke. "Out of prison and off to class?"

"Off to the kitchen. I'm starved," she said as her voice echoed around the silver stairs.

Mark looked down the stairs. "You have a long way to go. Is the elevator broken?"

"No, but she'll take me right to class," she said reminding him the golden woman knew everyone's class schedule and was always very concerned with the students getting to class on time.

Once, Olivia had to desperately use the restroom and she was late for Slayer History. She tried to go back up to her room but the floor would not light up unless it was the one where her class was located. Today she wasn't taking any chances. That day, she missed an entire class because she was too busy arguing with the elevator.

"Surf down," Mark suggested.

As tempting as it was to light up into a ball of fire, Olivia didn't want any more trouble. "I'll take my chances with the endless staircase," she uttered.

"Want me to take you?" the kind question escaped his lips.

Mark wasn't doing a good job at keeping his distances from the captivating girl.

But how could he? Her blood drew them closer with every passing second. Every minute spent in her sight he was more taken by how amazing she had become and everything she was capable of doing. It was hard to contain the joy he felt in being able to share his thoughts with her and lending her a helping hand whenever she needed.

Olivia searched his eyes for the reason behind his sudden willingness to be her cornerstone and found none. It was enlightening for her. "Sure."

Mark took her by hand and as he did their hands became a soft sand. Their bodies were soon taken by the wonderful trick; the little bits of sand grew smaller and smaller until they were all gone. It all happened very quickly, but if one were watching in slow motion on a large screen, it would have been quite the scene to see.

Their bodies came into the kitchen as the same white sand they left with. Olivia thanked her new trusted friend and he walked away from her.

She turned with delight and looked at the cooks, her eyes watering for whatever they were preparing now. It was like a multi-million dollar restaurant kitchen— men and women in white clothes with tall hats walking around tasting and stirring and mixing. Laughing and joking. Water dancing in the air into pots and pans. Random winds blowing in from nowhere cooling deserts. Tomatoes growing instantly. It was phenomenal!

Eating at Trio-Genesis, whether in a cafeteria or at a fancy party, the food was five stars. And how could it not be? Imagine freshly cut lettuce as a bed for a salad, crispy, with small drops of water still keeping the beautiful greens moist. Think for a moment cutting into a juicy steak from the animal that grew right in the backyard farm.

"Darren!" She shouted at her favorite cook. He turned and smiled at her as he made his way over to greet her.

As he closed in on her, he embraced her with every muscle on his body. His towering figure protected every inch of skin Olivia had. She had never been welcomed so warmly into the kitchen before, and she had the feeling it wasn't because he had come up with the next greatest recipe. He pulled away from her, smiling down and looking deep into the eyes he had looked into for two months now.

"I should have known. You're the only person in this place who gets her steak rare," he joked, clearly stating that the word was going around. His humor was much like her own and his kindness was like that of Patrick's.

That's who he reminded her of: Patrick. The way he looked out for her under any circumstance, still managed to be her friend after finding out the truth, and could still find humor in everything.

He wasn't one the big guys around but he made the food. That gave him some power. He never did get into Trio Army so Darren became one of the most talented chefs. He was well-known and treated with respect. If Darren said Olivia was cool, she was.

Olivia leaned back on the counter and laughed at Darren's cute comments about her identity. He joked with her over and over, called her a hothead, and even asked if she wanted cow's blood. She didn't. He promised to keep cooking for her as long as she promised to keep her grubby little teeth on his food and never on him. She smiled.

"Let me see 'em," Darren said, motioning at her mouth.

She wanted to show him. "I can only do it in my room." She sighed.

"They are going to have to come up with a way to fix that for you," he said moving over to his workstation to throw away the food he was recklessly burning.

"I understand the threat," she walked to the other side to look at him better. "Trio-Genesis can't risk other vampires being able to come in unnoticed so I can feel more at home."

Darren walked to the trash and flipped the pot over into the bag. The little pieces of chicken fell into the garbage. "They can take your DNA and put it in the system so that you can surf and feed and whatever. That way, the building is still safe and you are still free," he said never looking up at her.

"That's not what I was told." She rolled her eyes.

"Leave it to me," he told her.

It was incredible how she always seemed to end right where it'd help her most. It was going to be so easy taking her place in Trio-Genesis. Those mindless morons would soon see her true power. With every step she was closer to the slayers and further from the bloodsucking monsters she grew up with.

Darren sat down to eat breakfast with her. The scrambled egg and cheese sandwiches he made were incredible.

She looked over at the clock. She had completely forgotten about her class at that point and time had gone by so quickly. It didn't matter anyway; it's not like there was ever anyone there to teach her. Olivia hesitated for a moment, then she dabbed her lips with the cloth napkin on her lap and placed the white cloth on the table next to her plate.

"Time flies, when you're having fun," he said as he grabbed their plates and stood. Olivia looked at him. He knew her too well too quickly. She smiled and stood.

"Thanks, Darren," she said and turned her back to leave.

Olivia would attempt going to class. Maybe arriving late would mean someone would be waiting for her. She could hear Darren's exhaling as he placed the dishes in the large metal sink.

Olivia pushed the button for the golden elevator. It came instantly. The doors closed behind her and the elevator shot up.

"You're late," the elevator barked. She opened at the end of a familiar hallway with nothing but a staircase to the right.

Once again, Olivia climbed the stairs to make her way to the only class with no teacher or other students. Unknown. She had this class three times a week, and she would wait for 10 minutes at least, every time she went.

Olivia climbed the narrowing stairs. It must have been the top of Trio-Genesis and a closet space that was left and made into a classroom. Not even the elevator went up there. There was always one desk attached to the chair sitting in the middle of the room and an old brown desk, which must have been the teachers. The whole room smelled of molding wood after a storm. There was only one window; it let light in from behind the desk of the teacher. Olivia opened the rusty door to find no one. She went inside; the door creaked close behind her.

Every week there was more dust on the floor and more spider webs on the corners of the walls. She walked behind the desk to look out the window. She was very high up. All she saw was a green patch of grass down below and the gleaming light blue waters coming from the left.

She turned and placed her hands on the desk. "Class, today we are going to learn about nothing. Due to my constant absences and possible death." Olivia walked to the door and turned to knob to leave.

There he stood. He was an old man whose little legs barely held up his body. His back curved slightly and his wrinkled hands shook at the weight of his brief case. The bits of hair left on his head were gray and white; the glasses on this face rested on the bridge of his nose and his smile was the most comforting smile she had ever seen.

There was a certain mystery behind his light brown eyes. Olivia was even more beautiful than he had ever imagined. Her shaped brown brows curved around the top of her eyes while her full lips hid her large smile. Her skin had no flaws, no scars, no battle wounds, and no stitches. A few very light beauty marks graced her face and neck, and her messy hair was tucked behind her ears. She still hadn't showered from the island, food was more important and her room had no running water.

Olivia jumped a little. "It's so hard getting up all those stairs and finding that you aren't here. Today I'm glad to see you've waited for me," his little voice said. "Please take a seat." Olivia walked over to the little desk. It was made for a large child but her figure wasn't big and she wasn't more than 5 feet and 3 inches, so for her the desk was quite comfortable.

At first, the sight of the bending chair frightened her; it could never hold her up.

But she walked around the other side and sat, pleased to find it didn't break on her.

He stumbled over to his desk and put his things down on it. Then he walked behind it and pulled up the chair, having a seat.

First, he opened his briefcase and pulled out several blank papers and some with words on them. He took out one number two pencil and a little bottle of whiteout.

Next, he retrieved his pencil sharpener and put a defined point on his dull pencil. He then took out an ivory candle and placed it to left of his desk. The man closed the briefcase and moved it to the floor. He sat there looking Olivia in the face for a good minute or so.

"Good morning. I am Mister MLB. Like the basketball," he said, smiling.

"You mean baseball," she corrected him.

He nodded. "Now it's your turn."

He must be joking. "Good morning. I'm Countess Olivia Brook Montgomery."

"You are Dracula's daughter," he said.

Olivia was sure all her teachers had known at this point, so why should she lie anymore? Besides, how much harm can this little man do, and how much information can he really know? He must be senile at his age.

She nodded at his statement. He proceeded to stare at her again.

She looked at him, smiled stupidly, and shook her head. "I'm sorry, but I'm not sure I'm learning anything. I came to this class every week for two months, and you weren't here. Today I came a whole 45 minutes late and you thank me for waiting for you. Was I really supposed to wait an hour for you every class so I can teach you that MLB stands for Major League Baseball." Her words didn't hurt his feelings. Olivia was too quick to judge.

It wasn't a bad thing that he wanted to get to know her. He had made every class; late, but he still made them. And it was pointless to start teaching someone who kept the most important part of their identity hidden. He couldn't come out and tell her he knew who she was. He wanted her to feel good about herself. She looked too much like her parents for her to be anyone else.

"I'm not teaching you, you are teaching me," he said calmly. She rolled her eyes. "What are we learning today, Ms. Montgomery?" he asked seriously.

"You're not kidding," she said as her laugher ceased. Olivia exhaled a bit and scratched the back of her neck. She pulled the rubber band off her hand and tied her hair in a ponytail. She looked around a bit confused and made her confession. "You really aren't joking," she said again.

MLB instructed her to start with something easy: her parent's names, her date of birth, her favorite color, things about herself. The most important part was for him to know her, to meet her, to understand her. He could never learn where her comfort zone was if she wouldn't open up to him. He recognized her sarcasm and her lack of patience, so he addressed it.

With every passing minute, Olivia understood the lesson was her life and personality. As he taught her how to teach and what to teach, it became increasingly clear that he couldn't and wouldn't teach a stranger.

His passion for teaching her was great but her resistance would only get in their way. His intentions were pure and his mind was much more advanced than she had imagined from his old physique. And that was the real lesson she had learned in those 30 minutes he spoke to her. Her judgment came too suddenly and without grace.

Never judge a book by its cover because while a plain black cover can hold the secrets of life, a masterpiece of a cover can be filled with vague thoughts.

Once he was done his side of teaching, Olivia tried to remember all he asked of her to say. She spoke some on her mother, but what she remembered was so little that the time spent on the subject was no longer than five minutes.

Her father was her pride and joy, her driving force, her super hero. She didn't say any of these things but it was clear by the way she spoke of him. MLB knew the man very well.

She filled him in on the exciting events that had happened in the two months she was there.

"Everyone has an element; even a vampire," he stated. "It's a common misconception that we teach here. Elements are not created by other elements, they are enhanced."

"The reason vampires carry Fire as their element is because their blood is so hot and their tempers are very short," he went on. "The will to be alive again is so strong in them that it makes the organs heat up, and their bodies are always running on a deep adrenalin and a lust that is never fulfilled. Most humans have different elements and they simply never learn to tap into it. Born vampires are taught anger and hate. Their element of Fire comes from the human tendency of their true desire of purification; after all, it's what fire does."

"My element is air. We airheads are deeply intelligent, but we can be easy to turn. Our minds are not hard to penetrate. The wind is always switching directions. But our ability to 'go with the flow' is what makes us incredible leaders. What's your element?" he asked her noticing he was teaching again.

Olivia thought a while. She wasn't sure. She always knew she had some hold of every element, but her strongest by far was Fire; she wasn't certain, though, because it was the only one she had learned. It ran deep in her veins and came most natural to her. Like a burning love waiting to consume and devour all with a cleansing touch of passion. "I'm most familiar with Fire. But I've tapped into them all."

"Now it's my turn to teach you," he said slowly as he stood and walked to the other side of the desk and let the weight of his body rest against it.

Mr. B watched her quietly and gazed upon the beautiful child he was teaching. It was like teaching one of his own. "Mastering an element is not an easy thing. But I suspect that you are close to the finish line of your first element. I would like to work on each element with you until you have reached your full potential, but that could take years, and I don't have much time left in me," he said playing with the white hair on his head. Olivia smiled.

"Have you ever heard of the four fables of the elements?" he asked the very attentive student. Olivia shook her head. "Many believe it only to be an old wives tale. But I was told by my grandfather, and he by his grandfather before me. And so on. Would you like to hear it?"

She smiled, it was enough of an answer. How quickly he had grabbed her attention to a hypnotizing stage. How particularly strange it was that she was so interested in the words he was saying. It brought him much joy to see one of his few students so thrilled to learn from him. It brought him even more joy knowing the identity of this one girl.

Mr. B stood and walked over to the table. He opened and closed the draws and looked around in his things. "I have it written down here somewhere," he told her as he looked around. "Don't want to tell it wrong." He finally opened a draw in which he suddenly remembered had a secret compartment. With a fist to the table, the compartment opened and he grabbed only the book, disregarding all other items in his hidden section.

He pushed his glasses up closer to his eyes and opened the small brown book. It was torn and old. "Long before the age of evil gained the power to kill with the strength from their hands..." He paused and looked up at her. "...it's speaking of the vampires here. I'm reading fable one. It's closest to you..." he then looked down and continued.

"...an intelligent man along with his three closet friends gathered for a wondrous night of fishing. At the light of the moon, the four fell asleep in the boat and as dawn woke the man up, he found himself alone on the boat. The waters crashing his small vessel against the unforgiving rocks. Without fear, he climbed out of the boat and unto the rocks. The man held on to the boat and used his strength to pull it up on the rocks. There he sat in his anger wondering where his companions had run off to, leaving him in such position. He looked for land around the black rock he sat on but was blocked by a large mountain with only a cave as refuge for the cold night that came upon him. All his life's lessons had taught him nothing to survive this. His only trick was making fire from rubbing stones and wood together. Being that the only wood he carried was his boat, the man broke it and built himself a fire. As the light of fire filled the cave, a female bat came from the darkness. In anger, she bit the scalp of his head. The man, filled with rage, took the female by her wings and broke them. The blood ran down his arms as he burned her in the flames from his fire. But the fire drank from the bloodsoaked sleeves he wore and took him to his death."

Olivia had never heard such a story before. "Is all that true?"

"I believe it," he said. They sat in silence for a few seconds.

Finally he spoke. "Let's pick this up next class. Maybe you can wait for me again," he said as he smiled, moving his things behind the desk. Olivia laughed and stood. She moved to the door and turned to face him again.

"I'll be on time next class." She smiled at him and thanked him for the lesson.

The old, crazy man kept his eyes on the things he collected. "I won't." He smiled, raising only his little eyes to her. Olivia laughed and walked out closing the door behind her.

"...the blood soaked sleeves he wore took him to his death," she said to Patrick and the other listening vampires who sat at the bar of Eclipse.

They looked at her in amazement and each took a sip of their drinks. Patrick kept his mouth open a while longer and then snapped back to reality. He looked down at the dishrag he was holding and kept cleaning the countertop behind the bar that faced the door.

The man to her left used his words first and soon after everyone started asking questions. "That can't be true," he said.

Following this were doubts and judgment from the others who heard her story.

She had said the story word for word, remembering every detail her teacher said to her a few hours before. One man grew angry of her tales and walked away. They left until it was only Patrick and Olivia.

Occasionally, they would all sit around into the late hours of the night and laugh together. Other nights they knew Olivia liked her privacy with her dear friend. Sometimes they knew she wanted to be left in the booth in her own kind of privacy and in her quietness.

It was nights like those that Patrick made her a drink and brought it to her without saying a word. He would heat up the blood so it would be calming and soothing. It was nights like the ones she sat alone that Olivia was most human.

But tonight was her normal night—her sharing the day events with Patrick and whomever was around who wanted in. She never gave away her whereabouts to the others or where she heard the stories from. And although she was on an important away mission, they knew that every once in a while they would see and hear from her. Joshua would come every night and ask Patrick if he had seen her.

Joshua wanted her to report to him and it killed him that she stayed away. He needed her blood. He had his own supply, but fresh from her sweet veins was always better and deepened the connection more. That was always a plus for him.

They laughed. "I'm not sure he was sober," she said. "At first he was lost, then there, and then lost again. He kept looking at me as if I was some kind of prize sitting on his mantel," she said taking the last sip of the xixi in front of her. Patrick filled her glass some more and looked at the clock on the mirror behind them. It was almost time for her to go. Joshua was sure to come soon.

"I'd love to talk all night, but we are pushing the clock here," he told her softly.

Olivia's mood changed. She wanted dearly to stay and talk and laugh some more. She wanted to share more of the stories. "I didn't

184

mean to stab you with goodbyes. Your mission is bigger than the hours we sneak in every now and then," he said lifting her chin and tapping her nose. Olivia stood from her chair, the vampires in Eclipse stood with her. Her body burned red in hot flames, and all that was left was the smoke from where her body once was, for she was no more.

He sat there very calm looking into the flames that burned on her hand. The fire danced in their eyes. Olivia sat across from him with a new chair he had brought up the flight of stairs. It was dark brown like the floor beneath them and old like the desk he sat at. Her hand was above his desk resting on the wooden surface.

"Think of the hottest flame you can bare. Imagine that flame against your skin. Burning deep into the flesh of your arms. Picture the wick of a candle when it's a flame. The color of the flame at the very bottom…" Mr. B took another pause to make sure his favorite student was following along his directions. "…Burn hotter."

Without a moment's hesitation, Olivia's blood boiled faster. The flame on her hand turned to a light shade of blue and a certain smile came over Mr. B. "You've been able to do this for quite some time."

She had. In fact, it was among many of the party tricks she carried up her sleeve. But it wasn't hate that made the fire burn hotter. It wasn't anger, jealously, or any other evil thought she could have had. It was passion. Consuming inspiration was driving her whole life.

In her spare time she sat in the wilderness knowing there was more to her power than she could unveil. Once before she had heard that the elements could be mastered. Since then, she found it useful to tap into that power. Not many would learn to control their element with such detail. Becoming one with an element many times caused self-destruction; brought many to the brink of death. Nothing else mattered but the power that they could and would have with practice. But it wasn't power that was the driving force in mastering an element, it was the realization that they were one with the element they received at birth or death.

The flames burned blue still and then the words left his lips. Maybe he was moving too suddenly. Maybe it was all too much for one day. Being able to contain a small hot flame without setting the room in flames was enough for one class.

After seeing Olivia for only a month, perhaps it would make her teachings fall short a little. But then again what's a class without a risk?

"Turn the flames into water," he instructed. Olivia looked at the flames and remembered the ocean and the salt water she was choking on almost a month ago. "Think water…" She already was. It was the trickiest—perhaps the toughest—thing she would do all year. Turning burning passion into streams of healing.

The flames turned from burning fire to swirls of water right before her eyes. The water kept the same motion as the flames and danced like nothing she has ever seen before. It was a fire of water, it seemed. A beautiful sight that might only be seen once in a lifetime by those who were very lucky and smart enough to be around the right people.

Water moved for a few seconds on her hand, and as Olivia lifted her eyes to look at Mr. B the water collapsed on her hand and all over the papers he had on his desk.

Olivia and he chuckled a while and dried off the papers. "It's quite alright, we'll try again soon," he reassured.

Olivia nodded. Soon more classes had passed. Olivia went from seeing him on their regular scheduled time to seeing him after school on the days she did not have him, and spending time with him on the weekend.

She could usually find him in the little room or in the back garden. They watched the leaves change colors together, he would read to her different tricks that could be done with fire.

Once, he greeted her with cookies, saying he made them himself; but by the taste of the sweet chocolates, Darren had something to do with it. That day they spoke without teachings. He gave her more stories and she took the information with open ears.

Olivia thought to ask him of another element. Earth.

"Your accident in defense class could mean you master Earth next. Or it could be the last you learn. Earth is a delicate power."

Mastering the elements doesn't mean having good fighting skills, it means being aware that it is all around you whenever you need it. There may be no plants or dirt in a room but someone who has mastered Earth or is mastering Earth will sense it all around them. The same with Water and Air. They work together when they are used together. But over the years it was easier to learn how to use them against the other.

Fire and Water against each other. Water and Air. Earth and Fire.

"I disagree," she said quickly. "Air fuels a fire." There it was, the passion that burned in her. "The earth holds the other three elements within it. It's impossible to say they really are meant to work against each other."

"Then again, you might master Earth better than you can even imagine mastering Fire," he said as he noticed the child he was teaching was no longer a little girl in the graveyard crying over the loss of her parents.

"She mastered Earth. Your mother. What's your favorite memory of her?" he asked and gave her the news all at once.

She remembered the feeling of the cool grass on her feet as if it were only a few minutes ago that she was running in the fields with her mother chasing her up the hills—her little legs struggling to stay away from her mother's arms. It was all a game then.

Now she would give anything to be caught in those arms, rolling in the grass and letting her mother brush the hair off her face and behind her own small ears. The sun would beat down on them as the figure of her father would watch from the distance.

Now she wasn't sure if it was a dream or if it was real. It would be so great if it had been real, but what child would remember such memories so vividly? Certainly if there was such a child, she would be Olivia.

"Close your eyes. Concentrate and cover the floor of this room with what you are thinking." He had been reading her mind.

Was he prying in her private thoughts all along? Was that all he wanted? Not even Patrick knew her dreams of her parents or her nights of torment from the blood leaving her body as Joshua fed off her flesh. It was all hers and hers only.

Mr. B was in her soul, deep beyond the thoughts that haunted her and amazed her at the same time. He knew her mother much better than Olivia did. He knew Savanna's favorite place was any backyard with a patch of grass. She loved to run in it, smell it, cut it, roll in it.

Olivia dropped her hands down by her sides and thought of the grass and running on it barefoot. "Olivia, open your eyes,"

She did. The dusty wood floors weren't dust and wood anymore, it was grass.

Real, live grass. "Pull the grass," he instructed. She was off her chair, crouched down by her seat in seconds, letting her hand run over the tip of the grass. Intoxicating. Breathless. In awe.

She let the grass run in between her fingers, but never let it touch another part of her body. If she lacked concentration it would disappear. Then she held on and pulled the grass right off the dirt. Real, live dirt. Worms and little critters.

Her eyes grew wider.

"If there is grass, there must be dirt," he gleamed. "You will learn quickly, Olivia." She stood up. "You may go now,"

She looked at him walked over to the door and opened it. Olivia stepped out of the class and closed the door behind her. The grass was gone. The room's floors returned to their dusty form.

The little old man sat there smiling. He looked down at his paper and went back to doing the crossword puzzle he had pulled out of his bag in the beginning of class.

The sun was coming in from the window behind him. He put down his pencil and looked at the picture in the case he carried. There was a man who looked much like a younger version of himself and a small child, about three with dark eyes much like the night sky, shining black and glimmering white like the stars. He held the child in his arms close. He looked right into the child's eyes as the child somehow found the focus of the camera. The old man closed his case, took a deep breath, and surfed out of the small closet class.

CHAPTER 11

Lots of Cars

The flames danced in his fireplace as he sat on his green leather couch and spoke into his phone. Mark's voice was raspy and faint. Over on the other side of the room, Kelly stood looking at clothes hanging in his closet. Her mind was half-attentive on his words. He wanted his privacy.

"No change," he said rubbing his eyes as if not to cry. "He calls when he can." His voice was like a sob. "Yes, I'll see her again this week. I will. Goodnight, Pop. You too." He never said the full words back to him. But it would do. One day when death reached his bed, Mark would regret never speaking the words back, but there was time until that day.

Kelly walked over to him seeing he had hung up the phone. "How is he?" she asked trying to lighten the mood with her tone.

She handed him a jar of chocolate balls. Whites, milks, and darks. Mark smiled up at the caring girl before him. If anyone was ever in need of a friend, Kelly was the person to go to; once you had her, she was loyal to you. She would stand by your side no matter what.

"He's, well, aging." With this, Mark and Kelly heard a knock on his door. Mark whistled, and a warm wind came into his room filling the air with the fresh smell of after-shave as Jason surfed in.

"I have two chili dogs with mustard and relish, a pumpkin crusted apple pie, two cheeseburger with no onions, two small fries, and a mango milkshake for me, and a blackberry milkshake for you," Jason said walking over to the fireplace. He looked up once he reached the chairs and saw Kelly. "I thought it was Broendsday…"

Kelly looked down at Mark who was still sitting but was now salivating at the mouth. It would lighten his mood; she was sure it already had.

"It is. I was just saying goodnight," Kelly said, giving Mark a kind smile as a bed a flowers showered down on her. At that, she was gone.

Jason sat down on the chair next to Mark and made himself right at home. He removed his shoes and put the food down on the twine leafy coffee table before them.

Mark immediately opened the bags and went for some fries and hot dogs.

"Hey, one of those is mine," Jason said, still unzipping his sweater to free himself of the heavy sleeves that rested on his arms. It was warm enough by the fire anyway.

The boys ate the food and shared jokes and laughs into the late hours of the night, never letting the mood of joy and happiness die off. Jason kept Mark's spirits up and Mark helped Jason lighten his mood about Olivia; it was all Jason seemed to talk about after a new topic was done.

Part of him wanted to believe her while the other part was on Alison's team of hate and disbelief. For the most part, Mark always brought Jason back from the deep thoughts he fell into, but sometimes his eyes filled with a certain anger.

"Do you love him?" Rick asked Olivia, as they walked down the hallway.

On one hand, he was evil and cruel; dashing and brave. On the other, he was a coward, unable to make up his own mind about what he wanted. He could never be a real leader, as much as he wanted the role. His voice wasn't loud enough, nor his ideas grand enough. He could bring a certain fear, but his power did not overcast those around him. He was another shadow in Olivia's small figure—a tall tower with all the lights off, abandoned, left for demolition, if anyone would do such kindness.

"I've known him all my life. It would be ridiculous not to," she fabricated.

It wasn't hard to become friends with Rick. He was kind and followed Olivia every second he got. They would sit together whenever he found her at the dining hall or the library. He would come up behind her in the corridors and accompany her to her next destination. He woke her every Sunday morning if it was past 10 and he had not seen her. And he kept every secret she had not yet told him. In a way, she did confide in him.

Everything reminded her of Patrick. After becoming closer with her teacher, Mr. B, Patrick was left in the dust. Time after time again, she would promise herself to see him. Tell him everything! But every day she would find her way into another compartment she had not known of, or in a new conversation with her new found "friends." Now as she walked, it seemed as if she was replacing Patrick with Rick or anyone else in her life.

"Could I have some time to myself?" she implored. Rick said "yes" to everything out of her mouth. So he placed a soft touch on her shoulder and surfed away leaving the vampire girl with a wet patch on her shoulder.

It was dark and the weather grew colder with each passing night. The long, never-ending ceilings were somber, but Olivia could see stars through the glass. The skies were covered in them. This was only an illusion. She was nowhere near the highest floor.

After what seemed like hours of walking, she came to the place she finally wanted to go. It was where Jason had first held her captive. The room held one silver chair, a control system, and a cage. She walked over to the control system and snorted to herself.

It was all too easy sometimes. She pulled a little vial of blood from the pocket of her pants and pressed the numbers 431 on the screen before her. A small tube slipped up from the control table and Olivia placed the vial into the tube. She pushed a green button and the tube slid down and hid away. It wasn't long before the table made a small buzz sound and Olivia let a smirk dance on her lips.

She then pushed a blue button. Nothing. She turned to leave but was stopped by the door that opened on the other side of the room. Olivia walked over to the door and poked her head inside. It was empty and dark.

Her voice rang in the compartment she stepped into. "Hello?" Nothing. No response.

A bright light went on, after a few short seconds of adjusting to the light, Olivia saw only an empty, white room. The door creaked closed. The room returned to its former darkness.

Olivia lit a fire in her hand and moved about the room. White walls, white floors, and white ceiling all were reflecting the glow from the fire burning brightly on her hand. She turned around and faced where the door once was but was now covered by a male figure. He smiled, showing all his teeth.

It worked.

She was smiling no more. Olivia sighed and placed a finger over the mouth of her glass. The red liquid left on the edge, where she had placed her lips to drink, caught her finger and she dragged the blood along the edge of the glass. The crystal did not sing.

Olivia looked up at Patrick on the other side of the bar. It was empty there that night. Maybe it had been a slow night, maybe he asked everyone to leave, maybe everyone got up and left on their own, but it was empty.

The tables had rings from the sweat of the cups and it was already staining the brown wood. The booths had bloody napkins stuck in the corners. The radio was turned on very low, so much so that music could not be heard.

Olivia breathed in gently. Her eyes never left Patrick's. He smiled softly at her and she remained serious. If someone were to surf in, they would say Olivia and Patrick were lovers on the break of their relationship, realizing what they have been doing was wrong and that it should end. But no one would surf in or walk in either. The front door was locked and there was no back door from the outside.

The lights were slightly dimmed. Patrick took Olivia's empty glass from her hands, pulled the dirty rag from his side, and cleaned the stain.

"You've been away a while," he said cleaning away at his work so he did not have to look into her eyes.

A hushed sorry escaped her lips.

"You're not." The cold reply was more honest than her apology. She was never sorry. Patrick knew better than to cling to Olivia when she was on a mission. But he cared for her too deeply to leave her drowning out at sea.

She didn't look at him. "I've changed, Patrick." He stopped cleaning and turned back at her. He raised her face by her chin with his hand and looked into her eyes.

"No, you haven't," he said and let go of her face.

"I've tried to."

That was more than enough for him. "That means what exactly?" he placed his beautiful hands on the counter and lowered himself into the bar stool behind the bar.

"Your iniquities have been cleared? You've changed perspectives? You're leaving for good?" he stopped but Olivia did not speak. "You've not changed."

"I don't want this anymore," she said under her breath.

"I'll die for you!" he said loudly, overpowering the tone of the conversation. "I am ready to die for you. But you can't turn on me and say things like 'I've changed.'"

Olivia's voice was calmed, sad, and almost desperate. "Will it be worth it in the end?"

"In the end...? You're talking like you're going to die... relax. It's just a little war, Olivia," he stood and kept cleaning. "Don't be mad. You have no idea what kind of pressure I've been under. Joshua is here every day." Patrick breathed out his worries. "He asked me why you don't go to him instead, 'Why does she cling to you?'" Patrick stopped cleaning to watch Olivia's reactions. "The bar has been empty," he said then averted his eyes.

"I thought you had enough to quench it, I'm sorry." This apology she did mean.

Their eyes met. Patrick needed some time to return to his normal self.

She stood placing a brown shopping bag on the bar top and left. Patrick looked into the bag, pleased with the gooey red liquid inside.

The sunset was shining brightly on the grounds of Trio-Genesis. She sat on the grass looking around at the slayers reading and talking, children running around, parents attentive to whatever their children were doing.

She was sitting with her legs out in front of her, soaking up the sun, bathing in its light. When she was little, her mom used to take her outside and sunbathe her for Vitamin D. Of course, Savanna couldn't do this at The Vampire Mansion. She brought her to Trio-Genesis, where Olivia was free to run around with her little friends and play in the sun without vampires surrounding her thinking she was going to burn without the right ointments on her skin. SPF 200!

Jason sat down next her. "Hello there, Olivia," he said putting a bit of emphasis on her name and smiling.

"You make it sound, like I've only told you yesterday," she said not smiling as he did to her, "when are you going to let it go?"

"When I'm convinced you're not lying to me," his smile faded. He sat like her, looking at the children running on the open grass. Jason inhaled then exhaled. It was a quiet moment, except for the noise around them. He looked up at the sun and covered his eyes with his arm.

"It's kind of hot suddenly, for mid-October," she said breaking the silence between them. "I wouldn't mind a cold breeze right about now."

Jason looked to the right, inhaled, and blew out slowly. Olivia smiled. "I meant a real breeze, but thanks." The cool air hit her face and arms.

They sat there again in silence. Jason lay down on the grass and closed his eyes. It was moments like these when he had no idea what came over him. Someone else was controlling his actions. He meant Olivia no good by his own means.

The sleepless nights reflected on his face. Besides keeping an eye on Olivia and studying for his classes, he did nothing else. The dreams of her attacking him kept coming in his sleep. He would wake up holding his family picture and sweating like a mad man. After he woke from the dreams he would refuse to sleep, but his eyes would always drift off and again he would find himself in a different place, blood running from his neck. Blood running from her neck also. The nightmares kept him on his feet but off his guard.

There was a power that ran in him when he was near her. But there was a hate that grew stronger, even if only in his mind. He wasn't sure what possessed him to speak now. "I can never actually trust you." He didn't rise from the grass and Olivia didn't look at him. Her focus remained in the absence of the spaces ahead. "You're the tide. Always changing,"

She recalled Joshua's words very clearly now. "I will always, trust you first. You're the fire, Olivia. And fire always burns. It's unpredictable, but you always know the outcome." He wasn't power thirsty then.

Mark watched her from the distance, standing under the doorway. His arms crossed at his toned chest. Their smile were identical, his and Olivia's. He would die for her. He would kill for her. He would lie for her. And for now, he would lie to her. And for always, he would lie to her.

Light filled Jason's eyes when he opened them and sat up to look at Olivia. There's something about her. He never knew what was coming next. He never knew what to expect out of her mouth.

"I never want you to," she said and paused in time. Then, like the wind, she was another person. "Do you want to go for a drive?"

Mark could see their mouths moving but from afar he could not see what they said. "Are you thinking of telling her?" Kelly asked as she crept up on Mark. He shook his head and they made their way over to the two enemies on the lawn.

From the distance, Olivia and Jason hear Mark's voice. "There they are," he said, as if he didn't know.

"Jason and I were just going for a car ride. You guys should come," Olivia said standing after Jason, who looked at her with amazement. He never agreed to anything. "Better than sitting here and getting skin cancer." She looked up at the sun.

There was a moment, and so Kelly took it. "I think she's right," she said looking at Mark trying to lighten his mood a little.

He was stressed after Olivia came to Trio-Genesis. He wouldn't rest, couldn't sit still, could barely eat, or get his work done. He kept watching her. Any moment now, she would vanish and her absence would leave a crater in his soul. "We need to get out more. Have some fun." Kelly wrapped an arm around Mark.

Olivia didn't see where this new Kelly came from. But she didn't have a problem with it.

"Fine." Jason quit.

She came from nowhere, Alison fueling her fire as she opened her mouth. "Where are we getting a car from?" the blonde woman asked a less-than-surprised Olivia. Everyone else seemed to be startled by her surfing in a few inches away from their faces. Rick wasn't far behind her entrance. He had been keeping her company at the door with Tom.

"Surely daddy has bought his little princess a nice pink Porsche." Olivia batted her lashes at Alison. She was burning with hate. The silver stake she kept strapped to the belt that tied around her waist under her shirt was ready to kill the blood-sucking Countess.

"Speak one more word of my father and I will find a way to kill you," she said closing in on her face.

Once more Kelly jumped in for the rescue. "What Alison is trying to say..."

"And failing miserably," Olivia added.

"... is we surf everywhere."

Olivia nodded. "That's what I thought. Do you even know how?"

"We aren't stupid," Alison said disgusted.

"I don't know how to drive," Rick said under his breath. Olivia smiled and raised an eyebrow at Alison.

"I'll teach you," Olivia said smiling. "Anybody else need a lesson?" They looked around at each other.

There was another opening to say something smart at the worshiped Countess. "Anyone crazy enough to get into a moving vehicle with you should be put in a mental institution." The blonde girl laughed.

Olivia's comeback was just as fast. "The car will be parked when we get inside, Goldie Locks." She surfed a ring of red, burning her body as she did. Olivia had to leave before Alison could say anything else. Rick surfed shortly after her, not to miss the opening of the surf.

Surfing was a delicate thing. If one surfed fast enough after another's surf they could follow the spark of the first. Like a chain, the surfs would lead to the same location. The person surfing would never find the place on their own from that method of travel, but they would always reach the destination as the first person surfed. It was something that was done with the clearest of minds. Anger and hate blocked the path. The spark was too fast to miss. All other emotion would get in the way.

"I want to watch this," Kelly said surfing off of Rick's spark hand in hand with Mark. Alison looked back at Tom who still stood by the door, and when she turned back Jason was gone. She had missed the spark and her opportunity to join them.

Olivia watched as the others quickly surfed into the shadow of Eclipse. They waited for Tom and Alison for a second, but knew that they were no shows after just a few seconds had passed. Olivia didn't mind her very best enemy staying away. She didn't want Patrick to meet the woman starved for attention.

"Before we go inside here's a few rules you might not want to break: Don't speak, if possible try not to breathe too much, look at no one, touch nothing and no body, and be nice to me." She smiled at the last rule of survival.

"This is where you have a car?" Mark asked.

Olivia grabbed the door handle and turned it looking back to him. "No. This is where I keep the keys."

They walked in. Everyone gave the Countess a meaningful look and went back to their drinks. They knew the others with her weren't welcomed, but they also knew Olivia must have a reason to be carrying her own personal posse of slayers. They had their guards up; nevertheless, they trusted her before themselves.

Olivia walked over to the bar and sat down. The slayers stood behind her. "XIXI, crumbled ice, no fat." Olivia looked at her vampire friends sitting on the bar next her. A hand wiped the table in front of her with a dirty rag then placed down her drink.

"I'm not giving you the code," Patrick said letting go of the drink. "Don't try and be all nice and sweet either; it's not going to work. You can take the one in my garage, or you can take the bike on the roof. I'm not giving you code."

Patrick locked her extensive collection of cars, standard and automatic, in the mansion's underground private garage. It looked more like a car lot with shiny new cars for sale. Few ever used. Many were a sparkling black or a deep blue. A few reds popped out and some whites that were never touched for fear of dirtying them. The cars ranged from the 1920's to the next year's new model. Of course, the old and restored ones were merely for show. It gave her a wonderful feeling looking around at all of them, sitting in the new ones, and smelling the new car smell. From pick-up trucks to mini coopers. Olivia had just about every car driven on the road.

"Who said I wanted a code?" She was keeping her cool as she sipped her drink.

"Olivia."

Now these words, he said slowly too make sure she understood him. "I. Am. Not. Giving you the code." Her eyes shrunk and she gave him the puppy look. "Give it up babe; it's not going to happen," he said looking at Olivia's new friends.

He looked them all over asked them if they wanted anything to drink. They shook their heads. Patrick exhaled. "What's with the fan club behind you?" Olivia broke her doggy eyes and brushed her right brow with three fingers once.

"No...no...no." he said and sucked his teeth a bit. "Olivia, get them out of here. Get them far away from here. Don't bring them back. Don't bring them close," he whispered calmly so only she could hear. "Have you lost your senses?!"

"Relax, will you? They aren't even breathing a lot." She sipped the drink again.

"I can tell, that one is turning blue," he said pointing. "Olivia, I just fixed the booth from last week's fight."

She looked back at the slayer he was pointing to: Rick. "He's not turning blue that's just his element. Water," she answered him trying hard to be a wise guy.

"Will you shut up?!" he whispered in a serious voice. "Now, get these 'vampires' out of here before something bad happens. I don't want blood in the bar." He looked at her closely. Sure, everyone knew and suspected Olivia was with a slayer army behind her, but they hoped it was dinner.

"A little late for that, don't you think?" she noted nodding her head to the bottles behind him.

"Hey Pat, another round of A- shots for me and the guys here!" a vampire yelled.

"Coming right up, Steve," he said, cool again. "Get your little friends out of here, before they start asking for fresh blood. Not that they can drink it anyways," Patrick said taking shot glasses and placing them down in front of himself to pour the drinks.

"I'm not leaving until you give me the code." She raised the stakes for him.

"You said you didn't want... fine. 5554. Now go," Olivia smiled, leaned over and gave Patrick a kiss on the cheek to thank him.

Olivia got up, so did the rest of the vampires in the bar. She walked out the front door. Rick inhaled.

"Olivia, I'm trying to be on your side here. But you can't make us bait in a place like that. I walked in there and was praying to remember the friendly advice you gave us once I smelled the foulness in the air. You have to warn us of these things. We are trying to be your friends." Kelly was doing well today.

"I'm sorry." The deadly words slipped her lips and her eyes widened.

Jason could not believe his ears. Olivia... had apologized. "Next, all we have to do is go to the Vampire Mansion."

There went any glimmer of hope Jason had for her. He laughed a little. "You heard nothing Kelly said. We can't stroll into the

Vampire Mansion. We'll die. We're Slayers," he said taking back his place as group leader. He soon remembered how Kelly spoke to her, like a mother explaining to a five year old why she can't touch the stove. "Olivia, we can't go to the mansion. It's hidden. It's dangers. It's off limits to all slayers. We wouldn't be able to find it if we tried," Jason explained to her calmly. It worked, to an extent.

"You don't need to find it, I know where it is. But you're right, you wouldn't find it, and I'm the only one who could surf there. Even if you followed me, entering with another element wouldn't work," she said, very proud of the security she and Patrick along with Michael—the brains of the security team—had placed on the large house.

It wasn't covered with Elements like Trio-Genesis. And a main computer didn't run it either. Michael said the best place to hide something is in plain sight. "Unless, you don't mind becoming a vampire for like an hour or two?"

"You can do that?" Rick asked right away. He was in! Vampire for an hour? He would conquer the world... or just Olivia's heart. It was all the same to him.

"No!" Jason lost it. Now he was the angry father telling the bad dog he couldn't pee in the house, much less on his couch! "No one is becoming a vampire for an hour." His whole body posture had changed.

The bar door opened. A tall, scruffy vampire walked out. "Countess!" He screamed. Olivia jumped out her skin. "I am so happy to see you." His words were slurred and his voice high. He walked off too drunk to even surf.

"I told Patrick to stop giving them alcohol. The two just don't mix." Olivia thought for a second. "There is another way. It will get a little hot."

"You're delusional if you think I'm going to surf with you," Jason barked at her.

"Fine, don't come," she said.

"Come Rick." She grabbed onto his hand and Jason broke them apart.

He pushed Rick away from Olivia and looked into her eyes, deep down into her soul. "No one is going! We will show up in ashes," Jason said.

"It's perfectly safe. I know what I'm doing, Jason." Olivia was tired of his nagging.

"I'm not going to let you get my team killed for a joy ride!" he screamed.

"Your team?! You're the worst leader I've ever met," Olivia pointed out.

"At least I'm not running away from my responsibilities!" he shouted back.

"What responsibilities? You're just a hot air balloon!" She smirked proudly using one comment to hurt two sides of him.

"At least I'm not a hothead!" He yelled louder than she had before.

"I'll go." Mark spoke at them. Jason stopped. How could Mark be on her side? He was his friend, not hers. Deep down Jason was right; it was a stupid risk to take for a few moments of fun.

"I trust you. I'll go," Mark said again, this time to Olivia only. And before Jason could tell him he didn't give permission, Mark fought him with his words. "I don't need your approval." Mark walked over to Olivia and took her hand.

Kelly wouldn't let him go alone, so she too took one of Olivia's hands. Jason watched in horror. What was happening? Everything was turning on him, and he was losing all the trust of his team to the vampire girl beloved by all.

Her father's power truly ran in her veins. The power to possess the mind of even the strongest people and have them wrapped around her little finger. The same power made him act without thinking. It was the venom of all vampires—the venom that took freewill and turned it to mush. It was stronger with a bite. But Olivia could spread her poison with her voice, with her big brown eyes, and the touch of her soft hands. She reeked of power.

"But I could use your company," Mark said extending his hand to Jason. Rick walked around him and took a hold of Kelly's hand. They waited patiently for Jason to take the hand or reject it.

He took it.

Olivia took in a deep breath and exhaled slow. A small flame covered her body and moved down her hands until she breathed again and lights of red, orange, and yellow took the oxygen to feed the fire and ate their bodies.

"I'm blind! I'm blind!" Rick started screaming. His arms flying out in front of him, hitting Kelly.

"Rick! You're not blind, the lights are off!" Kelly said pushing in the general direction his hit came from.

Olivia wandered off slowly without them noticing. It would have been a perfect time to attack, and she could have taken them all down as easily as she had surfed them there. They were talking amongst themselves and would have never seen it coming.

She would first take out Jason, their little leader. Without him, they would let their anger consume them, become them, and she would use it to kill them. Once she had them attacking her, defending would be easy.

Jason's parents were gone, his only brother thought to be dead. Rick was an exchange student who didn't call home very often. Kelly's parents abandoned her when she was small because she was different from her brothers and sisters.

Olivia knew from Mark that his parents weren't around much. There would be nothing to find. Their bodies would completely obviate.

"Olivia?" Jason called out. Feeling her presence was getting further and further away made him uneasy.

She made him uneasy.

"We shouldn't have come," he said under his breath.

The lights came on and they hid their eyes. Olivia's hand was on the power box across the room; next to the lights was the main alarm. One push at the orange button and every vampire fit to fight in the Mansion would be in the garage. But treason would come at too high a price if put into motion at the wrong time. And this was the wrong time. Many things had to be prepared first.

"Pick a car," she said opening her arms out.

So many cars! All licensed, with plates from all over the U.S.A, England, South America, Canada and all over. "There is no limit. You can pick manual or automatic. Black, white, gray, blue, red. Last year's model, a 1950's model."

They looked around and their eyes widened. There must have been a thousand cars there. There were cars as far as the eye could see: the best cars, the most amazing trucks, cute buggies, and even old mustangs.

Olivia must have driven at least 20 of them. As much as she loved driving, she didn't have time to take out every car.

She had lost a few from careless racing. She'd just surf right out of the car and watch it drive itself off a cliff into the water or explode once it hit a tree.

A few times, the police would come after her and most of them would retire after chasing her down. One minute Olivia was there, the next she and car were gone. The plates would be put into the system, but with all the cars she had, she never had to drive one twice. And none of the plates were registered under real names. Besides, she didn't like seeing a lot of miles on the cars. After the rate of retired cops went up and Olivia had ruined seven or eight cars, Patrick started changing the code on the garage so she couldn't take them out. She could sit and look, touch them, but if one car surfed it would set the alarm off, and Patrick was sure to drop whatever he was in the middle of to stop Dare Devil Olivia.

Mark was completely in love. He made the first move walking away from the group. His eyes wide and his mouth watering with joy. It was a silver Bugatti Veyron. Olivia had never driven it. Mark could marry the car. It didn't take him very long to start looking through the whole car.

Olivia didn't think he'd be so into cars. But he happened to pick one of her favorites. Mark took a second to look up at Olivia and looked over to his right; there were three more Bugatti Veyron in black, white, and blue.

This was heaven and Jason knew it. He was itching in his skin to run around shopping for his pick; his pride kept him.

"How many dealerships did you hit up to steal all these?" he asked bitterly.

Olivia saw the envy on his face. It rolled off his tongue when he spoke. It was painted in his skin. "These priceless beauties were all birthday presents. Excuse me if no one likes you enough to buy you something," she answered him smirking.

"Have you been receiving cars since you were one?" Rick asked for an explanation.

It was rightfully so that he did. Thousands of cars. At one point someone had to know she would like to receive something else. "Sweet sixteen. The perfect present, completely over done," she said shortly.

"Ah, everyone wants to impress the Countess," Jason said sarcastically eyeing the shining rims nearest him.

Olivia was enjoying his hate all too much. There wasn't anything in the world that gave her more pride than the look on someone's face when they were over filled with jealousy at all her beautiful cars.

"You know, Jason, maybe if you stop being such a stick in the mud, you can take the time to experience this wonderful moment that's been placed before you." Olivia took a short breath and kept spitting words at him. "So, stop being a green monster and pick a car."

She looked at Rick. "So an automatic or a manual?"

"You are the master, I am just the apprentice," Rick bowed.

Olivia smiled. It was about time someone trusted her with something she clearly knew more about. "Real car enthusiasts like to do the driving. How much do you know about a shift stick?" she said dragging him away from Jason and Kelly.

"I'm not jealous!" Jason screamed at her.

"Didn't say you were!" she said smiling.

Rick looked down at her and whispered, "He's jealous."

"I know," she whispered back.

There they stood, Kelly and Jason; the two losers. She didn't know much about cars and Jason was swimming in his pride, but his blood was dancing in him to sit in one. "Well, I'm not," he said trying to convince himself.

Kelly shook her head and walked over to a Porsche Carrera GT. It was pretty to her and she recognized the name Porsche. But that's all she really knew.

Olivia ran over to her favorite car, the red Lamborghini Reventon. It was licensed "Eagle." She had named the car based on its peak-looking front and majestic look. This she would not let Rick drive; she would show him first. Olivia got in on the driver's seat and Rick on the passenger side. It was incredible inside. This was the one car Olivia did not crash. It was the one car she did not get caught speeding in. This was her baby.

Despite their differences, it was none other than Michael Bow who graced Olivia with the beauty. This and the motorcycle Patrick gave her were the favorites. She looked at her mirrors and then looked in the backseat of the car. "Is that my jacket?" she said reaching over and grabbing the leather jacket. "It is my jacket." She came out of the car and put her jacket on. She walked over to Jason, who stood there still! How stubborn could one man be?

"This isn't a good idea," he said to her again. Over and over he would parent Olivia, and yet he could never realize that she didn't need his advice; nor did she want it. No one else did either for that matter. He was wasting his breath. Jason had one goal in mind, to tolerate her and to get as much information on her for his own gain. If only he knew how close he physically was to what he sought.

"Do you ever let go?" she questioned honestly. Her face changed; she was completely sincere and friendly for a moment. "Or are you always going to be a pain to be around?" There it was, one sweet second in her blood. It's all she had in her.

Jason didn't change his hard and proper stance; he just looked at her with the same blank look in his eyes. Nothing really mattered to him anymore since he had lost all that mattered most to him, and nothing took him out of the state he was living in.

As a slayer, Jason killed to avenge his family. Every child he saved from the bloodsucking teeth of another vampire was a point at victory that went to his big head. Proud, arrogant, and always right, his friends hardly knew the carefree Jason they fell in love with.

"Go pick a car and I promise none of us will look at you differently for having fun," she said and stood there with him a minute. Rick broke the elongated moment when he beeped the horns.

"Are we driving or what?" he shouted.

Olivia was disappointed in him. Jason was disappointed in himself. Is this what his family would have wanted? For him to turn into a cold unforgiving killer? He was no better than a vampire, no nicer than the Grinch, and no better than Olivia. That was enough to drive his mind into chaos.

"I'll go put the code in," she said and walked away from him.

After the number had gone into the large main frame in a small room Olivia surfed into, she surfed over next to the car. Three engines roared in delight from being turned on. Olivia stuck her head out of her window and spoke. "Surf the car to route 16 over by Avalanche Mountain; we'll meet up there." Her eyes glanced over at Rick as she asked if he were ready and told him to hold on tight. His hands grabbed on to the leather seats and his eyes shut quickly. Olivia's hands held on tight to the wheel. The car erupted in flames and they were gone.

Route 16 was lit only by the night sky and the large crescent moon. The water glimmered on the right and Avalanche Mountain rose on the left. Olivia waited in the car for Mark and Kelly to surf up. It wasn't long before a burst of dirt came swooping in on her left and then another on her right. The road ahead was empty.

"The race ends at the turn. There's only one, you can't miss it. Three rules!" she said shouting out the windows again. "One: If a cop comes, surf the cars and yourselves out. Two: If another driver shows up, surf the cars and yourselves out."

"Seems like the same thing to me. Where do we surf them to?" Mark asked revving his engine.

Big locations like, Avalanche Mountain were known to everyone. But it's not like they could take the cars to the Mansion back in Schroon Lake, or to Patrick in Toronto. They had no idea how far they had traveled in the short period of time.

"Surf to Trio-Genesis."

"What's rule three?" Mark asked.

Olivia smirked and wrapped her hand on the shift stick, checked her mirror and looked at Rick. "Don't play nice." She smiled and went into first gear and sped off, quickly switching gears and picking up speed.

The two were completely left back in her dust. The road was narrow, long, flat. She looked over at Rick who found this side of the Vampire Slayer very sexy. Olivia looked into the mirror; from the distances, she could see four lights approaching her quickly. Olivia wasn't aware that Mark and Kelly were such good drivers. They met up with her cherry red ride. Mark cut her off from the inside and managed to keep Kelly and Olivia stuck behind him. Olivia finally met around on the outside, near the short wood fence that kept the safer drivers from plunging to their death into the water below.

"You drive like a girl!" she screamed at Mark. "Who taught you how to handle a vehicle?"

"My grandfather," he said and saw Kelly take the lead around them as they were busy conversing; she was finally in the lead, but it wasn't for long.

"Okay, Rick. This is where driving gets fun. Hang on tight." Olivia's hand erupted into hot flames and her red-hot car was taken in the fire. She surfed in front of Kelly causing the two drivers to come to a slow enough lag to give her a great advantage of the free road ahead of her. It was about two miles away—the sharp left turn Olivia knew was coming—and she needed a good lead to slow down and make the turn without going for a dive.

They could see her lights before them. It was all over now. She would make the turn and beat them by a long shot.

Rule Three: Don't play nice.

Mark only saw a wind of blue fly past him on the left. Then he was graced with looking at the back of blue Koenigsegg Agera R. It was licensed "Force."

Olivia touched her left thumb to the volume button on the wheel of her car and turned off the volume, pleased with her near victory. Then it happened; something that's never happened before. Olivia was in shock. Did her eyes deceive her? This couldn't be happening! It was hurricane wind followed by the screeching of tires making her left turn before she could.

Mark and Kelly rode side by side and came to a bracing stop at a dirt patch on the right of the road across from the left turn. Olivia was in her car beating herself up for losing and the winner sat in the Force waiting for the other drivers to get out.

"He's back," Mark said climbing out of the car and glancing over at Kelly.

"Don't be a sore loser. He's always been a great driver," Rick said getting out of the car. Olivia finally worked up the courage to face the victor. She opened her door, came from the car, and closed it angrily behind herself. Who took her victory?

It was unbelievable. His dark blonde hair peaked out the door and his toned body stood next to the Force with the door still open. His arms rested in front of him on the car door. His blue eyes matched the car and night sky. Their lights lit the space around them.

"Slayer?" Olivia asked in shock. "You beat me?"

Jason smiled. Mark walked over to the best friend he had missed. It's amazing that it took the Vampire Slayer to bring him back to his normal self. Jason did walk with a stick up his butt; he also knew how to have a good time. That was before.

Maybe it was now again.

"What can I say?" he shut the door and leaned on the car.

"Who taught you how to drive?" Olivia asked. She had to be taught by the same man, woman, Slayer, person, machine...

Mark turned to look at her. "My grandfather." He smiled, rubbing Jason's head with his hand laughing.

CHAPTER 12

Control

It wasn't long before Rick was sitting in the driver's seat and Olivia was holding on for her life on the passenger seat. It took him a few days driving on the empty Eclipse back parking lot to get the hang of a manual car. Olivia offered to teach him automatic, but he was determined to race with them; and he wasn't going to beat anyone in an automatic. It took him a little longer, but he was pleased with the turn out.

Olivia needed time for herself. Now that she discovered Jason's passion for driving, she could just tell him she was going for a drive and hope he didn't want to tag along.

He didn't.

Her eyes looked up at her rear view mirror; a yellow sports car was behind following her at the same speed. Olivia pulled over to the right of the road and slowed down a little. The car behind her pulled over to the left and rolled down his window. "Running away?" a man with dirty blonde hair, tough cheekbones and blue eyes shouted.

"Something like that!" she shouted back. Olivia sped off while the man followed. Her eyes kept the continued glances at the mirrors as she looked for the man with the yellow car.

The road curved, turned, and went straight for another mile and a half. Olivia kept her speed at 95 as she dangerously followed the path of the road. After a small curve of the road, she looked up at her mirror. The man with the yellow car was no longer behind her; her foot came off the accelerator a bit and her speed dropped down to 70. Her right hand dropped from the wheel for a moment. As she reached for the mirror, Olivia spotted his headlights. The road was straight now. Avalanche Mountain was on the left. A smile formed on her lips and she stepped harder on the gas once more.

He got closer and closer until he was right next to her, window down, shouting: "To the right of the road at the end of this mile there's a dirt patch; you get there before me and I won't bother you anymore."

"You seem to be looking for a reason to race," she answered him. She had found him out and it was written on his face. "You don't need one,"

Olivia was on the right lane, he on the left. Their cars flew down the road; both of them spotted the cliff. The man cut off in front of Olivia to get a better shot at the right side of the road cliff. Olivia moved to the left and sped on. The cliff was 8 seconds away. Olivia stepped on her brakes turning her wheels to the left; her car swerved in front of his and he had no choice but to break. Her tires burned as her car went right and onto the patch of dirt. The car came to a dramatic stop a foot away from the edge. Olivia turned off her radio and got out of the car.

The man was impressed. He stood leaning on his car facing her direction. "By a foot, you would have died," he said to her.

"No, by a foot..." Olivia looked back at her car not saying by a foot she would have surfed out of the car and to safety. "By a foot, that car would have been a total loss," she smiled.

"So this is where I leave you alone?" he asked.

"I could use the company," she told him.

The sun had gone up; Olivia and the man from the yellow car sat a foot apart with their feet hanging from the cliff side. He leaned his body forward and placed his elbows on his knees, sighing. Olivia put her arms out behind her and placed her hands on the dirt. She nodded as though they had come to some agreement. The wind was blowing softly on and off. The waves crashed below them and splashed. There was fog on the ground and the car windows were wet with the night's dew.

The man let his hands hang between his legs beside his knees. Olivia looked over at him and watched him for a while. She wondered what it would be like to be human. No worries of who to fight and how to live, no troubles with family who she didn't know, and powers she couldn't control. She watched as he looked from the cliff down to where the sky met the ocean. She had wished many times that she was just like him, free to ride wherever she wanted, going from state to state, only caring about herself.

It wouldn't be such a farfetched idea. People already thought she only cared about herself. Olivia fights on Olivia's side, with her best interest in mind, forget about what her father would have thought of the nonsense she is up to all the time. No, she only thinks of herself. She doesn't care, she never will.

It's what every vampire said about her behind her back, to her face, it didn't matter.

The fear she once had from her people was fading.

The man felt her eyes on him and he turned. "I better get going," he said getting to his feet. He put out his hand to help her up. Olivia shook her head, but thanked him with a smile.

She looked to her left out to the open road that curved on the mountainside.

Olivia wanted to get up and into her car; she would drive it as far as the road took her, worry-free. She sighed. "Well… Countess, as you would say. Good luck with that problem, and whatever you decide, it's going to be the right decision," he said and began for his car.

"Todd?" Olivia spoke.

He turned to face her, "Yes?"

"I'm sorry about your girlfriend," she said gently.

Olivia wasn't looking at him but he looked away, his eyes wanting to fill with tears. "You're not to blame," he said as he headed for his car. He opened the door and got inside. "It was nice meeting you, Olivia," he spoke and shut the door. Todd drove off, leaving Olivia to decide on her own.

She pulled her phone from her right back pocket.

Olivia stood up and cleaned the dirt off her hands. She dialed Patrick to come take the car back so she could return to Trio-Genesis.

She remembered herself as a child, both her parents out in front of her on a grassy field. She would run over to her father and hug him as he picked her up in his arms. Then she would look at her mother laughing and extend out her arms to her until Savanna would take her little hands in her own then receive her from her father into her tired arms. Olivia gave Savanna a kiss on the cheek and then Savanna would tickle her beautiful baby on the side of the neck with her nose.

She opened her eyes and remembered she was still on the cliff side motherless and fatherless. She moved away from the car and walked over to the side of the cliff.

"The Elements are all connected in you and through you. To master an Element you must become the Element," she recalled the voice of Mr. B in her head.

Olivia waited a minute until Patrick came. He surfed up next to her, a tired look in his eyes, along with an, I hate you look. He yawned and rubbed his eyes. "Olivia, it's six in the morning. Ever since I gave you that stupid code, you've been undeniably reckless."

"Did you know that when you have fully mastered an element you feel it around you all the time, or you don't feel it at all because it's become so much a part of you." To him it was insanity.

Why was she standing off the side of a deep dive, teaching him about Elements? "When I master fire it will either never hurt me or I was always feel it. Same for you." She took a breath. "Do you think it means that if I master water, I'll always feel cool, or I'll be able to breathe in water without drowning myself?"

"Did you know that you made me surf all the way over here to take your car even though you can do it yourself?" he noted.

Patrick took in the deep breath and just as he did, Olivia looked back at him. "The only way to know how far you are from mastering an Element is to test your limit against it. I need you to find Jessica Trahold for me, she's a friend of a friend," she said, finally, right before she dove for the cliff side.

"Oh sweet, Lord!" he gasped. "OLIVIA!" Patrick screamed at the top of his lungs running to the cliff side. He watched her fall and fall, then he watched in horror as her body hit the water.

Patrick ran his hands through his hair. He paced the dirt, cupped his hands around his lips, and shouted her name again three times. Patrick looked up at the heavens then back down at the water. He paced some more and brushed his brows looking desperately down at the water. He would shout her name repeatedly. Nothing would come up. No sign of her, not even her floating body. Maybe the sharks ate her alive.

He was most definitely awake now. Cowering under his skin, he remembered a very important person would know Olivia was gone. He would feel it. The first person Joshua would ask would be Patrick. And what was he to say?

She was sorrowful in her thoughts of marring you, so she plunged to her death. That seemed fit. But it was hardly true. What was she rambling on about before she went for a swim? Elements… something about mastering Elements. It was possible Olivia would guinea pig herself to find how much truth was in her lessons.

"She's immortal. Olivia can't die. She's the Vampire Slayer. She's not dead…" Patrick thought frantically. "Olivia!" he screamed again looking down at the deadly water in which she wasn't coming up from. Patrick kept his eyes where Olivia had hit.

He stayed there a while waiting to see if she would surface. Something came bubbling out of the water. Patrick watched the bubbles rise. "Olivia?" A shoe surfaced. Her shoe. "Ok, Olivia! I'm leaving. No more games. I'm taking your car like you asked and I'll be waiting to see if you can manage to act like a grownup," he screamed at the waves crashing on the rocks.

Patrick looked at the water another second and left. He figured that she was long gone by then; he wasn't going to sit around and wait for her to come up out of the water. He convinced himself Olivia had surfed away right before hitting the water.

She had surfed, just not before she hit the water. She surfed into Jason's room and sat next to his sleeping body.

"Did I pee the bed?" he asked rubbing his eyes. Jason sighed; his mind was still half-asleep. He yawned; his eyes became watery. Jason continued to rub his eyes. He stopped to look at his hand where Olivia had poisoned him. The mark of the bite had disappeared, but he still felt its presence. It was now the stigma he would have to his friends; this missing mark was the proof of the deception he led.

Olivia sat there, her dark brown eyes looking deep into his mind. She focused on his evocative eyes; they were the waters she dove into. Jason noticed her retrospective look and couldn't help but awe at her.

Olivia's hand was still on his bicep where she had been grasping at to shake him senselessly out of his slumber. As the look in her eyes changed, her hand managed to travel from his arm to his shoulder.

Jason jerked his shoulder at the cold tingle in his skin; his hand moved to meet Olivia's hand where the cold sensation was coming from.

They looked into each other eyes, and for the first time, really met each other's gaze. He did nothing but look into her eyes; Olivia did nothing but return the favor. Their minds clicked together for a very short second and Olivia no longer possessed control.

"Come to me." The voice was strong. The urge to leave was immense. "Come back to me, Olivia. Come home, I want you to…" Olivia fought it as much as her body could stand. Being there next to Jason helped. He held her grounded.

"Why are you wet?" Jason asked pulling her from the trance.

"Let's come clean here," she said getting right to the point. "You and I both know you don't trust me, completely."

Small talk never made much sense to her. If you want something from someone just ask right away. Unless you need something, which you know they won't give, then by all means persuade them till the cows come home.

"If there was a way to stop me, would you trust me?"

"I'm not sure that's the definition of trust," Jason said, still groggy and growing highly upset Olivia was dripping dirty ocean water on his clean sheets. She smelled of angler and bait.

Then he noticed it. Olivia's arm was cut. She was bleeding, something very peculiar for her to do. It was a deep wound from the top of her right shoulder to the tip of the elbow. It was dirty and little particles of gray rock lain around the wound and inside the cut.

She smiled at him foolishly. "This morning I cut my arm. I took a sharp rock to it, picked it up right from the ground, germs, dirt, and all. As always, it took a while to heal. So I thought, why does that happen?"

She began explaining. The dirt infects the wound, and keeps the blood platelets from being able to close it quickly. Washing the wound, washes away the dirt; letting the blood platelets in Olivia's body rush to the healing. Water good, dirt bad.

After re-cutting her arm and going for a dive, the force of wind on the wound, plus the salt in the water, along with the very sharp rock that hit her arm when she hit the water that deepened the wound, kept the cut open longer.

The salt burned into it and the little pieces of rock stuck in it. It was red and oozing blood.

"I just woke up. Please say that all over," Jason said.

"Everyone has a weakness. The elements are mine," she said looking oddly happy about the discovery that could lead to her own destruction.

Jason laughed, "Olivia, you can't be serious. You possess all the elements. They shouldn't harm you."

"They also possess me," she said, her eyes wide with excitement.

Jason finally caught on to the idea and he jumped out of the bed. His light blue pajama pants matched everything else that was blue and white in his glassy room. His white shirt fit tight on his tone body. She couldn't help but admire him for a second as she stared right at his chest.

"What?" he asked looking down at his shirt.

She looked away. "Nothing. I was pleasantly annoyed at your love for all things in white," she lied.

"I happen to be attracted to darker women," he smiled. "Sorry," the slayer smirked at her.

Olivia rolled her eyes and cleared her throat.

Jason ran to the bathroom and began brushing his teeth. He gave her some kind of instruction to get the others and head down to one of the labs and he would find them. Most of it was a bunch of mumbles covered by a mouth full of toothpaste.

Olivia ran out of the room to collect the others.

When he reached the lab, Olivia and the others were already waiting for him.

Alison studied his toned muscles in his gray t-shirt. Jason's hair was perfectly combed to the side, like he was off to the ball to meet with Cinderella or something. The handsome gentleman.

Tom watched her silently from the other side of the metal bed Olivia was to lay on.

Jason came in talking all kinds of nonsense about elements, control, trust, power. No one really understood what he was saying until his words were more direct. "It's the only thing we'd have to stop her."

Mark chimed in knowing it was the right moment for questions. "Excuse me? Stop her from what?"

Their eyes found each other in the question; Jason and Olivia's mouths were taped shut. Locked. The thought would take them to their graves or further.

"From killing us." Alison smiled her most evil grin. "This idea is in case our little blood sucker gets too close for comfort; we have to stake her heart and make sure she doesn't magically pull it out so she can heal." Alison's words were toxic, filling the room with the energy for the raging argument that was about to come.

"To kill her?" Rick couldn't believe his ears.

He reached closer to Olivia and wrapped an arm around her. He had dubbed himself her protector, her savior, her most loyal ally. "You want us... me... because something tells me some of us have no problem with it... Alison! Anyways, you want us to summon our elements; the harshest parts of water, air, earth. Into a scientific experiment called the TIC that we can use to hurt or kill, Olivia. By slowing down the human body's natural healing process and Olivia's un-human healing process of closing a wound so that if we have to kill her she can bleed to death?"

The Countess looked up at Rick. When he put it like that it was kind of hard to want to go through with something so destructive.

"How many of you honestly trust Olivia?" Jason shocked them to silence.

His face changed as he walked to the table with a syringe and gloves. Jason pulled on the gloves and turned over to Olivia who rested comfortably in Rick's arms. The guy would bench press a cow for Olivia, all she had to do was ask. Jason waited; after no one spoke, he took the syringe and elastic to wrap around Olivia's arm for blood. They watched him approach the Countess and her trusty beach babe.

"Get that thing away from her." Rick's arm came across Olivia's body. He was her human shield. Through thick and thin, Rick would give his life for her; he already made that very clear to everyone. He turned to look at Olivia, whose pondering mind kept her from deciding whether to go through with the deadly idea. "I trust you, Olivia," he whispered to her.

Those words moved her. People like Rick trusted Olivia; wanted the best for her and cared for her safety. There were many people like Rick at the Mansion; many Olivia didn't know. But they were there. And it was for those people she wanted this.

Olivia looked up at him, Rick's eyes begged her not to do it. "If I ever were to hurt you…"

"You wouldn't," he pleaded. "I wouldn't let you. I'd take myself out of equation before you had the chance," he confessed. It's like he knew her soul and the thoughts in her mind. Rick loved Olivia like a brother loves a sister; he treated her like family, which was much more than could be said for another in the room.

She moved from around him and sat on the bed so Jason could take her blood.

There was no turning back from it if he took that blood. He would do it with or without her permission after that. "I want to do this," Olivia said finally. That's all he needed.

Rick backed away from the bed. "I won't be here for it, then," he said and walked out into the hall.

Kelly looked over at Jason and understood she should go retrieve him. Jason tied the elastic around Olivia's arm and was ready to take blood.

The TIC would contain salt water, acid rain water, rock and stone particles, dry hot air, and her blood. It was tricky conjuring these certain elements and placing them in such a small environment.

Jason removed the needle from her arm; instantly the small hole closed. He topped off the little vile of blood which contained the blood vampires would only dream to get their fangs on, and then took note. The effects of the elements worked only on the spot in which they lay.

Her wounded arm sat on the side of the bed, resting uncomfortably waiting to be cleaned or banged—anything that would take the pain away. Tom noticed the uneasiness in her eyes, pulled up a stool, and sat by her and the wound.

Inspecting it, he asked Alison for a sponge and some water.

That was Tom's gift; he was very handy with the sick, the wounded, and the helpless. If born a human he would have fallen into medicine very quickly, would have made a hell of doctor or surgeon. But here he was, an Air Head, using his natural born skills to heal his enemy.

Tom loved that about medicine: no matter who it is, no matter how much you might despise them, at the very moment, all that matters is saving their lives. There was a certain point when the enemy became the grateful ally, and the ally a bitter enemy.

Tom cleaned the wound, and what was left to heal healed right before their eyes. Mark made his way over to Jason who was already looking at Olivia's blood through a microscope and writing things down.

"Please tell me we are making an antidote." Mark took the attention from his friend.

"These aren't to be used in case she's throwing a tantrum," Jason said looking at his friend. Mark's mind kept filling with unanswered questions.

"If it gets into the wrong hands…" he started but Jason cut him off, assuring him it wouldn't. No one else would know but them. It was a way for them to protect themselves. Mark couldn't object that Olivia could be dangerous. But in his heart, he knew good intentions could always be turned around.

The door opened and Rick walked back in with Kelly. He still disagreed with the procedure, but Kelly convinced him it's what Olivia wanted; he couldn't disapprove of Olivia's wishes.

As soon as he reentered the room, Rick asked the same question Mark did. Would there be an antidote? Jason explained once again, loud and clear for everyone to hear this time.

This wasn't an object they would be testing on Olivia for fun. It was a serious poison that would infect her body, either letting her bleed to death or making its way to her heart and pumping it through her system and poisoning her to death. It wasn't a game or a toy. It would be secured safely on to every one of them; only to be used if the occasion called for it. That was enough to get even Tom worked up.

"Suppose one of these vials break and the glass cuts her and TICs make their way into her flesh. Out of complete accident, we've just killed the Vampire Slayer and started a war," Tom stated.

It wasn't a likely scenario that this would happen. Humans accidentally die every day. If it's her time to go then it's her time to go. That didn't work either, because they weren't people. Someone doesn't accidentally die from poison; it's completely intentional. They argued; the odd part was seeing Olivia and Jason on the same side.

"How are we going to test it?" Kelly asked stopping all the voices from further sounds.

Jason opened his mouth but words didn't come out. He exhaled instead and looked down at Olivia who was enjoying the argument more than the attention.

"How do we know if works for sure, lest we test it on her? And if we do test it, which is necessary considering what this is going to be, we don't want to kill her to know it works. So we have to make an antidote. If only for the sake of knowing it really works," the nimble girl pointed out.

Jason finally agreed, but only if the antidote had to be kept in a certain temperature that they wouldn't be allowed to carry or it would be useless. It would make them more cautious with the TICs knowing they'd have to go back for the antidote with only seconds to spare of Olivia's life.

So it was settled. They would work on the poison, and would fix up an antidote.

Jason walked back to the vial of blood he had taken from Olivia. Jason gave orders. "Mark, take Olivia to her room. We'll come for her when we're ready."

"Excuse me?" Olivia questioned him without hesitating.

Jason walked over to her and looked her square in the eyes, "If you want to destroy your enemy, would you keep him in the room as you discuss with others your plans for his downfall?"

It made sense. She didn't have an argument. Olivia didn't want Mark to escort her out either. She could take herself to her room. Actually, she can do whatever she wanted for a few hours while none of them would be supervising her.

As soon as her back was out the door Jason locked the room and they began working. Jason, Mark, and Alison worked on the TICs, while Tom was in charge of making the antidote with Rick and Kelly. The three antidote markers decided without Jason's permission they would make something that could be held at any temperature but would be more effective cold because it could be injected into her veins. The warmer version of the antidote could be rubbing on the wound to keep the TICs from spreading until the cold injection could be applied.

Jason took out a jar, blew into it and closed it off quickly. He placed the air into the heater and kept it there for an hour. He did this several times with different jars until he became lightheaded from his output of air. While the air cooked, he sat down in front of the computer and worked on fixing the setting so that the elements could be mixed by machine and so that very small drops of the final product could be freeze dried and safe to carry.

On the other side of the room, Mark took the dirt from the bottom of a shoe and blended throne bushes. The sound was irritating and the hairs on his back were standing. Goosebumps rolled down his arms and legs. Alison came over and took him to fill the blender with hot salt water. It would help the noise, blend it faster, and make the mix more deadly.

Acid rain was hard to conjure up, but Alison knew where there was sure to be some in the province of Saskatchewan, Canada. Their northern lakes had been proven to have acid rain. She surfed off quickly and came back with two gallons of it. She knew she wouldn't need that much, but it brought her comfort bringing back something that would help kill Olivia.

Once the computer was set to mix the elements and liquefy them to then freeze them, Jason walked over to check the progress everyone else had done.

Since the elements were also part of Olivia, they would use the same thing that killed her to treat her.

Rick knew were the best springs were hidden around the mountains and rocks; he collected water from these fountains and heated them to body temperature.

Kelly collected Aloe Vera and Yarrow; it was all she would need. The gel from the Aloe Vera plant would block infections and coat the wound, while the powder from Yarrow leaves would help stop the bleeding. Just to be safe, she also mixed together St. Johns Wort to increase the healing process.

Tom's job seemed the silliest of them all; he had little jars that he opened and closed once air was let in. He did this by the window; the basic idea was to collect fresh air as to air out a wound.

They mixed gels and powder from the plants with the fresh air and spring water. After cooling it, Tom removed some from the refrigerator for testing. To test the antidote Tom placed Olivia's blood under the microscope and watched its reaction when the mix they created was dropped on the blood. It was missing something, the blood was reacting faster, but not fast enough to rush over and heal a wound and kill the poison. But to know what it was missing they needed the completed TICs.

When the machines mixed the boiled air, blends of earth, acid and salt water together, Jason walked over to the glass of deadly-looking brown goo and dropped his own homemade mix of holy water. If nothing they had mixed killed her, the holy water should take the part of Olivia that is vampire and chill her blood.

He was happy with the reaction of the holy water with the brown goo. It boiled and turned black. All that was left to do was freeze dry it into little balls smaller than a millimeter so they could carry small vials full of them.

On skin, the TICs would be harmless; Olivia would able to hold them right in her hand. But if she were stabbed with a stake covered in TICs, death would come quickly.

Their gooey consistence was so they could stick to wood, metal, and silver. The TICs had to be held in glass vials for it would eat away at plastic. It's like they were still alive.

The machine made strange noises as the black slime went through it and was dropped through very small holes into trays and then placed into the freeze dryer. Once the first batch was done, Jason took one small TIC with a pair of tweezers and dropped in a glass vial where the remaining contents of Olivia's blood rested.

The blood boiled in the glass. Tom brought some of the antidote over and placed some drops into the boiling blood. Its boiling slowed down but it wasn't enough.

They watched it. If they couldn't come up with an antidote they couldn't use the TICs. It was already agreed on. All their hard work would be destroyed.

Mark walked away from the others and over to the antidote in the refrigerator.

The five were busy thinking of ways to make the antidote stronger, going over what the three had done and what they could do to counter the effects. Mark opened the large jar with the liquid antidote, took the knife he always carried on his belt and cut his hand. He let the blood fall into the jar and mixed it carefully not to make any noise. Once mixed, he took a needle and filled it.

"Try this." Mark said giving the needle to Jason. He didn't understand, but he trusted his friend and put two drops of the new antidote into the boiling of the blood under the microscope. It boiled faster and then it stopped. They were silenced.

"It's perfect," Jason said. All eyes were on Mark. What could he have possibly done to make it work?

"It wasn't mixed," Mark convinced them with his silence. His bloody hand was in his front pocket. "It works. I'll go get Olivia," he said and surfed out of room in quite the rush. Outside he inspected his hand and went over to the medical wing to get it patched up. Hopefully no one suspected anything.

He sat patiently waiting to be taken care off. It was just like a real hospital, except everyone had a chart from day one in Trio-Genesis.

There were the sick, the wounded, the ER, the visiting quarts, even prenatal care.

He sat in the ER waiting room and soon enough his name was called. Mark went into a small white room where his temperature was taken, his blood pressure checked, his vitals looked at, and finally, his hand stitched, by none other than his father who said very few words to him.

The hallways on the 37th floor were empty; the creaking coming from the floor echoed loudly in the silence. He walked down to Olivia's door and knocked gently on it. Mark heard a fuss in the room and knocked again. A minute or two went by, the doorknob turned, and the door opened.

She looked at him with sleepy eyes. Her hair was down around her face, her eyes were glassy and her skin white. She was still in the same dirty clothes, but they were now dry and wrinkled. Olivia rubbed eyes and yawned. "What time is it?"

"We've finished. We need you," Mark said looking behind her to see the mess in the room. The sheets were on the floor, the drawers were open, and there was broken glass next to the still misplaced bed in the very odd temporary bedroom. It looked like a battlefield. "Olivia, what happened?" He pushed her door to look in better. She stood in the doorway and pulled the door shut.

"I'm a messy vampire," she lied and looked into his eyes. Mark couldn't be more awake. Olivia looked drugged out. "Let's not keep them waiting," she said and started walking away.

He saw her white socks and mentioned to her she had no shoes on, but Olivia didn't care. Shoes weren't a problem right now. Mark caught up to her and surfed them down to the front of the door of the lab. He knocked five times and the lock was undone. Jason opened the door and the two walked in.

"What took you so long?" Alison asked right away giving Olivia cold hard stares.

"It's 1 a.m. princess. Get off your high horse. I was in bed," Olivia answered. They couldn't believe it was that late. The whole day went by and they did this. It was insane. They hadn't even eaten.

Olivia was a little off balance; her eyes blood shot. She wasn't acting normal and her body kept getting the urge to leave.

"It's one in the morning?" the blonde girl shouted. She was furious; she wasted a whole day, a day she would never get back, helping Olivia. Well, helping to kill her. But now that they had made an antidote it wasn't the same. If they got Olivia back to it fast enough for a cold dose of it, she would live. She would be in pain and a little off for a few days, but she'd live.

They took the time Mark took to bring her back, to fill up all the vials with the red sticky liquid. Amazing enough after all the mixing even without Mark's blood, the antidote still came out red.

"I'm not picking sides here, Jason. But it's late, let's get this over with," Kelly said. He nodded. They were well aware of the time. He looked over at Tom and Alison, who was extremely happy at what she was about to do. They had cleared a space in the middle of the lab. Jason glanced at Rick.

"Can we just cut her and kill her already?" Alison asked bluntly enough to twist Olivia's arm a little further than she should have.

"Wow, well. Don't hold anything back!" Olivia barked at her.

"Fine, I won't." Then Alison walked right up to Olivia and slapped her in the face.

The mark of her hand rested on Olivia's cheek as her hand brushed the spot. Olivia looked at the others as if to ask for a little bit of back up, but it wasn't coming.

So she did what any girl would do: called her a female dog and raised her fist to punch her on the jaw line. Jason caught her hand and pushed her back. Olivia's body came colliding with Mark. He held her up.

Alison looked over at Jason as he gave her full permission to drown the half-sleeping Countess. Alison flew on Olivia, the lioness. Her hands came crashing on Olivia's soft face. Mark pulled Alison off the vampire girl and pushed her back at the others. Olivia was fired up she began fighting the blonde, little by little the others started to help Alison.

Mark was so confused, he didn't know who to help; so he did what made most sense to his heart and fought side by side with Olivia. It was the first time he got the chance to defend her this way, and it brought him a great sense of meaning now.

Olivia was having too much fun winning. Jason grabbed Mark's arms behind him and spoke in his ear. "Go along with it," he hushed his friend. Mark stopped and looked at Jason. He trusted the man with his life so he stopped helping her and nodded in agreement.

"They're gone, Olivia!" Alison screamed. She stopped hand in the air with a fireball. Olivia froze in her steps and looked into Alison's blue eyes across the room. "Your mother is dead because of you. Your father? That poor man. Didn't he die trying to save your life?" She kept the words coming, sharp knifes hitting Olivia where it hurt most.

"You parents couldn't stand the sight of a Halfer, they would rather die than be with you. How proud you must be. Not even the people who are supposed to love you the most can stand to look at you," Kelly said.

"And all this time, you've done nothing. You're not even worth enough to avenge their death, or does family honor even matter to you?" Jason spoke.

This was getting the job done much faster. "That's right, you never had a family. They died before you learned what that was," Jason said before she released the fireball in her hand at him. The flame had already been dying in her hand. When the ball was close enough Jason just blew it out like a candle.

"What would your father say? You here, fighting against your own people?" Tom asked her. Olivia looked at Mark for help.

"He would be so disappointed," Rick added.

They couldn't have meant any of those things, but they seemed awfully true in the state she was in.

"No one wanted you," the blonde laughed. "And no one wants you now. Not here, not there. That's why you stick around with us, isn't it? Little Countess Olivia doesn't have any friends of her own. You're pathetic. You're worthless, Countess…" Alison said mocking her title.

"You know very well this TIC idea is suicide, but that's what you want: to die. You're all alone and you think that if you die you'll go and be with your parents in heaven…" The smile on her face was satisfactory. It was everything Alison had ever wanted to say to an enemy. Maybe she meant some of them, maybe she didn't; but coming from her, Olivia would never know what was meant that night and what was a cruel joke.

"That's enough, Alison," Jason spoke noticing Olivia's red eyes. She was going to blow at any minute, and if Olivia blew up no one would hold her back.

"But guess what, darling? They won't want you there either. The devil doesn't want you. You're a reject. Don't give that sob-faced look, you know it's true; deep down, you know it. None of us actually care about you. Think about it: has any one come to look for you? Their precious Countess missing for months now… no one came. They are happy you're gone." She laughed with every ounce of evil in her body. "They wanted you out! They left you, Olivia!

In the Park! On the Island! Here…" Alison smiled coldly glaring daggers at Olivia.

Her eyes were watery and her fangs had come from their hiding place. Alison had her right where she wanted her. Alison needed her to feel pain, to lose all control, to try to kill her; then they would all see the monster Olivia was.

"That's enough, Alison! I said stop!" Jason hushed. He looked at Olivia who began running to attack Alison, he put his hand out in front of her, air came out of his palms and it hit Olivia, pushing her back; she didn't fall, but it kept her from walking for a while.

"I'm not DONE! But you are… aren't you Brook?" Alison said, and the moment she did, she wished the words would come back into her big mouth.

Olivia broke from Jason's wall, pushed him aside, and jumped on the blonde.

Olivia didn't bite her or hit her with any fire. She could have burned her to death or sucked her dry. But this was much more satisfying.

She punched her face and slapped her soft checks as she screamed into her ears. There was blood coming from Alison's mouth and nose; she could feel Olivia's weight on her lungs.

Alison pulled a dagger from her pouch and stabbed Olivia on the side. The vampire screamed. Jason pulled Olivia off Alison. He held her back while Tom helped the bleeding blonde to her feet. Jason ordered Kelly to get the TICs from the freezer. She popped out a handful, he pulled his hand away from her wound, and received the TICS into his blood-filled hand.

"I'm sorry," he whispered the words as he placed his hand back on the still open wound. Olivia screamed and Jason let her body fall to the floor.

They watched her body sprawl on the floor and heard the Countess scream. Jason picked her up and placed her on the bed. Olivia was shaking, her body was cold and her skin became ghostly.

It was boiling on the skin around the wound, burning layers of skin, slowly cutting into the flesh. Tom and Rick held her body down. Jason felt her pulse and it was fading.

"Mark, the antidote," Jason said awaking the slayer, who stood in shock.

He ran over to the refrigerator to the antidote. Hold on, Olivia, he kept thinking.

Mark filled a syringe with the liquid from the vial and ran back over to Olivia's dying body, injecting the needle into her veins. The blood ran in her veins like a strong current on the water. The current rushed to the wound on her side. Olivia's back lifted off the table as she gasped for air, screaming a blood-curdling screech that echoed in their ears. The wound boiled around the black TICS then closed with a soft blue light.

The blood she had lost lain on the side on the bed and the puddle was untouched on the floor. Jason blew a soft cool breeze on her face and felt for a pulse.

CHAPTER 13

A New Plan

It was always dark outside the big Mansion gates, for only dark deeds happened inside.

The Mansion was busy in preparation for The Countess' birthday. The fact that she wasn't around didn't count as reason enough to keep from celebrating.

Every year her birthday was celebrated differently. The year of her 16th birthday, she had a big, out-of-control bash. It was a large beach party on the very same beach Olivia found herself this year. It was the year they built a garage for all her cars. Last year her party had a theme: the seven deadly sins. This year the theme would be masquerade, a fascinating idea considering many vampires took this as a costume party.

Olivia loved the idea of a room full of people in ball gowns and black ties with their faces covered, hidden from the world. It was mysterious without being cliché. To her at least. And it kept the atmosphere light. She needed that. With each passing birthday, she had something more dramatic.

The words "Happy Birthday" were never used at the Mansion. There was nothing to be joyous for. The 29th of October was a day of grieving. Olivia never celebrated anything on the 29th of October. She kept to herself. And then two days after the 29th, she celebrated turning a year older.

Every vampire prepared for the celebration. It was still a few days away, but the Mansion was large and it took a lot of time to get the whole place ready for any event.

Joshua Lenson, came from the forbidden corridors.

"It was delightful, Michael," he breathed out to his friend. "The look on his face once he heard everything and how it all was progressing. It's like he could hear me." It was a dream come true for Joshua.

"I might be selfish, but sometimes it's who you need to be to get a job done. I have the best for us in the end." He sighed in relief. "She's going to hate me, but she'll change her mind once she sees all I've done. For both of us. Besides, sometimes being around her around is…"

"Unbearable? Suffocating?" Michael jumped in for the help.

"Yes!"

They walked down the long hall discussing the estate of the project that Joshua was so pleased with, conversing about the missing Countess; how she would be back soon for her par… celebration.

They walked down further and started noticing decorations and ribbons. Dark shades of crimson spread throughout the walls and down the halls.

"Had my father passed on my birthday, I'd skip the celebration too." Joshua touched the velvet cloth as he passed.

Olivia didn't mind others having parties on their birthdays. She encouraged it if they remembered the date or cared enough to do so.

Patrick's birthday never went forgotten. He never had a party, but Olivia always took him out. As for Joshua's big day, he never remembered the right date or where his birth certificate was placed so he could check. Were it not for Olivia, his birthday would go by without thought. She always got him presents and delicious foods. His birthday was the third largest event that happened every year, and the attendants went out of fear.

His egregious deeds were what made every vampire frightened of him. Behind closed doors, Olivia never knew what Joshua was up to. And unlike only slightly harmful Olivia, fully harmful Joshua was not being as gracious. The residents were panicked.

He found a sick liking to people standing for him when he entered and left a room. He enjoyed hearing his own name out of the mouth of every vampire he crossed by. He liked having his coffee brought to him in the morning, and enjoyed the bodies of vampires moving out of the way on his account. Joshua didn't tell any of them to do this, but he said that his treatment would be the same, if not better than the treatment, Countess Olivia received.

To the Mansion, there was a likely chance the Countess was dead somewhere, killed by her own Joshua, in thirst and lust for power. "A lime tree will only produce sour limes," one Janitor said to the other. "Only sour limes," he would say, cleaning the black floors with the dirty mops. "Ugly children don't have parents." He laughed to the janitor working at his side.

It's true what he said about the ugly children. No one claims the troublemakers as their kids or wants to be the parent who gave a bad seed to the world.

That's what some would say Joshua was: a bad seed. No one really loved him, but that didn't affect the way he turned out. He was an evil little boy from the day he was born. He was a sour lime from the moment he was on the tree. He was the ugly child no one claimed.

He was walking into the meeting room with the long table. All who had to be there already were. Joshua sat in Olivia's chair and Michael took his left side. Joshua sat there for a second taking in all the expressions on each face. Another body was missing as well. Patrick was not told about the meeting.

While some smiled and smirked, others crossed their arms over their chest, biting their jaws down.

The room was quiet; from the far left, all the way at the end of the table, a vampire coughed. It was the last thing he did before he was ashes on the ground. No one moved. Joshua pulled back his hand and put it in his pocket. His mouth opened but no words came out. Joshua took in a breath and exhaled.

"We are living in new times. Our numbers grow and then suddenly decrease; this process repeats year after year. Why is that?" the self-appointed Count Joshua asked haggard faces.

He spun around and got up from his chair. "For some time now, I believed everything was every man for himself. Hop on the life boats, screw the women and children," he said as he began to walk around.

"With all of our intelligence, strength, and willpower, we are still losing men." Joshua reached where the man's ashes laid. "We try to overpower each other, we try to outsmart one another. We kill each other. This!" he said pointing to the ashes on the ground, "this is why we decrease in numbers! We push buttons, until one of us just... pops."

His voice echoed in the room as he walked around once again.

"We fight for food. They fight to keep us starved. The only difference is we fight each other also." He sat back down.

Spinning around in Olivia's chair, he felt the leather on the arm rest. Joshua touched his hand to his face and then picked the corner of his eyes. "I may have put in motion a few changes." He grinned at Michael. "Changes, some of you might not agree with. But as your new leader," he paused to see if anyone would disagree, "I'm afraid they had to be done. I've spoken to your fearless Countess and she gave me this signature."

Michael pulled out a scroll from his jacket pocket and opened it, showing everyone Olivia's name written in her prefect cursive. Above her name were the words, I hereby grant all powers to Joshua E. Lenson in the duration of my absences. All powers are stripped from Patrick Knight Tyler and all members of the court until my return.

Olivia B. Montgomery

"All powers have been relinquished to me."

The room rose with gasps and frowned eyes.

"Until further notice..." Joshua smirked an evil smile and tapped his fingers on the table.

The voices of the vampires were a panic fire in the forest, with the roar of hurricane winds, and tones of a beached whale.

Joshua silenced the men and women and proceeded to explain the forthcoming plans.

CHAPTER 14

First Time

Olivia opened her eyes, to meet an ocean of blues in front of her. She gasped and sat up on the bed quickly.

Her head collided with Jason's forehead making a thump sound. He stepped back a little, rubbing his head asking Olivia if she was okay.

She looked around the room. Her vision was blurry. "Great. I'm going to need glasses."

The slayer laughed and explained she must wait for her eyes to adjust to the light awhile. She hated waiting. Her voice was raspy and dry, so she asked for some water. It was already next to the bed. Jason poured her a glass and Olivia drank like a mermaid.

She kept blinking and rubbing her eyes. She worked on looking at closer objects and found the rip on the side of her shirt were Alison had stabbed her before.

The blouse was covered in her rich, red, blood; still moist but no longer sticking to her body. She ran her hand alongside the rip as she felt for a cut. The skin was completely healed.

The blood puddle on the floor was cleaned up, but the red stains remained on the white tiles. She then looked off to the side were the others were mixing chemicals and elements again.

"It didn't work?" she asked, almost certain of what Jason would say back.

He shook his head and scratched the side of his eye. His hand moved in front of his mouth and rested on his upper lip. Jason gazed off into the distance. He looked back at the others, hard at work.

The handsome slayer took a deep breath. "Mark was right. It's too dangerous." He exhaled a long breath he had been holding. His eyes moved to meet hers. "You've been out cold for the last four hours. You hardly had a pulse. There were times it looked as though you weren't breathing. It's too strong, so we're mixing up a new batch."

So it worked; there wasn't a problem. They were a bunch of cowards trying to help her. They've killed before, why worry about killing now? They must really like her at this point if they don't even want to keep the only drug that can kill her as strong as they have it. This wouldn't be a problem at the Mansion. Vampires had more backbone then these skimpy little fools.

Olivia looked at him and laughed. She got up from the bed. "I'm sorry, I didn't know lethal poison should be less harmful," she turned to Jason. "We don't need a new batch. What are we going to do, make one to kill me less?"

"You were unconscious for hours!" Mark dropped his work.

"If it's meant to kill me, I should be unconscious forever."

Alison couldn't help but agree. Her black eye and swollen lip didn't disagree either. Olivia looked at the blonde and shook her head. Sure she hated her, but she didn't have to beat her face off. Now she had to look at her, and she looked uglier than before.

Of course that wasn't true. Alison was a beautiful slayer; even magical looking.

Stunning eyes, the perfect oval face, and glowing skin.

"This is what we wanted."

She walked over to Alison and rose her hand to the blonde's forehead. Olivia's hand hovered over Alison's eye. A soft blue light came from the palm of Olivia's hand. Alison jerked her body back slightly, grunting and closing her eyes.

"Hold still," the vampire ordered friendly.

When she removed her hand, the bruises from Alison's face had gone.

There wasn't a mirror for the blonde to see the magic, but the uneasy feeling of her eye coming off the socket was no more. Sure, she wasn't Olivia's biggest fan, but she wasn't her worst enemy either. "If the enemy gets their hands on the poison and one of us isn't there to hit you with a handful of antidote, until we can get you back to Trio-Genesis, you will die."

There was stillness in the room. They shared many of these moments when the air wasn't comfortable around them and walls seemed to be listening.

"This is what we made, this is what we have. We work with what we have." Olivia didn't wait for an argument.

She excused herself by saying she wanted to rest before class and they should as well. The others were left to maul over the truth.

They had in their hands a powerful weapon for those who pledged their allegiance to her. They also had a powerful weapon against their most powerful weapon.

In the wrong hands all of the weapons would be used for ultimate power and destruction.

Once in her quarters, Olivia made her way over to the bed, which she built in the middle of the open area.

She hadn't yet sorted through the boxes, or looked around the complex long enough to discover its three floors, suites, private library, and living spaces to spare.

All she had done was move the bed to a wall, gotten the water in the bathroom fixed so she could bathe, and moved her clothes and dresser to the open space where the bed was. There she sat on the gray sheets, she took from her previous room, exhausted and fatigued.

She used all her energy to turn Alison's face into a punching bag.

"So worth it." Olivia looked at her blood-splattered fist—finally being able to take her by the hair and make her bleed from the mouth, almost begging for mercy.

But she revoked the blue glow coming from that same hand. The hand used to hurt she also used to heal.

Olivia dropped the rest of her weight on the bed and closed her eyes, automatically pulling the puffy comforter over her body and rolling on her stomach. There wasn't much time, but she used the few moments to rest some more. Sleeping on a lab table was not the same as her queen size mattress. And her queen size mattress was not the same as her king size, plush, memory form, mattress kept at the mansion.

The sky was bright and the blinds were open in the classroom.

Ms. Browse sat on her chair calling students up to present their paper on a famous vampire, written in first person.

She gave her students many papers that she did not grade. They were merely to occupy them as she prepared for the real assignment. This year, the personal essay was said assignment.

Student upon student bored the Countess to death. They were ill informed, and some just pathetic—the cocky boy, for example, who went up in front of the class with a paragraph about Dracula:

"I was a disturbed creature. Lurking in the darkness. Thirsty for the blood of man. Before my death took me, I married a breathtaking angel, whose wings were as wide as an ocean and as deep as the sea." He tried very hard to be poetic. "Savanna, I called her. Her name was a beautiful trance. In this unity we gave birth to a daughter, with whom I find no comfort, as I wait in my tomb to be resurrected by my little angel."

Olivia raised an eyebrow at Ms. Browse.

"Touching, Jeffery. Not the proper length, but touching. C minus."

"What about lack of intelligence? What grade does he get for that?" the Countess asked loudly.

The students laughed in unison.

"Ms. Morton. Since you're so inclined to speak, why don't you go next?"

She stood and started walking down towards the front. "Ms. Morton...Your paper," she reminded her. "Unless you memorized it,"

The class chuckled again.

Olivia turned back and took the notebook from a top her desk; she opened to a blank page in the middle and held the white paper against her chest as she walked down again.

She turned and looked around the room then down at her paper.

"My parents met in battle," she snickered. "A common place to meet where I come from. Only there was nothing common about my mother. Her name was Savanna; was, because she has already joined the afterlife."

Olivia looked up to see if anyone was listening. Some eyes were on her, others gazed into the light of the window, and some drooled in their sleep. The rude students joked in the back.

"My father, too, has passed. His tragic end came at the hand of his most trusted ally. I still remember it." Her eyes blanked into the back of the room. "The raging voices coming from the room. I couldn't move. I felt the blood freeze in my chest and I could hear the echo of his words as he ran in front of me. There I stood helpless and useless; waiting for the end that was enviably coming." There wasn't a breath in her speech or a pause in her movement.

She went on. "David's eyes filled with hate, regret, sorrow, and misery. All I could think was why I hadn't moved. Why I was incapable of stepping inches to my left or to my right," every eye was on her now.

"It was different when my mother died. There was no cure for whatever illness she had. But that night, with my Dad laying there, his shattered eyes looking up at me, his broken voice whispering 'run...'" Here, she paused and looked down at her paper again.

"I could have stopped it," Olivia said quickly combing the hair from her face. "There's not a day that passes that I do not wonder if he would have been proud of me now. And I would give anything," she said breathlessly, "to hear him say it one time. That I'd let it ring in my ears forever."

The bell rang as it always does and the bodies stood conventionally. They walked passed her, not giving the slightest glance at her face.

She turned for Ms. Browse. "B. Minus," she said nodding from her chair. "A bit disappointing, might I add,"

"Excuse me?"

"Had I asked Mr. Sharpie to write a paper on himself and his tragedies, I'm sure he would too excel," Browse said as Jason walked by stopping at the sound of his name.

"You're wrong," the slayer quietly spoke without turning. Their heads lifted in Jason's direction. "I would never open myself to people I know."

"No one knows Mr. Sharpie."

"I do. So do you." Jason finally looked. "Brook, we only have an hour for lunch and I thought the team could have a quick practice, let's bouce," Jason said to excuse the two from the prying teacher.

The Countess did not pass down the invitation. Now, this was more like it. She was getting some respect back. Not from everyone, but from the people who mattered at least. Not that Jason mattered.

Olivia skipped lunch and headed else where once she was out of the class rooms door.

The grass was covered by the orange and red leaves. Some green patches were spotted here and there. The bark on the trees was dark brown and wet from the rainy week.

It was empty.

There were no visitors on Wednesday, or any other day of the week. Most of the residents were dead for a second time and their loss carried no meaning. But for those people with families, the graves were visited. New flowers brought in once a year, nothing fancy. Unless the vampire visiting a grave was Olivia.

A large pond graced the center of the cemetery with a red maple tree growing from an uplifted island in the middle of the pond. Tall, black, decorative iron fencing surrounded from every side. Marvelous tombstones in all shapes filled the fields.

Dracula's tombstone was a simple marble black engraved with 24k gold letters.

There was a hole for flowers, which Olivia never brought. The disturbing smell of dead roses mixed in the dirty rainwater; it was only adding insult to injury. Colorful flowers for the dead, flowers that would die by the dead, then replaced by the living. It was a waste of a beautiful, God-made creation.

Today the wind was still and the clouds covered the skies. Only a moment ago, when she sat in class, the sun couldn't be any more radiant. Not here; it was always cold and gloomy. The sun did not shine on the dead souls of the lost, cursed creatures who fed on the blood of innocent people. Maybe it was the shadow of the mansion, the cemetery was horribly close to the dark building.

Olivia was in for a rude awakening when visiting his grave. She would share her days with him, her stories, her pain, her laughter, but he had nothing to give in return. She never left that place with a smile on her face, and she never surfed out near his grave. It was rude to be there and the next minute be gone. If she could one day find death and was given the chance to rest, she would rather no one surf in and out of her grave. Why bother coming if one is in such a rush to leave?

Although sadness struck her when she came to visit, she wasn't complete without her moments by his gold-plated name.

One day it would bring her trouble. The walls have ears, the trees are spies, and the grass is a large recording device taping all of their conversations. All her secrets could be heard here. If followed, Olivia would be giving up every truth and every lie. The damage her truth could do would be irrevocable.

She had been lethargic, all her energy put into her plans, and today she lacked vigor. She never had gone so long without visiting. Were it not for her "paper" she might not have come. No, her birthday was close. She would come.

Why do people visit graves? All it does is bring up old memories that they shared with a loved one. They visit and leave melancholy. Would these people want others to be crying at the grave site day and night? Or ever?

"I want people to remember me and laugh," she once told Patrick.

Patrick, on the other hand, didn't find meaning in being remembered, especially if he ended up in hell. "Let's suppose there is a God who created everything. If I'm lucky enough to end up where He is, I don't want to be missed. I would be in such a wonderful place. I'll go far enough to say I don't want anyone wearing black at my funeral."

"What should we wear?" She sipped her drink and he sipped on his.

"Pink?"

Patrick put down his glass. "What a marvelous idea!"

"I hate pink."

"But if I'm not lucky enough." He looked around at the emptiness of Eclipse. "I hear hell is a giant pit of horrid anguish. Weeping and gnashing of teeth." He shivered. "...if I end up there, don't sit at home crying and remembering me. I'd rather you spend your time discovering how to keep out of hell." He chugged his drink and started to clean up.

"There is," he paused, "one person I would miss. I don't know what I would do if said person died. Think I would lose my mind." He lifted her chin. "So don't go dying before I do." He smiled sweetly.

Olivia looked back down at her empty glass, and when she looked up she was sitting on the leaves by Dracula's grave again.

"Hi dad." Her mouth spoke the words but her ears did not receive the message.

Olivia sat there playing with the leaves on the ground.

"I never have new words to give you. I wish you were here," she mumbled in between her breaths. "It's hard to decide what to do next. I made a promise to a room full of people. I know if you were here, things would be different. I can never say or do the right thing and every day it's more difficult to remember your voice, to recall your face." The lump on her throat had grown to a nice size rock.

"I'm almost 20. I... I'm not celebrating this birthday again. In your honor. There was a hot summer this year; hardly ever rained. The roses were crimson red. Mom would have loved a garden... I think." Olivia looked at the ground and ran her hands over her blue jeans. "I didn't bring any flowers, sorry. You know when things are going so well you keep waiting for the other shoe to drop? I helped them to construct a powerful poison to destroy me. If the time comes, they will use it. It's their only chance." Her head was a messy pile of word vomit!

"I haven't raked any leaves this year. I remember you used to take me out back and we'd rake the leaves so I could jump in them. You said it helped me grow. Didn't understand that until a few weeks ago." She giggled and tossed a few leafs up.

When the leaves stopped falling she blew at the ground and they flew up again.

Olivia stood and rotated quickly, moving the leaves around her in a hurricane motion. She danced, hopped, and a real laugh even escaped her lips.

The figure of a man watched her from a fat tree with arms crossed over his chest. "Never pegged you for a dancer," he stated.

She stopped and armed herself with fire at his direction.

"Easy there, Pocahontas. It's just me." The handsome slayer ruined every moment she had of joy.

"What are you doing here?" her smiled faded and voice panicked. Her checks and nose were red. Strands of hair fell on her face and over her eyes. Olivia pushed back some pieces with her hand and fixed her shirt.

"I asked you a question."

He didn't say a thing, but his eyes never pulled away from hers. He kept moving closer and closer to her. He noted that she wasn't moving. It seemed as though he had the power this time around. Oh sweet revenge!

"Are you going to answer me, or are you just going to attack me like a psycho?"

"You looked terribly depressed this morning," he said stopping a foot away from her. "Aren't you cold?"

She had goose bumps up and down her body. He moved closer to her and rubbed her arms with his warm hands.

"How did you find me? How much did you hear?" The word vomit was rising again.

"Nothing. By the time I found you in this hell hole, you were already putting on a good show," he admitted.

"I asked you two questions not one."

"I thought about you, about being wherever you were. Hoped it would work." He looked around, "I'm glad it did."

She wasn't. He was dangerously close to the mansion, it wasn't in sight but it was walking distance and just over the hill behind them. At any given moment a vampire could stroll by to visit a grave, and the slayer would be gravy.

"You're not the only one with leather jackets," he goofed, looking at his black leather animal.

Olivia took a deep breath in. "You can hug me if you want." He smirked at the displeased Countess.

Olivia broke the trance of his faint sweet smell to mock his genuine generosity with a witty phase. "I'd rather fall into the town sewer than touch bodies with you."

She looked at his hands still on her arms. "Well..." wasn't he going to stop touching her or intoxicating her with his beckoning eyes and manly stance?

Maybe it was because he wished to see how far he could push her before she slapped him. Maybe he really enjoyed pissing her off, maybe he liked having this little power he was sure he had over her, or maybe he wanted her to hug him. So he went against her wishes and pulled her body close to his and rested his chin on her head.

"Breathe," Jason spoke. "Friends hug each other; that's all this is. Two friends. I'm consoling you."

She muttered words, but their bodies were too close and he couldn't hear her. He pulled away and looked down at her brown sparkling eyes. They breathed in each other's faces for a second.

Jason looked down at Olivia's lips and back up at her eyes.

Oh great, this was really happening. This was that moment when two people who hated each other fell madly in love as they shared a first kiss. Their lips were centimeters apart.

"You smell like dead squid," she said and they both pulled apart from the embrace he was giving.

"Do you run away from everyone?" he stepped back.

"No." There was a rustle in the leaves. "Just from peeping strangers." She looked around and then at Jason. "We should go."

CHAPTER 15

⚜

Voices

Mark and Kelly sat in silver chairs playing mercy. He giggled at her girlish attempt to hurt him. The girl then narrowed her eyes and pushed back his fingers in a swift motion.

"Ah! Mercy! Mercy!" the slayer shouted as she released his hands.

Jason and Olivia surfed into the training room where the others were already waiting their arrival.

The glimmer was still dancing in Jason and Olivia's eyes. He looked down at her perfect face, memorizing the shape of her pupils and the round of her nose.

"Finally!" Alison barked. "We only have half an hour before Kerrigan's class,"

Jason looked at Olivia and walked over to the white wall. *We'll talk about that later*. He opened his thoughts to Olivia.

"Talk about what?" Alison butted in.

Jason focused on the blonde girl. "Talk about what, Jason?" she asked again. Red filled his cheeks, and he swallowed hard.

"I didn't say anything," he answered honestly and walked away from the crazy girl.

Alison looked at Olivia and the blonde's eyes clouded, her chest rose with air, and she exhaled. Olivia snickered.

"What is your problem?" Alison asked.

Olivia shook her head and began walking away also. But Alison grabbed Olivia's arm and stopped the vampire girl to ask again.

Olivia responded telling her that she hadn't said anything either, she should have left it at that, she could have left it at that, but she didn't. Olivia went on, "I'm minding my own business, unlike some people; butting into other people's thoughts." She breathed and pouted her bottom lip. "Alison, really... sweetie?" Olivia grabbed hold of Alison's hands. "...build a bridge and get over it," she said, smiling at her.

Kelly's jaw dropped to the ground as Rick clapped and laughed. Tom slapped the beach blonde slayer upside the head to cease his clapping.

Alison walked over to the wall where Jason was standing by and pulled down two swords. She threw one to Olivia, and the sword fell on the floor.

"Let's settle this like big girls," Alison said, nodding her head at the sword.

The brunette picked up the sword and swung it to the right in a half circle pointing it down. She studied her weapon briefly. It had a silver pommel and an iron grip lined decoratively with golden white swirls. She looked at Alison's weapon and noticed it was the opposite of hers, with an iron pommel and silver grip.

"Are you sure you want to do this, Princess?"

Alison was asked by the sword masters of Trio-Genesis to teach upon graduating in two years once reaching level 20. But her heart was set on Trio Army.

She had her arm extended out, pointing the sword at Olivia. This time, she would be on the attack; the Countess would naturally have to be on the defense. Alison would fall on the defense letting Olivia gain the upper hand to distract her before disarming the vampire. It wouldn't take long; a couple of swings of the arm, a minute or two of concentrated fighting. It was an easy task.

Olivia swung the sword up the rest of the circle from the left and met Alison's sword with hers. Alison twitched her arm muscles to move her sword while, in one quick motion, Olivia pushed her sword in a swift circular motion, placing the tip of her sword underneath the tip of the hand Alison had on the grip.

It was a half a second, and the sword knocked clear off Alison's hands. In the time it took for her to notice that she was unarmed, Olivia's sword was already at Alison's neck.

"Maybe you should become a big girl before you start settling things like we do," Olivia said.

She stepped back and released the weapon at Alison's feet. The sound of the sword rang in the room. Olivia looked at Rick and walked over to him. His mouth was a flytrap. She smiled at him and closed his mouth with her hand.

The room was quiet for a second. Alison was standing in the middle covered in shame and wallowing in defeat. Her blood was a teapot ready to scream.

"Ali," Jason whispered to her as she walked out of the room, passing him by in total negligence.

She may have lost to Olivia, but she was by no means a dumb woman. She knew the battle plans well and had all the potential to become a good leader. Her intelligences would lead her to great places in her future; if she were a human, she would be senator or even president. Her intelligences didn't come from pure study but from her family also.

Actually, Joshua and Alison would make a great couple. The best part about it was, they didn't need someone else to love them, they could love themselves. If Alison kept up her good behavior, maybe Olivia would introduce the slayer to the vampire. Far be it from her to keep two people so perfect for one another apart. And although she wouldn't mind giving Joshua away to Alison when he was really pissing her off, she wouldn't want to be away from him.

They had something special—like a force, an energy, a connection. Another felt that connection to the Countess.

Jason's concern with keeping an eye on the bitten girl was quickly turning into an obsession. Her smell was evocative, her eyes paralyzing. He counted the breaths Olivia took and watched the back of her head in class as the voice of his teachers would resign into blahs in the background of his imagination.

Upon entering the room he would watch her sneak a breath, then either cross her arms over her chests, or scratch her stomach, or clear her throat.

In the evenings, he would lay awake looking at the ceiling of his room, recalling the day she poisoned his blood. His nightmares transforming into blissful dreams, swarmed with ecstasy. When he'd wake up from the dreams at 3 or 4 am, he would smile and cover his face with the cold side of the pillow.

Few nights he slept without waking. Few nights he slept without dreaming. No one knew of the secret visions from his sleep. No one knew why the glasses in his room kept disappearing.

In the morning, he would step carefully on the wooden floor to avoid cutting his feet on the missed pieces of glass hiding about. Then he'd make his way into the shower to lean his head against the tile and exhale every possible breath in his body.

The meditations were no longer working. He couldn't hover above the floor more than five minutes before he'd come crashing down on wood. He began levitating over his bed to keep from breaking a leg.

The dark circles under his eyes were fooling everyone except Alison.

"He's falling for her," she said in hushed tones to Tom, who sat across the desk from her in the library. Students surrounded them, stuck in their own worlds, worried about their grades and what teams would choose them.

Tom looked up from his book and put down his pen. "If you mean he's falling for her lies, then yes, he is falling. If you mean in love, no, he's not."

"He can't be falling for her lies without falling for her. She's..." and it pained her very much to say this, "perfect."

Tom raised his brows at her.

"You know she's flawless." Alison took a deep breath and smiled her little fake smile. "I saw how he looked at her yesterday, after we fought."

"Did you see the way he looked at you?" Tom asked honestly. "He knows what he lost when you walked out of that room. Besides, you're much more beautiful than she is."

"I saw them later that day. I thought he would come after me, but he went after her," Alison told her friend. "He was comfortable with her, close to her, laughing. He pushed her a little. The kind of the gentle love, play fighting."

Tom grabbed her hands from across the desk and looked into her eyes. He spoke comfort to her and gave her some examples of why Olivia could be trusted. She did, after all, take them to the Vampire Mansion. Maybe not all of them, but that was on Alison and Tom. They could have gone, but they chose not to. But she shared enough information. She helped create a weapon to destroy herself.

Alison always seemed to forget despite Olivia's reputation, she was trying to fit in.

Maybe she didn't tell anyone of her presence because she didn't want the attention.

And because the system already knew. She did put her blood into the heart of the building. Everyone that needed to know of her existences knew.

"For the time being, she is on our side. It's going to have to be enough, Ali."

Rick was walking down the aisles of the library looking for a book on vampire history when he heard Alison's voice saying, "For all we know that bite she gave him at the beach turned him into one of them. She's a vampire. Isn't that what they do? Take their victims and turn them and have them fall madly in love? Before we know it, it's going to be all over the school, and then it's going to come back to haunt us."

The book was before him. He reached for it and left back to sit where Kelly was waiting.

"I just heard that Jason loves Olivia, and that he wants her to turn him so they can move into the Vampire Mansion and have a family together so they can take over the world. And we helped!"

Kelly laughed.

Rick nodded his head quickly. "Laugh now, but it's all over the school. Everyone is going to find out she's a vampire and that we all helped her get in here."

Kelly's eyes widened. She pulled out her phone and dialed the familiar number she called several times before.

"Mark, Rick is convinced that our favorite little vampire," she whispered the word, "has turned Jason, and that they are off running into the sunset to be married and have a wonderful family in the Vampire Mansion after taking over the world. And to add to the festivities, all of Trio-Genesis knows we brought her here," she spoke into the phone. Kelly pulled the phone away from her ear so that Rick could hear Mark's laughter.

"I told you," she said, looking at Rick.

On the other side of Trio-Genesis, Mark was causing his own pandemonium surfing up and down in search of Jason. He finally stopped and thought he must be in his room. Sure enough, he was.

He surfed in and saw Jason laying on his bed staring at the ceiling. The sheets were messy, and Jason was sweaty. He lay in his pajama pants and had his arms crossed behind his head, grinning like a fool.

"Why did Kelly call me to warn me that everyone knows about Olivia—and that you want her to turn you so that you can live happily ever after and destroy the world?" he screamed.

Jason jumped up from his rest and laughed uncontrollably once the fright of Mark entering his room had passed.

"It's not funny. The whole school knows that 'Brook' is really Olivia, and that you are a vampire," Mark said, panting.

Jason shook his head. "Why are you sweating... dude... were you running? Did you run all the way here to tell me all that?" Jason asked, laughing still.

He began his long explanation. Sure, he was different around Olivia, but it wasn't the magical feeling of love.

"Olivia and I are friends. I'm learning to trust her, and she me. Nothing else is going on."

As the last words came out of his mouth, Jason's bathroom door opened and strong fog came out along with a just showered Olivia, wearing a button down shirt belonging to Jason and a towel in her hand drying her hair as she spoke, "Well that was fun." Olivia looked up and saw Mark.

"I can't imagine any more happening." Mark's eyes rolled around his head twice over.

The slayer stood out of bed and looked at Olivia. He was red. Mark had seen Jason blush before, but he had never seen him this red. "This is not what it looks like." Olivia smiled.

"You can't go sleeping with Dracula's daughter! She is engaged to be married," he boiled at Jason. He turned to Olivia. "What would your fiancé say, do, or think? Don't you care about him at all? Not to mention when he finds out, Jason is toast. And I mean toast—he'll incinerate him!" he screamed and reprimanded them. "And you're both getting it easy from me! Imagine if Alison had walked in here."

A short laugh came from Olivia's mouth. She would give anything to see Alison's reaction. They understood they weren't in the best position to argue, well... Jason understood. Olivia would argue with anyone.

"Jason and I were practicing. I was teaching him how to use a sword properly." Mark paced the room.

"Well, I can see that."

Jason's hand met his forehead with a slap.

"After I completely disgraced one of your best swords person, I offered some of my training to him."

"Is there a perfectly good explanation as to why you used his shower and are wearing his clothes, too?"

"I cut her with my blade and there was blood everywhere," he started explaining, realizing quickly nothing was sounding proper. "Before the alarms could go off," his eyes widened, "I took off my shirt to dry the blood and Olivia ran off to the bathroom to wash her clothes. Resulting in a naked..." he paused, "...I saw nothing. She was in the bathroom. Olivia."

"He threw me a shirt and his shirt is out the window in the yard," she added. Mark nodded once, and as a few seconds passed, Jason pointed to the window.

Mark walked over, opened the window, but saw nothing. It was too dark. "I can surf down a get it for you, if you need proof," Jason suggested.

"Wait, why are we trying so hard to convince him nothing happened?" Olivia asked and tossed the towel on the chase by the fireplace. As the towel flew to hit the chase, a hot wind came from Jason's hand and engulfed the towel, drying it before it rested by the soft burning light.

Mark moved from the window, closing it suddenly. "Because I'm... Jason's best friend."

"Would you like to sleep with him?" Olivia jerked her head back.

The silence was her answer. She excused herself from the awkwardness of it all.

Once she was gone, Mark sat and rested his feet on the sofa by the window. He looked out into the yard and covered the smirk on his lips. They were silent. Jason walked to the chase and picked up the towel taking in the scent left behind.

"I've seen you gazing at her." Mark's voice was gentle. "You're hypnotized by her power. This started as a quest to profit you. What has it turned to now?" These words were not as kind.

The bitterness of Mark's voice sat in Jason's mouth. Mark rose from his seat and moved toward his friend.

"You think I've lost focus," he said.

"I know you've lost focus!"

"I gather more information from Olivia in one sitting than you get in questioning my authority." Jason was shouting.

"You're falling for her."

"I AM NOT THAT NAÏVE!" Jason's voice echoed in his room.

Mark took the towel from Jason's clutching hands, "You are becoming..."

"The vampires are planning a war. We don't have time for you to guilt me to depression."

Patrick was standing by the test tubes, while Olivia pulled out some TICS from the freezer. She popped some out and put it in a little glass container smaller than the ones they use to carry them. Small enough so it would not be recorded as missing.

"Here, keep this on you at all times." She placed the container in Patrick's hand. "Go to Joshua. Everything here is ready. He may begin." Olivia reached into her pocket and pulled out a piece of paper. "Coordinates. As soon as I can, I will meet him at Browns Wing Park. Send my love and best wishes," Olivia whispered.

"You're sure this will work?" Patrick held her face in his hands and looked into her eyes.

"How can it not? We have the upper hand. I know everything about them," Olivia said and hugged Patrick goodbye before he surfed off in red flames. She held on to the ash of his exit and surfed off herself.

Outside the door, blue eyes filled with water. A pale hand covered graceful pink lips and blonde hair framed the face of a frantic girl. Her entire body was shaking. It all made sense, and as much as it brought her joy, it pained her to know she was right. Alison backed away from the door and surfed away with quiet waters.

CHAPTER 16

The Storm

Alison pounded Jason's bedroom door, screaming for him to come out.

Door after door opened with angry students emerging from their rooms. The blonde girl did not stop the uproar.

Shouts and screams came from others now, telling the girl to quiet herself. Finally, a student grabbed her by the arms and shook her body about.

"Trio-Genesis will be under attack," she screamed back at his face. "We are all going to die." Her eyes watered.

The hallway roared with laughter. He released his grip and walked away. "You're crazy," he mocked. "I hope that Jason guy does come out so he can take you to the mental rooms." The fat, white boy reached for his bedroom doorknob, and the red light blinked brightly. The alarm sounded loudly. He turned and looked at the blonde girl in silence, then around at the others.

"Trio-Genesis is under attack. Please do not panic. We have everything under control." The familiar voice of the elevator came over the intercom.

The fat boy's eye widened, his lips trembled, and spit came out his open mouth as he screamed "everybody panic!"

Bodies ran left and right. Doors shut with thuds and bangs. Screams and cries filled the hall.

The voice again repeated the announcement, this time adding that all level 15 and up slayers were to report to the main training station on the fourth floor.

The woman over the intercom repeated the message twice and then told everyone else to report to the main Ball Room on the first floor she repeated the messages once again.

Alison stopped beating on the door and surfed back to where Olivia was. She surfed in the lab screaming and shouting that Olivia was a traitor and that she would kill her. She shouted at the top of her lungs. She kicked things and broke things, but the Vampire Slayer was long gone by then.

Alison glared at the white box with their only salvation inside; she was on the move as the thought came to her. The TICs were the only things strong enough to protect them all.

A warm wind filled the room and Jason spoke. "Good. You're hiding them." He ran over to her.

Her motion ceased. "Hiding them?!" She was livid. "Jason, I'm taking them to use. If these things can kill Olivia, it can kill all of them. This is our only chance. She's told them everything."

Jason lunged at Alison trying to take the TICs from her, but she used her fist on him, hitting him many times. Like a woman swatting a fly.

"We are under attack! I heard her talking with another vampire not too long ago in this very room." She was blood red. Her eyes watered but no tears were falling.

"This is our only chance, Jason. Please." He let go of her.

His skin was cold and his eyes were empty. "I have to take these out of here," he said finally and put a hand to the refrigerator. A strong wind filled the room. Alison reached out in front of her to follow him, but it was too late. He took most of it with him, but she had some still. She had enough to give to her group.

"The training station." Words spilled from her mouth.

There were bodies everywhere. Moving and screaming. Everyone looking for friends, groups, teammates, lovers.

She shouted their names into the room along with others. "Tom!" she screamed in one direction.

She screamed for Kelly in another. All of their names came out of her mouth over again; all but Olivia's and Jason's. Her head jerked behind her as she heard her name loud and clear through the screaming slayers.

"Here!" Her voice carried.

"There. I see her." Tom's voice echoed in her direction.

Finally, someone who would believe her and who would fight Olivia with her.

She was opening her mouth to tell him everything she had seen, but the evil brunette was already with them, standing under Mark's protection.

Alison was a lion and Olivia was the lamb. She advanced on her prey, but Jason held her back.

"It's her fault! She's working with them. It's part of her plan. It has been all this time!" Alison pleaded.

The words were one big mess of thoughts and anger and violent screams. "Let go of me." She shook her arms. Despite her strength, Jason was stronger than she.

Naturally, Olivia denied every word Alison threw at her. And it worked. No one believed the blonde. Alison kept screaming of how she overheard Olivia talking to a vampire about it being time. She finally pushed Jason away and attacked Olivia.

The crowed moved away to watch the two girls fight.

"Alright, a girl fight!" Shouted the same white boy from the hallway.

Mark, Jason, and the others tried to stop the fight, but when the watching circle was formed they got pushed away from each other and away from the girls.

It was quite a sight. No powers; just hair pulling, scratching, and a few punches— a real girl fight.

Everyone watched with pleased looks on their faces.

Alison hit Olivia several times, but got back twice more what she put out.

When Olivia's hair was out of the way and her neck fully exposed, Alison grabbed it from right under the jawline and beneath the ear lobes then pushed up with her thumb and index finger.

Like pushing a button, Olivia's eyes turned bright red and her fangs came out of their hiding place, a force she could not control.

Alison backed away from her, took her chance, and screamed "she's a Vampire!"

Jason surfed behind Olivia and held her back. At this point there wasn't much that would stop Olivia. Tom also surfed in the circle and held back Alison, but there was no need.

The slayers all around got ready to fight; their weapons pulled out and their elements were ready on the attack.

The voice of a man came over the vociferous crowd of slayers that were ready for the kill. "STOP!" the voice roared.

Silence hit them like a wave crashing on a surfer.

He stood on a glass platform and spoke to every slayer in the room. "This is Countess Olivia," he said.

Whispers came from every corner, followed by gasps.

"She has been staying with us for quite some time now. To some of you, she is no stranger. This is the same girl, who for the past four months, has studied with you and eaten with you." He screamed again to silence the noise.

"You may know her better as Brook Morton. Her attendance here has nothing to do with this war. She came to warn us and to learn to master her full powers, which is her birthright." He addressed the last bit looking at Alison.

"I've been keeping a close eye on her." The man surfed into the circle of slayers. "Disarm," he said to the remaining slayers still ready to kill.

"Tomas, let her go." His voice was soft and reassuring.

He turned then to Jason, who held onto an angry vampire, his muscles ripping through his shirt as the heels of his feet dug into the ground beneath him. He exhaled quickly as Olivia kept pulling out of his hold.

"Jason, that is no way to treat a Countess," he said, looking at the slayer.

"She won't be able to control herself if I let go."

"Your trust in me is shaken," the man said.

"Not stirred." Rick whispered to Kelly standing next to him. She slapped him on the abs.

Jason looked around and then at Olivia before letting her go.

She stood breathing heavy for a second, looking around at the frightened slayers.

There were many of them and only one of her. Her eyes returned to their natural brown color and her sharp biters went away.

"Welcome Countess, we've long anticipated your arrival." He made his way closer to her and bowed his head. "Please accept my apologies. I do not reveal myself often. Nor do I condone this insanity." He raised his head and looked about.

"Those of you to my left report to Brown's Wing Park. There is a frenzy there awaiting your arrival. Those of you to my right report to the front entrance and down the hills. Half of my best men and women are giving their lives there already. They must not get any closer to the building." His voice was loud enough for all to hear but no one moved.

"Are we cowards in the face of war? All of you in here wish to join Trio-Army. Now is your chance. My slayers do not hesitate when given orders!" The anger filled the ears of every slayer and each surfed off with his own element.

The eight remained, waiting for instructions as well. He walked and they followed. "There is something else I must apologize for." The pause seemed like hours. "I should have looked for you. Olivia, you're arrival had been delayed greatly, when Jason came back with you," there was another breath in his speech, "I was soothed. Then I let the events unfold. I knew you couldn't keep your secret forever."

Olivia found her way into having a word. "That's all fine and dandy. But who the hell are you?"

Jason's eyes were fearful, for he knew this man. Olivia might be top dog at the Mansion, but this was not her castle. Although this man's ways weren't always "right" he was the president, the senator, the governor, the pope, of Trio-Genesis. His word was law, he read of the law, and only he had permission to change the law.

Beneath him were many counsel man and woman. These selected few were scattered in Trio-Genesis. Some were teachers; others were staff, doctors, cooks, janitors, and some in Trio Army.

"He's Gabriel Elliot Ominoes," Jason whispered to Olivia.

"And I am Countess Olivia Brook Montgomery. My name has a title in front. You seem to be a man of law. What law do you follow that gives you the right to speak above me?" Olivia sounded like an old governess sometimes, more mature than her years, and she could persuade many with her words.

"A thousand apologies, Countess. Between our rules, yes, you are higher than I. But given that you know very little about this place, I would gladly appreciate your blessing to continue my rein of mere Head Sever before the law." He bowed his head to her again.

"Granted."

Only he and Olivia knew what was happening. A bunch of old words and strange laws. How was Olivia possibly above him? She was Countess over the vampires, yes.

But did her half slayer breed make her Countess over slayers? It would be, in fact, that since Savanna married into royal blood she would become Countess of the Vampires, but not Countess of the slayers.

Marriage Law of the Vampire and Slayer Court Section 9.27

Lest the royal couple produce an heir, the spouse's title remains the same.

After climbing the white spiral stairs to the mirror ball, Gabriel, Olivia, and the six slayers reached an automatic sliding door. It opened and the group of eight entered.

From the inside of the mirror ball, there was a 360 view of the area where Olivia stood previously fighting with Alison.

"Gabriel, I know you see everything that happens in Trio-Genesis, but I heard her talking to a vampire about everything being ready and to take something to them. Please, you have to believe me," Alison begged. "I know what I heard,"

"I've had my eye on Olivia since she's arrived. Believe me when I say, nothing happens without my approval. Trust me, Olivia is our best bet right now. She will prove her loyalty to you if given the chance," Gabriel whispered back to the terrified blonde girl.

Alison breathed deeply to calm herself from doing something drastic. Gabriel needed her to trust Olivia right now.

The only light came from the various screens and controls on the operating tables.

There were buttons with all different colors and of all different sizes.

"We must move Trio-Genesis," Gabriel said. "It takes about two hours to relocate the building." He continued, looking at Olivia, his eyes glistening with a trail of old unwiped tears. "Olivia," he breathed, "if you could stall the vampires, talk to them, delay them." She did not respond with the hasty speed the moment called for. "Think of the women, the children. And yes. Think of the men who live here. Trio-Genesis is their only home." Gabriel's words rang with a definite truth.

Olivia turned from them and watched one of the screens showing a picture of the front gate. She could not see the fight, but the flashes of light from the different powers were very visible.

"Once we've moved I'll send Jason for you." Gabriel affirmed her.

"So, what? You want me to go fight at the gate, go to the park have a picnic, make a fire, round up the family, and sing kumbaya? How exactly do I stall an army of vampires, Gabriel?" She turned back around.

Jason walked over to Olivia and looked her in the eyes sternly. "Olivia, you're their leader. Make them stop."

"It's not that simple. They are still individuals with their own thoughts and actions. Think of it as a president running a country. He or she doesn't control what the citizens do."

"Olli, this is our home. If you can't do something, we are all going to die," Mark said, using a nickname she has gone long without hearing. "Please help us."

Olivia glanced around at the others, and then at Jason. She briefly caught Alison's eyes, tearing and hopeful. Again, she looked at the screen. There were less red lights flashing with every passing second. Her brows frowned and she exhaled softly so that only she could hear. But the motion of the breathing was visible so Jason laid a warm hand on her shoulder and squeezed gently.

"I'll do what I can." She faced a relieved crowd. "Jason, you'll have to be captured in order to find me. Then you'll have to pray you're brought to me before you're executed." The information wasn't the most pleasant to receive.

"The rest of you will help the council members and I to move the building," Gabriel said. "Mark, Rick and Tom: you three head to the park and find the ones there."

Rick smiled, slapping Tom's back but keeping his attention focused of Gabriel, "Any advice, Head Server?"

"Speed is your friend."

With this, the three surfed away according to their own element. "We'll find the remaining ones here," said Jason.

They, too, surfed off.

A ring of blue fire surrounded Olivia and the flame ate her body. All that was left was smoke when the fire had gone, transporting the vampire slayer.

The alarms rang in the halls and bounced off the walls. A horrid noise made the children cry and the old people annoyed. It seemed to be ringing louder and louder by the second. The only place without the blasting sound of the warning was Goldie, but even then, the ringing played from the distance.

Jason ran into the registration hall and found the sweet woman sitting on her chair waiting to register another student.

It was no trouble finding Mr. B. He was sitting in his little chair by the fireplace reading to his catatonic daughter in one of the hospital rooms. Kelly was most familiar with him and breaking the news of the attack was easier coming from her lips. It wasn't a secret in the hospital by any means. But the old fart had lost his mind a bit and the alarms didn't set him off in the slightest. It was just a loud noise and red flashing lights. His hearing aid wasn't turned up all the way anyway, so the noise really wasn't all that loud. But he rose from his wooden chair and took a sip of his orange juice before standing, kissing his daughter on the forehead, and following Kelly slowly down the hospital hallway.

Alison rounded up counsel people faster than she could surf. She sent out a general message through a few janitors and ran through the kitchen collecting the remaining cooks left behind. If they stayed behind, they were either helpless slayers or council people.

The sky was dark and cloudy. On a regular night, the park would have been deserted, quiet, and cold. The night dew would be freezing on the grass and the quiet sound of crickets would softly rise from the brushes. This was not a regular night.

Fire was crossing between vampires and slayers, the earth was shaking, and the trees were attacking, vampires and slayers running around wet. Some were choking from lack of air. Others were burning in the heat of the fire while some were even drowning. Slayers caught in the crossfire were hurt by their own side. Things started changing in all of their minds. This was just the beginning.

For every slayer there were two or three vampires. They were greater in number.

They were stronger and more motivated, but their battle tactics were lacking.

Everyone fought someone at all times. More vampires would come in to replace the others who had died.

Their best fighting tactic was leaving the strong to fight last, wearing out the slayers with the new blood, and then bringing in real soldiers.

Olivia surfed into the middle of the pandemonium, instantly putting up shields to protect herself.

Wooden stakes worked on the weaker vampires. Silver stakes worked on all of them. But one drop of vampire blood could make the skin boil and hiss. Staking was uncommon now that vampires learned to protect their chest.

Strength and fire broke and burned slayers while slayer blood on the flesh of vampires was painful. It was purifying to their skin—a horrible dry feeling. In anguish, vampires with blood on their hands would scream and run from bleeding slayers.

She watched vampires she knew die; she witnessed the death of many classmates she sat close to. She watched Mark get badly hurt and sweet Rick kill a vampire she knew. It was all happening too fast.

Worst of all, she couldn't find the needle in the haystack: Patrick.

She closed her eyes, but that didn't stop the hatred surrounding her. She became weary, hearing the screams and shouts. Her eyes danced, looking in every direction.

The streets were deserted. The buildings around her were vacant for the night, and the closest house with people wasn't for miles. No one else could hear the hurting. Nobody stopped to listen. She focused her eyes on a vampire child attacking a slayer much older. The slayer was a pregnant woman, and she took no pity on the boy.

Before she could pull the ground from under the boy's feet, Mark rushed by and picked the child up in his arms, running away with him. The boy was restless and tried several times to bite the man who had saved his young life. Mark put the boy down by a tree and wrapped him with branches.

Mark's bleeding arm hung by his side and his breathing was quick as he worked on pacing himself. All of the living slayers he was told to get had gone. His mission there was done. The shadow of the tree gave him enough of an opportunity to escape, and he did. His better half told him to stay and fight, but his warrior side knew there were other plans for him. Tom and Rick, too, found chances to escape, and so they did.

Olivia's breathing quickened. She dropped one hand to her knee and lifted her hand slightly. Her face was dim and her other hand trembling. The force field she held fell down and a strong pair of hands came from behind her, holding her close. A man's voice spoke and told her not to panic and not to move. A blazing fire took them as Joshua surfed off with Olivia.

CHAPTER 17

Falling Walls

"Your arm!" Kelly ran to Mark who was leaning on the wall. He smiled at her and attempted to rise from his position but it was hard to mask the pain when the skin from his shoulder to his elbow was burned off. The blood was pouring from his wound. "Rick, get him a medic, will you?"

The blonde slayer surfed off to find help.

As the water from Rick's surf dried on the ground, the wind from Jason's arrival was present. Slayers accompanied him from the counsel.

There was a pause as Jason's eyes studied Kelly and Mark sitting on the floor. Looking at the blood beside them and then at Mark, he sat bent down by his closest friend. "That looks painful." He grinned, making the bloody slayer chuckle.

"Oh, I don't feel a thing." Mark's eyes watered and he rested his head against the wall once more.

"Get a medic," Jason said looking at Kelly.

"She's already sent for one," Mark said.

Gabriel arrived with another group of council members.

Mark took shallow breaths and spoke again. "Olivia was there. She was just watching."

"She'll be fine." The words came from Gabriel's mouth. "We need to move before more of them come. Mark, we will still need your assistance." The medic surfed in with Rick and a very small first aid box.

"You told me it was a little scratch," the man said. He knelt by Mark to take a closer look.

"Can you fix him up, son?" Gabriel asked from behind the young man. He rose as he saw Gabriel and shook his hand grinning from ear to ear.

"Sir, it's an honor…"

"There will be time for chit chat later, Evan, focus. We need this man."

"He needs to see a doctor, sir," Evan told him. "He needs antibiotics and a bed. Rest. All I have is some gauze."

"That will have to do for now."

Evan opened his first aid box and started wrapping up the arm. The blood ate through the bandages quickly. It wasn't long before all he had was used up. "It's all I have, I'll have to run for more."

"No time for that," Gabriel informed. "This is plenty. You've outdone yourself." He placed a hand on the young man's shoulder.

Evan surfed away.

"We don't have time to do a proper swear in, for now you six are part of this counsel." They whispered "oh my gods" and "holy cows."

A council member for a night; no one would believe this. This must be what Olivia feels like at all times: important.

"We need a body on every floor," Gabriel announced. "There are 32 of us here, so we will be short. My hope is that instead of putting someone on every floor we can put two people on 16 floors; the respective floor with the same element will come along." He took a breath and motioned to a woman. "Dianna has made us a list of the floors we will work from. You can pair yourselves."

Mark and Kelly grabbed hold of each other's hand.

Dianna looked around the familiar faces once, then at her list and read. "Floor One: Earth. Floor Two: Earth. Floor Three: Water. Floor Five: Air. Floor Nine: Water. Floor 12: Air. Floor 14: Earth. Floor 18: Water. Floor 20: Air. Floor 22: Water. Floor 25: Earth. Floor 28: Water. Floor 30: Air. Floor 32: Water. Floor 36: Earth. Floor 40: Air."

She then read off the coordinates of the new location which place them in the forests of Inlet NY and off they went two by two.

Jason stood side by side on the fortieth floor with Gabriel. The elevator doors opened and they stepped inside.

Trio-Genesis had an elevator on each floor, each resting always on its respective floor. The whole system was a fortress cornerstone. On the blueprints, the elevator made a large square in the center of the building.

Goldie's door closed automatically once the slayers had entered their respective location.

For the most part, Goldie sounded like a recording of an operator, but tonight there was a slight hint of fear in her voice. She took extra time with the words and quick, almost unnoticeable, breaths between thoughts.

"Please place a hand on the back wall while we scan your identity. In the event that the floor you are on does not surf, please surf out of the building and into safe ground. The remaining parts of the building may collapse on you, so do not remain in the building. Make sure that all other parties are safe on one of the first two floors before surfing Trio-Genesis into a new location. Please refrain from making loud noises. Surfing must take place at the same time, so we ask that you use the shortest form of surfing possible and keep transportation under one second. If possible, please discuss what method to use for each of the three elements. Please remember not to remove your hand until surfing is complete. Trio-Genesis would like to thank you for your bravery and valor. Please hold for further instructions."

Mark laughed with Kelly. This was the first time the building had to move in their life time.

Laugher was the best medicine in tense situations. It broke the ice, it calmed the heart, and it fed the spirit. Alison too was laughing up a storm with Rick.

Tom stood firm next to a stranger. Silence was between them. The man made no attempts to get to know the new counsel boy.

"Face recognition complete. Surfing countdown will begin shortly. Ten. Nine. Eight. Seven. Six. Five. Four. Three. Two. One."

There was a slight shaking. From the outside, the walls dissolved into water, wrapped in leaves, and became clear as air. Then within the blink of an eye, the whole building was gone. Not one second had passed and Jason was opening his eyes to the sound of Goldie's voice:

"Surfing Complete."

In the ballroom slayers cheered, clapped, and shouted. They, too, had instructions to remain silent, still, and to refrain from surfing out of the building lest their floor not surf.

Gabriel embraced Jason as an ugly laugh roared from deep within their throats.

The men tapped each other on the back several times as the doors opened.

They pulled apart and their laughter died suddenly when Gabriel placed a hand to Jason's shoulder and nodded his head once.

A hot wind filled the elevator and Jason was gone.

Water poured from the heavens and the ground below him was cracked and shaking. The fire burning all around illuminated the night. The wind was strong but it was no bother to him.

Others, however, were blown away into the sky or hurled against park benches or trees.

It was a graveyard. Bodies laid on the grass covered in mud and blood. The cries echoed from their mouths, wailing into the night.

Jason's chest was rising and falling rapidly. He ran in different directions trying to tend to broken slayers screaming in agony, instructing others of the same elements to aid their brothers and sisters.

His pleading was useless. There was no help for the wounded.

He had read before in his history books of battles such as these, but his eyes had never seen the damage up close.

"Please, Jason. Help me." It was the soft moan of a student from his class. From neck to torso, the boy had been burned.

Jason moved to his aid, and as his feet rushed to the wailing boy, a weight fell on Jason's body.

Fists met his face repeatedly. Two hands grabbed his shouldered and drove him deeper into the wet grass.

The man holding Jason by the shirt lifted his body high above the ground and took a good look at his face.

"I remember you," Michael said.

Jason shook the blood from his eyes and looked down at the vampire holding him. "That makes one of us." As the words left his mouth, Jason spit the blood out on Michael's face.

The vampire screamed and turned his face to the heavens so the rain could wash off the burning poison. It was the moment Jason had to escape, but Michael returned his attention to the slayer crawling away.

Michael's hand grabbed a hold of Jason's dirty blonde hair and the vampire began to drag the slayer across the field. He kicked and shouted.

Jason's hand rolled over a rock and the slayer held tight to his only way out. But the vampire yanked at Jason's head, pulling the slayer and the rock from their position. Michael let go and leaned down to look at the beaten man.

"If you're looking for the Countess, you won't find her here. Joshua has her and he is never letting her go again." Michael spat in Jason's face.

Jason curled the rock in his hand and raised it to Michael's face. The vampire knocked from his balance fell to the muddy terrain. Jason climbed on the man and beat him with the rock in hand.

Blood splattered from Michael's face and boiled on Jason's hands, but he was not stopping. Michael's scream reached the ears of a vampire nearby who came to his rescue.

Sarry pulled Jason away from Michael and held the bloody blonde to his knees with a stake close to Jason's chest.

"Now you will know the death you deliver," she said.

"Stop," Michael's voice roared, and he smiled as he rose up. "Another wishes to have the honor."

Olivia sat on her white stone throne.

Red cushioning covered the seat, back, and arms. A majestic chandelier hung from the white ceiling in the center of the room.

The floor was one large piece of a gray and white marble. Three steps covered in crimson carpet led to the throne.

To Olivia's right was a glass dining table covered in a sheer white cloth with red silk crocheting along the edges. On top of the table lay two swords sharpened and ready for battle. One sword had a silver blade and braided grip. The other had a flat white gold cross-guard and a plain grip but a sizable diamond on the pommel.

On her left were a few potted plants and a glass double door that led to an outside den. The door had no curtains, and light from the moon shone directly into the throne room. It was a rectangular room and the double door entrance was a dark brown wood that required shining and cleaning twice a day. Not one speck of dust ever sat on those doors or their beautiful carvings.

Her clothes had marks of dirt and grass on it. And although her body posture was straight and poised, Olivia looked like a peasant.

Joshua entered the throne room with a large rectangular box in hand. He sat the box on the table, opened it, and lifted out a long royal blue gown with sapphire gems across the back.

"A ball has been planned for your arrival, despite the dreary date. This seemed suiting," he said presenting the dress.

"I wish to rest," Olivia said "and to feed."

He walked over to his Countess and looked upon her. She smiled at him. He approached her. His hand moved slowly to her face and brushed away the hair that covered her neck. He helped the Vampire Slayer to her feet and once she stood, he sunk his teeth into the skin of the back of her neck.

He pulled back and exposed his neck for her feeding. Olivia's eyes turned bright red and her fangs where no longer hidden. She, too, went for the same spot on the back of his neck and took a long and much desired drink from his sweet, hot blood.

She pulled away and wiped the blood from her mouth. Olivia sat once more on her throne and rubbed the velvet arm covering under her hand.

The door banged open and a dirty, bleeding Michael entered with no apologies. "Ah, Michael. How unpleasant of you to make an appearance. Do you have anything useful to say, or do you simply enjoy pissing me off?" Olivia asked.

"I've a prisoner to bring Joshua." He swallowed hard. "Countess."

"Well, don't keep this man a secret. Bring him in." Joshua laughed.

Michael clapped his hands and two guards dragged in a dirty homeless looking thing. The body of the slayer was thrown at Michael's feet.

The slayer began to lift himself but Michael kicked him down. Once on his knees, he turned around and saw her sitting motionless on her thrown.

Olivia did nothing but blink.

Joshua rested the weight of his body on the arm of her chair. "You're Jason, right? I am Joshua. You may call me Count Elect Joshua. I am the future Count of the beautiful Vampire people."

The two guards who dragged Jason in stood behind him, towering over his kneeling form. They were easily over six feet tall, and Jason could see their shadows on the ground before himself.

"You are quickly becoming the talk of the Mansion." Joshua began walking towards Jason. "The man who kidnapped the Countess, brainwashed her and is slowly..." and this he let linger as he said it, "falling under her incredible charm."

His heavy, shiny, black boots met Jason's chest, and the handsome slayer fell on his back.

Jason concentrated on the light hanging from the ceiling.

The vampire looked back at Olivia. "Would you care for a drink, my love?"

Olivia smiled back and motioned with her head for one of the guards to bring them some glasses and a bottle of blood. "Do you have a preference?"

Joshua shook his head, and so Olivia asked to be surprised. "On your feet, slayer," Joshua spoke again.

Jason lay there motionless, his ears still ringing from the sound of his head hitting the floor.

"Michael, give our guest a hand will you?"

The brute started clapping. "Should I give him a round of applause next?"

He finished clapping and filled his hand with Jason's shirt, lifting the man to his feet. Jason stood as tall as he could and planted his feet firmly on the ground. Joshua walked back over and placed a hand on Jason's shoulder.

"Brave man," Joshua said and punched Jason on the stomach.

Twice more he hit Jason, each punch stronger than the other. The guard returned.

"So tell me, why have we been graced with your company?" Joshua took the glasses and the bottle over to the table.

He poured half a cup for Olivia, half a cup for himself, and then brought a glass to her. The smell of the blood filled the air.

The guards standing in the background began slightly waving from side to side. "What's the matter? Cat got your tongue?" He took a sip. "Break him."

Jason never moved. He stood his ground. The guards approached, but they were uneasy and dizzy.

Again Olivia's voice, their only salvation, was heard. "Stop."

She stood and the guards bowed. One look at Michael and he too withdrew to his knees.

"Back away from him," she ordered.

By this time, Michael and the guards were turning blue. They backed away to the doors and Olivia commanded they leave.

"Can you breathe, Joshua?" she asked.

"It is a bit stuffy in here," was his reply.

"How long do you plan on holding your breath, Jason?" She walked over to the slayer and they stood face to face. Olivia had no problem breathing under the protection of her shield.

"Isn't there a way to break it?" an extra pale Joshua complained.

The slayer did not quit, his motivation only growing stronger after seeing Joshua stumble back and sit on the steps rubbing his temple.

"Make him stop!" Joshua barked.

Not so tough now, Jason thought.

With the right control and with the right amount of energy, Jason could hold his breath for a good long while, but he was tired and Olivia wasn't helping. Her closeness was distracting, he was running low on his own air supply, and he had to break, releasing the air in the rest of the room.

Joshua welcomed a breath of fresh air into his dying lungs. Olivia let down the force field and ran her hands over Jason's shirt. Security had sure been compromised since she was gone.

"The guards here need to be fired." The Countess reached under his shirt and unbuckled the armed belt every slayer had hung tightly across their chest and back at all times in battle.

Jason was fully packed with heavy artillery: two daggers, one wooden stake, two silver stakes, four vials of TICS, one bag of un-chilled antidote—which was only enough to get her back to more antidote and wasn't at all enough if more than one of the vials were to be used—and a small first aid kit. There were three empty compartments to fill, but Jason grabbed all he had time for.

Joshua couldn't help but agree with Olivia's suggestion. She held the belt out for Joshua to see and dropped it on the ground behind herself. Unarmed and too tired to make more moves for the time being, the cards were in their hands.

She walked to her chair and sat down again.

The vampire man stopped his walking at the dining table with the two swords, picked up both swords and walked over to Jason. Joshua dismissed the belt on the floor and held a sword up by Jason's neck.

Joshua's mouth opened and more garbage came out. "My original plan involved decapitating you right where you stand. However, I have come up with a better plan."

He dropped the sword to his side. "Olivia has always enjoyed those medieval duals where the winner gets the hand of the fair maiden. And being that today is her birthday, I want to give her a treat."

Olivia clapped and cheered like a silly schoolgirl.

"So the rules are: if I kill you, I win. If you, by some chance in the heavens, come across the miracle of killing me—which as you may have figured won't happen— Olivia there…" he said pointing at her with the sword. "Wave to us darling."

She did.

"…will kill you. In which case, you still lose."

Joshua handed Jason the sword with the braid grip and kept the diamond one for himself.

Jason held up his sword. Joshua did the same. Olivia's voice came from the back as she told them to begin.

Jason swung right, but Joshua met his sword. They swung left and right and left again. Their feet moved quickly and their hands swung swiftly.

Jason tried Olivia's trick to unarm Joshua, but it didn't work.

Olivia snickered at his pitiful act, but clapped for his miserable attempt.

Joshua kept pushing onward toward Jason, backing him away with every move. Jason gave one hard unexpected swing at Joshua's sword, and made the vampire lose his grip of the delicate weapon.

Jason surfed in front of the laughing Olivia and held his sword to her neck. "Quite the birthday gift, I say." Jason spoke at a mortified Joshua.

CHAPTER 18

Deaths and Birthdays

Joshua turned around to see the dreadful act. Jason was going to kill her right before his very eyes. Jason pulled back his sword to meet her neck with greater force. Just as he did, Joshua surfed behind him and swung his own weapon at Jason.

Olivia screamed his name, making Jason move out of the way of what should have been certain death, but the tip of the blade caught across his back. It tore through his flesh cutting his skin.

Jason fell back on the small set of steps, were it not for Olivia, he would be laying there cut diagonally.

Olivia surfed out of her chair and behind Jason. She held on to him as his fell. Joshua looked back at her. "Whose side are you on?" he asked angrily.

"My side," Olivia said while Jason looked up at Olivia, almost questioning her words.

He handed her the sword. "Here, it's your kill," he said backing away from them. Joshua shook his head in disbelief. Olivia smiled. He ran at her for the attack.

Olivia didn't use defense; instead, she attacked back, forcing Joshua to fight the only way he didn't know how.

Olivia swung her sword with all her might, advancing on him faster and faster.

Olivia was a proficient swords master, but the particular blade she was holding was not proper for her size, and it took extra thought to fight properly.

Joshua studied her sword careful.

In practice she used weapons much smaller, he would know, they practiced every afternoon. After hours of endless fighting they declare a winner based on physical exhaustion. The loser would have to pay for a human lunch where they enjoyed each other's company.

This wasn't practice. The stage was set and the curtains were up, someone would emerge victorious and someone would bleed to death.

Her hand grasped tightly around the grip.

Joshua opened his hand and fire from his open palm came at her, which she reflected back to him.

With a swirling movement of his hand, he made the incoming fire hazard a fire dagger mid-air and pushed it back in her direction along with an extra ball of fire. It hit Olivia on the shoulder, taking her attention off the fight. He came back to the attack, but the wound would soon heal itself and Olivia would do everything to gain the offensive once more.

Joshua made another ball of fire and threw it her direction. "Ah-ha! You missed!" she screamed at him.

"No I didn't," he said.

Olivia's smile faded. She looked back at Jason to make a run for him, but he was fine; he managed to collect one of the daggers from the slayer's weapons belt, and it was his protection when the hurling ball of flame came at his face.

Some slayers have a magically powerful shield and some use their best resources.

Jason dropped the hot dagger and Olivia's feet couldn't stop until she was face to face with the slayer to make sure he was okay.

She picked up the silver dagger in her left hand and held it. "How could I be so stupid?" the whispered words escaped her lips.

The realization of the situation hit her. She swallowed hard and blinked slowly. She rose quickly from the ground and turned back to Joshua to get it over with. The tip of Joshua's sword met her abdomen, and the blade went right through her.

She didn't scream or cry. Olivia held in her breath and dropped her sword.

Jason only saw Olivia's back and the tip of the sword dripping with her blood. As it fell on the white marble, Jason noticed the little black TICS. His eyes shot to the belt on the ground. All four vials had been broken. He looked at Olivia's back, her shirt quickly soaking with her blood.

An evil smile formed on Joshua's face. "Happy Birthday, Olivia. Say hi to your father for me," he said and pulled her close to his body. Her hands flew behind the vampire.

Olivia's eyes grew wider. Her breath was caught up inside her, and she never broke eye contact with Joshua. She held up her left hand and plunged the dagger into his flesh.

The vampire released the sword and the Countess. Olivia backed away from him as the silver burned inside his flesh.

Olivia looked down at the splitting sword stuck in her body and raised her eyes at Joshua. She held onto the sword with both hands and pulled the long, bloody blade from inside her while blood fell to the floor. Jason rose up slowly to help her.

Olivia raised the sword and ran it through Joshua, right above his belly button.

Blood dripped from his mouth and Joshua looked up at Olivia.

"How about you say 'hi' to yours, for me?" she mocked and withdrew the blade from his insides.

Joshua fell on his knees and forward on his face.

Olivia stepped back. Her face was bleached. She only had minutes to continue her mission for the night. Jason made his way to the belt, grabbed the bag with the antidote, and poured it on his hand.

"Take a deep breath if you can and close your eyes. This is only enough to transport us once." He wrapped his arms around her and placed his hand on her back over her wound. Then with a blink of his eyes, he and Olivia were gone with the wind.

There was one more task to complete before they could return to Trio-Genesis. Jason surfed her into the middle of battle at Brown's Wing Park.

"You can do this." He held up her arms out beside her and Olivia shot a force field throughout and all around the battle. The slayers were still outnumbered. This was their chance to surf off and they knew it, so they fled in surrender.

She saw the bright lights of the ceiling fly passed them as they rushed her into the hospital. Someone pushed Jason on another bed and into another room to tend to his wounds.

The hospital was in pandemonium with slayers injured from battle and crying in pain, but when Olivia went by on her bed with her heart barely beating, the hallways were silent.

Word traveled quickly in Trio-Genesis.

Olivia fell into a deep sleep and they injected the antidote to her six times before the wound looked any better. After eight applications, Olivia's skin started healing on its own, but the Vampire Slayer was still sleeping.

Jason was recovering easily with the 17 stitches on his back and the several on his face.

He and Mark visited Olivia every day at least once a day. Every time they walked in, Rick was coming out. Only the nurses and the doctors knew how much Rick would visit her.

He brought her fresh flowers to replacing the dying ones and read to her from his favorite children's book. He always had food for her in case today was the day she would wake up. But there was no guarantee she would wake, and the slayer usually left the room in a deep depression.

Another few days passed and Rick begged the staff to return her to her room, plug her in there, and let her wake up to a nicer setting. Finally, they allowed him to move her. A team of doctors and nurses helped the Countess settle into her room.

Once there, even Alison was caught visiting her. "I know we hate each other, but Rick's depression is wearing us all down," the blonde told the sleeping vampire girl.

"Besides, now that everyone knows about you, there are a group of people who hate you and don't trust you as much as I do. I want you to meet them." She laughed but Olivia was still.

Mark and Jason weren't getting sleep, so they took turns sitting outside her door in case she woke up and needed help.

After another week, Rick stopped coming to read. It wasn't his choice, but the team decided it would be best for his health if he stayed away for a while. With the lack of sleep from Jason and Mark, and Rick's spiraling sadness, the others lost hours in their days too.

Patrick had lost all hope that she would come to visit him ever again. He even went as far as to look for Trio-Genesis and find her himself. But the only grounds he knew them to be on were empty.

Then, suddenly, no one came to visit. No one waited outside her house door.

One morning, when the sun was rising on the fields, a ray of light shone on her gentle face. The light rested there a few minutes and her brows moved. A small moan left her still closed lips. Then her entire face squinted, and she moved the sheets over her face.

Under there was darkness but no air. She moved the sheets away with a quick motion and parted her lips. She smacked them together repeatedly and reached to her bedside table where there was always a glass of water.

There was nothing within her reach. Olivia kept pushing her hand forward until it met a vase and the vase met the floor. The sound of the glass made her retrieve her hand slowly back under the sheets like a child in trouble.

A few more seconds passed and the Vampire Slayer sat straight up in bed shouting, "I'm thirsty!"

She finally opened her eyes then covered them with both hands angry at the sun, "It's too bright," she complained.

Olivia dragged her hands down her face, pulling the skin away from her eyes and rolling them upward. Then she picked the eye boogers from each eye and yawned. Her stomach made a very unusual sound.

"Holy cow!" she shouted at the ceiling. There was a pause. "I'm so hungry," she said.

She rose out of bed and walked to the bathroom. Olivia hadn't yet taken the time to admire her new house. Well, not new. Everything still needed fixing. Maybe she would fill her day with that.

She would enter each room in the "house" and look through all the things her parents left her, and stop living in just the entrance and bathroom.

The Countess kept thinking about what to do in the house as she brushed her teeth. Every tooth she brushed carefully and then flossed and gargled.

Showering was the best part of her morning so far. The hot, burning water bounced off her skin, and the soap was very fragrant-heavy.

She dressed in blue jeans and a green shirt with a pull-over hoodie that had Trio-Genesis written on the front with designs of the different elements. The hoodie was light blue, and her long hair she pulled to the front around her neck.

Losing her balance from hunger, she sat on her bed and put on gray sneakers. Nothing really went together, but it looked good enough to run down for some eggs and bacon and go back to sleep before class. She had no idea what day it was, and since the built-in alarm hadn't woken her, she figured she had enough time.

As it turned out, it was Saturday.

Olivia made her way to the golden doors of the elevator and pushed the button.

Goldie opened her doors and the Countess stepped in. The buttons for the floors lit up and the golden box spoke, "Welcome back, Countess. Will you be going down for breakfast?"

"Yes. And thank you."

The light for the dining hall floor lit and they were off. "How are you feeling?" the voice asked.

"I'm great. How do you like the new location? By the way I need to know where we are eventually."

"It's beautiful here. You should go for a walk once you regain your energy. There are mountains on the other side; white snow on the peaks. We are in Inlet NY."

She described the glorious view to Olivia. The stream off the right side that fell into a lake. The summer would be warmer but not by much. Snow covered the fields. Olivia reached the floor and the doors opened.

"Goodbye Countess."

"Bye."

Olivia walked out. This hallway was full of slayers. She walked, picking under her nails.

This was home now. Trio-Genesis was her place of residence and even the others seemed to be more used to her. She was getting many looks from many different eyes. Whispers as she walked by. Smiles and nods from heads out of respect. Once more people noticed she was walking among them, they went silent.

Olivia's eyes looked around from side to side.

Finally, the cafeteria doors were in sight, and she couldn't wait to be away from the public eye.

She walked in and headed right to the buffet line. The noise powered the room, and Olivia was able to find her way to the start of the line without too many eyes on her.

Hot plates were stacked on each other. She grabbed a blue tray and a white round plate and started going through the long buffet.

Eggs, bacon, sausage, ham, turkey, cheese. Then pancakes: chocolate chip, banana, blueberry, strawberry, buttermilk, apple. French toast made from wheat and white bread. Waffles: apple, banana, chocolate. Wheat bread, white bread, rye bread, hard rolls, hamburger rolls, cinnamon bagels, everything bagels. Muffins: raisin, corn, cranberry, blueberry cinnamon, white chocolate chip. Then pastries: donuts, and danishes. Followed by cereals. Next was fresh fruits: grapes, blackberries, blueberries, strawberries, cherries, apples, pears, oranges, bananas, honeydew, raspberries, watermelon, and grapefruit.

On her plate were two eggs, three pieces of bacon and two links of sausage, one slice of white French toast, and three pieces of oranges.

There was a new addition to the drinks section: a bottle of blood. It was type A positive. Trio-Genesis staff figured A positive or A+ was an "A plus," so it was best.

Olivia didn't hesitate as she pulled a hard plastic cup from the stack and poured herself a full glass. She brought the cup to her lips and took a few huge gulps. The blood wasn't as fresh as container blood should be, but it was cold and satisfying. Her thirst was not quenched, and she longed for water.

She saw a bottle and placed it on her tray. The countess looked around for her team. Maybe they were around eating. She found them sitting in the middle of a long table.

Six slayers sat in silence, the world happening around them while they were still. Rick pushed his eggs about his plate. His toast was soggy and his orange juice warm. His face was dim and black circles rounded his red eyes.

Mark looked worst of all, lost in his cold coffee.

Kelly rested her head on his shoulder and looked into the blackness of the cup also.

Tom wasn't Olivia's biggest fan, but the weight of her absence was ever present. His eyes had bags under them, and he slowly picked at the food on his plate.

Out of respect and some unexplained sorrow, Alison sat quietly. Her eyes were empty and there was some trace of distance tears.

Many times, Jason told Mark how he felt the tip of the sword cutting his back when he laid down to sleep. In his dreams, he would see a pool of blood and black tics swimming in her blood.

Jason woke up in a cold sweat every night since the fight. On nights he didn't dream with a pool of blood, he dreamt she was on the field with her arms out, blood weeping from her back as her shield grew around the battle. Then her body collapsed in his arms and he fell down holding a half-dead Olivia, crying into her hair; not knowing if he should surf or stay where he was. If he stayed she would bleed out, if he surfing home her wounds would open and the damage could be permanent.

His decision to surf saved her life, but with the news of her coma, maybe if she had died it would have been easier.

Slayers came back in groups for the dead before their bodies vanished home. Vampires old enough turned to dust and washed away with the rain, other immortals were taken to be burned. The born vampires were taken to their families for the three day wait, they would return as immortals for the second chance. There was mutual respect when it came to collecting the dead.

Jason made his choice to leave. At Trio-Genesis there was medicine and more antidote. There at the park, he had nothing.

Everyone tried to convince Jason he had done the right thing.

There was no coffee in between his hands; no plate of food before him. Jason was thinner, sickly looking, and his eyes were dead. His vision focused on nothing while his head faced straight. He only sat with the team because he was their leader and under their supervision. After the screams from his nightmares woke up the students in the rooms parallel his, Jason's team was ordered by Gabriele to keep an eye on him 24/7. They took turns.

Olivia sat down next to Rick. "Good Morning," she said casually.

Rick lifted his head looked at her. "Morning," he said in a hush voice then looked back down at his food.

"Did you see the little drink addition? They put a bottle of blood there just for me. I thought that was cool." She began eating.

Rick slowly lifted his head again and watched Olivia eat. His mouth was open and his eyes were gleaming.

He began nudging Alison on the side. After a few nudges she answered him angrily. "What?" she looked over. "Holy sh…" The blonde cut herself off.

Tom also looked over. He needed to know what all the fuss was about. His whole complexion changed.

"You're alive," Tom said, leaning over the table to see her better.

Kelly was next to notice, she shook Mark wildly laughing and never removing her eyes from Olivia.

The slayer looked up. Olivia was still eating. He shot up from his seat and grabbed Olivia's face in both hands checking her eyes. It was just like her mother's sparkle.

"Jason, look who it is," Mark yelled.

Jason was sitting right across from her, staring dead in her face but looking right through her. He blinked and saw her. There were no smiles from him, no jokes, and no motion. He kept looking at her. Everyone waited for his reaction. His mouth was open, and for the first time in days, Jason was breathing again. His breath picked up, and his heart rate rose as his eyes almost filling with water.

"Olivia." The name escaped his.

"Yes?"

The handsome slayer jumped from his seat. It was really her. It was. She was there: alive, eating, talking, moving.

"You're awake!" he shouted.

"Well, it is morning." She bit her French toast.

"You've been in a coma," Jason came out with the answer to her confusion. Olivia brushed off the words as if comas were normal and blissful states of sleep.

"I'm awake now," she said way too casually.

Surely, it would have bothered anyone else, but Olivia didn't make it into a big deal. She looked at them. "You all look awful." She laughed.

Of course they did. They hadn't slept, hadn't eaten, and were completely restless and starved. Their team was broken with her gone. Olivia was touched; she didn't know she'd be missed so much.

"You've been in coma for ten weeks," Jason said and everyone standing sat down.

"No wonder I was so hungry!"

"You sleep for two months, and when you wake all you have to say is you're hungry?" Alison screamed.

"I see you haven't changed." Olivia smiled at the blonde girl. "What do you guys want me to say?" Olivia stopped eating and asked.

They looked at each other and then at her. "It was quiet without you. We want to hear you talk..." Kindness escaped Alison's mouth. "So I can shut you up." She laughed.

They all laughed.

"Don't start liking me now, Blondie," Olivia joked and went back to eating her breakfast. "Goodness, Jason. Eat something. You look uglier than usual."

They laughed some more.

Olivia talked about what happened at the Mansion. In return, they shared with her the moving of the building. Laughs and smiles filled them. Olivia brought their moods right back up.

After eating breakfast they parted ways to give her a chance to take in the new location.

The Countess walked to the balcony doors of her living room and opened the curtains. The fields were beautifully covered in white snow just as Goldie had described. As the Countess stood there looking out her doors, she felt for the place on her stomach where Joshua had pierced her. She had noticed the scar in the shower early that morning and ran her hand over it. It was different now that she knew how much time had passed.

A wind filled the room and Olivia knew she was no longer alone. She fixed her shirt, and before Jason could speak her mouth was releasing words. "How long was I asleep again?"

He stood by the front door. "Ten weeks and two days."

"I have a scar." She turned and showed him the wound mark. Jason reached over his head with his left hand and pulled off his gray shirt. She saw how thin and sick he looked. Jason turned, revealing the large diagonal scar on his back. She ran her hand over the scar. "But I've never had a scar," Olivia mentioned.

The slayer faced her. Their bodies were very close; almost touching. "Neither have I," he said looking down at her suddenly succulent lips. "There's a first time for everything."

"You've never had a scar?" It was hard to believe someone who spent so much of his time fighting never got a significant wound. Jason shook his head. Olivia backed away from him and faced the window. Jason put his shirt back on.

"I need to give up vampirism," she said like she was speaking about a religion. The slayer wasn't sure that was a choice she could make. Didn't she need to feed occasionally? "Maybe resign my title too."

"Won't you miss the Mansion? Maybe miss your throne and your royal servants? You would be just another student here. People would bow to you one week and your fame would be gone the next."

It was true. Their interest in her would die, as would her fame. Olivia wasn't the leader Gabriel was to them. To some, she was still the enemy.

"I don't want to be in the spotlight." She took a breath. "I still feel very weak," she lied.

"I'll let you rest," he said and left with the wind.

Her eyes grew red and her teeth came from their hiding place. The room became hot before the temperature went back to normal.

His hand pulled the hair that hid her neck, and he saw the little bite marks on the back of her neck like he had so many times before.

Olivia closed her eyes and waited for the bite that would never come. He wrapped his arms around her and his sweet voice asked, "Do they suspect?"

She shook her head, opened her eyes, and smiled. "I have them eating out of my hands."

CPSIA information can be obtained at www.ICGtesting.com
Printed in the USA
BVOW03s2002271015

424429BV00001B/5/P